GIRL, FORGOTTEN AND
KARIN SLAUGHTER

"All of Slaughter's books . . . are satisfyingly surprising and plausible, but it's Slaughter's prodigious gifts of characterization that make her stand out among thriller writers."
—*WASHINGTON POST*

"Like touching a live wire that continues across three generations."
—*KIRKUS REVIEWS*

"If you're into mystery thrillers, then you're into Karin Slaughter."
—*THESKIMM*

"Her heroines are believable, flawed, and courageous."
—OYINKAN BRAITHWAITE, AWARD-WINNING
AUTHOR OF *MY SISTER, THE SERIAL KILLER*

"Expect from a Karin Slaughter crime thriller . . . just the right amount of twists, turns, shocks, surprises, and domestic thrill and shrill."
—*PARADE*

"Genuinely startling twists. . . . This is Slaughter at her best."
—*BOOKLIST* (STARRED REVIEW)

"One of the boldest thriller writers working today."
—TESS GERRITSEN, *NEW YORK TIMES* BESTSELLING AUTHOR

"Her characters, plot, and pacing are unrivaled among thriller writers."
—MICHAEL CONNELLY, *NEW YORK TIMES* BESTSELLING AUTHOR

"Her talent is the equivalent of an Edgar Allan Poe or a Nathaniel Hawthorne. . . . One of the great talents of the twenty-first century."
—*HUFFPOST*

"The queen of explosive thrillers." —*GOOD HOUSEKEEPING*

GIRL,
FORGOTTEN

Also by Karin Slaughter

Blindsighted
Kisscut
A Faint Cold Fear
Indelible
Faithless
Triptych
Beyond Reach
Fractured
Undone
Broken
Fallen
Criminal
Unseen
Cop Town
Pretty Girls
The Kept Woman
The Good Daughter
Pieces of Her
The Last Widow
The Silent Wife
False Witness

EBOOK ORIGINALS
Snatched
Cold, Cold Heart
Busted
Blonde Hair, Blue Eyes
Last Breath
Cleaning the Gold (with Lee Child)

NOVELLAS AND STORIES
Like a Charm (Editor)
Martin Misunderstood

KARIN
Slaughter

GIRL,
FORGOTTEN

A Novel

WM

WILLIAM MORROW

An Imprint of HarperCollins*Publishers*

HB 02 22 2023 0233

HarperCollins books may be purchased for educational, business, or sales promotional use. For information, please email the Special Markets Department at SPsales@harpercollins.com.

A hardcover edition of this book was published in 2022 by William Morrow, an imprint of HarperCollins Publishers.

FIRST WILLIAM MORROW PAPERBACK EDITION PUBLISHED 2023.

Library of Congress Cataloging-in-Publication Data has been applied for.

ISBN 978-0-06-285897-9

23 24 25 26 27 LBC 5 4 3 2 1

For Mrs. D. Ginger

APRIL 17, 1982

Emily Vaughn frowned at the mirror. The dress was as beautiful as it had been in the store. Her body was the problem. She turned, then turned again, trying to find an angle that didn't make her look like she'd thrown herself onto the beach like a dying whale.

From the corner, Gram said, "Rose, you should stay away from the cookies."

Emily took a moment to recalibrate. Rose was Gram's sister who'd died of tuberculosis during the Great Depression. Emily's middle name was in honor of the girl.

"Gram." She pressed her hand to her stomach, telling her grandmother, "I don't think it's the cookies."

"Are you sure?" A sly smile rippled Gram's lips. "I was hoping you would share."

Emily gave her reflection another disapproving frown before forcing a smile onto her face. She knelt awkwardly in front of her grandmother's rocking chair. The old woman was knitting a sweater that would fit a child. Her fingers dipped in and out of the tiny, puckered collar like hummingbirds. The long sleeve of her Victorian-style dress had pulled back. Emily gently touched the deep purple bruise ringing her bony wrist.

"Clumsy-mumsy." Gram's tone had the sing-song quality of one thousand excuses. "Freddy, you must change out of that dress before Papa gets home."

Now Gram thought Emily was her uncle Fred. Dementia was nothing if not a stroll through the many skeletons lining the family closet.

Emily asked, "Would you like me to get you some cookies?"

"That would be wonderful." Gram continued to knit but her eyes, which never really focused on anything, suddenly became transfixed by Emily. Her lips curved into a smile. Her head tilted to the side as if she was studying the pearlescent lining of a seashell. "Look at your beautiful, smooth skin. You're so lovely."

"It runs in the family." Emily marveled at the almost tangible state of knowing that had transformed her grandmother's gaze. She was there again, as if a broom had swept the cobwebs from her cluttered brain.

Emily touched her crinkly cheek. "Hello, Gram."

"Hello, my sweet child." Her hands stopped knitting, but only to cup Emily's face between them. "When is your birthday?"

Emily knew to offer as much information as possible. "I'll be eighteen in two weeks, Grandmother."

"Two weeks." Gram's smile grew wider. "So wonderful to be young. So much promise. Your whole life a book that has yet to be written."

Emily steeled herself, creating an invisible fortress against a wave of emotion. She was not going to spoil this moment by crying. "Tell me a story from your book, Gram."

Gram looked delighted. She loved telling stories. "Have I told you about when I carried your father?"

"No," Emily said, though she'd heard the story dozens of times. "What was it like?"

"Miserable." She laughed to lighten the word. "I was sick morning and night. I could barely get out of bed to cook. The house was a mess. It was a scorcher outside, I can tell you that. I wanted desperately to cut my hair. It was so long, down to my waist, and when I washed it, the heat would spoil it before it could dry."

Emily wondered if Gram was confusing her life with "Bernice Bobs Her Hair". Fitzgerald and Hemingway often crossed into her memories. "How short did you cut your hair?"

"Oh, no, I did no such thing," Gram said. "Your grandfather wouldn't allow me."

Emily felt her lips part in surprise. That sounded more real life than short story.

"There was quite a rigmarole. My father got involved. He and my mother came over to advocate on my behalf, but your grandfather refused to let them enter the house."

Emily held tight to her grandmother's trembling hands.

"I remember them arguing on the front porch. They were about to come to blows before my mother begged them to stop. She wanted to take me home and look after me until the baby came, but your grandfather refused." She looked startled, as if something had just occurred to her. "Imagine how different my life would have been if they had taken me home that day."

Emily didn't have the capacity to imagine. She could only think about the realities of her own life. She had become just as trapped as her grandmother.

"Little lamb." Gram's gnarled finger caught Emily's tears before they could fall. "Don't be sad. You'll get away. You'll go to college. You'll meet a boy who loves you. You'll have children who adore you. You'll live in a beautiful house."

Emily felt tightness in her chest. She had lost the dream of that life.

"My treasure," Gram said. "You must trust me on this. I am caught between the veil of life and death, which affords me a view of both the past and the future. I see nothing but happiness for you in the coming days."

Emily felt her fortress cracking against the weight of impending grief. No matter what happened—good, bad or indifferent—her grandmother would not bear witness. "I love you so much."

There was no response. The cobwebs had fractured Gram's gaze into the familiar look of confusion. She was holding a stranger's hands. Embarrassed, she took up the knitting needles, and continued the sweater.

Emily wiped away the last of her tears as she stood up. There was nothing worse than watching a stranger cry. The mirror beckoned, but she felt bad enough without staring at her reflection for a second longer. Besides, nothing was going to change.

Gram didn't glance up as Emily grabbed her things and left her room.

She went to the top of the stairs and listened. Her mother's strident tone was muffled by her closed office doors. Emily strained for her father's deep baritone, but he was probably still at his faculty meeting. Still, Emily slid off her shoes before carefully picking her way down the stairs. The old house's creaks were as well-known to her as her parents' warring shouts.

Her hand was reaching for the front door when she remembered the cookies. The stately old grandfather clock was ticking up on five. Gram wouldn't remember the request, but nor would she be fed until well after six.

Emily placed her shoes by the door, then propped her small purse against the heels. She tiptoed past her mother's office to the kitchen.

"Where the hell do you think you're going dressed like that?" Her father's stink of cigars and stale beer filled the kitchen. His black suit jacket was thrown over one of the chairs. The sleeves of his white dress shirt were rolled up. An unopened can of Natty Boh was beside two crushed empties on the counter.

Emily watched a bead of condensation roll down the side of the can.

Her father snapped his fingers as if hastening one of his grad students to get on with it. "Answer me."

"I was just—"

"I know what you were *just*," he cut her off. "You're not content with the damage you've already caused this family? You're going to completely blow up our lives two days before the most important week of your mother's entire career?"

Emily's face burned with shame. "It's not about—"

"I don't give a glorious goddamn what you think it *is* and is *not* about." He pulled the ring off the can and threw it into the sink. "You can turn back around and get out of that hideous dress and stay in your room until I tell you otherwise."

"Yes, sir." She opened the cabinet to retrieve the cookies for her grandmother. Emily's fingers had barely brushed the orange and white packaging on the Bergers when her father's hand clamped around her wrist. Her brain focused not on the pain, but on the memory of the handcuff-shaped bruise around her grandmother's frail wrist.

You'll get away. You'll go to college. You'll meet a boy who loves you . . .

"Dad, I—"

He squeezed harder, and the pain took her breath away. Emily was on her knees, eyes tightly shut, when the stench of his breath curled into her nostrils. "What did I tell you?"

"You—" She gasped as the bones inside her wrist started to quiver. "I'm sorry, I—"

"What did I tell you?"

"T-to go to my room."

The vise of his hand released. The relief brought another gasp from deep inside Emily's belly. She stood up. She closed the cabinet door. She walked out of the kitchen. She went back up the hallway. She placed her foot on the bottom stair, directly above the loudest creak, before putting her foot back on the floor.

Emily turned.

Her shoes were still beside the front door alongside her purse. They were all dyed a perfect shade of turquoise to match her satin dress. But the dress was too tight and she couldn't get her pantyhose past her knees and her feet were painfully swollen so she bypassed the heels and grabbed her clutch on the way out the door.

A gentle spring breeze caressed her bare shoulders as she walked across the lawn. The grass tickled her feet. In the distance, she could smell the pungent salt of the ocean. The Atlantic was far too cold for the tourists who would flock to the boardwalk in the summer. For now, Longbill Beach belonged to the townies, who would never stand in a snaking line outside of Thrasher's for a bucket of French fries or stare in wonder at the machines stretching colorful strings of taffy in the candy shop window.

Summer.

Only a few months away.

Clay and Nardo and Ricky and Blake were all preparing for graduation, about to start their adult lives, about to leave this stifling, pathetic beach town. Would they ever think of Emily again? Did they even think of her now? Maybe with pity. Probably with relief that they had finally excised the rot from their incestuous little circle.

Her outsiderness didn't hurt now as much as it had in the beginning. Emily had finally accepted that she wasn't a part of their lives anymore. Contrary to what Gram had said, Emily was *not* going away. *Not* going to college. *Not* meeting a boy who loved her. She would end up shrieking her lifeguard whistle at obnoxious brats on the beach or passing out endless free samples from behind the counter at Salty Pete's Soft Serve.

The soles of her feet slapped against the warm asphalt as she turned the corner. She wanted to look back at the house, but she refrained from the dramatic gesture. Instead, she conjured the image of her mother pacing back and forth across her office, phone to her ear as she strategized. Her father would be draining the can of beer, possibly weighing the distance between the rest of the beer in the fridge and the Scotch in the library. Her grandmother would be finishing the tiny sweater, wondering what child she could've possibly started it for.

An approaching car made Emily move from the center of the road. She watched a two-tone Chevy Chevette glide by, then saw the bright red glow of the brake lights as the car squealed to a stop. Loud music pounded from the open windows. Bay City Rollers.

S-A-T-U-R-D-A-Y night!

Mr. Wexler's head swiveled from the rearview mirror to the side mirror. The lights blinked as he moved his foot from the brake to the gas, then back again. He was trying to decide whether or not to keep going.

Emily stepped back as the car reversed. She could smell the joint smoldering in his ashtray. She assumed that Dean was supposed to chaperone tonight, but his black suit was more appropriate for a funeral than a prom.

"Em," he said, shouting over the song. "What are you doing?"

She spread out her arms, indicating her billowing turquoise prom dress. "What does it look like I'm doing?"

His eyes flickered over her, then did another, slower take, which was the same way he had looked at Emily the first day she had walked into his classroom. In addition to teaching social studies, he was the track coach, so he'd been wearing burgundy polyester shorts and a white, short-sleeved polo—the same as the other coaches.

That was where the similarities had ended.

Dean Wexler was only six years older than his students, but he was worldly and wise in a way that none of them would ever be. Before college, he'd taken a gap year to backpack across Europe. He'd dug wells for villagers in Latin America. He drank herbal tea and grew his own weed. He had a thick, luxurious Magnum P.I. mustache. He was supposed to teach them about civics and government, but one class he was showing them an article about how DDT was still poisoning the groundwater and the next he was explaining how Reagan cut a secret deal with the Iranians on the hostages to swing the election.

Basically, they had all thought that Dean Wexler was the coolest teacher any of them had ever known.

"Em." He repeated the name like a sigh. The car gear went into neutral. The emergency brake raked up. He turned off the engine, cutting the song at *ni-i-i-ight*.

Dean got out of the car. He towered over her but, for once, his eyes were not unkind. "You can't go to the prom. What would people think? What are your parents going to say?"

"I don't care," she said, her voice going up at the end because she cared quite a lot.

"You need to anticipate the consequences of your actions." He reached out for her arms, then seemed to think better of it. "Your mother's being scrutinized at the highest levels right now."

"Really?" Emily asked, as if her mother hadn't been on the phone for so many hours that her ear had taken on the shape of the receiver. "Is she in trouble or something?"

His audible sigh was clearly meant to indicate he was being patient. "I think you're not considering how your actions could derail everything she's worked for."

Emily watched a seagull floating above a cluster of clouds. *Your actions. Your actions. Your actions.* She had heard Dean being condescending before, but never toward her.

He asked, "What if someone takes a photo of you? Or there's a journalist at the school? Think about how this will reflect on her."

A dawning realization put a smile on her lips. He was joking. Of course he was joking.

"Emily." Dean clearly wasn't joking. "You can't—"

He turned into a mime, using his hands to create an aura around her body. Bare shoulders, too full breasts, too wide hips, the stretching seams at her waist as the satin turquoise failed to conceal the round swell of her belly.

This was why Gram was knitting the tiny sweater. This was why her father hadn't let her leave the house for the last four months. This was why the principal had kicked her out of school. This was why she had been cleaved away from Clay and Nardo and Ricky and Blake.

She was pregnant.

Finally, Dean found words again. "What would your mother say?"

Emily hesitated, trying to wade through the torrent of shame being thrown at her, the same shame she had endured since word had gotten out that she was no longer the good girl with the promising life ahead of her but the bad girl who was going to pay a heavy price for her sins.

She asked, "Since when do you care so much about my mother? I thought she was a cog in a corrupt system?"

Her tone was sharper than she'd intended, but her anger was real. He sounded exactly like her parents. The principal. The other teachers. Her pastor. Her former friends. They were all right and Emily was always wrong, wrong, wrong.

She said the words that would hurt him most. "I believed in you."

He snorted. "You're too young to have a credible system of beliefs."

Emily bit her bottom lip, struggling to rein in her anger. How had she not seen before that he was completely full of shit?

"Emily." He gave another sad shake of his head, still trying to humiliate her into compliance. He didn't care about her—not really. He didn't want to have to deal with her. He certainly didn't want to see her making a scene at the prom. "You look enormous. You'll only make a fool of yourself. Go home."

She wasn't going to go home. "You said we should burn the world down. That's what you said. Burn it all down. Start again. Build something—"

"You're not building anything. You're clearly planning some stunt in order to get your mother's attention." His arms were crossed. He looked at his watch. "Grow up, Emily. The time for selfishness has passed. You've got to think about—"

"What do I have to think about, Dean? What do you want me to think about?"

"Jesus, lower your voice."

"Don't tell me what to do!" She felt her heart beating inside her throat. Her fists were clenched. "You said it yourself. I'm not a child. I'm nearly eighteen years old. And I'm sick and tired of people—men—telling me what to do."

"So now I'm the patriarchy?"

"Are you, Dean? Are you part of the patriarchy? We'll see how fast they circle the wagons when I tell my father what you did."

Fire razed up into her arm, shot into her fingertips. Her feet left the ground as she was spun around and slammed into the side of the car. The metal was hot against her bare shoulder blades. She could hear the *tick* of the cooling engine. Dean's hand was clamped around her wrist. His other hand covered her mouth. His face was so close to hers that she could see sweat seeping between the fine hairs of his mustache.

Emily struggled. He was hurting her. He was really hurting her.

"What lying bullshit are you going to say to your father?" he hissed. "Tell me."

Something had cracked inside her wrist. She could feel the bones chattering like teeth.

"What are you going to say, Emily? Nothing? Is nothing what you're going to say?"

Emily's head moved up and down. She couldn't tell if Dean's sweaty hand was moving her face or if something deep inside of her, some survival instinct, had made her acquiesce.

He slowly peeled away his fingers. "What are you going to say?"

"N-nothing. I won't—I won't tell him anything."

"Damn right. Because there's nothing to tell." He wiped his hand on his shirt as he stepped back. His eyes flickered down, not appraising, but calculating the price of her swollen wrist. He knew she wouldn't tell her parents. They would only blame her for being out of the house when they had ordered her to stay hidden. "Go home before something really bad happens to you."

Emily moved out of the way so that he could get into the car. The engine chugged once, then twice, then caught. The radio sparked, the tape cassette coming back alive.

S-A-T-U-R . . .

Emily cradled her swollen wrist as the bald tires spun for traction. Dean left her in a fog of burned rubber. The smell was putrid, but she stayed in place, her bare feet stuck to the hot asphalt. Her left wrist throbbed along with her pulse. Her right hand went to her belly. She imagined the rapid pulses she had seen on the ultrasound keeping tempo with her own quick heartbeat.

She had taped all of the ultrasound photos on the mirror in her bathroom because that felt like something she was supposed to do. The images showed the tiny bean-shaped splotch slowly developing—sprouting eyes and a nose, then fingers and toes.

She was supposed to feel something, right?

A swell of emotion? An instant bond? A sense of awe and majesty?

Instead, she had felt dread. She had felt fear. She had felt the weight of responsibility, and finally, that responsibility had made her feel something tangible: a sense of purpose.

Emily knew what a bad parent looked like. Every day—often several times a day—she promised her child that the most important duties as a parent would be fulfilled.

Now, she said the words out loud as a reminder.

"I will protect you. No one will ever hurt you. You will always be safe."

The walk into town took another half hour. Her bare feet felt scorched, then flayed, then finally numb as she traversed the white cedar of the boardwalk. The Atlantic was to her right, waves scratching at the sand as they were pulled back by the tide. The darkened shop windows on her left mirrored the sun as it crept over Delaware Bay. She imagined it passing over Annapolis, then Washington DC, then through the Shenandoah as it prepared for the journey out west—all while Emily trudged along the treadmill of the boardwalk, the same boardwalk she would probably be walking for the rest of her life.

This time last year, Emily was touring the Foggy Bottom Campus at George Washington University. Before everything had so magnificently gone off the rails. Before life as she knew it had irrevocably changed. Before she had lost the right to hope, let alone dream.

This had been the plan: As a legacy, her GWU acceptance would be a formality. She would spend her college years nestled between the White House and Kennedy Center. She would intern for a senator. She was going to follow her father's footsteps and study political science. She was going to follow her mother's footsteps into Harvard Law, then work five years at a white-shoe firm, then get a state judgeship, and eventually, possibly, a federal judgeship.

What would your mother say?

"Your life is over!" was what her mother had screamed when Emily's pregnancy had become apparent. "No one will ever respect you now!"

The funny thing was, looking back on the last few months, her mother had been right.

Emily left the boardwalk, cutting down the long, dark alley between the candy shop and the hot dog shack, crossing Beach Drive. She eventually found herself on Royal Cove Way. Several cars drove by, some of them slowing down to take a look at the bedraggled beachball in the bright turquoise prom dress. Emily rubbed her arms to fight the chill in the air. She shouldn't have gone with such a loud color. She shouldn't have chosen something strapless. She should've altered it to accommodate her growing body.

But she hadn't considered any of these good ideas until now, so her swollen breasts were spilling out of the top and her hips swung like a pendulum on the clock inside of a whorehouse.

"Hey, hot stuff!" a boy screamed from the open window of a Mustang. His friends were shoved into the back. Someone's leg was sticking out a window. She could smell beer and pot and sweat.

Emily's hand cradled her round belly as she walked across the school quad. She thought about the child growing inside. At first, it hadn't seemed real. And then it had felt like an anchor. Only lately had it felt like a human being.

Her human being.

"Emmie?"

She turned, surprised to find Blake hiding beneath the shadow of a tree. He was cupping a cigarette in one hand. Improbably, he was dressed for the prom. Since elementary school, they had all scoffed about how the dances and the proms were a Pageantry of Plebs clinging to what would probably be the best nights of their pathetic lives. Only Blake's formal black tuxedo set him apart from the bright white and pastels she had seen the other boys wearing in passing cars.

She cleared her throat. "What are you doing here?"

He grinned. "We thought it would be fun to sneer at the plebs in person."

She looked around for Clay and Nardo and Ricky, because they always traveled in a pack.

"They're inside," he said. "Except for Ricky. She's running late."

Emily didn't know what to say. *Thanks* seemed wrong considering the last time Blake had talked to her, he'd called her a stupid bitch.

She started to walk away, offering only a stray, "See ya."

"Em?"

She didn't stop or turn around because, while he was right that she could be a bitch, Emily wasn't stupid.

Music pulsed from the open doors of the gymnasium. Emily could feel the bass vibrating in her back teeth as she walked across the quad. The prom committee had apparently decided on the theme of "Romance by the Sea", which was as sad as it was predictable. Paper fish in rainbow colors darted between rows of blue streamers. Not one of them was a longbill, which was the fish that the town was named after, but who was Emily to correct them? She wasn't even a student here.

"Christ," Nardo said. "You've got some balls showing up like this."

He was standing off to the side of the entrance, exactly the kind of place she would expect Nardo to be lurking. Same black tux as Blake, but with an I SHOT J.R. button on the lapel to make it clear he was in on the joke. He offered Emily a sip from a half-filled bottle of Everclear and cherry Kool-Aid.

She shook her head. "I gave it up for Lent."

He guffawed, shoving the bottle into his jacket pocket. She could see the stitching had already torn from the weight of the rotgut. A hand-rolled cigarette was tucked behind his ear. Emily remembered something her father had said about Nardo the first time he'd met him—

That kid's gonna end up in jail or on Wall Street, but not in that order.

"So." He slipped the cigarette out and searched for his lighter. "What brings a bad girl like you to a nice place like this?"

Emily rolled her eyes. "Where's Clay?"

"Why, you got something to tell him?" He wagged his eyebrows as he stared pointedly at her belly.

Emily waited for his cigarette to catch. She used her good hand to rub her stomach like a witch with a crystal ball. "What if I have something to tell *you*, Nardo?"

"Shit," he said, his eyes flickering nervously behind her. They had drawn a crowd. "That's not funny, Emily."

She rolled her eyes again. "Where's Clay?"

"Fuck if I know." He turned away from her, feigning interest in a white stretch limo pulling into the parking lot.

Emily headed into the gym, because she knew Clay would be somewhere near the stage, probably circled by a group of slim, beautiful girls. Her feet registered the drop in temperature as she walked across the polished wood floor. The seaside theme continued inside the building. Balloons bounced against the rafters of the high ceiling, ready to drop at the end of the night. Large, round tables were laid out with sea-themed centerpieces glued together with shells and bright pink peach blossoms.

"Look," someone said. "What's *she* doing here?"

"Damn."

"The nerve."

Emily kept her eyes trained straight ahead. The band was setting up on the stage, but someone had put on a record to fill the void. Her stomach rumbled when she passed the food tables. The sickly-sweet syrup that passed for punch. Finger sandwiches fat with meats and cheeses. Leftover taffy that last summer's tourists hadn't bought. Metal bins of limp French fries. Pigs in a blanket. Crab cakes. Bergers cookies and cakes.

Emily stopped her progress toward the stage. The din of the crowd had died down. All she could hear was the echo of Rick Springfield warning them not to talk to strangers.

People were staring at her. Not just people. Chaperones. Parents. Her art teacher who'd told her she showed remarkable skill. Her English teacher who'd written *I'm impressed!* on her Virginia Woolf paper. Her history teacher who had promised Emily she would be the lead prosecutor on this year's mock trial.

Until—

Emily kept her shoulders back as she walked toward the stage with her belly sticking out like the prow of an ocean liner. She had grown up in this town, attended the schools, gone to church, summer camp, field trips, hikes and sleepovers. These had been her classmates, her neighbors, her fellow Girl Scouts, her lab partners, her study buddies, her pals that she'd hung out with when Nardo took Clay to Italy with his family and Ricky and Blake were helping out their grandfather at the diner.

And now—

All of her used-to-be friends were backing away from her as if they were afraid what Emily had might be catching. They were such hypocrites. She had done the thing they all were either doing or wanted to do, but she'd had the bad fortune to get caught at it.

"Jesus," someone whispered.

"Outrageous," a parent said.

Their admonitions no longer stung. Dean Wexler in his shitty two-tone Chevy had peeled back the last layer of shame that Emily would ever feel about her pregnancy. The only thing that made it wrong was these judgmental assholes telling themselves it was wrong.

She blocked out their whispers, silently repeating her list of promises to her baby—

I will protect you. No one will ever hurt you. You will always be safe.

Clay was leaning against the stage. His arms were crossed as he waited for her. He was wearing the same black tux as Blake and Nardo. Or, more likely, they were wearing the same tux that Clay had picked out. That's how the boys had always been. Whatever Clay did, the rest of them followed.

He said nothing when Emily stopped in front of him, just raised an expectant eyebrow. She noticed that despite his derision of cheerleaders, he was surrounded by them. The rest of the group had probably told themselves they were attending the prom ironically. Only Clay would know that they were attending the prom so he could get laid.

Rhonda Stein, the head cheerleader, spoke when no one else would. "What is *she* doing here?"

She had looked at Emily but asked Clay the question.

Another cheerleader said, "Maybe it's a *Carrie* thing."

"Did anybody bring the pigs' blood?"

"Who's gonna crown her?"

There was nervous laughter, but they were all looking for Clay to set the tone.

He took a deep breath before slowly letting it go. Then one shoulder casually went up in a shrug. "Free world."

Emily's throat bristled against the dry air. When she had thought about how this night would go down, when she had delighted at the idea of their collective shock, she had reveled in the story she'd tell her child about her mother the radical, bohemian temptress who'd dared to dance at her senior prom, Emily had expected to feel every emotion but the one she was feeling now, which was exhaustion. Mentally, physically, she felt incapable of doing anything but turning around and walking back the way she'd come.

So she did.

The crowd was still parted, but the mood had turned decidedly toward pitchforks and scarlet 'A's. Boys gritted their teeth in anger. Girls literally turned their backs. She saw teachers and parents shaking their heads in disgust. *What was she doing here? Why was she wrecking the night for everyone else? Jezebel. Whore. She had made her bed. Who did she think she was? She was going to ruin some poor boy's life.*

Emily had not realized how stifling the air in the gymnasium was until she was safely outside. Nardo was no longer lurking by the doors. Blake had recessed into another shadow. Ricky was wherever she was in times like this, which was to say nowhere useful.

"Emily?"

She turned around, surprised to find Clay. He had followed her out of the gym. Clayton Morrow never followed anyone.

He asked, "What are you doing here?"

"Leaving," she said. "Go back inside with your friends."

"Those losers?" His lip was curled. He looked over her shoulder, his eyes following something that was moving too fast to be a human being. He loved watching birds. That was the secret nerd part of Clay. He read Henry James and he loved Edith Wharton and he was making straight 'A's in advanced calculus and he couldn't tell you what a free throw was or how to spiral a football but no one cared because he was so goddamn gorgeous.

Emily asked, "What do you want, Clay?"

"You're the one who showed up here looking for me."

She found it odd that Clay had assumed she was here for him. Emily hadn't expected to find any of them at the prom. She had wanted to mortify the rest of the school for ostracizing her. Frankly, she had hoped that Mr. Lampert, the principal, would call Chief Stilton and have her arrested. Then she'd have to be bailed out and her father would be furious and her mother—

"Crap," Emily muttered. Maybe this stunt was about her mother after all.

"Emily?" Clay asked. "Come on. Why are you here? What do you want from me?"

He didn't want an answer. He wanted absolution.

Emily wasn't his pastor. "Go back inside and enjoy yourself, Clay. Hook up with some cheerleaders. Go to college. Get a great job. Walk through all the doors that are always opened for you. Enjoy the rest of your life."

"Wait." His hand rested on her shoulder, a rudder turning her back in his direction. "You're not being fair."

She looked into his clear blue eyes. This moment was meaningless to him—an unpleasant interaction that would disappear from his memories like a puff of smoke. In twenty years, Emily would be nothing but a lingering source of uneasiness Clay felt when he opened his mailbox and found an invitation to their high school reunion.

"My *life* isn't fair," she told him. "You're fine, Clay. You're always fine. You're always going to *be* fine."

He gave a heavy sigh. "Don't turn out to be one of those boring, bitter women, Emily. I would really hate that for you."

"Don't let Chief Stilton hear about what you've been doing behind half-closed doors, Clayton." She raised herself on her toes so that she could see the fear in his eyes. "I would really hate that for you."

One hand snaked out and grabbed her by the neck. The other reared back into a fist. Rage darkened his eyes. "You're going to get yourself killed, you fucking cunt."

Emily squeezed her eyes closed as she waited for the blow, but all she heard was nervous laughter.

Her eyes slitted open.

Clay released her. He wasn't stupid enough to hurt her in front of witnesses.

That one will end up in the White House, her father had said the first time he'd met Clay. *If he doesn't end up swinging from a rope.*

Emily had dropped her purse when he'd grabbed her. Clay retrieved it, wiping the dirt off the side of the satin clutch. He handed it to her as if he was being chivalrous.

She snatched it out of his hand.

This time, Clay didn't follow Emily when she walked away. She passed by several clusters of prom-goers in varying shades of pastels and crinoline. Most of them only stopped to gawk at her, but she got a warm smile from Melody Brickel, her one-time friend from band practice, and that meant something.

Emily waited for the light to cross the street. There were no catcalls this time, though another car full of boys did an ominously slow drive-by.

"I will protect you," she whispered to the small passenger growing inside of her. "No one will ever hurt you. You will always be safe."

The light finally changed. The sun was dipping down, casting a long shadow at the end of the crosswalk. Emily had always felt comfortable being alone in town, but now, goosebumps prickled her arms. She was uneasy about cutting through the alley between the candy shop and the hot dog shack again. Her feet ached from the punishing walk. Her neck hurt where Clay had grabbed her. Her wrist still throbbed like it was either broken or badly sprained. She shouldn't have come here. She should've stayed home and kept Gram company until the bell rang for dinner.

"Emmie?" It was Blake again, coming out from the darkened entrance of the hot dog shack like a vampire. "Are you okay?"

She felt some of her mettle break. No one ever asked her if she was okay anymore. "I need to get home."

"Em—" He wasn't going to let her walk away so easily. "I'm just—are you really okay? Because it's weird that you're here. It's weird that we're all here, but particularly because, well, your shoes. They seem to be missing."

They both looked down at her bare feet.

Emily barked a laugh that gonged through her body like the Liberty Bell. She laughed so hard that her stomach hurt. She laughed until she doubled over.

"Emmie?" Blake put his hand on her shoulder. He'd thought that she'd lost her mind. "Should I call your parents or—"

"No." She stood up, wiping her eyes. "I'm sorry. I just realized that I'm literally barefoot and pregnant."

Blake reluctantly smiled. "Was that on purpose?"

"No. Yes?"

She honestly didn't know. Maybe her subconscious was doing weird things. Maybe the baby was controlling her hormones. She would easily believe either explanation because the third option—that she was batshit crazy—would be an unwelcome development.

"I'm sorry," Blake said, but his apologies always rang hollow because he kept making the same mistakes over and over again. "What I said before. Not before, but way before. I shouldn't have said . . . I mean, it was wrong to say . . ."

She knew exactly what he was talking about. "That I should flush it down the toilet?"

He seemed almost as startled as Emily had been when he'd made the suggestion so many months ago.

"That—yes," he said. "That's what I should not have said."

"No, you shouldn't have." Emily felt her throat tighten, because the truth was, the decision had never been hers. Her parents had made it for her. "I need to—"

"Let's go somewhere and—"

"Shit!" She jerked her injured wrist away from his grasp. Her foot landed awkwardly on an uneven stretch of sidewalk. She started to fall, clutching uselessly at Blake's tuxedo jacket before her tailbone cracked against the asphalt. The pain was excruciating. She rolled to her side. Something wet trickled between her legs.

The baby.

"Emily!" Blake fell to his knees beside her. "Are you okay?"

"Go away!" Emily pleaded, though she needed his help to stand up. Her purse had been crushed in the fall. The satin had ripped open. "Blake, please just go. You're making things worse! Why do you always make things worse?"

Pain flashed in his eyes, but she couldn't worry about him now. Her mind was buzzing with all of the ways that falling so hard could've hurt her child.

He said, "I didn't mean—"

"Of course you didn't mean it!" she yelled. He was the one who was still spreading rumors. He was the one pushing Ricky to be so cruel. "You never mean anything, do you? It's never your fault, you never screw up, you're never responsible. Well guess what? This is your fault. You got what you wanted. It's all your damn fault."

"Emily—"

She stumbled, catching herself against the corner of the candy shop. She heard Blake say something, but her ears were filled with a high-pitched screaming sound.

Was it her baby? Was it crying for help?

"Emmie?"

She shoved him away and stumbled down the alley. Hot liquid dribbled down the insides of her thighs. She pressed her palm against the rough brick as she tried to keep herself from falling to her knees. A sob choked her throat. She opened her mouth to gulp in a breath. Salt air burned her lungs. She was blinded by the sun bouncing off the boardwalk. She stepped back into the darkness, leaning against the wall at the base of the alleyway.

Emily looked back at the street. Blake had slunk off. No one could see her.

She bunched up her dress, using her injured arm to hold up the folds of satin. With her good hand, she reached between her legs. She had expected to find blood on her fingers, but there was nothing. She leaned down and smelled her hand.

"Oh," she whispered.

She'd wet herself.

Emily laughed again, but this time through tears. Relief made her weak in the knees. The brick pulled at her dress as she sank to the ground. Her tailbone ached, but she didn't care. She was shockingly overjoyed that she had peed herself. The dark places her brain had gone to when she'd assumed that blood was gushing between her legs were more enlightening than any ultrasound she could tape to her bathroom mirror.

In that moment, Emily had desperately wanted her baby to be all right. Not out of duty. A child wasn't only a responsibility. It was an opportunity to love someone the way that she had never been loved.

And for the first time in this whole shameful, humiliating, helpless process, Emily Vaughn knew without a doubt that she loved this baby.

"It looks like a girl," the doctor had told her during her most recent exam.

At the time, Emily had catalogued the news as another step in the process, but now, the realization broke open the dam that had for so long held back her emotions.

Her girl.

Her tiny, precious little girl.

Emily's hand went to her mouth. She was so weak with relief that she would've fallen over if she hadn't already been sitting on the cold ground. Her head bent toward her knees. Big, fat tears rolled down her cheeks. Her mouth gaped wordlessly, her chest so filled with love that she couldn't form sound. She pressed her palm to her belly and imagined a small hand pressing back. Her heart lurched as she thought about one day being able to kiss the tips of those precious fingers. Gram had said that each baby had a special smell that only their mother knew. Emily wanted to know that smell. She wanted to wake up in the night and listen to the quick in and out of the beautiful girl that she had grown inside of her body.

She wanted to make plans.

In two weeks, Emily would be eighteen years old. In another two months, she would be a mother. She would get a job. She would move out of her parents' house. Gram would understand, and what she didn't understand she would forget. Dean Wexler was right about one thing: Emily had to grow up. She had more than herself to think of now. She had to get away from Longbill Beach. She had to start planning her future instead of letting other people plan it for her. More importantly, she would give her baby girl everything that Emily had never had.

Kindness. Understanding. Security.

Emily closed her eyes. She conjured the image of her baby girl joyfully floating around inside of her body. She took a deep breath and started to recite the mantra, this time from a place of love rather than duty.

"I will protect—"

The sound of a loud snap made her eyes open.

Emily saw black leather shoes, black socks, the hem of a pair of black pants. She looked up. The sun flickered as a bat swung through the air.

Her heart clenched into a fist. She was suddenly, inescapably, filled with fear.

Not for herself—for her baby.

Emily curled inward, arms wrapped around her belly, legs pulled up tight, as she fell to the side. She was desperate for another moment, another breath, so that her last words to her little girl would not be a lie.

Someone had always planned to hurt them.

They had never been safe.

PRESENT DAY

1

Andrea Oliver willed her stomach to stop churning as she ran along the dirt trail. The sun pushed down on her shoulders. Wet earth sucked at her shoes. Sweat had turned her shirt into Saran Wrap. Her hamstrings were steel banjo strings that jangled with every pounding strike of her heel. She heard grunts behind her as the stragglers pushed themselves to keep up. Ahead were the strivers, the Type As who would ford a stream full of piranhas if there was at least a one percent chance that they could come in first.

She contented herself with the middle of the pack, neither a dawdler nor a cliff diver, which was an achievement in and of itself. Two years ago, Andrea would've been firmly at the rear, or more likely still sleeping in her bed while her alarm blared for the fifth or sixth time. Her clothes would've been strewn around the tiny apartment above her mother's garage. Every piece of unopened mail on her kitchen table would've been stamped PAST DUE. When she finally crawled out of bed, she would've seen three texts from her father asking her to check in, another six from her mother asking her if she had been abducted by a serial killer, and a missed call from work telling her this was her last warning before she was fired.

"Shit," Paisley mumbled.

Andrea looked over her shoulder as Paisley Spenser peeled off from the pack. One of the stragglers had tripped. Thom Humphrey lay flat on his back looking up at the trees. A collective groan filled the forest. The rule was, if one of them didn't finish, they all had to go again.

"Get up! Get up!" Paisley yelled, circling back to either encourage him or kick him until he stood. "You can do it! Come on, Thom!"

"Let's go, Thom!" the rest of them shouted.

Andrea grunted the sounds, but she didn't trust her mouth to open. Her stomach was pitching like deck chairs on the *Titanic*. For months, she'd been doing sprints, push-ups, jumping jacks, rope climbs, burpees, and run approximately eleven million miles a day, but she was still a lightweight. Her throat filled with bile. Her back teeth ratcheted down. She clenched her fists as she rounded the last curve in the trail. Home stretch. Another five minutes and she would never have to run this grueling hell-course ever again.

Paisley flew by, going balls to the walls toward the finish line. Thom was back in formation. The line tightened. Everyone was digging deep.

Andrea had nothing left to dig. She knew her stomach would probably shit out of her throat if she pushed herself any harder. Her lips parted to suck in some air, but she ended up swallowing a cloud of gnats. She coughed, cursing herself because she should've known better. She'd spent twenty weeks killing herself at the Federal Law Enforcement Training Center, in Glynn County, Georgia. Between the mosquitos, sand fleas, gnats, palmetto bugs the size of rodents, rodents the size of dogs, and the fact that the Glynco FLETC was basically in the middle of a swamp, she should've known better than to try to breathe.

The sound of distant thunder roiled into her ears. She concentrated on her footsteps as the trail dipped down. The thunder turned into a distinctive staccato of claps and shouts of encouragement. The strivers had broken through the yellow tape. They were being cheered on by family members who'd shown up to celebrate their graduation from the grueling, Dante-esque torture that seemed designed to either kill them or make them stronger.

"Holy shit," Andrea mumbled, her voice filled with genuine

astonishment. She hadn't been killed. She hadn't dropped out. Months of classroom training, five to eight hours of hand-to-hand combat every day, surveillance techniques, warrant executions, firearms training and so much physical exertion that she'd gained four pounds of muscle, and now, finally, unbelievably, she was twenty yards out from becoming a deputy in the United States Marshal Service.

Thom streaked by on her left, which was such a fucking Thom thing to do. Andrea's second wind rallied to spite him. Her brain felt dizzy from the burst of adrenaline. Her legs started pumping. She passed Thom and caught up with Paisley. They grinned at each other in triumph—three guys had dropped out in the first week, another three had been asked to leave, one had disappeared after making a racist joke, another after he'd gotten handsy. She and Paisley Spenser were two of only four women in the forty-eight-person class. Just a few more steps and it would all be over but for walking to the stage for graduation.

Paisley nosed just ahead of Andrea as they crossed the line. They both raised their arms in celebration. Paisley's giant extended family whooped like cranes as they surrounded her in a warm embrace. All around her, Andrea could see similar scenes of joy. Every single face in the crowd was smiling but for two.

Andrea's parents.

Laura Oliver and Gordon Mitchell both had their arms crossed. Their eyes followed Andrea as strangers congratulated her and patted her on the back. Paisley playfully punched her in the arm. Andrea punched her back as she watched Gordon take out his phone. She smiled, but her father wasn't trying to take a photo of Andrea's momentous achievement. He turned his back as he took a call.

"Congratulations!" someone yelled.

"I'm so proud of you!"

"Well done!"

Laura's mouth was a thin white line as she watched Andrea move through the crowd. Her eyes looked moist, but these were not the tears of pride she had wept after Andrea's first school musical performance or blue-ribbon win at the art show.

Her mother was devastated.

One of the senior inspectors offered Andrea a cup of Gatorade. She shook her head, teeth gritted as she jogged toward the row of bright blue porta-potties. Instead of choosing one, she walked around to the back, opened her mouth and basically threw up the lining of her stomach.

"Sh-hit," Andrea sputtered, annoyed that she had figured out how to take down a bad guy using nothing but her fists and feet but she couldn't control her own weak stomach. She wiped her mouth with the back of her hand. Her vision swam. She should've brought the Gatorade back with her. If she had learned anything at Glynco it was to hydrate. And also to never, ever let anyone see her throw up because this was the place you got your nick-name for the rest of your career. She was not going to be known as Puke Oliver.

"Andy?"

She turned, unsurprised to find her mother offering her a bottle of water. If Laura was good at anything, it was rushing in to help without being asked.

"Andrea," Andrea corrected.

Laura rolled her eyes, because Andrea had been telling her for the last twenty years to call her Andy. "Andrea. Are you okay?"

"Yes, Mom. I'm okay." The water was ice cold inside the bottle. Andrea pressed it to the back of her neck. "You could at least pretend to be happy for me."

"I could," Laura allowed. "What's the procedure on throwing up? Do the criminals wait until you've finished vomiting before they rape and murder you?"

"Don't be gross. They do it before." Andrea twisted open the cap on the water bottle. "Remember what you told me two years ago?"

Laura said nothing.

"On my birthday?"

Laura still said nothing, though neither of them would ever forget Andrea's thirty-first birthday.

"Mom, you told me to get my shit together, move out of your garage and start living my life." Andrea held out her arms. "This is what that looks like."

Laura finally broke. "I didn't tell you to join the fucking enemy."

Andrea poked her tongue into her cheek. A ridgeline had formed along the inside of her mouth from clenching her teeth. She hadn't thrown up in front of anybody. Not once. She was the second shortest student in the class, eking out an inch over Paisley at five-six. Both of them were fifty pounds lighter than the nearest guy, but they had both finished in the top ten percent and they had both just outrun over half of their class.

"Darling, is all of this Marshal bullshit some form of payback?" Laura asked. "You're trying to punish me for leaving you out of the loop?"

Out of the loop was an understatement, considering Laura had kept it hidden for thirty-one years that Andrea's biological father was a psychopathic cult leader bent on mass murder. Her mother had even gone so far as to concoct an imaginary biological father who'd died in a tragic car accident. Andrea would probably still believe her lies if not for the fact that, two years ago, Laura had finally been backed into a corner and forced to tell the truth.

"Well?" Laura demanded.

Andrea had learned a very hard lesson over the last two years, and that was that saying nothing could be just as hurtful as saying everything.

Laura gave a heavy sigh. She wasn't used to being on the other side of the manipulation. Her hands went to her hips. She looked back at the crowd, then up at the sky, then finally turned her gaze back on Andrea. "My love, your mind is so amazing."

Andrea filled her mouth with cold water.

Laura said, "The willpower and drive you've shown to get here tell me that you could do almost any job you wanted to. And I love that. I love you for your grit and determination. I want you to do what you're passionate about. But it can't be this."

Andrea swished the water around her mouth before spitting it out. "Clown school said my feet weren't big enough."

"Andy." Laura stamped her foot in frustration. "You could've gone back to art school or become a teacher or even stayed at the nine-one-one call center."

Andrea took a long swig of water. Thirty-year-old Andrea would've taken everything her mother said at face value. Now, she only saw misdirection. "So, more debt, being surrounded by bratty kids, or listening to senior citizens whine about their trash not being picked up for nine dollars an hour?"

Laura was undaunted. "What about your art?"

"That's lucrative."

"You love drawing."

"The bank loves me paying off my student loans."

"Your father and I could help—"

"Which father?"

The silence between them took on the texture of dry ice.

Andrea finished the water while her mother regrouped. She felt bad about taking that last swipe. Gordon had been—was still—an incredible father. Until recently, he was the only father Andrea had ever known.

"Well." Laura turned her watch around on her wrist. "You should clean up. Graduation is in one hour."

"I'm impressed you know the schedule."

"Andy—" Laura caught herself. "Andrea. I feel like you're running away from yourself. As if you think being in another town, doing this crazy, dangerous job, will make you a different person."

Andrea wanted desperately for the lecture to end. Her mother of all people should have understood the need to blow up your life and build something more meaningful out of the ashes. Laura had not sought membership in a violent cult at the age of twenty-one because her life was in perfect balance. Nor had she turned in Andrea's biological father to the police because she'd had an epiphany. And that wasn't even accounting for two years ago, when she had gone ballistic at the mere thought of Andrea's life being in danger.

"Mom," Andrea said. "You should be happy that I'm on the inside."

Laura looked genuinely puzzled. "The inside of what?"

"The System," Andrea said, for lack of a better description. "If he ever gets out of prison, if he ever tries to mess with us again, I'll have the entire United States Marshal Service behind me."

"He won't get out of prison." Laura's head was shaking before Andrea finished. "And even if he does, we can take care of ourselves."

You can, Andrea thought. That was the problem. When shit had gone sideways, Laura had been a bad ass while Andrea had cowered in the corner like a kid playing hide-and-seek. She was not going to feel that helpless if—when—her father turned his deadly focus back on them again.

"My darling," Laura tried again. "I like the person that you are now. I love my sensitive, artistic, kind little girl."

Andrea chewed at her lip. She could hear more shouts as the last of the stragglers crossed the finish line. Students Andrea had trained with. Students she had bested by almost a full ten minutes.

"Andrea, let me give you the same unsolicited advice that my mother gave me." Laura never talked about her family, let alone her past. She didn't have to wait for Andrea's undivided attention. "I was younger, but exactly how you are now. I approached every challenge in life as if it was a cliff that I had to constantly keep flinging myself over."

Andrea didn't want to admit that sounded familiar.

"I thought I was so brave, so daring," Laura said. "It took me years to figure out that when you fall, you're completely out of control. You're just letting gravity take over."

Andrea forced a shrug. "I've never minded heights."

"That's almost exactly what I told my mother." Laura smiled at the secret memory. "She knew I wasn't running toward something. I was running away from everything—especially myself. And do you know what she told me?"

"I think you're going to tell me."

Laura was still smiling when she gently placed her hands on either side of Andrea's face. "She said, 'Wherever you go, there you are.'"

Andrea could see the concern in her mother's eyes. Laura was afraid. She was trying to protect Andrea. Or maybe she was trying to manipulate her the way she always had.

"Gee, Mom." Andrea stepped back. "It sounds like she would've made a fantastic grandmother. I wish I'd had the opportunity to meet her."

Laura's pained expression showed the cut was too deep. This was new to them, this nasty back and forth that turned their tongues into razors.

Andrea lightly squeezed her mother's hand. They never made up with words anymore. They slapped on a Band-Aid and let the wound fester until the next time. "I should go find Dad."

"Yep." Laura's throat worked against tears.

Andrea silently reprimanded herself as she walked back toward the crowd. And then she reprimanded herself for reprimanding herself, because what was the fucking point?

She tossed her empty bottle into the recycling bin, accepting more pats on the back and congratulations from total strangers who thought she was awesome. Andrea's gaze traveled across a sea of mostly white faces until she found her father standing alone in the back. Gordon was taller than most of the dads, with a lean body and a scruffy beard and mustache that gave him an Idris Elba vibe, if Idris Elba was a nerdy trusts and estates attorney who was president of his local astronomy club and talked way too much about jazz.

Andrea was soaked with sweat and Gordon was in one of his Ermenegildo Zegna suits, but he pulled her into a tight hug and kissed the top of her head.

"Dad, I'm filthy."

"That's what dry cleaners are for." He kissed her head again before letting her go. "I'm very proud of what you've accomplished here, sweetheart."

She noted the precision of his words. He wasn't proud of her for becoming a federal agent. He was proud of her for doing the work, just like he had been proud of her when she'd traced an outline of her hand to make a drawing of a turkey in kindergarten.

She tried, "Dad, I—"

He shook his head. He was smiling, but Andrea knew her father's smiles. "Let's talk about how uncomfortable your mother is. I think we can both find some humor in that."

Andrea turned, watching Laura nervously pick her way past a line of armed men. The senior inspectors were dressed in navy polos with the official seal of the United States Marshal Service sewn onto the pockets. Tan pants showed the USMS Silver Star badge gleaming on their belts. Glocks were strapped to their hips.

One of the friendlier instructors started talking to Laura. Gordon chuckled at her agitated demeanor, but Andrea had been too much of a shit to her mother to take any pleasure from watching her squirm.

"I don't know," Andrea said.

Gordon looked down at her.

"If you're wondering why I'm doing this, the answer is that I don't know." Andrea felt unburdened by the admission. She had never let herself say the words out loud before. Maybe Laura's unsolicited advice had pried loose her tongue. "Mentally, in my head, I keep grabbing onto explanations like, being a Marshal gives me a sense of purpose or I should try to make up for the destruction my biological parents tried to cause, but the honest truth is that all I'm doing is putting one foot in front of the other and telling myself that running forward is better than falling backward."

As usual, Gordon contemplated his words before speaking. "Initially, I assumed that you were trying to piss off your mother, and well done because you certainly have, but over four months of physical discipline and intensive study aren't generally hallmarks of rebellion."

He had a point. "Snorting fentanyl and getting knocked up by a biker gang didn't really appeal to me."

Gordon's expression said he didn't appreciate the joke. "It makes sense that you would want answers about your early life."

"I guess," Andrea said, though the possible explanation was only one of many.

The United States Marshal Service, which Andrea was now a part of, controlled the Witness Security program, or what was colloquially called witness protection. Laura's deal to testify against Andrea's father had landed them both in the program, though Andrea was not yet born when her mother had signed on the dotted line. In return for testifying against Andrea's father, Laura had been able to create the story of her tragic widowhood in a coastal Georgia town. Instead of being labeled a stone-cold criminal, she had created the legend of herself as a small-town speech therapist whose anti-government sentiments made her a perfect fit for the disillusioned veterans she worked with at the VA hospital.

Unfortunately, Andrea had learned during her second week of Marshal school that all the USMS Witness Security records were tightly sealed. Absolutely no one could gain access to them without a solid, legally defensible explanation. This wasn't the Illuminati. You didn't gain all the secrets of the world by joining the club.

"Anyway." Gordon knew when to change the subject. "The Marshal badges are impressive. Very Wyatt Earp."

"It's called a Silver Star. And Wyatt Earp didn't become a US Marshal until someone tried to assassinate his brother." Andrea couldn't stop herself. The instructors had drilled the USMS history into every corner of their brains. "Virgil Earp was the deputy in charge during the Gunfight at the O.K. Corral."

"My compliments to your teachers for getting you to crack open a textbook." Gordon's smile still looked strained, but he said, "The starting salary provides a living wage. A step-raise is guaranteed after the first year. Subsequent raises will come after that. Paid time off. Sick days. Healthcare. Mandatory retirement at fifty-seven. You could roll your experience into a consultancy until you're ready to put yourself out to pasture."

He was trying, so she tried, too. "We only go after the really bad guys."

His eyebrows rose.

"We know who we're dealing with," she explained. "It's not like the local police where they pull up on a speeding driver and don't know if they're stopping a cartel member or a guy who's late to softball practice."

Gordon waited.

"We've got their names, their criminal histories. A judge gives us a warrant and sends us out to find them." She shrugged. "Or we're transporting prisoners to the courthouse. Or we're doing civil forfeiture on white-collar criminals. Or making sure pedophiles are doing what they're supposed to be doing. We don't really investigate. Not unless we're assigned to very specific details. Mostly, we deal with people who have already been convicted. We know who they are."

Gordon nodded again, but more like he was acknowledging that she had spoken than agreeing with what she was saying.

She asked, "You know that painting, *The Problem We All Live With*?"

"Norman Rockwell. 1964. Oil on canvas." Gordon knew his art. "The piece was inspired by a six-year-old named Ruby Bridges who integrated an all-white elementary school in New Orleans."

"Did you know that the men who escorted her were US Marshals?"

Gordon asked, "Is that so?"

Andrea gave him all the facts she'd learned for this exact moment. "Marshals provide security for supreme court justices and foreign delegations. And they're tasked with protecting Olympic athletes. And scientists in Antarctica. They're the oldest federal law enforcement agency in the country. George Washington appointed the first thirteen Marshals himself."

Laura chose this moment to join the family. "They also hunted down fugitive slaves and returned them to their owners. And they ran the internment camps that imprisoned Japanese Americans during World War Two. And—"

"Laura," Gordon warned.

Andrea looked down at the ground. She could hear other parents having conversations with their children, and none of them felt as uncomfortable as this.

"Honey?" Gordon waited for Andrea to look up. "You have my support. You've always had my support. You don't have to convince me."

"For fucksakes," Laura mumbled.

Gordon put his hand on Andrea's shoulder. "Just promise me that you will always remember who you are."

"Yes," Laura said. "Don't forget *exactly* who you are."

They were clearly talking about two different things, but Andrea wasn't going to open that up for debate.

"Mr. Mitchell. Ms. Oliver." Another Marshal appeared out of nowhere. He was wearing a sharp suit with his gun concealed under his jacket. Mike winked at Andrea as if two seconds had passed rather than the one year and eight months since she'd last seen him. "I'm Inspector Michael Vargas with the USMS. You must be so proud of your daughter."

"Vargas?" Laura had visibly recoiled at the sight of Mike. He was her handler in Witness Security, and she trusted him about as much as she trusted anybody who worked for the government. "Is that another alias or are you finally telling the truth?"

Andrea shot her mother a look. "The truth about what?"

"Agent Vargas, nice to meet you." Gordon shook Mike's hand, pretending they had never met before because that was how WitSec worked. Even Andrea's instructors had no idea that she had grown up in the program. She doubted the director himself was aware.

"Ms. Oliver." Mike knew that Laura wasn't going to shake his hand. "Congratulations. I can see you're beaming with pride."

"I need a drink." Laura left to find a bar at a federal training center at 10:30 in the morning. She had always bristled at authority, but Andrea joining the very people who had policed her every action for over thirty years had turned Laura into a porcupine with a bazooka.

Mike waited until she was out of earshot. "Nobody tell her that the Marshals helped enforce Prohibition."

Gordon squeezed Andrea's shoulder again before making his own exit.

Mike watched him go, telling Andrea, "At least your mom showed up, right? That's something."

She kept her mouth shut as she tried to find some semblance of composure. Andrea was disgusting and sweaty from the run but the heat rushing through her body was all Mike. They had dated for four very intense months before she had ghosted him. The decision had been as excruciating as it was necessary. Mike was part of Andrea's old life back when, as her beloved mother had just pointed out, Andrea had never met a cliff she couldn't tumble over. She didn't need a man with a savior complex swooping in to break her fall. She had to learn how to save herself.

So maybe *that* was why she had joined the Marshals.

It was as good an explanation as any.

"What do you think of the sexy new look?" Mike scratched his beard, which was lush and dark and full. "You like it?"

She fucking loved it, but she shrugged.

"Let's take a stroll." Mike bumped her shoulder to get her

going, but not before glancing back at Laura and Gordon, who were clearly involved in a heated discussion. "Are they seeing each other again?"

They were, but Andrea wasn't going to feed her mother's handler any information.

Mike tried again. "I'm glad Gordon is supporting your decision to join the good guys."

Gordon was a black man with an Ivy League law school degree who broke out into a sweat every time he saw a police officer in his rearview mirror.

She said, "My father has always supported me."

"So has your mother." Mike grinned at her skeptical look. The fact that he was taking up for Laura when she'd nearly cost him his job a few years ago was either a testament to his resilience or a sign of traumatic amnesia. "You should cut her some slack. This can be a risky job. Laura knows that better than anybody. She's scared you're going to get hurt."

Andrea steered the conversation away from her private life. "I bet your mom threw a huge party when you graduated."

"She did," Mike said. "And then I found her bawling her eyes out in the pantry because she was terrified something bad would happen to me."

Andrea felt a tinge of remorse. She had been so hell-bent on completing her Marshal training that she hadn't stopped to think that Laura might have more reasons to hate this recent life choice than the obvious one. Her mother was a lot of things, but Laura Oliver was not a stupid woman.

"Tell me something." Mike nudged her toward the administrative building. "Are we pretending like you're not eaten up with regret for bailing on me a year and a half ago?"

More like Andrea was pretending like he hadn't edged her so hard that she didn't know whether to scream his name or burst into tears.

If memory served, they had each done a little of both.

"Hey." He playfully bumped her shoulder again. "I think that question deserves an answer."

She came up with one. "I thought we were keeping it casual."

"Were we?" Mike reached ahead to hold open the glass door.

"Casual doesn't usually include me driving over to West Jesus Alabama so you can meet my mother."

His mother had been the exact opposite of Laura, like June Cleaver wrapped up in Rita Moreno with a side of Lorelai Gilmore.

Still, Andrea said, "*Casual* encompasses many things."

"I don't remember getting that message. Was it in a text? Voicemail?"

"Carrier pigeon," she quipped. "Didn't you get the tweet?"

The lights were off inside of the utilitarian office building, but the air conditioning made it the most beautiful place Andrea had ever been. She felt her skin tingle as the sweat dried.

Mike turned uncharacteristically silent as he walked down the hall and opened the door to the stairwell. Andrea let him go ahead of her for the sake of feminism and also to enjoy the view from behind. The lean muscles of his legs stretched against his tailored pants. His strong hand gripped the railing as he pulled himself up two steps at a time. Andrea had slept with boys before Mike, but he was the first man she had ever been with. He was so smart, so damn sure of himself. There hadn't been a lot of room for her to be the same when she was around him.

He opened the door at the top of the stairs. "Tweets before twits."

Andrea guessed she was the twit because Mike went first. She squinted down the dark hallway wondering what the hell they were doing here. This was Mike's gift—he made her brain tune out the sensible things. She should be out of the shower by now. She was going to be late for her own graduation.

She asked, "Where are you taking me?"

"You're the one who likes surprises."

She was the exact opposite of the one who liked surprises, but she followed him into an empty conference room anyway.

The lights were off. Mike opened the blinds so that sunlight streamed in.

He said, "Have a seat."

He technically outranked her, but Andrea was never going to follow Mike's orders.

She walked around the room, which was used for surveillance

and fugitive apprehension drills. The whiteboards were wiped clean now that classes were over. Framed portraits on the walls showed various Marshals of yore. Robert Forsyth, who in the 1790s was the first Marshal killed in the line of duty. Deputy Bass Reeves, the first black Marshal who served at the turn of the last century. Phoebe Couzins, who was not only the first female US Marshal but also one of the first women to graduate from law school in the United States.

The largest framed piece was a poster from the 1993 movie *The Fugitive* starring Harrison Ford as an escaped con and Tommy Lee Jones as the Marshal who tracked him down. Andrea supposed it was better than the giant *Con Air* poster with Nicolas Cage that adorned the break-out room in her dorm. Marshals didn't often get the Hollywood treatment.

Mike stood in front of a giant map of the world. Blue pins dotted the various USMS outposts. The service was a tight community of roughly three thousand agents serving worldwide. They all either knew each other or knew someone who knew someone. It wasn't lost on Andrea that her exile from Mike had landed her in a job where she was bound to run into him again.

He asked, "What'd you put in for?"

Andrea hadn't made a specific request. She would get her assignment after graduation. "I asked for somewhere out west."

"Far from home," he said, knowing very well that was the point. "Have you decided what you want to do?"

She shrugged. "Depends, doesn't it?"

To their credit, the USMS really wanted you to do the work that you wanted to do, so they put you through rotations your first year. For two weeks at a time, you got to do a little of each—fugitive apprehension, judicial security, asset forfeiture, prisoner operations and transport, sex offender management, the missing child program, and of course WitSec.

Andrea's hope was that a giant lightbulb would turn on once she found her calling. Failing that, there was always the excellent retirement package and paid time off.

Mike said, "Those offices are tiny out west. Not a lot of local manpower to lean on. You'll probably be hookin' and haulin' most of the time."

He was talking about prisoner transport. Andrea shrugged.
"You've gotta start somewhere."

"That's a fact." Mike walked over to the window. He looked
out at the practice field. "It'll be another few minutes. Why don't
you sit down?"

Andrea should've pushed for more transparency, but she could
only stare at his broad shoulders. The sexiest thing about Mike
Vargas wasn't his muscular body or his deep voice or even his
hot new beard. He had a way of talking to Andrea that made
her feel like she was the only person he had ever shared anything
with. Like that he loved magical realism yet didn't buy into books
with dragons. That his feet were ticklish and he hated being cold.
That he sometimes resented but always loved his three bossy older
sisters. That when he was a kid, his saint of a mother had worked
two jobs to keep the family fed but he would've gladly skipped
a meal in order to spend more time with her. That he had lied
to Andrea about his father the first time they had talked about
their families.

That Mike was ten years old when his dad had gotten up in
the middle of the night to confront what he thought was an
intruder and accidentally shot Mike's teenage brother in the head.

That sometimes Mike could still hear the harrowing *thump* of
his dead brother's body hitting the wooden floor.

That sometimes Mike thought he was hearing the other *thump*
of his dad's body when the man had killed himself with the same
gun one week later.

"Hey, I almost forgot." Mike was smiling when he turned back
around. "I was going to offer you some advice."

Andrea loved his teasing tone. "My favorite thing is unsolicited
advice."

His smile turned into a grin. "Wherever you land, do yourself
a favor and tell everybody that we're dating."

She actually guffawed. "How is that doing me a favor?"

"Well, number one, look at me." He spread out his arms. "I'm
fucking gorgeous."

He wasn't wrong about that. "And number two?"

"The guys in your new office are gonna wonder why you're
not sleeping with them." He leaned his back against the window.

"And they're gonna start wondering—is she from internal affairs? Is she spying on me? Can I trust her? Or is she a lesbian? Why won't she come out? What's she hiding? Is her girlfriend prettier than me?"

"Those are the only choices? Either I'm a rat or I'm gay? It can't be that I'm not interested?"

"Baby, they're US Marshals. Of course you're interested."

Andrea shook her head. The only thing at Glynco that reeked more than sweat and Skin So Soft was testosterone. "I think your ego swallowed my carrier pigeon."

His eyes twinkled in the sunlight. "That explains why I can't get the taste of you out of my mouth."

They both startled when a man wearing a black suit and a springy earpiece and showcasing the stick-up-the-ass posture of a federal agent poked his bald head into the room. He glanced around, nodded, then backed out.

"Sorry I'm late." An imposing older man walked through the doorway, effectively sucking up all of the oxygen. He reached out an elegant hand toward Andrea. "It's nice to finally meet you, Andrea. I'm so proud of what you've done here at the training facility. It's quite an accomplishment."

She had to bite her lip to keep her jaw from dropping. He hadn't introduced himself, but she knew his face—of course she knew his face. He'd been a serious contender in the last presidential primary until a scandal had knocked him out of contention. Fortunately, he'd managed to land on his feet and was now the junior senator from the state of California.

He was also, she had recently learned, Laura's older brother, which technically made him Andrea's uncle.

"Have you—" her voice caught. "You didn't see my mother?"

Jasper Queller's Botoxed eyebrows twitched. "She's here?"

"With my dad. Gordon. They, uh . . ." Andrea had to sit down. She had forgotten Mike was in the room until he introduced himself to Jasper. She wanted to kick his balls into the back of his throat for bringing her here. And she wanted to kick herself for walking into his trap, because Jasper hadn't shown up by happenstance.

All of this had been planned.

Andrea heard a question ping-ponging inside her brain, one
that had been posed to her two years ago when her life had turned
upside down—

*Jesus, kid, did you go through your entire life with a fishhook
in your mouth?*

She had answered in the affirmative then. There was no excuse
for the fact that she was still taking the bait two years later.

She asked Jasper, "What are you doing here?"

Mike divined this was a good time to slip out the door.

Jasper placed a slim leather briefcase on the table. The sharp
sound of the gold-plated locks clicking open was like money. She
didn't know who had made his suit, but someone had held an
actual needle while they were doing it. She was probably looking
at the physical manifestation of her combined student loan debt.

He indicated a chair. "May I?"

Andrea didn't need to consult the organizational flowchart on
the wall. The USMS was a bureau within the Department of
Justice, which was overseen by the Senate Judiciary Committee,
which consisted of twenty-two senators, including the man who
was asking if he could sit down across from her.

"Help yourself." She tried to wave her hand cavalierly but
ended up hitting the edge of the table. Despite the frigid a/c, a
bead of sweat rolled down her back. Her emotions were all over
the place. Laura would go nuts if she found out that her daughter
and her brother were in the same room together. No matter how
angry Andrea was with her mother, she didn't see a choice in
front of her. She would never, ever be on Jasper's side.

"Andrea, I'd like to start by saying I'm sorry we've not met
before." Even sitting down, Jasper had a military bearing, though
he'd been out of uniform for decades. "I had hoped you would
reach out to me."

Andrea looked at the fine lines crinkling around his eyes. He
was six years older than Laura, but they had the same patrician
nose and high cheekbones. "Why would I reach out to you?"

He nodded once. "Good question. I suppose your mother was
against it."

The truth was an effective weapon. "The subject never came
up."

Jasper looked at her from behind his open briefcase. He pulled out a folder. He placed it on the table. He closed the briefcase and set it on the floor.

Andrea forced herself not to ask about the folder because he clearly wanted her to ask about the folder. "I'm going to be late for my graduation."

"Trust me, they won't start without you."

Andrea gritted her teeth. The small world of the Marshal Service just got smaller. She'd soon be surrounded by a bunch of trained investigators who would be wondering why a US senator had held up graduation so he could talk to Andrea Oliver.

"It's really quite something to see you in person." Jasper was openly studying her face. "Your aspect reminds me so much of your mother."

"Why doesn't that feel like a compliment?"

He smiled. "I suppose it's better than being compared to your father."

She supposed he was right.

"He's why I'm here, actually." Jasper tapped the folder. "As you know, the additional charges filed against your father two years ago ended with hung juries. DOJ won't try him again. Meanwhile, time is winding down on his original sentencing. Conspiracy to commit acts of domestic terrorism was a novel charge pre-9/11. The murder conspiracy only has a certain number of teeth, and while your mother's testimony was helpful, it was not quite helpful enough, was it? We would be almost better off had your father succeeded in his crimes."

Andrea didn't appreciate the swipe at Laura, but she shrugged out her hands. Nick Harp had another fifteen years left on his forty-eight-year sentence. "So?"

Jasper said, "Your father is up for parole again in six months."

Something about his tone twisted Andrea's stomach into a knot. The only reason she was able to sleep at night was because she knew that Nick was behind bars. "He's had parole hearings before. He always gets turned down. Why do you think this time will be any different?"

"One could say that the general attitude toward domestic terrorism has taken a recent turn, especially among historically more conservative parole boards." Jasper shook his head as if a United States senator had little control over the world. "In past years, I've been able to prevent his parole from being granted but, this time, he might actually have a shot."

"Seriously?" Andrea didn't bother to conceal her skepticism. "You oversee the Bureau of Prisons."

"Exactly," he confirmed. "It would be unseemly for me to be seen putting my thumb on the scale."

Andrea's throat had gone bone dry. She felt shaky with fear over the possibility of Nick getting out and angry that Jasper had contrived this ambush. "Excuse me, Senator, but we both know you've done some unseemly things before."

He smiled again. "Very much like your mother."

"Fuck off with your comparisons." Andrea leaned across the table. "Do you know what he did to us the last time? He's a monster. People died. And that was while he was still in prison. Do you know what he'll do when he gets out? He'll come right for my mother. And me."

"Excellent." Jasper mimicked her shrug from before. "We all seem to have a vested interest in his continued incarceration."

Andrea readjusted her approach, because being an icy bitch didn't seem to be working. "What do you want from me?"

"On the contrary, I'm here to give you something." He pulled his hand away from the folder. She saw there was a label but couldn't read the words. "I'd like to help you, Andrea. And to help the family."

She knew he meant Laura though, so far, he had yet to utter her mother's name.

Jasper said, "You've asked for an assignment on the West Coast."

She vehemently shook her head. The last thing she needed was to be in her uncle's home state. "I'm not interested in—"

"Please hear me out." He held up his hand. "I was wondering if you wouldn't prefer somewhere closer, like the Baltimore office."

Andrea was silenced by a sudden rush of anxiety.

"There's a federal judge in the district who's been receiving credible death threats. Someone mailed a dead rodent to her Baltimore home." Jasper paused a beat. "You might have seen the story on the nightly news."

Andrea hadn't seen anything because no one her age watched the nightly news.

Jasper continued, "The judge is a Reagan appointee. One of the last few standing, in fact. There was quite a bit of pressure for her to retire during the previous administration, but she missed her window of opportunity."

Andrea had never been interested in politics, but she knew the USMS was tasked with protecting federal judges.

"Her judicial appointment has a tragic backstory. The week before her confirmation hearing, her daughter disappeared. Concurrently, a body was found inside a Dumpster on the edge of town. The woman's face was bashed in. Two vertebrae in her neck were fractured. They had to identify her using dental records. She was the judge's daughter."

Andrea felt the soles of her feet start to tingle, as if she was standing on the edge of a very tall building.

"Unbelievably, the girl survived the attack." Jasper paused, as if the fact deserved reverence. "Though, *survived* is a relative term. Medically, she was in a vegetative state, but she was also pregnant. To the best of my knowledge, they never found out who the father was. They kept her body alive using life support for nearly two more months—until the baby could be safely delivered."

Andrea bit down hard on her lip to keep her body from visibly shuddering.

"At the time, the girl's plight was a cause célèbre. Her tragic circumstances arguably helped grease her mother's confirmation. Reagan was the one who really pushed the anti-abortion stance onto the platform. Before that, no one on their side really cared. Bush had to turn his back on Planned Parenthood to get the VP slot." Jasper seemed to pick up on her desire that he get to the point. "The judge and her husband raised the child. I say child, but she's forty years old now. She has a daughter of her own. A teenager, in fact. I hear she's quite a handful."

Andrea asked the same question from before. "What are you doing here?"

"I think what you really want to know is, *what does this have to do with my father?*" His hand returned to the mysterious file.

"The federal courts are in summer recess. As is their usual, the judge and her husband have returned to their family estate, where they will stay for the next two months. The USMS has two teams working security, one night shift, one day, while the death threats are investigated by the special judicial inspector out of Baltimore HQ. The security assignment is no hardship, really. Think of it as babysitting. And Longbill Beach is a beautiful town. I gather you know where that is?"

Andrea had to clear her throat before she could answer. "Delaware."

"Exactly right," Jasper said. "In fact, Longbill Beach is the same town where your father grew up."

Andrea put together the remaining pieces. "You think that forty years ago, Nick Harp killed the judge's daughter."

Jasper nodded. "Murder has no statute of limitations. A conviction would keep him in prison for the rest of his life."

Andrea heard the words echo inside her brain—*in prison for the rest of his life.*

Jasper said, "He was rumored to be the father of her child. She confronted him in public the night that she disappeared. They argued in front of several witnesses. He physically and verbally threatened her. Then he left town shortly after her body was identified."

Andrea felt her throat work. She wanted to hold onto the details but, in her mind, all she could think about was that Nick Harp had fathered another child.

And then he had abandoned her.

"See for yourself." Jasper finally released the folder, sliding it in her direction.

Andrea let the closed file sit between them. She could read the label now:

EMILY ROSE VAUGHN DOB 5/1/64 DOD 6/9/82

Her eyes blurred on the young girl's name. Andrea's mind was still reeling. She tried to focus her attention—murder, no statute of limitations, Nick behind bars for the rest of his life—but what she kept coming back to was a single question: Was this somehow a trap? She couldn't trust Jasper. She had learned the hard way that she couldn't really trust anyone.

"Well," Jasper said. "Aren't you curious?"

Curious wasn't the emotion she was feeling right now.

Scared. Apprehensive. Angry.

A forty-year-old half-sister who'd grown up in a beach town just like Andrea had. Another child who would never solve the puzzle of her mother. A sadistic father who'd destroyed their lives, then moved on to his next victim.

Andrea's trembling hand reached for the file. The cover felt thick between her fingers. The first page showed a photograph of a pretty young blonde who smiled openly at the camera. Her tight perm and blue eyeshadow placed her firmly in the early eighties. Andrea turned to the next page. Then the next. She recognized the police report by its layout. Date, time, location, street map, crime scene drawing, possible murder weapon, witnesses, injuries on the body of an innocent seventeen-year-old girl.

Sweat made Andrea's fingers moist as she continued to flip through the pages. She located the investigating officer's notes. Computers were rare in 1982. Apparently, so were typewriters. The scribble was almost illegible, photocopied so many times that the letters looked furred.

Andrea knew she would not find the name Nicholas Harp anywhere in the file. That was the pseudonym that her father had been using when he'd first met her mother. He'd abandoned his true identity back in the spring of 1982, when he'd left Longbill Beach for good. The people there would know him by his real name. She found it on the last page, circled, underlined twice.

Clayton Morrow.

2

"Oregon is beautiful, Mom." Andrea ignored the confused look the Uber driver shot her as they crossed over the Chesapeake Bay. She turned her head, indicating this was a private phone call. "I think I'm going to like it here."

"Well, that's something," Laura said. Water shushed into the sink. She was making dinner for Gordon back on Belle Isle. "It's been so long since I was there. I remember the trees."

"The Douglas fir is the state tree. The state flower is the Oregon grape. But it's not like grape-grapes. The fruit is more like a berry." Andrea's thumb scrolled through the Oregon Wikipedia page on her work phone. "Did you know it's the ninth largest state?"

"I did not."

"And—" Andrea looked for something that didn't sound like she was reading a statistic. "There's a rainforest in the northwestern part called Valley of the Giants. That's cool, right?"

"Is it cold there? I told you to pack your jacket."

"It's fine." She pulled up weather.com. "Sixty-four degrees."

"It's still early in the day," Laura said, though Oregon was only three hours behind. "The temperature will drop with the sun. You should buy a jacket there. It'll be cheaper than me Fedexing yours. Summer weather is mercurial in the Pacific Northwest. You never know what to expect."

"I'll be okay, Mom." Andrea looked out the window as she listened to her mother describe the exact type of jacket she should buy for weather that was happening nearly three thousand miles away.

"Zippers that seal are very important," Laura said. "And elastic around the cuffs because the wind will cut straight up your arm."

Andrea's eyes closed against the early afternoon sun. Her internal compass was spinning too fast. Jasper hadn't just put an unseemly thumb on the scale. He had knocked the whole damn thing over. Andrea was supposed to get two weeks off before starting her first assignment. Thanks to her estranged uncle, she was just over twenty-four hours out from graduation and already working two different cases. One was babysitting a judge who'd gotten some death threats and been mailed a dead rat, the other was to keep her father behind bars by somehow finding proof that he was guilty of murdering a young girl who had been long forgotten.

As with every other decision Andrea had made in the last two years, she wasn't sure why she had taken Jasper up on his offer. Her first inclination had been to walk out of the room. But then she had allowed herself to do the one thing she had resisted over the last two years: think back to the moment her life had exploded.

Instead of rising to the occasion, Andrea had spun around like a wind-up monkey clanging together a pair of broken cymbals. There was nothing about that time she was proud of. She hadn't planned anything. She hadn't considered the implications. She had aimlessly driven thousands of miles trying to solve the mystery of her parents and uncover the truth about all of their crimes. For her impetuousness, she had nearly lost her life and almost gotten Laura killed in the process. And that didn't even include what Andrea had done to Mike. He'd tried to save her multiple times and she had literally and figuratively kicked him in the balls for his trouble.

So maybe that was why Andrea had said yes.

It was as good an explanation as any.

How exactly she was going to solve a forty-year-old murder was anyone's guess. Her first twenty-four hours as a United States Marshal had seen a less than auspicious start. Yesterday afternoon, she'd driven five hours in a rental car to reach the Atlanta airport in time for her 9:50 flight to Baltimore, but then bad weather had delayed her flight for two and a half hours, then more bad weather had diverted her plane to Washington DC, which meant she hadn't landed until two this morning. From Dulles, she'd taken a twenty-minute taxi ride to a cheap motel in Arlington, Virginia, where she'd slept for four hours, then slept another hour and a half on the train to USMS district headquarters in Baltimore, Maryland.

No one had been prepared for her arrival. All of the senior officers were at a conference in DC. An agent named Leeta Frazier who normally worked civil asset forfeitures had stuck Andrea in a conference room to sign a bunch of paperwork, given her a pamphlet on how not to sexually harass anybody, handed over her government-issued Glock 17 9mm along with her Silver Star, then told Andrea she'd have to come back later to meet her boss and the rest of the team.

To make matters worse, Leeta was unable to requisition a car, which was how Andrea had ended up in the world's most expensive Uber to Longbill Beach. The day already felt like an extended version of the most boring day in the history of the known world. Only now, at nearly two in the afternoon, was Andrea finally passing through coastal Maryland on her way to Delaware where she was supposedly—hopefully—going to meet her new partner.

"Send me a picture when you get it," Laura said.

Andrea had to rewind the conversation to understand that her mother was talking about the phantom jacket Andrea was supposed to buy for weather she was not experiencing. "I'll try to remember."

"And you promised you'd call me twice a day."

"I did not."

"Text me, I mean."

"Nope."

"Andrea," Laura said, but then Gordon started to speak so she muffled the phone.

Andrea clicked off the screen on her work phone, wondering if she had already managed to violate agency policy by googling Oregon trivia. She still couldn't believe they had given her a gun and badge. She was a plain ol' dewsum—a deputy US Marshal. She could arrest people. She could deputize her Uber driver if she wanted to. Maybe she could make him keep his beady eyes on the road, because the minute he'd clocked she was law enforcement, he'd started looking at her like she was a turd that had been dropped in his back seat.

She was reminded of a sentence one of her instructors had written on the whiteboard:

If you want people to love you, don't join law enforcement.

"All right." Laura was back on the line. "It's not required, but I would very much appreciate an occasional text from you, my darling, so that I know you're still alive."

"Okay," Andrea relented, though she had no idea whether she would comply. "I need to go, Mom. I think I see a western meadowlark."

"Oh, send me a pic—"

Andrea ended the call. She watched a sandpiper float along the breeze, doing that weird thing where it was moving forward but looked like it was treading air.

She closed her eyes for a moment and let out a long breath, hoping to release her exhaustion. She felt her body yearning to go to sleep, but if her previous attempts at rest had proven anything, it was that her mind was perfectly willing to race between trying to figure out her uncle's true motives, wondering if her father would find out what she was doing and try to blow everything up, and rehashing her conversation with Mike to see which felt better: telling him she had made a terrible mistake or telling him to fuck off.

Andrea couldn't play that same game for another two hours. At least not in the back of an Uber that smelled of Armor All and mountain pine air freshener. To keep herself from spiraling, she reached into her backpack and pulled out the Emily Vaughn file.

Her eye caught the worn, typewritten label. She wondered how Jasper had gotten copies of the police investigation. As a United States senator, she assumed he had a lot of access to all kinds of information. Also, he was shitifyingly wealthy, so anywhere his power didn't work, a large briefcase full of cash certainly would.

Not that any of Jasper's machinations mattered. Andrea's alternate investigation had only one purpose, and it wasn't to ingratiate herself with her rich uncle. She really, really wanted to keep her father locked up—not only for Laura's safety, but because a man who was capable of turning a handful of vulnerable people into a cult bent on destruction should not be out of prison. If that meant solving a forty-year-old murder, then Andrea would somehow have to solve a forty-year-old murder. And if she couldn't prove her father did it, or if she proved that someone else did . . . She would fall off that cliff when she got to it.

Andrea took another breath and hushed it out before opening the folder.

The photo of Emily Rose Vaughn was what got to her the most. It was clearly her senior picture. The not-quite-eighteen-year-old had been beautiful, even with her perm and heavily lined eyes. Andrea flipped over the photo and looked at the date. Emily was probably starting to show when she'd stood in line with the other seniors for her turn in front of the camera. Maybe she'd worn a girdle or control-top pantyhose or some other eighties-style female torture to try to hide the truth.

Andrea studied Emily's face again. She tried to remember what it felt like to be that close to graduation. Excited about college. Eager to get away from home. Ready to be an adult, or at least a version of an adult that was still wholly subsidized by her parents.

Emily Vaughn had served as a human incubator during the last seven weeks of her life. As far as Andrea could tell from the police report, Jasper was right when he'd said that the father had never been identified. 1982 was thirteen years before the OJ Simpson trial had made the general public and the court systems more accepting of DNA evidence. Back then, there had only been Emily's word to go on, and she had apparently taken her secret to the grave.

The question was, had Clayton Morrow been a suspect because he was a credible suspect, or had the crimes of Nick Harp made him seem guilty after the fact?

Andrea had done the expected googling and found very little publicly available information about the attack on Emily Vaughn. No true crime podcaster or TV producer had done a deep dive on the case, probably because there was no new thread to pick at. No new witnesses. No new suspects. What little trace evidence that had been collected from the various scenes had either been

lost to time or washed away by the inland flooding caused by
Hurricane Isabel in 2003.

Judge Esther Vaughn's wiki linked to twenty-one forty-year-old
newspaper articles about the circumstances surrounding Emily's
death. Sixteen were from the *Longbill Beacon*, an alternative
paper that had folded eight years ago and left nothing but a 404
when Andrea clicked through. The national stories were behind
paywalls that she wasn't going to access because she didn't want
to leave a credit card trail and, also, she wasn't sure her credit
card would go through. The USMS database wasn't an option
because it was a violation of policy—and federal law—to run
background checks on people without legitimate investigative
authority.

Which meant Andrea's internet sleuthing had hit a post-wiki
dead end. The death of Emily Vaughn had left almost no digital
footprint. In the multiple opinion pieces that Esther Vaughn had
penned over the years, there were no details beyond her "tragic
personal loss" that she twisted to justify exactly the kinds of
things about criminal justice that you would expect a Reagan
appointee to justify. As for the judge's husband, Andrea had found
a press release dated one year ago from Loyola University,
Maryland, a private Jesuit liberal arts school, announcing that
Dr. Franklin Vaughn was retiring as professor emeritus from the
Sellinger School of Business Management in order to spend more
time with his family.

Likewise, details about said family were not provided.

Also likewise, Dr. Vaughn's many pontifications on economics
and social justice seemed light on solutions that did not involve
the yanking up of your own bootstraps, never mind whether or
not you could afford to buy boots in the first place.

Most jarringly, the internet didn't seem to know the name of
Emily's daughter.

Andrea was unsure how much to read into this omission. There
were a handful of explanations for the woman's lack of an internet
footprint. She was an elder millennial, seven years Andrea's senior,
so social media was probably not her natural habitat. It was easy
to keep your name offline if you stayed offline, and Facebook
sucked as much as Instagram as much as TikTok as much as

Twitter. Or Emily's daughter could've legally changed her name or taken a spouse's last name or cut off contact with her grandparents or, more likely, she stayed away because her mother had been brutally murdered, probably by her megalomaniacal father, and her grandmother was a federal judge and as bad as people were forty years ago, they were absolute monsters now that they had the internet.

So all Andrea could do was wonder. Was Emily's daughter still in Longbill Beach or had she gotten out? Was she divorced? Jasper had said that she had a child of her own, a teenage girl who was a *handful*, but was she close to her grandparents? Had she been told the truth about Emily's death? What did she do for a living? What did she look like? Did she have Nick Harp's icy blue eyes, sharp cheekbones and slightly cleft chin, or her mother's more rounded, heart-shaped face?

Andrea's hand went to her own face. She had none of Jasper and Laura's patrician features, though Jasper was probably right about Andrea's *aspect* reminding him of Laura's. Her eyes were a light brown, not icy blue. Her face was narrow, though not triangular, with an almost imperceptible cleft at the chin that she assumed came from her father. Her nose was a genetic mystery— turned up at the tip like Piglet smelling a tulip.

She clipped Emily's photo back on the first page. She thumbed through the reports, though she had read them all countless times at the airport gate, on the plane, in the back of taxis, in her motel, on the train. Smudged fingerprints offered evidence of the orange peanut butter crackers she'd snarfed down for breakfast.

Andrea should be better at this.

All prospective agents at the Glynco FLETC went through criminal investigation school for an intensive, mind-bending ten weeks. Andrea had sat alongside an alphabet of future federal law enforcement as they were drilled in the finer arts of investigation—DEA, ATF, IRS, CBP, HHS. And then the wannabe Marshals had peeled off for ten more weeks of specialized instruction alongside the Sisyphean physical requirements that set the service apart.

The instructors had created intricately detailed dummy cases—a fugitive on the run, a child kidnapping, a series of escalating threats to a supreme court justice. Andrea's team had combed through faked CCTV from businesses and ATM machines and residential doorbells. They had gone online and pulled up building plans and maps, then run credit checks and public records searches looking for family members, friends and acquaintances with varying degrees of separation. There were social media accounts to scan, license plate readers to ping, photographs to run through facial recognition, cell phone carriers to subpoena, emails and texts to read.

In 1982, there was only your mouth and ears. You asked questions. You got answers. You put them all together and you tried to get to a resolution.

Andrea wouldn't say the Longbill police chief had done a stellar job, especially considering the killer had never been charged, but he'd put in the yeoman's work. There were line drawings with measurements of the Dumpster behind Skeeter's Grill where Emily had been found. A rough stick figure with 'X's documented the violence on her body. The alley where blood consistent with Emily's type was located had been measured off and processed for trace evidence. A possible murder weapon—a piece of wood from a splintered shipping pallet in the alleyway—was found discarded along the main road. A clump of black threads was found on the pallet back in the alley, but was returned by the FBI as too common to be conclusive. From the multiple witness statements alone, Andrea was able to generate a timeline that traced the last steps Emily Vaughn had taken before her life was cut short.

The most poignant part, the part Andrea couldn't get past, was a word that normally would've been deleted on a computer screen, a ghost lost to technology.

Andrea had found the word in the handwritten transcript of a 911 call that was generated when a kitchen worker at the fast-food restaurant had lifted the lid of the Dumpster and found the naked, very pregnant body of Emily Vaughn laid across broken bags of garbage. The operator's handwriting was shaky, probably because the Longbill Beach police mostly dealt with complaints about unruly tourists and aggressive seagulls. The first line probably encapsulated the first thing the caller had said.

Body of a woman found in trash behind Skeeter's Grill.

They didn't know that Emily was still alive at that point. That was a revelation that the EMTs would bring. What got to Andrea, what brought tears to her eyes, was that at some point, probably when they realized to whom the body belonged, someone had crossed out the word *woman* and changed the sentence to—

Body of a girl . . .

A girl who was filled with potential. A girl who had hopes and dreams. A girl who was found lying on her side with her arms wrapped tightly around her unborn child.

To Andrea, Emily would never be just *a* girl. She was *the first girl*—one of many her father had left in his violent wake.

Andrea felt the car start to slow. The two-hour ride had passed more quickly than she'd noticed. She closed Emily's file and slipped it into her backpack. They were driving down the main strip of what had to be Longbill Beach. She saw dozens of sun-stupefied tourists loitering outside fast-food stands and strolling down a wide, white boardwalk lining the Atlantic Ocean that for all appearances could've stretched six hundred miles south to the boardwalk in Belle Isle.

Annoyingly, she thought of her mother—

Wherever you go, there you are.

"Drop me—" Andrea winced, because the driver chose this exact moment to turn up the radio. "The library! Drop me off in front of the library!"

He pumped his head on his neck, keeping time with the blaring music as he took a sharp right turn away from the sea. He'd obviously chosen the song for her sake. N.W.A.'s "Fuk da Police."

Andrea indulged herself in an eye-roll as the car took another elbow turn that pushed her shoulder into the door. The Longbill Beach Main Library was on the backside of the high school. The building looked newer, but not by much. Instead of the solid red brick of the school, the exterior was a beachy stucco painted in salmon with Palladian windows that probably turned it into a kiln during the summer.

The driver didn't bother to turn down the music as they pulled to the front of the library. A wiry older man in a faded Hawaiian shirt, jeans and cowboy boots stood by the book deposit box.

He started clapping his hands to the music, which hit the chorus as Andrea was opening the car door.

"Fuck the police, fuck— fuck—" the man shouted along, doing a two-step toward the car. "Fuck the police!"

Before Glynco, Andrea had catalogued people as only younger or older than she was. Now, she guessed the guy was mid-fifties, around six feet tall, maybe 175 pounds. Military-looking tattoos swirled up his muscled arms. His bald head gleamed in the waning sun. His Van-Dyke was salt and pepper and came to a devil-point half an inch below his chin.

"Fuck the police." He spun around, his shirt riding up. "Fuck-fuck."

Andrea had frozen at the sight of a 9mm Glock clipped to his belt. His Silver Star gleamed beside it. She guessed she was looking at her new partner. And then she further guessed that he had worked in fugitive apprehension, because there were very few dress codes and regulations for agents tasked with hunting down the worst of the worst.

She extended her hand. "I'm—"

"Andrea Oliver, straight outta Glynco." He showed off an impressive Tex-Arkana accent as he shook her hand. "I'm Deputy Bible. Glad you finally made it. You gotta bag?"

She didn't know what to do other than show him her duffel bag, which held enough clothes to get her through a week. Any longer than that and she'd have to explain to her mother why she needed her things sent to Baltimore instead of Portland.

"Excellent." Bible gave two thumbs up to the driver. "Love what you're saying there with your music, son. Way to be an ally."

If the driver had a response, Bible didn't wait for it. He nodded for Andrea to follow him down the sidewalk. "Thought we'd walk and reconnoiter, get to know each other, come up with a plan. I been here maybe two hours, so I didn't get much of a head start. Name's Leonard, by the way, but everybody calls me Catfish."

"Catfish Bible?" For the first time in two years, Andrea regretted that her mother wasn't here. He'd practically stumbled out of a Flannery O'Connor novel.

"You gotta nickname?" He watched Andrea shake her head. "Everybody's gotta nickname. I bet you're just hiding it. Watch out."

A kid on a bicycle nearly clipped her.

"Take a gander." He turned his head so the light would catch the thin scars that slashed down both sides of his cheeks. "Got into a fight with a catfish."

Andrea wondered if the fish had a switchblade.

"Anyways," Bible walked as fast as he talked. "I heard your flight got delayed. Must've been hell jumping on a plane right after the push and puke."

He meant the Marshal Mile, the last run before graduation. And he also meant that he was aware of the highly unusual circumstances of Andrea's speedy assignment.

She told him, "I'm good. Ready to go."

"That's great. I'm good, too. Super good. Always ready. We're gonna be a fantastic team, Oliver. I can feel it in my bones."

Andrea tightened her grip on her duffel and moved her backpack to her other shoulder as she tried to keep up with his long strides. The going was not easy as they got close to the main strip. Both sides of Beach Drive were filled with tourists of varying sizes and ages looking at maps, stopping to text, gaping at the sun.

She felt incredibly conspicuous in her outfit. The polo was black with a giant yellow USMS logo on the back as well as over the breast pocket. All they'd had was a man's small, but the sleeves hung down past her elbows and the collar was so thick it scraped her chin. She'd pulled the seams out of the cuffs of her pants, but they were still half an inch too short and the waist was half an inch too large because women's pants had tiny pockets and no belt loops, so she'd been forced to buy boys' pants in the kids' department and a thick, woven belt so she could clip her gun, handcuffs, mace and Silver Star around her waist. For the first time in her life, she had hips. But not in a good way.

Bible seemed to pick up on her discomfort. "You got some jeans in that bag?"

"Yes." She had exactly one pair.

"I like wearing jeans." He punched the button at the crosswalk.

His head stuck up above the crowd like a meerkat's. "Comfortable, stylish, easy to move around in."

Andrea looked at the street signs as Bible debated relax vs. slim fit. She recognized the intersection from one of the witness statements—

At approximately 6:00 p.m. on April 17, 1982, I, Melody Louise Brickel, witnessed Emily Vaughn crossing the street at Beach Drive and Royal Cove Way. She appeared to have come from the direction of the gymnasium. She was wearing a strapless turquoise dress made of satin with tulle with a matching clutch but no pantyhose or shoes. She looked troubled. I did not approach her because my mom told me I should stay away from Emily and anyone in her group. I never saw her alive again. I do not know who the father of her baby is. I swear the contents of my statement are true under penalty of law.

Bible asked, "Who'd you meet at HQ?"

Andrea had to pull her brain out of a fog. "Everyone was at a conference. There was a woman working asset forfeiture who—"

"Leeta Frazier," he provided. "Good gal. Been around almost as long as me. But, listen, here's what's important—Mike told me to look after you."

Her heart sank. "Mike doesn't—"

"Now, let me stop you right there," he said. "Cussy, that's my wife, she's always telling me that chivalry is wasted on the young, but I wanna tell you straight up I've never believed the rumors. And I'm not just saying that because you're engaged."

Andrea felt her jaw wanting to hinge open.

"Glad we've got that out of the way." The light had turned. Bible started to cross the street inside a herd of sunburned teenagers. He glanced over his shoulder, asking Andrea, "You got a place in B'more yet?"

"No—I—" She jogged to catch up. "We're not—Mike and I—"

"None of my business. We will never speak of it again." His finger zipped across his lips. "Listen, though, what do you know about the judge?"

"I—" Andrea felt like she was falling through a black hole.

"Lookit, I remember what it's like to be a shiny new dewsum straight out of the box—just got your credentials slapped in your hand, don't even know which way is thattaway, but I'm here to coach you up. My last partner's on a beach sipping Mai Tais and counting manatees. You and me, we're a team now, like a family, but a work family because you've got your own family, I get that."

Andrea stepped up onto the sidewalk. She took a breath. When she'd first met Mike, he'd strafed her with a similar machine-gun volley of bromides. He'd been trying to throw her off, to get her to say something she didn't mean to say, and it had worked so many times that she'd felt like an idiot.

She had spent the two years since working on not being that woman anymore.

Andrea took another breath, then said, "Judge Esther Rose Vaughn. Eighty-one years old. Reagan appointee. Confirmed in 1982. One of two remaining conservatives on the court. She has a granddaughter and a great—"

Bible stopped so abruptly that Andrea almost bumped into him. "How do you know about the grand and great-grand?"

She felt caught out. Maybe there was a more deliberate reason that the forty-year-old daughter of Emily Vaughn had no visible online presence.

Instead of floundering, she asked, "Why wouldn't I?"

"Exactly." He started walking again.

Andrea didn't know what to do but follow him up the long sidewalk. The crowd thinned as the last of the sightseers peeled off to watch taffy being pulled behind a smudged plate glass window. The touristy end of the street petered out at a closed bike rental shop and a place to sign up for paddleboard lessons and parasailing. As with everything else, the outriggers felt extremely familiar. Andrea had spent many a summer on the beach watching tourists try not to flip their surfboards into a rip tide or smack their parachutes into a high-rise building.

"So, the judge." Bible's prattle started back as quickly as it had stopped. "She got some death threats. No big deal. Happens all the time, especially after she tossed out that election LOLsuit two years ago."

Andrea nodded. Death threats were so commonplace now you could get them at Starbucks.

He said, "The latest death threats are classified as credible because she got some letters mentioning some particular details about her private life. Snail mail letters. The judge don't do email."

Andrea nodded again, but her head started throbbing over the rush of new data. Her focus during her entire journey thus far had been on Emily Vaughn and her possible killer. Andrea had pushed aside thoughts of her real job because of the word *babysitting*, but now she realized that her real job was, in fact, a very serious job.

She tried to sound like a Marshal. "Where were the letters mailed from?"

"That blue collection box we passed on the way from the library. No cameras on it. No fingerprints that can be used," Bible said. "They were mailed over the holiday, one on Friday, then another on Saturday, then Sunday and Monday. They were all addressed to the judge's chambers at the federal courthouse in Baltimore, same building as the one you were in today. We all got a kind'a family up there between the federal judges and the Marshals. I've known the judge and her people for years. We look out for each other."

Andrea tried another question, "Was the rat sent to the courthouse?"

"Nope," Bible said. "The box with the rat didn't get mailed. It was left in the judge's mailbox at her city house, which is located in Guilford, an up-your-butt part of North Baltimore, a dog's leg from Johns Hopkins and Loyola."

"Where the judge's husband, Dr. Franklin Vaughn, taught economics before he retired last year."

Bible clicked his tongue, she guessed as a reward for Andrea doing her homework.

She asked, "Are they the same people? The death-threat-letter mailer and the rat-dropper?"

"Could be the same guy, could be it's two guys."

"Guys?"

"In my experience, if a woman's gonna kill you, she'll do it to your face."

Andrea had found that to be true in her experience, too. "Are you reading anything into the dead rat? Like, that sounds like a *Godfather* kind of thing—*you ratted us out.*"

"I appreciate your taste in movies, but no. The Baltimore Crew is dead and gone and the judge don't really work them cases anymore," Bible said. "Now, so, you're probably wondering why we ain't in Baltimore right now. Lucky for us, it's summer recess, otherwise the judge would still be going to work every day at the courthouse. No way she'd come running back home because of one dead rat. The lady likes a schedule. She's been spending the summer months at the Longbill house since her confirmation. Her car drove them here this morning at the crack of dawn, which is exactly what the judge has been doing for two hundred years. What you gotta keep at the front of your mind at all times is, the judge is gonna do what the judge is gonna do."

Andrea caught his meaning, not least of all because of the googling she'd already done. Every photograph of Judge Esther Vaughn showed a stern-looking woman staring down the camera, invariably wearing a beautifully colored scarf to accent a severe black suit. The descriptions in the articles were a stroll down #MeToo lane. Several articles from the nineties notably called Judge Vaughn *a difficult woman.* The early aughts saw her described in a far more squishy *complicated woman.* More recently, all the strong *I* adjectives were invoked: *imposing, imperious, intelligent,* and, most commonly, *indomitable.*

"Anyways, that's your nutshell on the judge," Bible said. "Don't really matter at the end of the day who mailed what and why, whether or not it was the same person or multiple persons. The judicial inspector back at Baltimore HQ is tracking that rabbit. We're not the investigators. Our only job is to keep the judge safe."

Andrea felt her throat tighten. Everything was starting to feel very life and death, not least of all because she had a loaded gun on her hip. Would a crazy person really come after the judge? Did Andrea have the nerve to stand between an eighty-one-year-old woman and a potential assassin?

Bible said, "You and me, we drew the short straw since we got here later in the day. We're on the night shift, keeping our peepers wide open in case the rat-mailer or the death-threatener shows up. Got it?"

Andrea could only focus on one part: night shift. She had been longing for a bed in a quiet hotel room since her flight had been delayed.

"First stop." Bible pointed to a squat, yellow brick building a few yards away. "We're gonna meet the chief of police. Marshal rule number twelve. As soon as you can, you gotta let the locals know we're here, make 'em feel appreciated. I wanted to wait for you before I made the introductions. You got any questions so far?"

She shook her head as they climbed the stairs. "Nope."

"Good deal. Here we go."

Andrea caught the door with the edge of her duffel bag before it closed behind him. She shifted her backpack over her shoulder and walked inside. The lobby was the size of a prison cell. Immediately, she smelled Lysol competing with the pungent odor of urine cake. The toilets were directly across from the front desk. Less than ten feet of space separated them.

"Good evening, officer." Bible gave a quick salute to the very tired-looking sergeant manning the desk. "I'm Deputy Bible. This is my partner, Deputy Oliver. We're here to see the big boss."

Andrea heard a groan come out of the cop's mouth as he picked up the phone. She directed her attention to the wall around the toilets, which was plastered with photographs documenting the members of the Longbill Beach Police Department going back to 1935. Andrea followed the dates with her eyes, crossing from one side of the bathroom doors to the other until she found what she was looking for.

The 1980 photo showed a Lego-jawed police chief with three men on either side of him. The caption read: BOB STILTON AND THE SQUAD.

Her heart did an odd flip.

Chief Bob Stilton had been the investigating officer on the Emily Vaughn case.

Andrea felt her throat work again. The chief was exactly how she'd pictured him—beady-eyed and mean-looking with the bulbous red nose of an alcoholic. In every photo, his fists were clenched so tight that his hands were bleached of color. Judging by his reports, he wasn't a fan of either grammar or punctuation. Or laying out his deductive reasoning. The statements and supporting documents and diagrams were all in order, but the man had excluded any field notes that might reveal his thoughts on the shape of the case. The only indication that Clayton Morrow was even a suspect appeared in two lines of text the chief had scribbled out at the bottom of the last page in the file, which happened to be the autopsy report—

MORROW KILLED HER. NO PROOF.

Andrea moved to the next photo on the wall, which was dated five years later. Then another five years passed to the next photo. She kept going down the line. The force grew from six to twelve men. Chief Bob Stilton became more bent with age until the 2010 photo showed a younger, less round version taking center stage:

CHIEF JACK STILTON AND THE SQUAD.

Andrea knew that name, too. Jack Stilton was the son of Chief Bob Stilton. Back in 1982, the younger Stilton had provided a witness statement in cramped, block handwriting, relaying the last time he'd seen Emily Vaughn alive.

At approximately 5:45 p.m. on April 17, 1982, I, Jack Martin Stilton, witnessed Emily Vaughn talking to Bernard "Nardo" Fontaine. They were standing outside the gym. This was prom night. Emily was wearing a green or blue dress and had a small purse. Nardo was in a black tux. They both seemed very angry, which concerned me, so I approached. I was at the bottom of the stairs when I heard Emily ask where Clayton Morrow was. Nardo said "F-k if I know." Emily walked inside the gym. Nardo told me "That bitch better shut her f-ing mouth before someone shuts it for her." I told him to shut up but I don't think he heard me. I went around the back of the gym to smoke a cigarette. I didn't see either of them again. I only stayed for half an hour, then I returned home and watched TV with my mom. One of the

Boys with Dana Carvey, then Elton John was on Saturday Night
Live. I did not see Clayton Morrow at the prom. I did not see
Eric "Blake" Blakely or his twin sister Erica "Ricky" Blakely,
though I assume they were all there because that is how they
operate. I do not know who the father of Emily's baby is. She
does not deserve all the bad stuff that has happened to her. I
wore a black suit once to my uncle Joe's funeral but my mom
rented it so it wasn't technically mine. I swear the contents of
my statement are true under penalty of law.

Andrea heard a door slam open behind her.

"Chief Stilton. Thanks for meeting with us so late in the day."
Bible was giving the real-life Jack Stilton a firm handshake when
Andrea turned around. "I promise we won't take up much of
your time."

Andrea tried to keep her composure as Bible made the introductions. Stilton's left eyebrow was bisected by a scar, a white line
sending a lightning bolt between the fine hairs, probably from a
long-ago scuffle. His pinky finger had clearly been broken at some
point and healed badly. Despite this, he didn't look like the kind
of guy who was spoiling for a fight. The extra weight he carried
gave him a baby-face, though Andrea knew he was the same age
as Clayton Morrow, the man who, three years after leaving Longbill
Beach, would introduce himself to Laura as Nicholas Harp.

She found herself almost split in two as she shook hands with
Jack Stilton.

Had he been friends with her father? Did he know more than
he'd let on in his statement forty years ago? He didn't look like the
kind of guy who stayed in and watched movies with his mother.

"You're both Marshals?" Stilton seemed dubious, probably
because Bible looked like a semi-retired skateboarder and Andrea
looked like she had found her pants in a boys' clothing bin at
Costco. Which was accurate.

Bible said, "We are indeed deputies with the United States
Marshal Service, Chief Stilton. Hey, I bet you grew up hearing a
lot of cheese jokes, am I right?"

Stilton's nostrils flared. "No."

"I'll try to think of some." Bible slapped Stilton hard on the back. "You two go ahead and get started. I gotta shake hands with my wife's best friend. Oliver, you good?"

Andrea could only nod as Bible disappeared into the bathroom.

Stilton exchanged an annoyed look with the sergeant. He reluctantly told Andrea, "I guess let's go on back."

Andrea had a feeling Bible was throwing her into the deep end to see if she could swim. She asked Stilton, "Have you been the chief of police for long?"

"Yes."

She waited for more, but there was nothing, just him turning his back to her as he walked through the door.

So much for swimming.

Stilton's leather equipment belt squeaked as he showed her through to the squad room. The space was utilitarian, a large, open rectangle with two smaller offices at the back, one marked with a sign that said INTERVIEWS, the other marked CHIEF STILTON. A conference table and kitchenette took up one side of the open space. On the other side, four desks were cubicled behind dividers. The overhead lights were on, but no one else was in the building. Andrea guessed the rest of the force was either on patrol or at home with their families.

"Coffee's fresh." Stilton waved his hand toward the kitchenette. "Help yourself, sweetheart."

"Uh—" She was caught off guard. The only man who ever called her *sweetheart* was Gordon. "No, thank you."

Stilton fell heavily into a large leather chair at the end of the conference table. "All right, honey. Are you gonna tell me what's going on or do we have to wait for your boss?"

Andrea had let the first time slide, but now, she gave him a sharp look.

"Don't get all woke on me," Stilton said. "They don't honey-pie you genteel ladies down south?"

His fake southern accent sounded like Scarlett O'Hara had twisted his balls in her corset strings. No wonder people hated cops so much.

Stilton said, "Come on, honey. Where's your sense of humor?"

Andrea dumped her duffel and backpack on the floor as she sat down at the table. She did the same thing she had done with the Uber driver. She pulled out her phone and ignored him. Her eyes blurred on the screen. She forced herself not to look up. At first, she could feel Stilton staring at her, but then he got the message. He stood up with a loud groan and went to the kitchenette. She heard the scrape of a mug as he lifted it from the shelf. The click of the coffee pot being pulled out from the burner.

Her eyes finally focused on the banner that had popped up on her lock screen. Predictably, she had two texts, one from each parent. Laura had sent a link to the Portland Art Museum's permanent Native American Art collection. Gordon had sent a text asking her to call him over the weekend, but only if she had time. Andrea pulled up her contacts and found Mike's number. She hadn't forgotten what Bible had said outside the library.

She texted—*WTF DID YOU TELL THESE PEOPLE????????*

The three little dots floated. And floated.

Finally, Mike texted back—*YOU'RE WELCOME!*

"Sorry about that." Bible let the door slam behind him. He clocked Andrea on her phone, but asked Stilton, "Coffee fresh?"

Stilton made the same broad gesture toward the kitchenette as he sank back into his chair.

"Thank you kindly." Bible's boots scuffed the tiles as he crossed the floor and poured himself a cup. "We don't wanna keep you too long, Chief Cheese. Why don't you hand us over your report and we can bring it back later?"

Stilton looked confused. "Report?"

Bible looked confused, too. "I thought you'd been here for a while? Maybe your predecessor left something we can take a look at?"

Stilton's tongue darted out between his lips. "Look at what?"

"Your file on the judge."

Stilton shook his head. "What file?"

"Oh, I see. My bad." Bible turned away from the chief, explaining to Andrea, "Most times, local cops keep an active file on anything unusual that's happened in the vicinity of a federal judge's home—strangers hanging around, cars parked on the street too long, that kind of thing. It's just something you typically do when you've got a high-value target in your jurisdiction."

Andrea slipped her phone back into her pocket, feeling a wave of shame for taking it out in the first place. Bible was showing her how it should've been done. Instead of ignoring the jerk, she should've reminded Stilton that she was a federal agent and he was a dipshit.

Bible asked the chief, "What about suicides? You got any lately? Don't have to be successful."

"I . . ." Stilton was thrown again. "There's been a couple of girls over at the hippie-dippie farm. One cut her wrists. This was about a year and a half ago. Then during the Christmas holidays, another one was pulled out of the ocean cold as an iceberg. Both of them ended up fine. They were just looking for attention."

"The hippie-dippie farm," Bible repeated. "What's that now?"

"It's about six miles off the coastal road, less than a mile as the crow flies. Smack on the edge of the county line."

"The place with all the rainbow-colored buildings?"

"That's the one," Stilton confirmed. "They've been doing some kind of hydro-organic shit out there for years. Lots of international students live there during internships. They've got dorms, a mess hall, a warehouse. Looks like an excuse for free labor if you ask me. We're talking mostly female students. Very young. Far from home. Recipe for disaster."

"Hence the two attempted suicides."

"Hence."

Andrea watched Stilton shrug. She wanted to shrug, too. She had no idea why Bible was interested in suicides.

"All right." Bible put his coffee mug on the table. "Thank you for your time, sir. Let me give you one of my cards. I'd appreciate it kindly if you'd let me know if another suicide pops up."

Stilton studied the card Bible slapped on the table. "Sure."

"We've got a twenty-four-hour detail at the judge's house, in case you hadn't noticed. Two all day long, two through the night. Me, I like to sit on the front porch with a shotgun. Call it an intruder deterrent. Off hours, we're quartered at the motel just up the road. Give us a holler if you need anything and we'll do the same."

Stilton looked up from the card. "That it?"

"That's it." Bible clapped him on the back. "Thanks for the help, Chief Cheese."

Andrea silently followed Bible back through the lobby and outside the building. She weighed her options as they walked down the stairs single file. He had thrown her into the deep end. She had sunk like a rock with an anvil chained around its neck. She was only a few hours into her real job and she was already failing.

Bible stopped on the sidewalk. "So?"

There was no way around the truth. The instructors had drilled it into them twenty-four/seven that the first thing they had to do was establish authority. If Andrea couldn't grab a small-town cop's respect, she'd never be able to do it with a bad guy.

Andrea told Bible, "I screwed up. I let him get to me when I could've worked to bring him on side. We might need him one day."

"What'd he do to piss you off?"

"Called me sweetheart and made fun of my accent."

Bible laughed. "Well, it's a hell of a thing, Oliver. Freezing him out is one way to go. I've seen it work before. I've seen some gals, they lean into it, call him honey right back, maybe get a little flirty."

Andrea didn't know a hell of a lot, but she knew that flirting with a man in a work situation was never going to gain her any respect. "What's the other way to go?"

"Marshal rule number sixteen: think of yourself as a thermometer. Look at what they're putting out and adjust your temperature accordingly. The chief was running a little warm, so you should'a been a little warm. No need to freeze him out. Give it a try next time. Practice makes permanent."

She nodded at the familiar refrain. Most of policing required fine-tuning your responses. Andrea was more used to extremes. "Okay."

"Don't sweat it too hard now. Put ol' Cheese in your rearview. Probably the last time you'll see him."

Andrea gathered lesson time was over. Bible started back up the sidewalk.

"My car's back at the library." Bible could clearly tell she was lagging. "We'll grab a bite to eat before we go to the judge's house."

The mention of food made her stomach growl. Andrea's feet

felt heavy as she trudged behind him. She looked down at the concrete. Every few yards, there was a small black box about the size of a shoebox. She recognized the traps from her own beach town. With tourists came rodents. She wondered if whoever had mailed the judge the dead rat had found it downtown. And then she put the question out of her mind because she was too exhausted to do anything but put one foot in front of the other.

"Diner's up here." Bible picked up the pace. "I called ahead and snagged us two seats at the counter. Hope that's good by you?"

"That's great." Andrea hoped like hell that food would bring her second wind. Her stomach rumbled again as the scent of French fries filled the air. Ahead, the neon lights of RJ's Eats cast a pink glow onto the sidewalk. MILKSHAKES-HAMBURGERS-OPEN TIL MIDNIGHT.

"Well whattaya know." Bible grinned as he held open the door for a woman carrying armloads of take-out bags.

"Cat?" She sounded surprised to see him. "What are you doing here?"

"Coach pulled me off the bench." He made the introductions. "Judith, this is Andrea Oliver, my new partner in crime prevention."

"Hi." Judith stared at Andrea, waiting for a response.

"Uh—" Andrea had trouble finding her voice. "Huh-hey."

"She don't talk much. Lemma help with these." Bible took the plastic bags and walked Judith the short distance to her car. A man waited behind the wheel. Andrea could see his Silver Star clipped to his belt.

Bible told Judith, "We're gonna grab a bite. Tell the judge we'll be there by five thirty so I can show my new partner the ropes."

"Make it six so we've finished dinner. Granny has us all on the early bird special." Judith opened the door and dropped her quilted saddlebag of a purse into the passenger's seat. She took the bags of food from Bible. In the streetlight, she looked slightly older than Andrea, about forty. She was dressed in a colorful blouse with a flowing kind of sarong for a skirt. There was an earthy, artsy air about her, though the car she climbed into was a sleek silver Mercedes.

Bible waved, "See you in a bit."

The door closed with a muted *thunk*. The engine purred to life.

Judith glanced out the closed window, giving Andrea a quizzical look. Andrea didn't know what to do. She unzipped her backpack and rummaged inside as if she was searching for something of vital importance. Finally, the car pulled away, but the woman's face was burned brightly into her memory.

Icy blue eyes. Sharp cheekbones. Slightly cleft chin.

Judith looked just like their father.

OCTOBER 17, 1981

Six months before prom

Emily shivered as a bitter wind sliced off the ocean. Her eyes closed against the sting of salt in the air. She felt teary and achy and tired but also weirdly awake. She had never had insomnia before, though her grandmother had told her it ran in the family. Maybe this was what it meant to be almost eighteen—almost an adult, almost a woman—the inability to shut off your brain so that you could rest.

College. An internship. A new town, new school, new friends.

Emily put a silent question mark behind the *friends* part.

She had grown up in Longbill Beach knowing the same people, places and things. She wasn't quite sure that she remembered how to make new friends, nor was she certain she wanted to. While she had other school-specific acquaintances on the periphery, since first grade, the essence of her emotional life had orbited around only four people—Clay, Nardo, Blake and Ricky. They had happily called themselves *the clique* after Mr. Dawson, the elementary school principal, had warned Ricky that she was part of one.

For as long as Emily could remember, the clique had spent every weekend and a good many nights together. They took a lot of the same classes. They were all enrolled in the honors programs. All of them but Blake was in Mr. Wexler's running club. They read amazing books and talked about politics, world events and

French films. They were constantly jockeying to make each other more intellectually pure.

And this time next year, they would all be scattered to different places and Emily would be alone.

She took a left onto Beach Drive. The empty shops lining downtown cut the harsh gale from the sea. The maddening throngs of tourists were gone, which was a relief but also sad in its own way. Emily's senior year had put so many things into perspective. She found it much easier to look back than to glance ahead into the unknown. Everywhere she turned she was hit with nostalgia. The park bench where Clay had confided in her about the car accident that had killed his mother. The tree she'd leaned against while Ricky put a Band-Aid on a scrape Emily had gotten from a stupid tumble down the two steps to the library. The alley between the taffy store and the hot dog stand where Blake, giddy after winning the county-wide debate competition two years ago, had tried to kiss her.

Emily heard shouts of boisterous laughter, and her heart did a little purrup like a kitten at the sight of the boys at the far end of the street. Clay walked alongside Nardo, both of them talking and enjoying the late afternoon sun on their windblown faces. Nardo was lean from running but his cheeks had always been plump, almost cherubic. Clay was taller, more serious and steady. His strong jaw cut through the air as he turned to look over his shoulder. As always, Blake trailed behind them, hands thrust deep into the pockets of his corduroys. He was looking down at the sidewalk so was taken unawares when Nardo came to an abrupt stop.

Emily heard the shouted "*Christ!*" from fifty yards away. She smiled as Blake shoved Nardo, then Clay stumbled, then they were all jostling each other back and forth along the sidewalk like pinballs bouncing around a machine. She was overwhelmed with love at the sight of them—their youth, their easiness, their abiding friendship. Without warning, tears sprang into her eyes. She wanted to hold onto this moment forever.

"Emily?"

She turned, surprised but not surprised to see Jack Stilton sitting on the steps outside the police station. He had a pen in his hand and a notebook in his lap with nothing written down.

"Cheese," she said, offering a smile as she wiped away her tears. "What are you doing out here?"

"Supposed to be writing a paper." He tapped his pen on his notebook, clearly agitated. "Dad and me have been staying at the station."

Emily's heart sank. Her own mother could be cold and imperious, but at least she wasn't a crazy alcoholic who occasionally changed the locks on the front door. "I'm sorry. That really sucks."

"Yeah." He kept tapping his pen, warily glancing down the street at the boys. As a group, they could be very unkind to him. "Anyway, don't tell anybody, okay?"

"Of course not." She thought about sitting on the steps beside him, but Clay had already seen her. There was sure to be teasing about what he called Emily's collection of broken toys. "I'm really sorry, Cheese. You know you can always sleep in our gardening shed. My parents never go back there. You don't have to wait for me to offer. I can put a pillow and blanket in there anytime."

"Yeah," he repeated, nodding his head. "Maybe."

"Em!" Clay bellowed from down the street. He was holding open the door to the diner, but he didn't wait for her because he knew that she would come.

She told Cheese, "I should—"

"Sure." Cheese put his head down, scribbling lines onto the notebook.

Emily felt bad, but not bad enough to do anything about it. She tucked her hands into her coat pockets as she jogged the distance to the diner.

The bell over the door clanged when she pushed it open. Too-warm air enveloped her. There were only three paying customers, all sitting far apart from each other on swiveling stools that lined the long counter. The clique had already taken up their usual semi-circular booth at the back. Ricky winked at Emily as she walked past with a tray full of sodas and milkshakes. Big Al glared from his perch in the kitchen. Even in the off-season, he didn't like the clique taking up space in his restaurant, but he'd decided it was worth the sacrifice to have his eyes on his two grandchildren. Also, Nardo always picked up the tab.

"You're not listening." Clay grabbed a milkshake off Ricky's tray, but he was talking to the boys. "Are you all being purposefully obtuse?"

Nardo had just jammed a fistful of French fries into his mouth, but he answered anyway. "I prefer being hypotenuse."

Ricky laughed, but everyone else groaned.

"That's exactly what I mean." Clay pulled a straw from the dispenser. "The world is falling apart, people are starving, I'm calling for a revolution, and all any of you jackasses can think about is sports cars and video games."

"That's not fair," Nardo said. "I think about sex quite a lot, too."

Blake said, "We always want what we can't have."

Ricky giggled, then slapped Blake on the shoulder. He sighed dramatically as he stood up so Ricky could take her spot between him and Nardo.

Emily quietly tucked in beside Clay but, as usual, he didn't move to make space for her, so she was forced to hang onto the booth with one butt cheek.

"You know," Blake said. "Now that you mention cars, did you guys see that Mr. Constandt got a DeLorean?"

"Actually," Nardo chimed in, "It's called a DMC-12."

"For the love of God." Clay dropped his head back and stared up at the ceiling. "Why do I waste my time with you senseless, boring plebs?"

Emily and Ricky exchanged a much-needed eye-roll. There were only so many times they could hear talk of revolution, especially considering that the worst thing that had ever happened to any of them was a few years ago when Big Al made Blake and Ricky work at the diner nights and weekends to help the restaurant get back on its feet after a devastating kitchen fire.

Clay groaned as he righted his head. His lips pursed around the straw. His Adam's apple bobbed as he swallowed. The setting sun in the plate glass window gave an angelic glow to his beautiful face. Emily felt a stir of desire at the sight of his features. He was undeniably handsome, with thick brown hair and a sexy, lush Mick Jagger mouth. Even as he drank, his cool blue eyes moved around the arc of the booth. First Blake, then Ricky, then

Nardo. His gaze avoided Emily, who was perched at his left elbow.

"All right." Nardo was always the first to break the silence. "Finish what you were saying."

Clay took his time, slurping the dregs of his milkshake before pushing it to the side, which happened to put the glass directly in front of Emily. Her nostrils flared. The smell of milk was noxious, almost spoiled. Her leg started to shake up and down. She felt slightly ill.

"What I was saying," Clay continued, "is that the Weather Underground *did* things. They trained like soldiers. They performed drills and practiced the art of guerrilla warfare. They transformed themselves from a bunch of college kids into a proper army for changing the world."

"They blew themselves up, along with a very expensive brownstone." Nardo was clearly delighted to be the bearer of this news. "That's hardly a winning strategy."

"They hit the Capitol." Clay counted out the targets on his fingers. "The State Department. They knocked over a Brinks truck. They threw Molotov cocktails at the pigs and went after a state supreme court justice."

Emily smoothed together her lips. Her mother was a state judge.

"Come on!" Clay said. "They bombed the fucking Pentagon, man."

"To what effect?" Nardo looked more imperious than usual as he pushed a lank of his wispy blond hair out of his eyes. He'd been the only one of the boys who'd gotten an ear pierced. The diamond was huge. "None of those actions accomplished anything. They blew up some empty buildings, they killed some people—"

"Innocent people," Emily interjected. "Who had families and—"

"Yes, all right." Nardo waved her off. "They killed innocent people, and it didn't do a damn thing to change anything."

Emily didn't like being dismissed. "Didn't they all end up in prison or on the run?"

Clay looked at Emily, the first time he'd done so since she'd walked into the diner. She normally basked in his attention, but now she felt weepy. He'd been accepted to a college out west.

Emily was going to school an hour away from home. They were going to be thousands of miles apart and she would pine for him while he probably forgot all about her.

Clay turned his attention back to Nardo. "Read the Prairie Fire manifesto. The point of the Weather Underground was to overthrow US imperialism, eradicate racism, and create a classless society."

"Wait up," Nardo parried. "I'm extremely fond of the current class structure."

"How shocking," Blake muttered. "The guy whose grandfather banked Standard Oil wants to keep the status quo."

"Fuck off." Nardo tossed a French fry in his direction, but it landed closer to Emily. "What I don't understand, Clayton, is how this isn't a cautionary tale. The Weather Underground. The Symbionese Liberation Army. Hell, even Jim Jones and Charles Manson—what became of them and their followers?"

Emily turned her head away, pretending to look out at the empty diner. Clay's milkshake was bad enough. Add in the catsup-glopped French fry and her stomach turned into a rolling wave. She felt a weird unsteadiness, as close to being seasick as you could get on dry land.

"What you don't understand, Bernard," Clay began, "is that Mr. Wexler is right. We've got a Goldwater-loving, geriatric B-movie has-been in the White House giving subsidized handjobs to his corporate pals while he slams so-called welfare queens and props up the military industrial complex."

"That is a lot for one sentence," Ricky said, instinctively circling around Nardo.

"It's called understanding the world, sweetheart."

Ricky caught Emily's eye again. The revolution very seldom advocated for women's rights.

"Okay, but—" Blake jumped in with his predictably pedantic tone. "I suppose an argument could be made that we're still talking about them, right? Or that we know about the Weather Underground and Charles Manson and Jim Jones all these years later, which means that somehow, they're still relevant."

"One builds off the other." Clay held up four splayed fingers. "That's the salute Bernardine Dohrn used to give to show solidarity with the Manson girls for sticking a fork in Sharon Tate."

"Oh, God." Ricky looked genuinely disgusted. "Come on, guys. That's not cool."

The boys each offered their own noises to signify apology or longanimity.

Still, Emily saw Blake move to take his sister's hand under the table. They were twins, but you'd hardly even mistake them for related. Ricky was small and round with a button nose and Blake was almost a foot taller and all elbows and lean muscle. Even their hair was different. Ricky's was a halo of springy curls. Blake's straight, shoulder-length hair was several shades lighter.

"Well." Nardo pushed back his hair again, sticking his already upturned, piggy nose into the air. "Let's talk about next weekend, shall we kids? Mummy and Daddy are finally taking a few nights in the city, so you know what that means."

"The Monthly Party!" Ricky raised her glass in cheer.

Emily looked down at the table. She could feel her hands start to tremble.

"Technically," Blake said. "Next weekend will be more than one month since the last party."

"Yes, all right, *technically* it's The Monthly Party plus one week," Nardo said. "The point is, old friends, the party is happening."

"Hurray!" Ricky offered up another toast.

Emily tried to make her lungs take in breath.

"Excellent news, old boy." Clay reached across the table and slipped one of Nardo's cigarettes out of the pack. "Who's coming this time?"

"Yes," Blake said sarcastically. "Who should we invite?"

Ricky snorted. They never invited anyone. It was always just the five of them, which was exactly how they liked it.

"If I might suggest—" Clay let the lit cigarette dangle between his lips. "Wouldn't it be nice if we had another session with our dear friend Mr. Timothy Leary?"

Everyone laughed, but the tremor spread from Emily's hands into her body. Sweat had broken out on the back of her neck. She shot Ricky another quick glance. Their monthly parties had been going on for years. They were less conventional parties and more alcohol and pot-fueled jam sessions where they solved world crises and made each other laugh.

Until last month.

They had tried LSD for the first time, and there were still parts of that night that neither one of them could remember.

"Come on, Emmie-Em." Clay had picked up on her hesitation. "Don't spoil the party before it's even started."

"You had a great time," Nardo said. "And I do mean *gree-e-e-eat.*"

Emily felt sick as she watched his eyebrows wag up and down suggestively.

"He's right." Predictably, Ricky rushed to Nardo's side. "Don't spoil it for everybody else, Em."

"Come on, Emmie," Blake joined in. "You know the deal. The three Musketeers."

This was Clay's perversion of *all for one and one for all.* Either they all got drunk and/or stoned together or none of them did. The fact that Emily was usually the only one who had to be cajoled seemed to be lost to their collective memory.

"Don't let one bad trip spoil the ride for the rest of us." Clay pushed her shoulder a little too aggressively. Her one ass cheek started to lose purchase. So of course he pushed her again.

"Clay!" She had to grab onto him so she wouldn't topple to the floor.

"I've got you." He had his arm around her waist, his face close. She looked down at her hand, which was pressed firmly to his chest. She could feel the hard muscle underneath. The steady beat of his heart. The same primal urge stirred deep inside of her body.

"Jesus, fuck her already," Nardo said, his tone equal parts disdain and eagerness.

Clay dismissed the suggestion with a snort as he effortlessly helped Emily back to upright. He flicked ash into Nardo's half-drunk soda.

"Ricky," Nardo said. "I'll have another milkshake, old girl."

Ricky rolled her eyes. "I thought Mr. Wexler said we should all lose a few pounds."

"I think he meant you in particular, my dear." Nardo took delight in her embarrassment. "Come now, little cow, fetch me a milkshake."

"Why don't you fetch my ass?"

He blew a plume of smoke into her face. "You wish."

Emily turned away again. The stench of smoke made her stomach squeeze. She put her hands to her face. Her cheeks felt as if they were on fire. She was still a little breathless from being so close to Clay, and she hated herself and her stupid body for the response. She stood up from the booth so fast that her head swam. "I need to go to the bathroom."

"Sympatico." Ricky bumped her shoulder against Blake so she could slide out of the booth. She told the boys, "Try not to blow yourselves up while we're gone."

This last missive was for Nardo, who wagged his eyebrows again in response.

"Jeesh," Emily muttered when they were out of earshot. "Why don't you just tell Nardo how you feel?"

"You know why," Ricky said.

Everyone knew why. Bernard Fontaine was a dick. He had always been a dick. He would always *be* a dick. Ricky's fatal flaw was that she knew this, had seen it in action every day for nearly her entire life, yet she still held onto the minuscule hope that he would change.

"Pop-Pop," she called to her grandfather behind the grill. "Nardo needs another milkshake."

Big Al gave her a wary look, but he went to the milkshake machine.

The funny thing was, Big Al thought Nardo was the bad influence when, in fact, it was Clay who was constantly leading them over the cliff. Every single stupid thing they'd ever done, from stealing booze to doing drugs to swiping cash and valuables from out-of-state cars, had been Clay's idea.

And he had never, ever been the one to pay the price.

Ricky said, "Let's go out back for some air."

Emily followed her down the long hallway. Tendrils of cold air pulled her along. She could smell the salty sea spray wafting in through the open door. Wind whipped at her hair. The boardwalk rolled like a carpet along the shore.

Ricky took a pack of cigarettes from her jacket pocket, but Emily shook her head. She still felt queasy, which was nothing new. Lately, any odor set her off, whether it was fresh flowers on the kitchen table or her father's stinky cigars. She was probably coming down with a stomach virus.

Light flared from the match as Ricky struck the box. She held the flame to the tip of her cigarette. Her cheeks sucked in. She huffed out the smoke with a harsh-sounding cough. Emily thought of something Blake had said the first time his sister had smoked: *You look like someone who's smoking because you think it's cool, not because you want to.*

Emily kept herself upwind, walking to the edge of the board-walk. She rested her forearms on the railing. Below, the sea swirled around the pilings. She felt a gentle spray of water on her skin. Her cheeks still felt hot from the sensation of Clay holding her so close.

Ricky could always read her mind. "You asked about me and Nardo, but what about you and Clay?"

Emily pressed her lips together. Four years ago, Clay had decided that sex would only complicate the group dynamic. Emily took the edict to mean that he wasn't interested, because Clay always found a way to get what he wanted.

She told Ricky, "He'll be in New Mexico this time next year."

"That's not so far, is it?"

"It's almost one thousand nine hundred miles." Emily had done the calculations using a formula she had found in her father's *Old Farmer's Almanac.*

Ricky coughed on a mouthful of smoke. "How long would that take to drive?"

Emily shrugged, but she knew the answer. "Two or three days, depending on how much you stop."

"Well, Blake and I will be up the street in Newark at good ol' UD." There was a sadness to Ricky's smile. The only positive that had come out of her parents' tragic death was a lawsuit that had put in place funding for Ricky and Blake's college. "Anyway, how many hours away will that be from you?"

Emily felt bad because she hadn't calculated the distance between Foggy Bottom and the University of Delaware. Still, she hazarded a guess. "Couple of hours at the most."

"And Nardo will be at Penn if his dad bribes the right people. That's only a few hours away from UD." Ricky had clearly done that equation. "So that's not far at all, is it? You can hop on the train and see us anytime."

Emily nodded, but she didn't trust herself to speak. She felt so unbelievably weepy, torn between desperately wanting her life to change and just as desperately wanting to stay safely inside the clique forever.

If Ricky felt the same, she didn't say. Instead, she smoked in silence. Her foot rested on the bottom rung of the railing as she scowled out to sea. Emily knew that she hated the water. Ricky and Blake's parents had died in a boating accident when the twins were four. Big Al was a good provider, but he was a reluctant parent. The same could be said for Nardo's folks, who were always on business trips in New York or vacations in Majorca or at a fundraiser in San Francisco or a golf tournament in Tahoe or anywhere, really, that didn't involve spending time with Nardo. As for Emily's parents—well, there wasn't much to say for Emily's parents other than that they expected her to succeed.

Weirdly, Clay was the only one who had two stable, loving adults in his life. He'd been adopted by the Morrows after his mother had died. He had four sisters and a brother who were out in the world somewhere, but he never mentioned them, let alone bothered to reach out to them. Probably because the Morrows treated him like a gift bestowed on them by the Lord Jesus Himself. Clay wasn't one to share.

"Em?" Ricky asked. "What's going on with you lately?"

"Nothing." Emily shrugged and shook her head at the same time. "I'm okay."

Ricky flicked ash into the ocean. She was too good at picking up on Emily's thoughts. "It's weird, isn't it? Like, we're all on the precipice of starting our lives, but we're still here, right?"

The railing shook as Ricky stamped her foot, indicating *here* on this spot outside of her grandfather's diner. Emily was glad that her best friend was feeling the same sense of fracture. She couldn't count the number of times they'd sneaked out the back door of the diner while the boys were arguing about which Angel was the hottest or quoting lines from *Monty Python* or trying to guess which of the freshmen girls at school had gone all the way.

Emily knew that she and Ricky would lose their sense of cama-
raderie once they'd all been away at college.

"Ugh." Ricky frowned at her cigarette, which was only half
smoked. "I hate these things."

Emily watched her flick the butt into the ocean. She tried not
to think about what it would do to the fish.

Ricky said, "You've been different since last month's party."

Emily looked away. The weepiness came back. The nausea.
The shakiness. She heard the ding a typewriter makes when it
gets to the end of the line. The clacks of the carriage sliding back.
Then one by one, she imagined the individual typebars popping
up, spelling out the words in all capital letters—

THE PARTY.

She had no memory of it. This wasn't like forgetting where
she'd left her keys or blanking on a homework assignment. Emily's
brain gave her context for those minor annoyances. She could
imagine herself dropping her keys on the table instead of her
purse or zoning out during class or forgetting to write down an
assignment. When she tried to recall the night of The Party, her
brain only took her so far. Walking up the concrete steps to
Nardo's looming front doors. The umber tiles in the foyer. The
sunken living room with its gold chandelier and massive console
TV. The large windows overlooking the swimming pool. The hi-fi
system that took up an entire wall. The speakers that were almost
as tall as Emily.

But those details weren't from that particular night, the night
of The Party. They were from countless nights before when Emily
had told her parents she was sleeping over at Ricky's or studying
with a friend she hadn't spoken to in years because they were all
going to Nardo's to get drunk and play board games or watch
movies or smoke Mary Jane and talk about how to fix the
screwed-up world they were all about to inherit.

The actual night of The Party was nothing but a black hole.

Emily remembered Nardo opening the front door. She recalled
Clay placing a tiny square of paper on her tongue. She remembered sitting on one of the suede couches.

And then she was waking up in her grandmother's bedroom
lying on the floor.

"Oh well." Ricky heaved a sigh as she turned her back to the waves. Her elbows rested on the railing, pushing her breasts out like a hood ornament. "I don't know anything about acid, but Clay is right. You shouldn't let one bad trip spoil things. Hallucinogenics can be really therapeutic. Cary Grant used them to heal his childhood trauma."

Emily's lower lip started to tremble. She felt a sudden disconnect, like her body was there on the boardwalk with Ricky, but her brain was floating off somewhere else—somewhere safer.

"Em." Ricky knew that something was wrong. "You know you can talk to me."

"I know," Emily said, but could she really? Ricky had this weird twin thing with Blake where telling one immediately meant you were telling the other. Then there was Nardo, who could get anything out of Ricky. Then there was Clay, to whom they all reported.

Emily said, "The boys are probably wondering what happened to us."

"We should go back in." Ricky pushed off from the railing and headed back toward the diner. "Did you get that worksheet from trig class?"

"I was—" Emily felt her stomach tighten. The salty breeze or the odors from the kitchen or the smell of cigarettes or all three hit her at once and she suddenly felt very sick.

"Em?" Ricky glanced over her shoulder as she walked up the hall. "The worksheet?"

"I was going to—"

Vomit hurled up her throat. Emily slapped her hands to her mouth as she stumbled toward the bathroom. The door popped open then slammed back into her shoulder. She lunged toward the toilet. The sink was closer. Hot liquid squirted between her fingers. She released her hold and a torrent of puke sloshed into the sink.

"Jeez Louise," Ricky mumbled. She yanked a handful of paper towels from the dispenser and ran cold water into the other sink. "God, that smells terrible."

Emily dry-heaved, eyes squeezed shut against the undigested cookies and soda she'd had with Gram before leaving the house.

Another dry-heave wracked her body. She was completely empty
but she couldn't stop.

"It's all right." Ricky placed the cold paper towels on Emily's
neck. She rubbed her back, making reassuring noises. This wasn't
the first time she'd performed the dubious task of vomit soother.
Of the group, she had both the strongest stomach as well as the
strongest nurturing instinct.

"Fuck!" Emily horked, using the word that she never used
because she had never in her life felt so sick. "I don't know what's
wrong with me."

"Maybe you caught something." Ricky tossed the wet towels
into the trash and took out her make-up bag. "How long has it
been going on?"

"Not long," Emily said, but then she realized it had been going
on for a while. At least three days, maybe even a week.

"You remember Paula from art class?" Ricky used her lighter
to warm up the end of her eyeliner pencil. "She kept puking
during third period and you know what happened to her."

Emily looked at herself in the mirror, watching the color drain
from her face.

"Of course, you'd actually have to get your cherry popped
for that to happen." Ricky freshened up the dark lines under
her eyes. "Did you lose your virginity without telling me? Oh,
shit—"

She was looking at Emily closely, reading the worst into her
shocked expression.

Ricky's throat worked as she swallowed. "Em, you're not . . . ?"

"No." Emily leaned down to the other sink and splashed cold
water onto her face. Her hands were shaking. Her body was
shaking. "Don't be stupid. You know I would never do that. I
mean, I would, but I would tell you when it happened."

"But if you did . . ." Ricky let her voice trail off again. "Shit,
Em, are you sure?"

"Am I sure I'm still a virgin?" She went back to the puke sink
and ran some water into the bowl to help it wash down the drain.
"I think I would remember if I'd had sex, Rick. I mean, it's kind
of a big deal."

Ricky said nothing.

Emily looked at her oldest friend's reflection in the mirror. The silence between them reverberated around the tiny, tiled space like the echo of a cannon.

The Party.

Emily said, "I got my period last Friday."

"Oh, fuck." Ricky huffed out a relieved laugh. "Why didn't you say?"

"Because I told you when it happened," Emily said. "I started right in the middle of PE. I told you I had to go back to the locker room to change shorts."

"Oh, right, right." Ricky kept nodding until she had convinced herself it was the truth. "Sorry. That's probably why you're sick. Cramps suck so bad."

Emily nodded. "Probably."

"Crisis avoided." Ricky rolled her eyes. "I should go take Nardo his precious milkshake."

"Rick?" Emily said. "Don't tell the boys I threw up, okay? This is embarrassing, and you know Nardo will make fish jokes or something gross."

"Yeah, of course." Ricky zipped her fingers across her lips and feigned tossing away the key, though Emily could already see the chain reaction—Blake to Nardo to Clay.

"I'll clean this up." Emily gestured toward the mess in the sink, but Ricky was already walking out the door.

Emily heard the latch click.

Slowly, she turned to look at herself in the mirror.

Her periods had always been erratic, following a schedule she couldn't predict. Emily was usually late or early or perhaps she was really bad at keeping up with her cycles because she had never had sex and Ricky always carried Tampax so why should Emily bother with tracking something that was a nuisance rather than a warning?

Her eyelids fluttered as they closed. She saw herself walking up the concrete stairs to Nardo's front door. Sticking out her tongue so that Clay would place a tab of acid in her mouth. Waking up on the floor beside her grandmother's bed. Feeling hungover and clammy and panicked because for some reason, for some very unknown reason, her dress was on inside out and she wasn't wearing any underwear.

Emily's eyes opened. In the mirror, she watched tears roll down
her face. Her stomach was still clenching but she felt ravenously
hungry. She was tired, but somehow invigorated. The color had
returned to her face. Her skin was practically glowing.

And she was a liar.

She hadn't had her period last week.

She hadn't had her period in the last four weeks.

Not since The Party.

3

Andrea stood at the sink in the bathroom at RJ's Eats and splashed cold water onto her face. She studied her reflection, thinking she didn't look nearly as freaked out as she felt. She had finally met Emily's daughter. Her possible half-sister. That it had happened due to sheer coincidence rather than Andrea's crack detective skills was something she was going to take as a gift rather than an omen of failure.

Judith.

Andrea fumbled for her phone in her pocket. She googled Judith Vaughn, but nothing came up but a pair of obituaries for some really old women and a Linked-In account that Andrea was not going to sign up for. Instagram, Twitter and TikTok were dead ends. She checked Facebook and found more older women and what she assumed were photos of older women's grandchildren. The name was from another century, so that made sense. Even when Andrea narrowed it down to Maryland and Delaware, she still couldn't find a Judith Vaughn matching the one she'd just gawked at in the street.

She held the phone to her chest. Her alternate investigation into Nick Harp wasn't going to fall apart because of some dead-end internet searches. Judith didn't seem like the marrying type, but she did have a daughter so maybe she also had a man's last name. Or a woman's, because that kind of thing happened too.

Andrea closed her eyes, took a breath and tried to focus on what, if anything, this new information meant. She had assumed that Bernard Fontaine, Eric Blakely and Erica Jo Blakely hadn't embraced social media for generational reasons, but that didn't make complete sense. Her mother was just a few years younger than Emily's former friend group and she had a Facebook account. Granted, Laura spent most of her time on Nextdoor but that was because people who lived year-round in beach towns were either busybodies, lunatics and/or possible serial killers.

The bathroom door opened.

A woman with a halo of salt-and-pepper curls raised her eyebrows at Andrea. She was wearing a red apron and white T-shirt. Madonna bangles looped around both wrists—black and silver bracelets stacked at least an inch up her arm. She stopped chewing her gum mid-smack to ask, "You okay, hon?"

"Uh—" Andrea's mouth suddenly didn't want to make words again. The woman was late fifties, five-six, around 140 pounds, with white roots showing under her dark hair dye. Andrea recognized the striped apron from the waitstaff, but the RJ on her nametag made a tiny bell start to trill inside of Andrea's head.

"Sweetheart?" The woman had a warm maternal air about her, like she always kept a bag full of emergency supplies and cookies in case anyone needed them.

"Uh," Andrea repeated. "Yeah, sorry. I'm fine, thank you."

"No problem." The woman resumed her gum-smacking as she walked into one of the two stalls.

Andrea resisted the urge to stare at her through the crack in the door. She had grown up in a small town, and the one thing she knew was that people tended to stay put.

She waited for the sound of peeing, then returned to Google, pulling up the diner's website. After bypassing a large HELP WANTED banner, she clicked on a page detailing the history of the diner, which started back in the 1930s when great-grandpa Big Al Blakely had started as a soda jerk. Then he'd bought the place, then passed it down to his son, Big Al, Jr, then there had been a fire that almost destroyed the business, then twenty years ago, the name had changed to RJ's when the woman currently occupying one of the stalls in the ladies' room had given up her job as editor of the *Longbill Beacon* to take over the joint. Andrea found her photo with her name underneath.

RJ "Ricky" Fontaine.

I, Erica Jo Blakely, wasn't at the prom last night. I stayed at home by myself until around six when my brother got back early from the prom because it was boring. We watched Blazing Saddles, Airplane and part of Alien on the VCR then went to bed. I know nothing about Emily Vaughn's baby. Yes I was her best friend since kindergarten, but the last time I talked to her was five months ago and that was to say don't talk to me anymore. We did not have a falling out or argument. My grandfather said stay away because Emily used drugs, which I knew to be true. I don't know what happened to her but that wasn't our scene. She turned out to be a really angry and bitter person. Everybody feels bad for her and her family because she is probably going to die, but that does not change the truth or the facts. I swear the contents of this statement are true under penalty of law.

Andrea stared at herself in the mirror again, wondering how she had failed to put together such an easy piece of the puzzle. Of course Ricky Blakely had married Nardo Fontaine. That was why all the searches for Ricky Blakely hadn't returned results. Ricky had taken her husband's last name. They were probably high school sweethearts. That's what happened in small towns.

Her reflection smiled back at her. She should've been kicking herself for not figuring it out sooner, but she was suddenly filled with elation. She had figured something out! She had actually located someone closely connected to Emily. No matter the snarky tone of Ricky's witness statement, they had been best friends for the majority of Emily's life. Adult Ricky would be over their little spat by now. She would know everything.

The elation sputtered out as quickly as it had come.

How would Andrea get Ricky to talk? She couldn't just knock on the stall door and ask Ricky to provide every single detail about a violent murder that had happened to her best friend forty years ago and hey, can you tell me if your other childhood best friend is the killer?

If Ricky wanted to spill dirt on Clayton Morrow, she would've done so decades ago when Nick Harp's terrible deeds had garnered national media attention. All of the stories Andrea had read outed him as Clayton Morrow of Longbill Beach. Ricky's own bio said she used to be in journalism, but Andrea had never come across a first-hand account from someone who'd actually grown up with her father. As far as she knew, no one in Longbill Beach had ever talked to the press. Clay/Nick's long-lost siblings had never been located or come forward on their own. His adoptive parents had refused to speak to reporters. They had both died over thirty years ago—one of breast cancer, the other of a heart attack—so any details they had about their son had died along with them.

Which left Andrea exactly back where she'd started.

She felt the familiar pull of Old-Andy-psyching-herself-up-for-failure. If Andrea had learned one thing at the academy, it was to break up tasks into manageable pieces. Right now, she was still in the information-gathering stage. She would come up with step two when the time presented itself. For now, one thing that might help was to stop thinking about her father as Nick Harp. Clayton Morrow was the person of interest in the Emily Vaughn murder. If Andrea could find a way to pin the charge on Clay, then Nick would be taken care of.

The distinctive sound of toilet paper coming off a roll put Andrea on alert. She knew that as weird as it had been to stand there the entire time Ricky was relieving herself, it would be extra weird to still be hanging around when the woman came out of the stall. Andrea made sure she was out the door before the toilet flushed.

She purposefully took a left out of the bathroom instead of a right toward the dining area. The kitchen was empty despite the rush. Andrea walked farther down the long hallway. The door was propped open. She could see the boardwalk beyond. The roar of the sea tunneled into her ears. A man in a fry cook's uniform appeared. He gave Andrea a curious look. He was about her age, and black, so definitely not Eric Blakely. Maybe a nephew or son?

She had her phone in her hands again. She put RJ Blakely through the searches and came back with a Twitter account: @RJEMSMF

RJ Eats Milkshakes Motherfucker.

Points for specificity. A quick scroll through the responses brought up tourists posting nice reviews alongside the usual number of assholes that were always on Twitter. Copious photos of milkshakes displayed on the counter in the diner. Most of them contained alcohol. Andrea would never get used to seeing liquor on a diner menu. She had grown up in the south, where you could score meth or a handgun on most any street corner, but alcohol sales were strictly controlled.

Behind Andrea, the bathroom door started to open. She hot-stepped it back up the hallway, but not before she heard Ricky on her cell phone anger-whispering like she was about to ask to speak to the manager.

"Certainly not," she hissed. "That's unacceptable."

A low-level hum filled the restaurant as older out-of-towners raked fried foods into their mouths. Andrea's stomach ached as she spotted Catfish Bible sitting at the far end of the counter. It was way too early for supper, but she hadn't eaten anything since the orange peanut butter crackers this morning. When she saw the hamburger and fries waiting for her at the empty bar stool beside Bible, she had to wipe the saliva from the corners of her mouth.

"Started without you," Bible said, chewing tiny bites around his hamburger like a kid. "Good place. I've been here before. Figured you'd want the special."

Andrea didn't bother to answer. She sat down and pushed the burger as far into her mouth as it would go. She sucked down some cola to help it travel. Then she scowled at the unexpected taste.

"Right?" Bible said. "All they got is Pepsi."

Andrea shook her head, because that wasn't right.

"So how'd you get into law enforcement?" Bible asked.

Andrea felt her throat stretch like a python's belly as she swallowed the glob of meat and bread. Every cadet had a story at Glynco—an uncle who had died in the line of duty, a family full of officers going back to the turn of the last century, a burning need to protect and serve.

Andrea could only offer, "Worked at my local police station."

His nod had an air of suspicion, and she wondered how deep the background check in her file had gone. For instance, did they make a distinction between being a uniformed cop in the streets and being a 911 operator who worked nights and zonked out like a vampire while the sun was up?

Bible said, "I was in the Marines. Stubbed my toe at the start of the Gulf War. Got sent home to recuperate. My wife, Cussy, made it clear she was gonna punch me in my soft bits if I didn't get the hell outta the house. Ended up joining the Marshals."

Andrea watched him shrug, but of course he was leaving out a hell of a lot, too.

He dabbed some fries in catsup. "You go to college?"

"In Savannah." She wedged more burger into her mouth, but was disappointed to see that he was waiting for her to continue. "Dropped out six months before graduation."

He chewed along with her. "I served in the Southern District my first go-round. They gotta real pretty HQ down there on Bull Street. You wouldn't be talking about the Savannah College of Art and Design, would you?"

She finished the last of her burger. Andrea had learned early on at Glynco that there was no elegant way to tell a Marshal that she'd washed out of a Production Design degree at SCAD after flunking *Illuminating the Narrative* without them turning slackjawed like they were watching butterflies shoot out of a unicorn's asshole.

She told Bible the settled-on narrative. "I got a job in New York. I lived there until my mother was diagnosed with breast cancer. I moved back home to take care of her. I worked at the local police department. I saw the posting for the USMS on the job board. I spent a year and a half hitting *reload* on the website until my application was accepted."

Bible cut through the deflection. "What kind of art did you do?"

"The not-good-enough kind." Andrea needed to change the subject and, other than her life story, there was only one thing Bible had shown any real interest in. "Why did you ask Chief Stilton about suicides in the area?"

Bible nodded as he finished his Pepsi. "If they're homicidal, they're suicidal."

At Glynco, they loved their rhymes almost as much as they loved their acronyms, but Andrea had never heard the phrase before. "What do you mean?"

He said, "Adam Lanza, Israel Keyes, Stephen Paddock, Eric Harris and Dylan Klebold, Elliot Rodger, Andrew Cunanan."

Thanks to a steady diet of *Dateline* reruns, she recognized the names of the spree killers and mass murderers, but she had never put together a theme other than monstrous. "They all killed themselves before they could be taken into custody."

"They were what's called intropunitive, which is a fancy way of saying they turned their anger, blame, hostility and frustration against themselves. There's documentation of homicidal and suicidal ideation in their pasts. They don't kill on a whim. They gotta work their way up to it. Write about it, dream about it, talk about it, land in the hospital over it." Bible wiped his mouth and threw his napkin on his plate. "Five years ago, there were maybe a thousand threats against judges every year. Last year, we were at over four thousand."

Andrea didn't ask for a reason. Everybody was pissed the hell off right now, especially with the government. "Any of them follow through with it?"

"There's only been four successful murder attempts on federal judges since 1979. One of 'em don't exactly fit the criteria because he happened to be at the Safeway where a congresswoman was targeted."

Andrea peppered her *Dateline* diet with true crime podcasts. "Gabby Giffords."

"I like that you're paying attention," Bible said. "All of the murdered judges were men. All the killers were men, which we know because we caught 'em. All but one judge was a Republican appointee." Bible paused a beat to make sure she was keeping up. "There are only two known cases where family members of a judge were murdered or badly wounded. In both those cases, the judges were women, and they were both the primary targets. Both were Democratic appointees. The assailants in each case were middle-aged white men. Both were suffering from debilitating depression—both had lost their careers, their families, their money. And they both ended up killing themselves."

"Homicidal and suicidal." Andrea could finally see where this was going. Another thing she had learned at the academy was that law enforcement loved their statistics. "Okay. Generally, past behavior predicts future behavior. That's why the FBI studies serial killers. They look for patterns. Those patterns are generally duplicated in other types of serial killers."

"Correct."

"That's why you asked Chief Cheese to notify you of any possible suicides in the area. A suicidal, middle-aged white male fits the profile of a person who might try to murder a female judge." She waited for Bible to nod. "But that seems like a wide net. I mean, how many guys matching that description who *don't* wanna kill a judge attempt suicide in any given day?"

"The US sees about a hundred and thirty successful suicides a day. Around seventy percent are middle-aged white men, most of them using firearms." Bible held up a finger. "Anticipating your next question, no—our guy didn't kill himself. I think he probably tried and failed. That's a pattern with these fellas, too. If they weren't failures, they wouldn't be so damn angry. And we know our bad guy didn't trot off to the hospital after his failed attempt, otherwise there would've been a police report, and of the eighty-four attempted suicide reports filed in the five-state area over the last five days, none of them have a connection to the judge."

Andrea felt her brain start to wake up. This wasn't just a curiosity. Bible was seriously invested in his theory.

She asked, "Why would there be a police report? It's not illegal to try to kill yourself."

"Technically, it is in Maryland and Virginia. Dates back to thirteenth-century English common law." He shrugged. "Perfectly legal in the state of Delaware, but generally, a lot of the ways folks try to kill themselves involve drugs obtained by illicit means or improperly discharged firearms. Not to mention there's an ex or a neighbor or a co-worker who calls in something funny."

That made sense, but still, she quoted Bible's words back to him. "'We're not the investigators. Our only job is to keep the judge safe.'"

"Well, sure, but I thought we were just shootin' the shit here, hoss. Can't investigate much over a greasy cheeseburger unless you're trying to Scooby-Doo some heartburn. Thank you."

Ricky was making the rounds with a pitcher to refill their drinks. Her molars worked the chewing gum like a piece of machinery. She started on Andrea's glass, giving her another wink. "Doin' good, hon?"

"Yes, ma'am." Andrea looked down at her glass as she tried to compose herself. She was still elated about discovering Ricky. She could only pray that Bible didn't notice.

He noticed. "Looks like you made a friend."

Andrea didn't answer his implied question. "'Particular details.'"

"What's that?" Bible took a swig of Pepsi.

She waited until his glass was back on the counter. "You said that there were some *particular details* about the judge's private life in the letters that were mailed to her chambers. That was why the death threats were deemed credible. So it would follow that whoever is threatening the judge knows her—at least well enough to know the *particular details*."

"Hot diggity damn," Bible said. "Mike was spot-on about you, Oliver. You're sharp as a tack. I wish I had your memory. Is that something you picked up in art school, an eye for detail?"

She sensed a rope-a-dope coming. "You seem to know Judith really well."

He picked up the glass again and finished the Pepsi before setting it back down on the counter. Then he slowly swiveled the stool until he was facing her. "All seriousness?"

"Sure."

"If this is gonna work between us, Oliver, I gotta know one thing about you and one thing only."

She could smell the bullshit coming, so she built her own pile to get in the way. "I'm an open book, Bible. Ask me anything."

"Are you a pie or cobbler person?"

"Pie."

He had been holding his breath, but now he let it out. "That is a damn relief."

She watched him spin back around and stick his hand into the air for a waitress.

Andrea stared out the car window at the never-ending clusters of giant vacation houses to the west of Beach Road. She didn't need to consult the town property records to know that the sprawling mansions had devoured the small cottages that vacationers had used for generations. The same type of overdevelopment had happened in Belle Isle. Laura's tiny beach home was dwarfed by what she called gargansions. She was constantly complaining about notes left in her mailbox offering her gobs of cash to sell.

"Asshats," she would mutter as she tore up the letters. "Where would I go?"

Andrea glanced at Bible, who had turned unusually silent since they'd left the diner. The dash lights gave the scars on his face an eerie glow. He drummed his fingers on the steering wheel along with the Yacht Rock mumbling from the radio. Andrea had often imagined her mother's generation would spend their later years in the nursing home shuffling along to a Duran Duran cover band and occasionally shouting "Whatchu talkin' bout, Willis?" at the staff.

Despite Bible's familiar taste in music, Andrea didn't know if she could completely trust her new partner. He clearly knew the Vaughn family better than he'd let on. At least well enough for Judith to greet him like an old friend. He was obviously trying to figure out who had threatened the judge, even though he'd made it clear that their job wasn't to investigate. And he wasn't sharing the why or how with Andrea, which seemed fair because she wasn't sharing her alternate investigation with him, either.

She opened her mouth, thinking that she should try to get him talking again, but then she remembered what he'd said about being a thermometer. He was running a bit cool, so she should run cool, too.

Her eyes turned back to the McMansions. She was still in the information-gathering stage of the Emily Vaughn cold case investigation. The fact was that no one knew for certain Clayton Morrow was guilty of murdering Emily Vaughn. Andrea hoped he was, because it would not only keep him locked up, but would likely give her family some peace. But she was also aware it was sloppy detective work to start with a solution and work her way back.

You didn't have to go through months of training at Glynco to know that looking for motive, means and opportunity was the starting point of every murder investigation. Andrea applied that formula to the brutal attack that had caused Emily's death.

Means was easy—a piece of wood that had been wielded like a baseball bat. The elder Chief Stilton had matched the weapon to a broken shipping pallet in the alley where Emily was attacked. It had presumably been tossed out of a car window, because a dog walker had spotted the splintered, bloody plank just off the main roadway between downtown and the Skeeter's Grill.

Opportunity was also fairly easy—almost every kid in the Longbill Beach High School senior class was downtown that night for the prom. As were the teachers who served as chaperones and the parents who wouldn't stay away. Considering the average age of the prom-goers, Andrea assumed they all had access to some form of private transportation. Emily's body didn't drive itself to the Dumpster on the outskirts of town.

That left *motive*, and there was no bigger motive than keeping a secret. The likeliest reason for Emily's attack was that the father of her child had wanted to remain anonymous. From all accounts, Emily had honored his wishes. The question had come up repeatedly in the witness statements and no one had known the answer.

There were no baby daddies in 1982. If you knocked up a girl, you either married her or you joined the army. If Clay wasn't the father, then Nardo or Eric Blakely were the next-best suspects. Several of the witness statements from prom-goers showed a decided jealousy toward the group. They were often described as arrogant and exclusionary and, in one telling, incestuous. Ricky had married Nardo. It made sense that one of the guys would be interested in Emily. It made slightly less sense that Emily would protect him.

Unless she was afraid to name him because she knew he would kill her.

To someone who hadn't just spent over four months training as a federal law enforcement officer, the easy solution would be DNA. Unfortunately, an over-the-counter option comparing Judith's DNA to Andrea's was not going to deliver an *aha* moment. Half-siblings were difficult to conclusively match without both of their mother's DNA, and obviously Emily's DNA was not on file. Sites like Ancestry. com were useful for tracking down familial DNA, but, again, you had to be in the system for a potential match to be made and all a match could show was a tentative genetic relationship.

Then there was CODIS, the Combined DNA Index System, a database of convicted offenders maintained by the FBI. As far as Andrea could tell, Nardo and Eric Blakely had never been charged, let alone convicted of a crime. As a violent offender, Clayton Morrow's DNA profile was already stored in the system. Even if Andrea managed to snag a buccal swab from Judith, there was no legal way for her to upload Judith's profile for comparison. You needed consent and warrants and no one, not even Jasper, was going to be able to swing it without Clayton Morrow finding out.

And if Clay found out, he would do something to stop it.

The trill of a phone broke Andrea out of her thoughts.

Bible glanced at the giant touchscreen on the dash, which read BOSS. He tapped the answer button. "You got Bible and Oliver on speaker, Boss."

"Noted." Surprisingly, the husky voice belonged to a woman. "Deputy Oliver, welcome to the service. I'm sorry I wasn't there to greet you personally, but as you know your assignment to my division was accelerated beyond the normal process."

Andrea realized that she didn't even know which division her boss was talking about. "Yes, ma'am. I understand."

"I'm sure you've read my email by now. Let me know if you have any questions."

"Yes—" Andrea felt her throat get sticky. She hadn't looked at her work phone since she'd waxed poetic on the trees of Oregon to her mother. "Yes, ma'am. Thank you. I will."

Bible watched Andrea try to open her work phone. She was used to her iPhone's facial recognition. The sliding number lock on the Android took some getting used to. When she finally got the damn thing to open, she saw sixty-two unread emails filled her inbox. A quick scroll down the subject lines told her she was attached to the Judicial Security Division, or JSD, which should have felt less surprising considering she was literally en route to provide security to a judge.

Bible said, "Thanks for checking in on us, Boss. We got night shift starting at six sharp. Gonna get there a little early to show Oliver the lay of the land."

"Excellent," the woman said. "Oliver, congratulations on the engagement. I've always thought Mike was good people. Never believed the rumors."

Andrea's teeth clenched as she scrolled through her emails. She was going to fucking kill Mike.

"Gotta jump," the chief said. "Oliver, my door is always open."

Andrea had finally located the boss's welcome message, which was a godsend because now she knew how to address Deputy Chief Cecelia Compton. "Thank you, Chief."

Bible grinned his approval. "I'll check in with you later, Boss. I'm expecting a call from my wife before I go on duty."

"Understood." There was a sharp click as the call ended.

Bible pressed the disconnect on his end. "Marshal rule number thirty-two: always check your emails before you ignore them."

"Good rule," Andrea mumbled, skimming the multiple missives from fellow deputies welcoming her to the service. Even Mike had chimed in with his usual bullshittery, writing a toneless work email that could've been devised by the head of HR.

Another phone rang.

"That's Cussy, my wife." Bible held his personal phone to his ear, his head slightly turned away in lieu of privacy, saying, "How was your day, beautiful lady?"

Andrea tuned out his disconcertingly soft tone as she kept scrolling through her emails. Every single Marshal in the immediate area had apparently reached out. Was she expected to answer all of these anodyne welcomes? Would they compare notes on her responses or could she just copy and paste?

Bible gave a suggestive chuckle. "Darling, you know I always agree with you."

Andrea turned her head toward the window again, figuring she could amplify his tiny bit of privacy. Bible had slowed for a stop sign. They had to be close to the Vaughn estate. She looked up at the street names, recognizing them from another witness statement.

At approximately 4:50 p.m. on April 17, 1982, I, Melody Louise Brickel, was talking to my mother in my bedroom about which dress I was going to wear to the prom. It was an argument, actually, but we made up later. Anyway, I walked to my window, which faces the intersection of Richter Street and Ginger Trail. There I saw Mr. Wexler's brown and beige car straddling the yellow line. He was dressed in a black suit but not wearing the jacket. His door was open but he was standing in the street. So was Emily Vaughn. She was wearing the bright teal satin dress I later saw her in downtown. I couldn't tell whether or not she had on shoes, but her clutch matched the dress. It appeared to me that she was arguing with Mr. Wexler. He was very angry. I should mention that my window was open because it's hot in my room because it's in the attic. Anyway, I saw Mr. Wexler grab Emily and push her against his car. She screamed, which I heard through the open window. Then he screamed back—not the exact words—something like "What are you saying? There's nothing to say!" At that point, I called my mother over to the window, but by the time she got there, Mr. Wexler was speeding off. That was when my mother reminded me that I was not allowed to talk to Emily Vaughn or any of her friends that she used to hang out with. Not because Emily was pregnant but because she felt like I shouldn't get mixed up with them because it was a bad situation and she didn't want me to get hurt because she knew it bothered me.

I saw Emily later that night outside the gym, which is in my previous statement, but after that I never saw her alive again. I didn't tell you guys this before because I didn't think it mattered. I really do not know who the father of Emily's baby is. I knew her a long time, since we were in kindergarten, but we weren't close like that. Actually, Emily wasn't close like that to anybody I know of except for maybe her grandmother who isn't well. Even with her group of friends before she was pregnant, it was like she knew them but they never really knew her. Not really. I swear the contents of this amended statement are true under penalty of law.

Bible rolled through the stop. Andrea watched the green street signs slip away. She wondered if Mr. Wexler was a dark horse in the paternity race. It wouldn't be the first time a teacher had dabbled in statutory rape. That might explain why Wexler wasn't mentioned on the *Where Are They Now?* portion of the Longbill High School's website, which claimed to offer a complete list of faculty who had come and gone since the school's founding in 1932.

Google wasn't much help, either. Wexler was a German surname meaning "money changer" and, apparently, a shit ton of Wexlers had dropped anchor in Chesapeake Bay back in the 1700s. Going by the area White Pages, you couldn't throw a rock without hitting a Rhinelander.

"This is it." Bible turned on the blinker, though they hadn't passed another car since leaving town.

Andrea leaned over so she could take in the tree-lined driveway that spanned at least half a football field. A set of iron gates was wide open despite the death threats. She wondered if they were broken or if the judge was just trying to annoy her security detail.

Bible asked, "You know what Yankee Cheap is?"

Andrea shook her head.

"Southern Cheap is, I'm gonna eat stale cookies while I serve you these fresh, warm buttered biscuits. Yankee Cheap is, I've got ten million dollars in the bank but I'm gonna cut off the thermostat during a blizzard and here's my great-great-grandpa's mothballed coat from the War of 1812 if you don't have the character and fortitude to generate your own body heat."

She laughed. "That should be one of your Marshal rules."

"I got another one for you." He swung the car around in the motorcourt and backed it into an open spot between two others. "Marshal rule number nineteen: never let them know you're intimidated."

Andrea's brain conjured up a photo of an imperious Judge Vaughn in one of her expensive-looking scarves. "Good rule."

The late afternoon sun put a sizzling glow on everything as they got out of the car. Andrea saw a black Ford Explorer that looked exactly like Bible's car parked nose-out to the driveway.

He provided, "Krump and Harri have day shift. Six to six."

"Great," she mumbled, because staying awake for another twelve hours straight would be super easy.

"Love your *can-do* attitude, partner." He gave her a firm salute. "Why don't you circle the grounds, get a lay of the land, then meet me inside? Go through the garage door and take a left."

"Will do."

Andrea waited for him to disappear into the garage. She was glad to get some fresh air into her lungs before she met the judge. Part of her felt wrong for knowing so much about what had to be the worst period of Esther Vaughn's life. Andrea wasn't sure how she was going to hide the fact that she knew more than she should know. Despite her duplicitous parents, being a liar didn't come easy.

She started to walk the length of the house, hoping Bible understood that *circling the grounds* would likely take a good fifteen minutes. The garage alone could house six cars. Andrea could barely see the road down by the open gates. The distant roar of the sea told her the backyard probably had a *La Terrasse à Sainte-Adresse* feel. The house itself lived up to the setting. From the outside, the Vaughn estate was not exactly Escher-esque, but impressive in a Tudor-beheading-your-wife kind of way. It stretched out in the middle like a large two-story house, then someone had added two massive wings on either side. She immediately understood what Bible had said about Yankee Cheap. Absent a meth and/or gambling habit, the family had to be pretty flush, but the house was clearly not being taken care of. Rot had set in.

Andrea turned at the corner and caught a tinge of the ocean as the wind shifted. A meandering stone path led to an English garden. The style was marked by an abundance of overflowing flora and fauna. Colorful flowers crowded the beds. Random clusters of shrubs and bushes hung over the twisting gravel path. An irregular stone wall bordered a small fountain. No weeds were in sight. Someone clearly saw the garden as a labor of love. Andrea could smell the earthiness from the freshly mulched soil.

She also smelled cigarette smoke.

Andrea kept herself in the shadows of the massive house as she walked the rear of the property. The garden gave way to untended patches of grass and overgrown bushes. The tree canopy tightened, blocking out the sun. Her foot stubbed a paver that was sitting sideways in the ground. She realized it was part of another winding path, so she took it, walking through overgrown plantings until she arrived at a clearing. A swimming pool was to her left. On her right, directly beneath a balcony off the top floor of the main house, a warm light spread out from what looked like a converted potting shed.

"Fuck!"

Andrea turned, spotting a teenage girl in a halter-top and cut-offs struggle between anger and fear at being caught with a cigarette. Given her age, it was unsurprising to see anger win out. She tossed the butt into the yard as she stomped back toward the house. She left a miasma of smoldering nicotine and hate in her wake.

"Don't forget to feed Syd!" Judith called from the shed's open doorway. She was still dressed in her flowy attire from before, but she'd pulled her long hair back into a loose bun.

Andrea fought the earlier awkwardness she'd felt outside the diner, asking Judith, "Syd?"

"He's our grouchy old parakeet, and that was Guinevere, my beautiful, tempestuous daughter. If you're wondering, she hates her name almost as much as she hates me. I try not to take it personally. We all hate our mothers at that age, don't we?"

Andrea had delayed her mother-hating years until the ripe age of thirty-one. "I'm sorry about before. It's been a long day."

"Forget about it," Judith waved it off. "I want you to know how much I appreciate what you're doing for my family. Granny would never say anything, but these last letters have really shaken her."

Andrea took the confession as an invitation to come closer. "Do you know what they said? The letters?"

"No, she wouldn't show them to me, but I gathered they were very personal. It takes a lot to make her cry."

Andrea had a hard time imagining the Judge Esther Vaughn she'd read about being reduced to tears, but that was the problem with all those imperious adjectives. You could forget that you were reading about an actual human being.

She asked Judith, "Do you live back here?"

"We're in the big house. I packed up Syd and moved us back home last year."

Andrea knew that Franklin Vaughn had retired a year ago. Maybe he really had quit to spend time with his family.

"Needless to say, Guinevere was not happy with the move."

Judith chuckled to herself. "She calls it House Slytherin, which is so unfair. That's our generation, isn't it?"

Andrea felt a lump in her throat. They could be half-sisters. In another world, they would've been thrown together after their parents remarried and hated each other.

"Through here." Judith gestured toward the shed. "This is my workshop. I sleep out here sometimes, but not when it's this warm. I'll give you the nickel tour."

Andrea felt her lips part as she walked into a very familiar space. Wooden shelves lined the walls. Stainless steel pots, strainers and funnels. Measuring cups. Nitrile gloves. Face masks. Tongs. Wooden spoons. PH test strips. Squirt bottles and droppers. A five-gallon bucket of sulfuric acid. Several large, clear plastic bags of white powder.

Judith said, "Don't worry, that's not coke, it's—"

"Mordant," Andrea provided. "What do you dye?"

"Silks, mostly," Judith said. "But I'm impressed. Most cops take one look at this set-up and think I'm running a drug lab."

"The judge's scarves." Andrea realized she'd missed an entire row of drying racks. Scarves of various colors were laid over the dowels. One was so deeply blue that the color looked like it had been refracted through a prism. "You really caught this indigo. Did you use the Gullah Geechee process?"

"Now I'm beyond impressed," Judith said. "How on earth does a US Marshal know about an ancient dyeing process brought over by slaves from Africa?"

"I grew up near the Low Country." Andrea worried she was giving too much away. "Did you go to school for this or are you self-taught?"

"Little of both." She shrugged. "I dropped out of RISD."

The Rhode Island School of Design was one of the top art schools in the country.

Judith said, "I always delight in inviting my former professors to my shows, but that's for my collage work. The scarves were something I started doing for my grandmother a few years ago. She had a tumor removed from her vocal cords. Thank God they caught the cancer in time, but she's very self-conscious about the scar."

Andrea felt sucker punched, but not about the cancer. She turned her back to Judith, pretending to look at the scarves as she fought a sudden rush of tears. She had always loved art, but it had never occurred to her that the love might have come from Clayton Morrow rather than Laura.

What else had he passed on?

Judith said, "The collages are in the studio. You might be interested in one of them."

Andrea sniffed as she turned back around. She was forced to wipe her eyes.

"Sorry, I've worked with acids so long that my eyes barely register the burn anymore." Judith motioned for Andrea to follow her into the next room. "There's a cross-breeze in the studio."

They walked through a door and into a large, welcoming space. Windows and fixed glass panes were everywhere, even in the ceiling. Easels showcased various stages of creativity. Judith wasn't a hobbyist or a crafter. She was an artist whose work brought to mind Kurt Schwitters and Man Ray. Paint spattered the floor. Pots of glue and scissors and cutting boards and spools of thread and blades and varnishes and spray fixatives were splayed on the tables besides magazines, photographs, and found pieces that would be refashioned into a new statement.

It was the most perfect studio Andrea had ever been inside.

"The sun can be brutal during the dog days of summer, but it's worth it." Judith had stopped in front of an easel that held what was clearly her latest work. "This is what I thought you'd want to see."

Andrea didn't let her eyes take in the details. First, she *felt* the piece, which gave her the sensation of standing on the deck of a tiny boat that was shifting against the waves of an oncoming storm. Judith had used solarization to create a sense of uncertainty. Bits of torn letters and photographs kaleidoscoped together to create a darkly ominous collage.

"This is one of my heavier pieces," Judith said, almost apologetic. "My work is usually called masculine or muscular, but—"

"They don't understand a woman's anger," Andrea finished. She had experienced a similar dismissiveness from some of her male professors. "Hannah Höch got the same bullshit when she exhibited with the Dada group, but she had her own exhibition at MoMa less than twenty years after her death."

Judith shook her head. "You're really the most fascinating Marshal I've ever met."

Andrea didn't tell her she'd only been a Marshal for a day and a half. She carefully studied the piece, reading the words that had been excised from letters, some handwritten on notebook paper, some clearly typed, some computer-generated.

Kill you fucking bitch die Jew slut temptress cunt jewess devil murderer ice queen motherfucker cocksucker pedophile blood-drinking ball-buster Soros-backed whore . . .

Andrea asked, "These are death threats that your grandmother received?"

"Not *the* death threats, but some of them from over the years. They're actually not bad, comparatively speaking." Judith laughed without really laughing. "My politics certainly don't align with my grandparents', but one thing we can agree on is that the current conspiracy theory whack-a-doos are pretty terrifying. My family isn't Jewish, by the way. I suppose the nuts think it's one of the worst things they can call us."

Andrea studied the photographs scattered around the nasty invective. Judith had used stitch and colored pencils to unify the theme. Franklin Vaughn with a Star of David drawn over his face. A younger Judith in a school uniform with the breasts cut out. Esther in her robes with 'X's scratched over her eyes. A dead rat with its feet in the air and foam coming out of its mouth.

"Found the poor thing floating in the pool." Judith pointed at the rat. "Granny put up a bird feeder last month and they showed up with their hands out."

Andrea shuddered. She didn't want to think about rats having hands.

"I paid some guy in New Zealand to Photoshop the foam around its mouth," Judith supplied. "It's amazing what you can find online."

"It is." Though Andrea knew that there were a lot of things—and people—who were invisible as far as the internet was concerned. She forced down her artistic jealousy and tried to remember why she was really here. Judith clearly had that small-town habit of oversharing with new people. Or maybe she was simply desperate for someone who understood what she was doing out in the studio. Either way, the woman seemed ripe for some directed questioning.

Andrea asked, "Do you use the Vaughn name for your art?"

"Oh, God no. I couldn't stand the scrutiny. I use my mother's middle name, Rose." She said, "Judith Rose."

Andrea nodded, pretending like her heart hadn't fallen out of her chest at the mention of Emily. "You're really good. She must be very proud of you."

Judith looked confused. "Cat didn't tell you?"

"Tell me what?"

Judith silently gestured for Andrea to follow her toward the back of the room. She stopped in front of the floor-to-ceiling storage racks that held large canvas panels. She thumbed through several pieces before stopping to look at Andrea over her shoulder. "Be kind. This was the first collage I ever attempted. I was Guinevere's age. I was full of angst and hormones."

Andrea didn't know what to expect when Judith flipped around a canvas that showed a very primitive collage. The feelings it evoked were still dark and troubling, but not as focused. It was clear that Judith had been working on finding her vision, just as it was clear to Andrea that the subject she'd chosen was her dead mother. Photographs of Emily framed the periphery, stitched together with heavy black thread like you'd see after an autopsy.

Andrea searched for something to say. "It's—"

"Raw?" Judith gave a self-deprecating laugh. "Right, well, there's a reason I don't show this to just anybody. Even my agent hasn't seen it."

Andrea tried to ask a question that a stranger would ask. "Is that your mother?"

Judith nodded, but the senior photo of Emily Vaughn in the corner of the piece was so familiar to Andrea that she could've described it with her eyes closed. Poofy permed hair. Light blue eyeshadow. Lips drawn into a bow tie. Mascara clumped like cobwebs.

Judith said, "Everyone always says that Guinevere favors her."

"She does." Andrea leaned in for a closer look. As with the more recent piece, Judith had broken up the images with strips of text. Lined school notebook was staggered around the canvas in no particular pattern. The missives were all written in the same loopy, round handwriting of a clearly emotional young girl—

People are SO MEAN ... You DO NOT deserve what they are saying ... Keep working it out ... YOU WILL FIND THE TRUTH!!!

Andrea asked, "Did you write the text?"

"No, they're from a letter I found in my mother's things. I think she wrote it to herself. Affirmations were big in the eighties. I really wish I hadn't torn it up. For the life of me, I can't remember what else it said."

Andrea forced herself to turn toward Judith. She didn't want to seem too eager or excited or nervous or afraid or show whatever emotion was making her feel like the soles of her feet were tingling. So many photos of Emily. Some with friends. Some with her caught in moments of searing aloneness.

What could sixteen-year-old Judith's art tell her about seventeen-year-old Emily's murder?

"Is it that bad?" Judith was clearly anxious. Andrea knew what it was like to value someone's opinion and have them look away.

"No, it's primitive, but it's obvious that you were working toward something important." Andrea's hand had gone to her heart. "I can feel it here."

Judith patted her hand to her chest, because she clearly felt the same way.

They stood like that, two women with their hands on their hearts, two women who could possibly be sisters, until Andrea made herself turn back to the collage.

She asked, "Do you remember doing this?"

"Barely. That was the year I discovered cocaine." Judith laughed lightly, as if she hadn't just confessed a crime to a Marshal. "What I remember was sadness. It's so hard to be a teenager, but to have such loss . . ."

"You really captured it." Andrea breathed deeply, trying to

quell her emotions as she took in the minute details of Emily's life. The frame of photos showed the young girl's personality—whether she was running on the beach or reading a book or dressed in her band uniform playing the flute, her sweetness almost pierced the camera lens. She didn't look fragile so much as vulnerable and very, very young.

A group photo was in the top-left corner. Emily was flanked by three boys and another girl. Ricky was easy to spot by her halo of curls, and also because she was the only other girl. Clay reminded Andrea of something Laura had said—that he'd been a breathtakingly beautiful boy. His piercing blue eyes sent a chill through Andrea even from forty years away. She assumed the guy standing beside Clay was Ricky's twin brother, Eric Blakely, though their hair was different in texture and color. Which left Nardo as the snarky-looking, slightly plump blond with the hand-rolled cigarette dangling from his lips like Delaware's own Billy Idol.

"Those were her friends." Judith still seemed clearly anxious for more feedback. "Rather, the people she thought were her friends. Pregnant teenagers didn't get their own reality shows back then."

Andrea had found herself transfixed by Clay's gaze again. She forced her attention onto a faded Polaroid. "Who's this?"

"That's my mom with my great-grandmother on my grandfather's side. She died shortly after I was born." Judith was pointing to a woman in a stern, Victorian-looking attire with a chubby, happy baby in her lap. "Granny was caught up in her career in those days. Gram practically raised my mother. That's where the name *Judith* comes from. I'm the sum of their parts."

There were more photos representing Judith's motherless life. First day of school with no one at her side. First school play. First art show. First day at college. All linked together with text from the letter and found objects—a piece of a report card, a diploma, an advertisement for training bras. Though someone was clearly behind the camera, Judith was always alone.

Weirdly, the photographs made Andrea realize how relentlessly present Laura had always been in her own life. Gordon was always taking the photos. Laura was the one helping Andrea frost cupcakes for the school bake sale, showing her how to pin the pattern onto the pieces of material for the dress she wore to her *Pride and Prejudice*–themed birthday party, standing beside her at every art show and graduation and concert and waiting in line outside the bookstore wearing a wizard's hat for the next Harry Potter release.

The revelation made Andrea feel oddly petty, as if she had scored a point against a rival.

"Obviously, that's me." Judith indicated a series of ultrasounds she'd fanned out in the center to represent the beginning of her life. "My mother had these taped to her bathroom mirror. I think she must've wanted to see them every morning and every night."

"I'm sure she did," Andrea agreed, but she found herself drawn to the liner notes from a cassette tape that anchored the bottom right-hand corner. Small, torn sections of colored photographs served as a constellation around the handwritten songs and artists.

Someone had made Emily a mixtape.

Judith said, "A lot of the music sucked in the eighties, but I have to admit these are pretty good."

The ink had smeared. Andrea could only read a handful of the cramped words—

Hurts So Good-J. Cougar; Cat People-Bowie; I Know/Boys Like-Waitresses; You Should Hear/Talks-M. Manchester; Island/ Lost Souls-Blondie; Nice Girls-Eye to Eye; Pretty Woman-Van Halen; Love's/Hard on Me-Juice Newton; Only/Lonely-Motels

She tried to make sense of the tattered constellation around the words, but then she realized the pieces were not from several photographs, but from one. Two icy eyes at diagonal corners. Two ears. A nose. High cheekbones. A lush, full mouth. A slightly cleft chin.

Andrea felt a knot in her throat, but she forced herself to ask, "Who made the tape?"

"My father," Judith said. "The man who murdered my mother."

OCTOBER 19, 1981

Emily sat on the exam table inside Dr. Schroeder's office. She was shivering so hard in the paper gown that her teeth were chattering. Mrs. Brickel had made her take off all of her clothes, including her underwear, which had never happened before. Emily's bare bottom absorbed the chill of the vinyl padding through the thin roll of white paper. Her feet were freezing. She felt nauseated, but she couldn't tell if it was the same nausea that had sent her running out of Bible Study last night or the nausea that had made her leave the breakfast table this morning without being excused. One had to be from stress. The other had to be from the sickly-sweet odor of maple syrup, which had always made her queasy.

Right?

Because there was no way that Emily was pregnant. She wasn't an idiot. She would know if she'd had sex because sex was a really big thing. You felt differently after it. You knew that things had irrevocably changed. Because they had. Sex made you a totally new person. You were really a woman then. Emily was still a teenager. She felt no different now than she'd been this time last year.

Also, girls missed their periods all the time. Ricky could never keep track of hers. Gerry Zimmerman had skipped months of periods because she was on some weird egg diet. And everybody knew Barbie Klein had played so much tennis and run so much track that her ovaries had shut down.

Emily silently told herself the same thing she'd said for the last two days while she waited for her pediatrician's office to open: she had a stomach bug. She had the flu. She was just regular sick,

not pregnant sick, because she had known Clay, Blake and Nardo
for as long as she had known herself and there was no way any
of them had done anything bad to her.

Right?

She tasted blood in her mouth. She'd accidentally bitten the
inside of her lip.

Emily's hand went to her stomach. She felt the contour of
her belly. Was that how it always felt? She'd lain in bed last
night rubbing her stomach like Jeannie's bottle and felt nothing
but the usual flatness. Was there always a slight bulge like this
when she sat up? She straightened her shoulders. She pressed
her hand to her tummy. The flesh curved into the palm of her
hand.

The door opened, and Emily jumped as if she'd been caught
doing something wrong.

"Miss Vaughn." Dr. Schroeder smelled of cigarettes and Old
Spice. He was normally gruff, but now, he looked irked. "My
nurse tells me you wouldn't say why you're here."

Emily glanced at Mrs. Brickel, who was also Melody's mother.
Would she tell Melody that stupid Emily Vaughn had a stomach
bug and thought she was pregnant even though she'd never had
sex? Would Melody tell everyone at school?

"Miss Vaughn?" Dr. Schroeder looked at his watch. "You're
delaying the patients who bothered to schedule actual appointments this morning."

Emily's mouth was dry. She licked her lips. "I—"

Dr. Schroeder's eyebrows narrowed. "You what?"

"I think—" Emily couldn't say the foolish words. "I've been
throwing up. Not much. I mean—I threw up yesterday. And then
Saturday night. But I think—"

Mrs. Brickel made a shushing noise as she rubbed Emily's back.
"Slow down."

Emily took a shallow breath. "I've never been with . . . I mean,
I haven't been with anyone. Not, like, married. So I don't know
why—"

"You don't know why *what?*" Dr. Schroeder's gruffness had
turned into outright hostility. "Stop making excuses, young lady.
When was your last period?"

Emily suddenly felt very warm. She had read the words *burning with shame*, but she had never experienced the sensation before. Her fingers and toes, her heart inside of her chest, her lungs, her bowels, even the hair on her head—every piece felt as if it had been set ablaze.

"I haven't—" Her breath caught. She couldn't look at him. "I've never been with—with a boy. I haven't. Wouldn't."

He started yanking open drawers and cabinets, then slamming them shut. "Lie back on the table."

Emily watched him toss items onto the counter. Surgical gloves. A tube of something. A headstrap with a small mirror on it. A metal instrument like a long duck's bill that clattered against the laminate.

She felt Mrs. Brickel's hand nudging her shoulder. Emily still couldn't look at the woman as she leaned back against the pillow. Below, two strange-looking bars swung up into the air. They curved at the ends like large spoons. Emily's heart lurched at the sight of them. This wasn't happening. She was trapped in a horror movie.

"Move to the edge of the table." Dr. Schroeder snapped on the gloves. Emily could see the hairs on the backs of his large hands take on the appearance of pelts under the vinyl. He grabbed her ankle.

Emily cried out.

"Don't be a baby," Dr. Schroeder barked. He grabbed her other ankle and yanked her down to the edge of the table. "Stop fighting."

Mrs. Brickel's hand was on Emily's shoulder again, this time bracing her. She had known. Emily hadn't said anything about why she was here, but Mrs. Brickel had told her to take off all of her clothes because she had seen the difference. She knew that Emily was no longer a child.

Who else could tell?

"Stop crying," Dr. Schroeder ordered, his grip tightening on her ankles. "My other patients will hear you."

Emily turned her head away, staring at the wall as she felt her heels being jammed into the stirrups on either side of the table. Her knees were braced wide open. She knew that if she looked up, she would find Dr. Schroeder looming over her. The thought of his gnarled, angry face glaring down at her broke Emily apart. A sob came out of her mouth.

"Unclench." Dr. Schroeder sat on the rolling stool. "You'll only make it worse."

Emily bit her lip so hard that she tasted blood again. She didn't know what he was going to do until it was too late.

He shoved the cold metal instrument inside of her. The pain brought another cry to her lips. Her insides felt as if they had been scraped away. Loud clicks opened the metal jaws. Instinctively, she pushed her heels to get away, but that only trapped her deeper into the stirrups. A lamp was rolled over. The heat was unbearable, but not as humiliating as Dr. Schroeder putting his face *down there.*

Emily gulped down another sob. Tears wept from her eyes. His fat fingers prodded inside of her. She gripped the table with her hands. Her teeth clenched. Her breath caught from a sharp cramp. The air was trapped in her lungs. She was paralyzed, unable to exhale. Her vision swam. She was going to pass out. Vomit spilled into her mouth.

And then it was over.

The instrument was wrenched out. Dr. Schroeder stood up. He pushed the lamp away. He took off his gloves. He spoke to Mrs. Brickel instead of Emily. "She's not intact."

Mrs. Brickel made a noise. Her hand tightened on Emily's shoulder.

"Sit up," Dr. Schroeder ordered. "Hurry. You've wasted enough of my time."

Emily struggled to lift her feet out of the stirrups. The metal clattered. Dr. Schroeder grabbed both ankles in his hands and lifted her heels up in the air. Instead of letting go, he clamped them together.

"See this?" he told Emily. "If you'd kept your legs closed, you wouldn't be in this mess."

Emily scrambled to sit up. The paper gown had ripped. She tried to cover herself.

"Too late for modesty." Dr. Schroeder had her chart in his hands. He started writing. "When was your last period?"

"It was—" Emily took the tissue Mrs. Brickel offered. "A—a month and a half ago. But I—I told you, I've never—I didn't—"

"You've clearly had intercourse. From what I saw, you've had it multiple times."

Emily was too shocked to respond.

Multiple times?

"You can cut the act. You've given yourself to a boy and you're suffering the consequences." Dr. Schroeder was matter of fact. "What did you think would happen, you foolish girl?"

Emily gripped the paper gown in her hands. "I never—I didn't do anything with—"

Dr. Schroeder looked up from his notes. He was finally paying attention to her. "Go on."

"I never—" Emily couldn't get the words out. "I was at a party, and I . . ."

She heard her voice trail off in the small room. What could she say? The party was with her friends, her clique. If she said that something bad had happened, that someone had drugged her or that she had passed out and there were only three boys there, then one of those three boys had to be responsible.

"Right." Dr. Schroeder thought he understood completely. "You drank too much or someone slipped you a mickey?"

Emily remembered Clay placing the tab of acid on her tongue. He hadn't slipped her anything. She had willingly taken it because she trusted him. All of them.

"So," Dr. Schroeder surmised. "You are claiming that you are blameless in this situation because some boy took advantage of you."

"I—" Emily couldn't say the words. The boys wouldn't do this to her. They were all good men. "I don't remember what happened."

"But you do admit that you had sexual intercourse."

It wasn't a question, and he had clearly seen the answer for himself. She was not *intact*.

"Well?" he barked.

All that Emily could do was nod.

The admission seemed to make him angrier. "Let me tell you this, young lady. You'd better work on a different lie to tell your father. I can tell from my exam that you've been sexually active for a very long time. You failed the two-finger test. There's a looseness that I would only expect to see in a married woman."

Emily's hand went to her chest. Had it happened more than once? Had someone been breaking into her room at night while she slept?

She tried, "I didn't—"

"You most certainly did." He dropped the clipboard on the counter. "Think very carefully about what you're planning to do next. Do you have the character to accept the blame for your actions or are you going to destroy some poor young man's future because you couldn't keep your knees together?"

Emily was crying too hard to answer him.

"That's what I thought." He glanced at his watch again. "Nurse Brickel, do the bloodwork to confirm what we already know is the truth. This girl is six weeks into her first trimester. Miss Vaughn, I will give you exactly one hour to tell your father what you've been up to before I call and tell him myself."

Emily felt her mouth working, but she couldn't form words.

Her father?

He would kill her.

"You heard me." Dr. Schroeder looked at her one last time, his head shaking in disgust. "One hour."

Mrs. Brickel gently closed the door behind Dr. Schroeder. Her lips were pursed. She used to make Emily and Melody cookies back when they were little and Emily's mother was working late at the office.

Now, Mrs. Brickel said, "Emily."

Emily stuttered out a sob. She couldn't take another verbal lashing. She already felt as if someone had put a knife in her chest. How would she face her father? What would he do to her? She'd been whipped so hard after she'd made a C in geography last year that the belt had left a scar on the back of her thighs.

"Emily, look at me." Mrs. Brickel held Emily's hand tightly. "The exam didn't tell the doctor anything about how many times you've been sexually active. He can only tell that your hymen is broken. That's it."

Emily was shocked. "He said—"

"He's lying," Mrs. Brickel said. "He's trying to shame you. But whatever happened, you are not a bad person. You had sex with someone. That's all you did. It might feel like it's the end of the world now, but it's not. You will get through this. Women always do."

Emily gulped down another sob. She did not want to be a woman. And she especially did not want to face her father. *Then* it would be the end of the world. He wouldn't let her go to college. He might not let her finish school. She would be stuck in the house with only Gram to keep her company and then Gram would be gone and there would be nothing.

What was she going to do?

"Sweetie, look at me." Mrs. Brickel wrapped her hands around Emily's arms. "I'm not going to lie to you. We both know this is going to be hard, but I know that you're strong enough to get through it. You are such an amazing girl."

"I don't . . ." Emily's mind was racing. She felt trapped. Her life was slipping away and there was nothing she could do about it. "What do you think my father will do?"

Mrs. Brickel's lips pursed again. "We'll see if the sanctity of Franklin Vaughn's politics holds up against the sanctity of his country club membership."

Emily shook her head. She didn't know what that meant.

"I'm sorry. I shouldn't have said that." Mrs. Brickel tightened her hold on Emily's arms. "Is it an option to talk to the father?"

The father?

"Emily, I know it's not ideal, but if you have feelings for this boy, you're not too young to get married."

Married?

"But if you don't want to, there are other options."

"What options?" Emily felt the question burst out of her. She was seized by panic. "What am I going to do? How am I going to get through this? I don't know who the—the father—I don't know who it is! I told the doctor—I told you—I said I don't know what happened. I promise you, honestly, I don't know because I took something and—yes, I took it, but I didn't know what would happen and I can't—I can't tell my father. He'll kill me, Mrs. Brickel. I know that sounds like I'm being hysterical but he—he'll—"

Emily cringed at the sound of her crazy voice bouncing around the room. Her heart was a snare drum. Sweat poured off her body. The nausea had returned. Her skin felt weird, like it had vibrated away from the bone. Nothing belonged to her anymore. Dr. Schroeder's appalled look had said it all. Emily had ceased being Emily. She was a transgressor. She was an other. Her hand went to her stomach—to that thing that someone had put inside of her.

Who?

"Emily." Mrs. Brickel's voice was calm, soothing. "You need to get in touch with your mother. Immediately."

"She's—" Emily stopped herself. Her mother was at work. She was never to be disturbed unless it was important. "I c-can't."

"Tell your mother first," Mrs. Brickel said. "I know you don't believe me, but Esther will understand. You are her daughter. She will protect you."

Emily looked down. Her hands were trembling. She'd sweated through the paper gown. Tears had glued the collar to her neck. They hadn't done the blood test yet. Maybe this was all a horrible mistake. "Dr. Schroeder said six weeks, but it—I think it was a month ago. That's four weeks. Not six weeks."

"The clock starts from the date of your last period," Mrs. Brickel said. "It's not from the date of intercourse."

Intercourse?

The weight of the word bowed Emily's shoulders. There was no mistake. This terrible nightmare had only just begun. She'd had intercourse with someone and now she was pregnant.

"Emily. Get dressed. Go home. Call your mother." Mrs. Brickel rubbed her back, coaxing her to move. "You will get through this, precious girl. It's going to be so hard, but you will get through this."

Emily could see tears in Mrs. Brickel's eyes. She knew the woman was lying. But there was no other option than to say, "Okay."

"Good. Let's do the blood draw, okay?"

Emily stared at the cabinet over the sink as Mrs. Brickel gathered the supplies. She was quick and efficient, or maybe Emily was numb because she barely felt the needle go in, hardly noticed the Band-Aid being taped to the crook of her elbow.

"All right, that's done." Mrs. Brickel opened another drawer, but she was not offering the usual lollipop that was handed out to good patients. She placed a maxi-pad on the counter. "Put this on in case there's any spotting."

Emily waited for the door to close. She stared at the pad. Her heart was pounding inside her skull, but her body still felt numb. The hands that pulled up her pants, buttoned her blouse, were not her hands. When Emily slipped her feet into her penny loafers, she had no sense that she controlled her movements. Her muscles were working on their own—opening the door, walking down the hall, through the lobby, outside. The eyes that watered in the morning sun were not hers. The throat that worked to swallow back bile was someone else's. The pulsing pain between her legs belonged to a stranger.

She stepped onto the sidewalk. Her mind reeled with nothingness. She imagined a carnival. The inner workings of her brain turned into a carousel. She saw the horses moving up and down—not the ice cream parlor or the beach chair rental place or the taffy machine standing dormant in the window as it waited for the tourists that would return in the summer. Emily's eyes squinted out tears. The carousel rolled faster and faster. The world was spinning. Her vision blurred. Her brain finally, blissfully, turned itself off.

Emily blinked.

She looked around, surprised at her new surroundings.

She was sitting at the booth in the back of the diner. No one else was there, yet she was still hanging off the edge the way she always did when the clique took up residence.

How had she gotten here? Why did she ache between her legs? Why was she dripping with sweat?

Emily shrugged off her jacket. Her eyes focused on the milkshake on the table in front of her. The glass was empty. Even the spoon was licked clean. Emily had no memory of ordering it, let alone drinking it. How long had she been here?

The clock on the wall read 4:16.

Dr. Schroeder's office had opened at eight this morning. Emily had been waiting outside when the doors opened.

Eight hours—lost.

She had missed school. Her art teacher was supposed to give her feedback on the drawing Emily had made of her grandmother. Then she had a chemistry test. Then band practice. Then she was supposed to meet Ricky in the locker room before PE so they could talk about—what?

Emily couldn't remember.

It didn't matter. None of it mattered.

She looked around the table, seeing but not seeing. Ricky, then Blake, then Nardo, then Clay. Her friends. Her *clique*. One of them had done something to her. She was not intact. She was no longer a virgin. The way that Dr. Schroeder had looked at her was the way that everyone was going to look at her from now on.

"Emily?" Big Al stood over her. He looked impatient, like he had been trying to get her attention for a while. "You need to go home, girl."

She couldn't get sound to come out of her mouth.

"Now."

His hand wrapped around her arm, but he wasn't rough with her. He tugged until she got to her feet. He picked up her jacket and helped her into it. He looped her book-bag strap onto her shoulder. He handed Emily her purse.

He said it again. "Go home."

Emily turned. She walked across the diner. She opened the glass door.

The weather had turned. Emily closed her eyes against a stiff breeze. Drying sweat prickled her skin. She had always loved escaping outside. When her parents were fighting. When things at school got too hard. When the clique was warring about something that had seemed very important at the time but was later laughed off or forgotten. She had always gone outdoors to get away. Even in the rain. Even during a storm. There was respite in the shadowy embrace of the trees. Comfort in the solid earth beneath her feet. Absolution in the wind.

Now, she felt . . .

Nothing.

Her feet kept moving. Her hands dug into her pockets. Emily didn't realize that she was going home until she looked up and saw the gates at the end of the driveway. They were rusted open. Her mother had wanted to repair them but her father had said it was too expensive so that was that.

Emily walked up the winding drive, head down against the wind. She didn't feel trepidation until the house came into view. Her legs didn't want to keep moving, but she forced herself forward. It was time for her to face the consequences of her actions. Dr. Schroeder was nothing if not true to his word. He would've called Emily's father hours ago. Her mother would know by now. They would both be waiting for her in the library. She imagined her father would already have his belt out of the loops, the leather slapping into his palm as he told her exactly what he was going to do.

The temperature dropped slightly inside of the garage. Her hand wrapped around the doorknob, and she suddenly became aware that she could feel the cold metal against her palm. Emily splayed out her fingers and, like that, she felt the sensation flow back into her body. First with her fingers, then up her arms into her shoulders and down into her chest, then hips, then legs, then feet. Oddly, the last part of her that awakened was her belly. She was suddenly ravenously hungry.

Her palm cupped the curve, and there it was. The gentle swell of pregnancy. The unmistakable sign of something growing inside of her. Gravity hadn't put the roundness there. A boy had.

Which boy?

The door flew open.

She saw her mother's strained face. Esther Vaughn seldom showed emotion, but now Emily could see her mother's mascara was running. Her eyeliner was so smudged that she looked like Tammy Faye Bakker. Emily would've laughed at the likeness, but then she realized her father was looming behind the door. His presence filled the cluttered hallway. If his anger had given off heat, they would've all burned alive in that moment.

As if by magic, the trepidation was gone. Emily felt awash in calm. She was resigned to what was about to happen, even eager to get it over with. She had learned from her mother that some-times it was best to just curl onto the floor, protect your face with your arms, and take the blows as they came.

And the fact was, she deserved it.

"Emily!" Esther dragged her toward the kitchen. She closed the hall door behind them in case the housekeeper was still there. Her tone was sharp, yet quiet. "Where the hell have you been?"

Emily's eyes found the clock on the stove. It was nearly five o'clock. She still had no memory of the time between now and leaving Dr. Schroeder's office.

"Answer me." Esther yanked her arm like the clapper on a bell. "Why didn't you call me?"

Emily shook her head because she didn't know why. Mrs. Brickel had told her to call Esther. Why hadn't she obeyed? Was she losing her mind? Where had the last eight hours gone?

"Sit down," Esther said. "Please, Emily, please tell us what happened. Who did this to you?"

Emily felt her soul trying to float out of her body again. She gripped the chair to keep herself grounded. "I don't know."

Franklin had quietly followed them into the kitchen. He crossed his arms as he leaned back against the counter. He'd said nothing. Done nothing. What was happening? Why wasn't he yelling, punching, screaming?

"Baby." Esther knelt on the floor in front of her. She held onto Emily's hands. "Please tell me what happened. I need to know. How did this happen?"

"I was . . ." Emily closed her eyes. She saw Clay putting the tab of acid on her waiting tongue. She couldn't tell them that. They would blame Clay.

"Emily, please," Esther begged.

Her eyes opened. "I drank some alcohol. I didn't know that it would . . . I passed out. I think I passed out. And then I woke up and I didn't know that anything had happened. I had no idea."

Esther pursed her lips as she sat back on her heels. Emily could tell that her mother's brain was working, drilling past the emotion in search of a solution. That was why there was no yelling or spanking or beating. Her parents had had eight hours to scream at each other.

Now, they were handling this like they did any threat to the Business of Being Judge Esther Vaughn—the same way they'd handled Uncle Fred when he'd gotten caught at that men's bar or when Cheese's dad, Chief Stilton, had brought Gram back after she'd wandered into the grocery store wearing her nightgown. Emily knew the steps as if they had been carved into the family crest. Acknowledge the problem. Pay off whomever it takes. Find a solution that keeps the family name out of the headlines. Move on as if nothing ever happened.

"Emily," Esther said. "Tell me the truth. This isn't about recriminations. It's about solutions."

"Recriminations aren't off the table," Franklin countered.

Esther hissed at him like a cat. "Emily. Speak."

"I-I never drank before." The more Emily lied, the more she believed herself. "I only took a little sip, Mom. I promise. You know that I would never do anything like that. I'm not—I'm not bad. I promise."

Her parents exchanged a look she could not decipher.

Franklin cleared his throat. "It was either Blakely, Fontaine or Morrow. They're the only ones you're ever around."

"No," she said, because he didn't know them like Emily did. "They wouldn't do that to me."

"Goddammit!" He banged his fist on the counter. "You're not the Virgin Mary. Just come out with it. Some boy put his cock in you and now you're knocked up."

"Franklin!" Esther warned. "Enough!"

Emily watched in shock as her father reined in his temper. She had never seen this happen before. Esther never asserted her authority at home. Yet somehow, she seemed to be in charge now.

"Mom." Emily's throat worked as she swallowed. "I'm so sorry."

"I know you are," Esther said. "Baby, listen to me. I don't care how it happened—whether you wanted it or not is immaterial. Just tell us who did it so that we can make this right."

Emily didn't know what was *right*. She thought about what Mrs. Brickel had said about options. And then she thought about Nardo blowing smoke in her face, Blake making some snide remark about the fit of her jeans, Clay completely ignoring her as she sat half-assed beside him at the table for nearly fifteen years.

She felt jolted by a sudden, stark realization. She didn't love them—not the way she thought she did. She didn't want any of them. Not even Clay.

"Emily." Her mother kept repeating her name like a mantra. "Emily, please."

Emily forced herself to swallow the glass in her throat. "I don't want to get married."

"And I don't want to be a fucking grandfather!" Franklin exploded. His fists were clenched, but he pressed his hands back down to his sides. "Jesus Christ, Esther. We talked about this. Just take her somewhere and get rid of it."

"We *did* talk about this." Esther stood to face him, taking Emily out of the discussion. "Someone will find out, Franklin. Someone always finds out."

He waved this away, skipping to the next step in the playbook. "Hire someone. Use cash."

"Who would I hire? One of my clerks? The housekeeper?" Esther was standing in her stocking feet, pointing her finger in Franklin's face. "You're the mathematician. Calculate for me how long it would take before someone came along with enough money to loosen their lips? How long before everything we've worked for implodes because of one stupid mistake?"

"It's not *my* mistake."

"It's *your* reputation," she shot back. "You're the one who goes to conferences and speaks at churches and—"

"For you!" he yelled. "For your sainted career!"

"Do you think the *Washington Post* would give two shits about a second-rate economics professor if it wasn't for his wife single-handedly bringing New Federalism to the state of Delaware?"

Emily had never seen her father look contrite before. He actually tucked his chin into his chest.

Then he asked, "Adoption?"

"Don't be ridiculous. You know how terrible the child welfare system is. We might as well cast the poor thing into the sea. And the number of people who would have to be read-in on the crisis would grow exponentially." Esther wasn't finished. "Not to mention that Reagan will permanently strike me from the list if there's even a whiff of this kind of scandal."

"As if his own daughter wasn't scandalously premature,"

Franklin huffed. "Here is some math for you, Esther. It could take years before someone talks. You'll be seated by then. A lifetime appointment. You can tell them to go fuck themselves."

Emily felt the glass return to her throat. She might as well not even be in the room.

"Do you not understand how devious the opposition can be? Look at what they're doing to Anne Gorsuch. She's barely been at EPA for a year and they've already put a target on her back." Esther gripped her hands in front of her face. "Franklin, I'm not a Kennedy. They won't brush a scandal under the rug when a conservative woman is involved."

Emily watched her father stare at the floor. Finally, he nodded his head. "All right, we'll get my mother to take her to a clinic somewhere safe, like California or—"

"Are you insane?" Esther threw her hands into the air. "Your mother barely even remembers her own name!"

"She knows enough to keep an eye on her own damn child!"

Esther slapped him across the face. The sound was like a limb breaking away from a tree.

Emily felt her mouth hanging open in surprise. A red welt spread down her father's cheek. Emily braced herself for a violent response, but Franklin simply shook his head before walking out of the kitchen.

Esther hugged her arms close to her waist. She paced back and forth across the room. Her mind was still racing. She was desperately searching for solutions.

Emily tried, "Mom—"

"Not a word." Esther held up a hand to stop her. "I'm not going to let this happen. Not to you and certainly not to me."

Emily tried to swallow the shards of glass again, but nothing would clear them away.

"You are not going to have your life ruined over this." She turned on Emily. "Why didn't you ask me to go on birth control?"

Emily was struck silent by the audacity of the question. Why would she go on birth control? Was that even allowed? No one had ever mentioned the possibility.

"Dammit." Esther resumed her pacing. "Are you sure you won't marry him?"

Him?

"You'll have to get married eventually, Emily. It doesn't have to be the relationship that your father and I have. You can grow. You can learn to love each other."

"Mom," Emily said. "I don't know who it is. I don't remember it even happening."

Esther's lips were pursed again. Her eyes scanned across Emily's face looking for deceit.

Emily said, "What I told you about how it happened was the truth. I—I drank something. I don't remember what happened next. I don't know who did it."

"Surely you have an idea."

Emily shook her head. "I don't think—they wouldn't do that. The boys. We've been friends since first grade and—"

"Your father's right about that, at least. They are boys, Emily. What happened to you is exactly what boys do to girls who black out from drinking."

"Mom . . ."

"At this point, the circumstances are irrelevant. Either you name the boy—any boy, I don't care. Just name someone and we'll fix all of this. Or you can live with the shame for the rest of your life."

Emily could not believe what her mother was saying. She was always talking about the truth and justice and now she was telling her own daughter to ruin someone's—anyone's—life.

"Well?" Esther said.

"I—" Emily had to stop for breath. "I can't, Mom. I honestly don't remember. And it would be wrong—I couldn't say something that I didn't know was true. I couldn't do that to—"

"Bernard Fontaine is a bigger con artist than his reprehensible father. Eric Blakely is going to end up slinging hash browns for the rest of his miserable life."

Emily bit her tongue so she wouldn't rush in to defend them.

"You've always liked Clay. Would that be so bad?" Esther visibly worked to moderate her tone. "He's very handsome. He's going to college out west. You could do much worse."

Emily tried to imagine a life with Clay. Always pushed to the side, hanging uncomfortably out in the air while he droned on about revolution.

She felt her head shaking before the answer came out. "No. I can't lie."

"Then that's your choice, Emily Rose. Remember that. You are the one who made the choice." Esther nodded her head once, signifying the end of one thing and the beginning of another. "We'll have to handle this as a family, the same way we always do. You shouldn't have gone to Schroeder. That's why our hands are tied. He's got a big mouth and he'll tell everyone if you come back from vacation with this little problem solved. Not to mention that nurse of his. Natalie Brickel was probably cackling like a witch when she found out."

Emily looked away. Mrs. Brickel had been nothing but kind. "I'm sorry."

"I know you're sorry, Emily." Esther's voice had caught. She turned her back so that Emily would not see her crying. "We're all sorry and none of it matters."

Emily felt her lower lip start to tremble. She hated when her mother cried. All Emily could do was repeat the same two words until she died. "I'm sorry."

Her mother said nothing. She had her head in her hands. She hated for people to see her at her most vulnerable.

Emily thought of all the things she could do right now—go to comfort her mother, hold her, rub her back the way Mrs. Brickel had rubbed Emily's—but emotional support exceeded their long-established duties. Emily always excelled at everything she did. Esther watched approvingly. Neither one of them knew what to do with failure.

All that was left to Emily was to stare at her clasped hands on the table while Esther collected herself. Dr. Schroeder, her father— they were right about one thing. This was solely Emily's fault. She could see every mistake she had ever made turn luminescent on the graph of her life. She wanted to go back in time with the insight that she had right now. She wouldn't go to any stupid parties. She wouldn't stick her tongue out like a dog and blindly swallow whatever was put in her mouth.

As flawed as Franklin Vaughn was, he had seen through Emily's clique in every way.

Nardo was as crooked as a stick in water. Blake talked big

about going to college on the money from his parents' wrongful death lawsuit, but they all knew he would drop out eventually. And Clay—how had Emily ever convinced herself that Clayton Morrow was worth her time? He was arrogant and soulless and so very, very selfish.

Esther sniffed. She blew her nose in a tissue from the box on the counter. Her eyes were red and raccooned. Devastation was writ into her marrow.

Again, Emily could only say, "I'm so sorry."

"I don't understand how you could let this happen." Esther's voice sounded rough. Tears kept rolling down her face. "I wanted so much for you. Do you know that? I didn't want you to struggle the way I had to. I was trying to make life easier for you. To give you a chance to be something without having to sacrifice everything."

Emily had started crying again. She was devastated by her mother's disappointment. "I know, Mom, I'm sorry."

"No one will ever respect you now. Do you understand that?" Esther gripped together her hands as if in prayer. "What you've done is you have wiped away your intelligence, your hard work, your drive and determination—everything you've done that's good until this moment is gone because of five minutes of—of what? You can't have enjoyed it. Those boys are barely out of puberty. They are children."

Emily nodded, because she was right. They were all a bunch of stupid kids.

"I wanted—" Esther's voice caught again. "I wanted you to fall in love with somebody who cared for you. Who respected you. Don't you understand what you've done? That's gone now. Gone."

Emily's mouth was so dry she could barely swallow. "I didn't . . . I didn't know."

"Well, you'll know now." Esther shook her head once, not to move on to the solution, but to indicate that a final decision had been made. "From now on, every time someone looks at you, all they'll see is a filthy whore."

Esther left the kitchen. There was a door to the hallway, but Esther didn't slam it. She didn't stomp her feet across the hardwood floor. She didn't scream or punch the walls. She simply left her words echoing around Emily's head.

Filthy whore.

That was what Dr. Schroeder was thinking when he'd jammed that cruel metal instrument between her legs. That was what Mrs. Brickel was secretly thinking. Her father had all but said the words. The label would be what Emily heard at school from her teachers and former friends. Clay, Nardo, Blake and Ricky would all say the same thing. It would be Emily's cross to bear for the rest of her life.

"Sweetie?"

Emily stood quickly from her chair, shocked to find Gram sitting on the cases of wine stacked inside the pantry. She had been there the entire time. She must have heard everything.

"Oh, Gram." Emily hadn't thought she could feel more ashamed. "How long have you been here?"

"I don't have my watch," Gram said, though it was pinned to the lapel of her dress. "Would you like some cookies?"

"I'll get them." Emily walked to the cabinet, opened the door. She couldn't look at her grandmother, but she asked, "Gram, did you hear what they were talking about?"

Gram sat down at the table. "Yes. I heard what they said."

Emily made herself turn around. She looked into her grand-mother's eyes, searching not for judgment, but awareness. Was this the Gram who had raised her, who was her champion, her confidante? Or was this the Gram who didn't recognize the strangers who surrounded her?

"Emily?" Gram asked. "Are you all right?"

"Gram." Emily sobbed out the word as she dropped to her knees beside her grandmother.

"Poor lamb," Gram said, stroking back her hair. "Such bad luck."

"Gram?" Emily pushed herself to speak while they had time. "Do you remember early last month when I woke up in your bedroom on the floor?"

"Of course I do," Gram said, but there was no way of telling if she did. Her memory was getting worse by the day. She often-times mistook Emily for her long-dead sister. "You were wearing a green dress. Very pretty."

Emily's heart jumped. She saw herself walking up to Clay, tongue out for the tab of acid, wearing the silky green dress that she'd borrowed from Ricky.

She said, "That's right, Gram. I was in a green dress. Do you remember that night?"

"The saddle-oxford was outside." Gram smiled. "Such a funny little bubble. Beep-beep."

Emily's heart sank. As quickly as Gram was there, she was gone. At least she wouldn't remember the conversation Emily had just had with her parents. Which meant that the more Emily's belly grew, the more surprised Gram would be every time she recognized her pregnant granddaughter.

"Sweetheart?"

"I'll get the cookies." Emily stood up to fetch the box. She wiped her eyes with the back of her hand. "Do you want some milk?"

"Oh, yes, please. I love cold milk."

Emily opened the fridge. She forced her mind to go back to the morning after The Party. She clearly remembered waking up on the floor of her grandmother's bedroom. Her dress was on inside-out. Her thighs had felt bruised. Her insides had throbbed from pain that she had passed off as breakthrough cramps.

Why couldn't she remember?

"Saddle-oxford, saddle-oxford, beep-beep-beep," Gram sang. "What's that called? The little bubble car?"

"A car?" Emily repeated, placing the glass of milk on the table. "What kind of car?"

"Oh, you know what I'm talking about." Gram nibbled at one of the cookies. "It's sloped in the back. Looks like something a clown would pop out of."

"A—" Emily sat down in the chair across from Gram.

She had another flash of memory, this time featuring the dark interior of a car. The dashboard lights were glowing. The song on the radio was turned down too low to catch the lyrics. Emily's hands were nervously working a tear in the hem of Ricky's green dress.

"They slope down in the back," Gram said. "The cars with the trunks you can see through the rear window."

Emily felt her breathing turn shallow the same way it had at Dr. Schroeder's office. She heard the song playing on the car radio again, but still couldn't make out the words. "A hatchback?"

"Is that what it's called?" Gram shook her head. "So strange to see a grown man in something like that."

"What man?"

"Oh, I wouldn't know," Gram said. "He dropped you off outside the house on the night you're talking about. I saw him from the window."

Emily felt her teeth grit. Again, her mind flashed up an image that felt as real as the one she kept seeing of Clay putting the acid on her tongue. It was hours after The Party. The night was so dark Emily could barely see her hand in front of her face. Suddenly, a car door closed. An engine turned on and a pair of headlights illuminated the front of the house. Emily stumbled. Her thighs chafed, the skin sticking together. She looked down to see the torn hem of Ricky's green dress. Then she looked up to find Gram standing in her bedroom window.

Their eyes met. Something passed between them. Emily felt different. Dirty.

The engine revved. The car quickly reversed. Emily didn't need to turn around to know what it looked like. She had been inside the car moments before, months before, at least a year before. Getting a lift home in the rain. Hitching a ride to track practice. The interior smelled of sweat and pot. The outside was bubble-shaped. The paint scheme was like a saddle-oxford shoe, light brown on the top, dark brown on the bottom. There was only one person in town who drove a Chevy Chevette that looked like that. He was the same man who had driven her home the night of The Party.

Dean Wexler.

4

Andrea felt an unexplained and possibly unfounded sense of rejection after leaving Judith's studio. The woman who was possibly Andrea's half-sister had no interest in their possibly shared father. Judith only knew the *People* magazine version of Clayton Morrow's later crimes. She had never dug deeper or tried to reach out to him. She did not want to know more. In fact, she seemed to want to know less.

"Why would I give him one second of my thoughts?" she'd asked Andrea. "Why would *anyone*?"

It was a good question, one that Andrea couldn't answer without giving everything away.

She held tight to her iPhone as she walked around the back of the house. She couldn't bring herself to look at the screen. She'd managed to take a few surreptitious photos of the Emily collage while Judith had closed up the studio. The ultrasounds, the group shot, the candids of Emily simply living her teenage life, the liner notes. Then Andrea had spent the remainder of their short time together nodding along while the woman talked about Guinevere, who was indeed a handful, and the judge, whom Judith managed to soften from granite into clay by revealing her interest in gardening and her unwavering support of her granddaughter's desire to pursue art rather than the law or economics or anything that could actually pay the bills.

"Granny is so driven," Judith had confided. "She told me that from the beginning, she was determined not to make the same mistakes with me as she did with my mother. It's a horrible way to get a do-over, but she made it mean something."

Andrea had not stuck around to hear what those mistakes were, though she'd had the feeling that Judith was eager to share. That was what living in a small town did to you. The isolation, the lack of ever meeting anyone new, turned you into a different person. You either talked too much or you didn't talk at all.

Despite Andrea's ulterior motives, she had found herself wishing that Judith fell into the latter category. It was too weird and dishonest to know so much about another person's life and pretend otherwise. For instance, she could tell Judith that she was very wrong about one seemingly random but important thing—

The handwriting on Emily's mixtape did not belong to Clayton Morrow.

As far as Andrea knew, it didn't belong to anyone in Emily's group. All of the witness statements from the original investigation had been written by the actual witnesses. So, Jack Stilton's almost illegible cursive and Ricky Blakely's childish use of circles to dot her 'i's were frozen in time. As was Clay Morrow's habit of randomly capitalizing letters in his block print. He'd pressed the pen down so hard into the paper that the Xerox had caught a shadow from the gouges.

At approximately 5:45 p.m. on April 17, 1982, I, Clayton James Morrow, was standing by the STAGE inside the gym when Emily Vaughn approached ME and my girlfriend, Rhonda Stein. Wordlessly, she stared at us, swaying back and forth with her mouth open. Everyone could tell that she was intoxicated or under the influence. Many people noticed that she wasn't WEARING any shoes and she seemed very disturbed mentally. Obviously, she was disoriented. She remained wordless before walking away. People were making jokes about her, which made me feel bad. We used to be friends until she went off the rails, thus I felt compelled by responsibility to make SURE she was all right. Outside the gym, I told her to go home. Anyone who claims I grabbed her is misrepresenting the actual facts. If these so-called witnesses were standing close enough, they would've seen her eyes roll back in her head. I caught her so she wouldn't fall. That's it. I do admit I yelled at her to be careful, and might have said that she was going to get herself killed, but that was only out of concern for her safety. Like I said, she was doing a lot of drugs and she was going around pissing people off, especially because every guy who ever LOOKED at her wrong got accused of raping her. This insanity is why I extricated myself from our previous acquaintance. I don't know who the father of her baby is and I frankly do not care. All I know is that it's not me, because I was never interested in her. If anything, she was more like a kid sister. If she wakes up from the coma, that is exactly what she WILL tell you. I am actually dating Rhonda very seriously. She is the captain of the cheerleading team and we share a lot of interests. I would never wish any ill will on anyone and I hope she gets better but honestly, this has nothing to do with me and I am glad I am leaving soon to go to college. I have actually built up enough credits to graduate and will leave soon. My parents can mail me my diploma, or they can hang it on their wall. I simply do not care. I was wearing a black TUX that night as were a lot of people, so I am not sure why that is relevant, but I was told to add that information. I swear the CONTENTS of my statement are true under penalty of law.

What stuck with Andrea the most about Clay's statement was the fact that, barring the first line, which was obviously the same coached line of all the witness statements, Clay had never used Emily's name again.

Andrea had reached the front of the Vaughn mansion. The dual Ford Explorers were still parked alongside each other. She assumed Harri and Krump were giving Bible the rundown as they handed over the shift. Instead of going inside the house, Andrea put her back to the wall. She unlocked her iPhone. Her fingers moved quickly across the screen as she ran a series of searches.

'Hurts So Good' by John Cougar was from the *American Fool* album.

'Nice Girls' was featured on Eye to Eye's self-titled debut.

Juice Newton's 'Love's Been a Little Bit Hard on Me' was from *Quiet Lies*.

Andrea looked up the rest of the list, from Blondie to Melissa Manchester to Van Halen. According to Wikipedia, all of the songs were from albums that had been released in April of 1982.

Which meant that whoever had made the mixtape had been in touch with Emily weeks if not days before she'd been attacked.

She smoothed together her lips. She swiped through the quickly taken snapshots of teenage Judith's first collage. She found the cassette tape liner notes and zoomed in.

Back in 1982, someone had used a fountain pen to write out the artists and titles. The ink had smeared. The letters were almost calligraphic, blending a book hand with roman writing alongside a Palmer-method precise cursive. Andrea had to guess that whoever had made the tape had either been overwhelmed by an artistic urge or gone to the trouble of trying to disguise their handwriting.

In light of Emily's brutal attack, the answer felt obvious.

The phone vibrated in her hand. Instinctively, Andrea's eyes rolled before she read her mother's name on the text, because of course Laura had texted her. She tapped open the message and found a photo of an Arc'teryx jacket that Andrea had to admit perfectly matched her style if not her current weather situation. Then another text popped up, this one a link to an outfitter in Portland, Oregon.

They've got your size, Laura had typed. *Talked to Gil, the mgr. He's there til 10.*

"For fucksakes," Andrea mumbled.

She texted back—*Can't read because of strong winds from helicopter blades.*

A door opened inside the garage. She poked her head around the side and saw Bible walking toward her.

"Sorry." She held up her iPhone. "My mother's going for helicopter parent of the year."

"No problem," he said, but she could tell it was a problem. "Harri and Krump wanted to give you a howdy-do before they hit the hay."

The two men appeared behind Bible, both well over six feet and, combined, almost as wide as one of the garage bays. She gathered from the exhaustion on their faces that they wanted to get the hell out of here.

Bible said, "Mitt Harri, Bryan Krump, this is Andrea Oliver, our new dewsum."

"Glad to meet you." Harri gave her a warm handshake. She

recognized him as the driver of Judith's Mercedes. He was taller than his partner, which meant he had to duck his head under the garage door. "Welcome to the service."

"Same here." Krump settled on a fist bump. "Don't let Foghorn Leghorn talk your ear off all night."

Andrea couldn't help but laugh. The description wasn't that far off. "I'll try."

"Mike's a solid guy," Krump said, and Andrea stopped laughing. "Never believed the rumors."

"Me, neither," Harri chimed in.

"Great," was the only word Andrea could force out between clenched teeth.

"Good deal. Thanks, fellas. Sleep tight." Bible patted Andrea on the shoulder, indicating she should hurry along. "Judge is about to go upstairs for the night. Come in and meet her first."

Harri and Krump gave her a salute before heading out. Andrea shoved her iPhone into her pocket as she followed Bible through the garage. There was another Mercedes parked in the far bay, a boxy 1980s S-Class with faded gold paint and cracked leather seats.

"Yankee Cheap," Bible whispered.

Andrea smiled, because he was being nicer than she had a right to expect considering he'd told her to check the periphery and she'd ended up taking a thirty-minute introductory class in the Dyeing Methods and Collages of Judith Rose.

She told him, "I ran into Judith again. And Guinevere."

"I'm guessing Guinevere was sneaking a smoke downwind to piss off her mama," Bible said. "You like Judith's stuff?"

"Uh—yeah." Andrea realized she sounded diplomatic when she was actually feeling caught out. And then she realized diplomatic probably wasn't a bad way to play this. "Art is subjective."

"I know that's right." Bible patted her on the back in comradery. "Judge is in the kitchen with Dr. Vaughn. I'm gonna take a look-see around. Meet me in the library. That's the place with all the books."

Again, Andrea had the sensation of being tossed into the deep end. She wasn't going to sink the way she had with Chief Stilton. She looked around, trying to orient herself in the long, dark hallway. Half-bath with newspapers on top of the tank. A shoe rack from the Dark Ages. Black and white Winslow Homer-esque portraits of rugged farm stock hung crookedly across a wood-paneled wall. Syd the parakeet's warbles echoed down the back stairs. Somewhere, a television was playing. It was less House Slytherin and more Miss. Havisham does Hufflepuff.

She heard silverware clattering against china and assumed that was meant to draw her toward the kitchen.

Thermometer, Andrea reminded herself as she walked down the hallway. The judge would be cold, so she needed to be cold, too. Andrea could do that. She was, after all, her mother's daughter.

She took a breath before entering the kitchen. Low ceiling with heavy oak beams. Corian countertops. White melamine cabinets. Faux-brick pattern in the faded linoleum. Gold chandelier over the farmhouse table. Someone had gone all out on the remodel back in the 1990s. The only update was one of Judith's very good collages hanging beside the fridge.

"Hello, dear." Esther Vaughn was sitting at the table with a cup of tea. Her husband was in a wheelchair beside her. His face looked completely slack. One of his eyes was milky. The other stared blankly up and to the right. "This is Dr. Vaughn. You'll have to excuse him for not speaking. He suffered a hemorrhagic stroke last year, but he's still fully compos mentis."

Andrea guessed the stroke was the real reason for his retirement. And also why his granddaughter had moved back home around the same time.

She said, "Nice to meet you, Dr. Vaughn."

The man offered no response, which was unsurprising. Because of Laura's work as a speech therapist, Andrea was very familiar with the different types of strokes and their consequences. Hemorrhagic was the worst, caused by an artery bursting in the brain, which could lead to hydrocephalus, which caused intra-cranial pressure that could destroy surrounding tissue, which was a polite way of saying brain damage.

Esther misread her silence. "Do wheelchairs make you uncomfortable?"

"No, ma'am. They make me glad that the people we love are still with us." Andrea fell back on her good southern manners.

"I should thank you both for having me in your home. I know this is a stressful time for your family. I'll do my best to stay out of your way."

Esther studied her a moment before asking, "Would you like something to drink?"

Andrea felt her thermometer struggling to acclimate. The imperious, impervious, indomitable Judge Vaughn was not nearly as imposing as advertised. Her hair was loose from its tight bun and hung almost girlishly around her shoulders. The craggy lines on her eighty-one-year-old face were softer in the kitchen light. She was tiny in person, maybe five-two in socks, which was what she was wearing with her light pink terrycloth robe.

Esther started to stand. "I've got tea or milk or—"

"Nothing for me, thank you, ma'am." Andrea indicated she should stay in her chair. The woman looked incredibly frail. Her wrists were as delicate as the bone china of her teacup. "I should get to work. Please let me or Deputy Bible know if you need anything."

"Please sit for a moment." Esther indicated the chair across from her husband. "We'd like to know a little bit about you since, as you said, you'll be spending so much time in our home."

Andrea reluctantly sat down. She couldn't remember what she was supposed to do with her hands, so she rested them on her thighs. And then she realized that might look weird, so she clasped them together on the table.

Esther offered a grandmotherly smile. "How old are you?"

"Thirty-three."

"Just under the wire for the Marshal Service."

Andrea nodded. The cut-off was thirty-seven. "Yes, ma'am."

"You don't have to ma'am me, Andrea. We're not in my courtroom and we're well north of Savannah."

Andrea forced herself to smile back. Bible had obviously given the judge her CV. That made sense. Andrea was in the family's private space. They were trusting her to protect them. Anyone would want to know more.

Esther said, "My granddaughter tells me you have an unexpected appreciation for art."

Andrea nodded, but she felt her body go on alert. Was there a warning in the judge's tone? If Franklin Vaughn picked up on it, he didn't say. His good eye still stared blankly ahead.

"Judith is extraordinary," Esther said. "Her mother had an artistic bent. Of course, you know what happened to her mother."

Again, Andrea settled on a nod.

"Tragedies can break a family apart," Esther said. "I'm fortunate that it brought mine closer together. And Guinevere is the icing on the cake. Though don't tell her I said that. She gets embarrassed when I praise her. I imagine you were the same at her age. Your mother must've had her hands full."

Andrea resisted the urge to gulp down all of the saliva that had flooded into her mouth. The judge was fishing for information. She couldn't know anything about Andrea—not anything that mattered. Esther Vaughn wasn't a mind reader. She did not have access to Andrea's file in the Witness Security database. Not even the president of the United States could unmask her true identity without a damn good reason. The only way Esther Vaughn would know something was off was if Andrea said something stupid.

She tried very hard not to say something stupid. "I'm glad for you, ma'am. That you're close to your family."

Esther picked up her teacup. She silently drank, not dismissing Andrea but not addressing her, either.

Andrea concentrated on keeping her breathing steady. She recognized the judge's game. They had practiced it at Glynco during fake interrogations. Nobody liked long silences, but guilty people were particularly susceptible to them.

"Dr. Vaughn?" A woman in a nurse's uniform broke the standoff. "I'll take you up for your bath. Judge, do you need anything?"

"No, Marta. Thank you." Esther leaned over and kissed her husband on the side of his head. "Goodnight, my dear."

If Franklin Vaughn was compos mentis, he didn't have the ability to show it. His gaze remained fixed as the nurse tucked in the blanket, disengaged the wheelchair brakes and rolled him out of the kitchen.

Andrea had stood to get out of their way. When she went to sit back down, she realized that she was better off standing.

Esther had straightened her spine. Her shoulders were squared.
The effect made her seem twice the size of the old woman who
had offered Andrea tea. The imperious, intimidating, indomitable
Judge Esther Vaughn had entered the room.

"Andrea, sit back down." Esther's lips were pursed. She waited
until her order was followed. "You must excuse my probing
questions. Your sudden appearance in my life interests me."

Andrea tried to dial down her own temperature to match the
ice cube in front of her. She quickly found out that there wasn't
a number inside of her that was low enough. She summoned her
old friend, Miss Direction. "I'm very sorry about the death of
your daughter, ma'am. I can see how not having a definitive
answer about the identity of the perpetrator might weigh on you."

Esther stared so openly that Andrea felt like her brain was
being dissected. Guilt flooded through the almost surgically filleted
chunks of gray matter. The urge to confess turned her fidgety.
She endeavored to maintain her composure, but the silence eventually became unbearable.

"Ma'am?" Andrea shifted in her chair. "Is there something
else?"

"Yes." Esther pinned her down with the word. "I've worked
alongside Marshals my entire federal career. I've never seen one
fast-tracked into service the day after graduation. Particularly, if
you'll excuse me for saying, a woman."

Andrea felt her stomach clench. She had met people like Esther
Vaughn before. They pushed you until you either quit or pushed
back. Old Andy would've folded immediately. New Andrea was
pissed off that this lady thought she'd be so easy.

"No need to excuse yourself," she told the judge. "I've been
called a woman before."

Esther's chin tilted up. She was finally realizing this wasn't
going to be easy. "I gather being engaged to another Marshal has
its advantages."

Andrea was going to take a hammer to Mike's balls if she ever
saw him again.

For now, she shrugged.

Esther said, "I don't like it when people maneuver their way
into my orbit. It makes me question their motivations."

Andrea stared at the deep lines in her face. The judge was just a person who knew how to push buttons. She was not so much indomitable as a Great Oz standing behind a curtain.

Esther prompted, "Are you going to tell me your motivations?"

Andrea channeled her cadet training. "I want to be the best Marshal I can be, ma'am."

"And you've chosen the glamorous world of Judicial Security to hang your hat on?"

"I'm trying it out, ma'am. The USMS allows you to—"

"I know the rotation procedure," Esther interrupted. "I've been around almost as long as the Marshals themselves."

Andrea tried to break her stride. "I didn't realize that you were a Washington appointee."

Esther didn't smile. "Reagan put me on the bench. I suppose you have no idea who Ronald Reagan was or what he meant to this country."

Andrea couldn't stop Laura's words from coming out of her mouth. "I know that it's fitting that Reagan died of pneumonia since so many of the homeless people and the people with AIDS that he ignored died of the same thing."

Esther's eyes locked onto her like two cannons.

Now Andrea remembered the value of keeping her idiotic mouth shut. The judge did have some actual power here. She could demand Andrea be taken off her detail. She could screw up Andrea's career before it even got off the ground. Andrea wracked her brain for a way to dig herself out of this hole, but all she could hear was the same word machine-gunning around her skull—

Fuck-fuck-fuck-fuck-fuck-fuck-fuck-fuck.

"Well." Esther's lips were so pursed that every line around her mouth seemed to be dedicated to that single purpose. "That was very funny, actually."

Andrea wasn't looking at a woman who had found something funny.

"I'll let you get to work." Esther stood from the table, so Andrea did, too. "I imagine Cat's in the library. That's at the far end of the hall on the left. Don't go up the stairs unless it's life or death. I understand you've got a job to do, but Dr. Vaughn and I expect to retain a modicum of privacy. Understood?"

"Yes."

Her spine turned to steel again. "Yes?"

Andrea caught the warning loud and clear this time. "Yes, ma'am."

Andrea had slept so restlessly in the crappy bed at the Beach, Please Motel that she woke up feeling hungover. Twelve hours of walking the darkened Vaughn estate was akin to trying to find Waldo inside Dante's first circle of hell. All she could do now was stare at the ceiling and pray that her headache would pass. She'd had a terrifying dream about sitting at the judge's kitchen table while a large spider unfurled its long, hairy arms. Andrea had been incapable of moving as the spider pulled her toward its wet, multi-fanged monster mouth. She'd jerked herself awake trying to scramble away. And then she'd slipped off the edge of the mattress and hit the floor.

Day two of her Marshal career was already off to a fantastic start.

Her iPhone dinged with a text. Andrea ignored it, assuming her mother had found another jacket in Oregon. She turned up the music she'd been listening to. Andrea had downloaded all of the songs from Emily's mixtape. She'd heard of some of the artists, but was mortified that her favorite was by a grown woman who went by the name Juice Newton.

Andrea closed her eyes, but she couldn't force herself back to sleep. Judith's collages floated into her brain. The newer one with the death threats against the judge, the earlier one that a teenage Judith had used to try to work through her conflicted feelings about her mother. The mixtape. The stray words—*Keep working it out! You will find the truth!!!* The group photo of Emily with three of the men who would later become prime suspects in her murder.

Chief Bob Stilton's notes stated that the attack had most likely occurred between 6:00 and 6:30 p.m. He hadn't explained how he had established that window, but Andrea had no other choice but to accept it. The weapon used to beat Emily was a slat from a shipping pallet in the alley, so it could be assumed that the attack was probably opportunistic or spur-of-the-moment rather than planned. Which tracked, because the attacker had obviously been furious.

Stilton had assumed that Emily's body had been removed directly after the attack, but Andrea wasn't so sure. The man's own diagram showed the alley as forty-one feet long and about three feet wide. Both buildings were approximately fifteen feet tall with one-foot-wide overhangs. Even in broad daylight, there were probably a lot of shadows you could hide a body in, not to mention that the three large, black plastic bags of trash from the diner provided excellent camouflage.

Andrea had looked up the meteorological data for that Saturday evening. Clear with no chance of rain. The sun had set around 7:42 p.m. If Andrea was trying to dispose of a body, she definitely would have waited until it was dark.

Which gave every suspect on her list plenty of time to be seen at the prom before returning to dispose of the body. No one had an iron-clad alibi. Even Eric Blakely, who admitted to being the last known person to talk to Emily that night, had corroborating witnesses. Two classmates claimed that they had seen him inside the gym during the timeframe of the attack.

Medical records recorded that Emily had weighed 152 pounds in the seventh month of her pregnancy. Lifting that much weight would not have been impossible for an eighteen-year-old boy, but it would not have been easy. Automobiles were forbidden on the boardwalk. The wooden piers probably would not support the weight of a car. The suspect would've parked on Beach Road. Then he'd have to go to the end of the alley, pick up Emily, then walk back to the car and put her in his trunk.

From there, it was a fifteen-minute drive to Skeeter's Grill where, as the statement from the boy who had found Emily in the Dumpster reported, most of the staff left around ten even though the restaurant closed at midnight. He had called in the body at 11:58 that evening. Emily was naked, probably because her teal satin prom dress would have been easily identifiable, or maybe because the killer was worried about leaving evidence. Either way, Emily's face had been unrecognizable. She'd had no identification on her, no purse or wallet. One paramedic had pronounced her dead, but then another had seen her hand move and started CPR.

And then seven weeks later, Judith Rose had been removed from her body.

Andrea rolled onto her side. Her brain had started buffering. There was not enough room to download all of this. She tapped her phone to check the time. She had missed a text from Mike at 8:32 this morning. Andrea felt a quiver in her heart, then another quiver somewhere else.

He'd sent her a photograph of a small herd of animals drinking from a lake, then followed it up with three question marks.

"What the—" She squinted at the animals, trying to figure out what they were. And then she decided it was too early in the morning for sleuthing. She rolled onto her back. She closed her eyes. Her brain filled with Juice Newton for a blissful minute before she opened her browser and pecked out—

Animal that looks like water buffalo and gazelle

Wiki answered—

Wildebeest, also called gnu

"Gnu?" she mumbled. Then, "News."

The read receipt had gone through, so Mike knew she'd seen his text. Andrea was trying to decide whether to respond or to throw her phone across the room when the three dots bounced, indicating Mike had more to say. She watched the text bubble pop up—

You forget my number again?

Andrea tapped the message space, but she didn't type. She wanted to think about Mike watching the dots bounce on his end. She let Juice finish wailing about love being a little bit hard before she wrote back—

Still 911, right?

The dots bounced again. And again. And again.

All for a thumbs up.

Andrea closed the app. She held the phone to her chest and stared at the ceiling again. She wasn't going to let herself get caught up in Mike right now. Instead, she focused her thoughts on the Vaughn family kitchen, summoning the gold chandelier and melamine counters, the spider-like judge unfurling herself across the table.

Andrea had been convinced last night that Esther Vaughn didn't know anything about Jasper's string-pulling or Andrea's connection to Clayton Morrow. Now, she was second-guessing herself.

A federal judge could get all sorts of information, and Esther Vaughn wasn't exaggerating by much when she said she'd been around almost as long as the USMS. Considering the average age of a congressman was nine thousand years old, she probably had tons of friends in high places. Sure, it was illegal to search the Marshals' private databases, but if the last few years had taught the world anything, it was that politicians did not play by their own rules.

She felt her muscles twitch impulsively toward her phone, but she stopped herself from searching—*who can find out if you are in witness protection?*

"Oliver!" Bible banged his fist on the door as he shouted her name. "Oliver! You up yet?"

She groaned as she pushed herself out of bed. She knew it was Bible, but she still peered out between the curtains on the window. The sun lasered into her corneas. She was so blinded that she couldn't make out the time on her phone. She opened the door, using her hand as a visor so that the sightlessness wouldn't become permanent.

"Still in your jim-jams?" Bible asked.

Andrea wasn't going to apologize for her shorts and matching T-shirt. "What time is it?"

He looked at his watch, though he had to know. "Pretty late. Thought you might wanna go for a run with me."

"A run?" She felt her head shake. It was like he wasn't speaking English. "What time is it?"

"Wa-a-a-ay past eleven. Like, almost noon practically." He started bouncing on his toes. "Come on, let's go for a run. Do you some good to get those endorphins pumpin' in your brain. Didn't wanna say this before, but if you put on the brakes after training, you'll never get back in shape."

"I—" Andrea turned back around to stare longingly at her bed. If it was just past eleven o'clock, that meant she had seven hours before she had to be back at work.

She looked at Bible again. "What?"

"Fantastic." He slapped his stomach, drumming out a beat with both hands. "You know what they say, Oliver. The skinny Marshals love their wives."

"Wh—" She couldn't ask *what* again. They'd both had maybe four hours of sleep. How in God's name did he have this much energy? "Bible, I—"

"The motel clerk told me there's a nice trail across the road that takes you into the forest. Puts you directly in back of that hippie-dippie farm ol' Chief Cheese was telling us about yesterday." He was pointing away from the motel, but she couldn't see past his finger. "We'll grab some breakfast after. Pancakes are my treat. Bacon, eggs—they don't have biscuits, but did I mention pancakes? Thanks for joining me, partner. I'll wait across the road."

Andrea was still trying to form a sentence when he reached out to grab the door knob and pull the door closed. His voice was muffled on the other side as he shouted a way-too-cheerful *good morning* to someone in the parking lot.

She leaned her back against the door. Her headache had been made worse by the unrelenting sunlight. She wanted desperately to go back to bed. Which was why she forced herself not to. Yet another cliff she let herself fall off.

Andrea was too lazy to change out of her pajama shirt, but she found a sports bra in her duffel for the sake of decency. Her running shorts were a wrinkled ball stuffed into one of the side pockets. She was looking for a pair of matching socks when the import of Bible's request finally hit her.

He wanted to check out the hippie-dippie farm.

This couldn't be idle curiosity. Bible was obviously investigating the death threats, no matter that he'd clearly said that was not their job. Maybe Andrea's alternate investigation into Emily Vaughn's murder would line up with his. She shoved her feet into her sneakers. Clipped her hair back behind her head. Her sunglasses were bent from being dropped into her bag. Andrea used her teeth to straighten the arm before sliding them on.

Outside, the sun was just as unrelenting as before, but now she had the heat to deal with. Andrea looked left, then right. The judge's house was roughly a mile away. Downtown was a five- or ten-minute walk in the opposite direction. The diner would be open. They would have pancakes. Hot coffee. Chairs that she could sit in. Tables she could lean her head on to fall asleep.

"Partner!" As promised, Bible was on the other side of the road. He was bouncing on his toes like Marshal Tigger. He clapped his hands together, shouting, "Let's go, Oliver!"

Andrea's feet dragged across the asphalt as she tried to get herself going. Bible happily disappeared down a packed dirt trail. There was no spring in her step as she followed. He was several yards ahead by the time her body remembered the mechanics of running. Every joint resisted the exercise. Still, she kept her hands loose, her elbows tucked to her sides.

Ahead, Bible took a sharp turn deeper into the forest. Andrea guessed they were on an old logging road. She tried to get her bearings. The path led away from the motel, almost perpendicular to the sea. The sun was directly on top of her head. Meanwhile, every tendon in her body screamed the same question—

Why the hell wasn't she in bed?

Andrea tried to drown out the noise as she propelled herself forward. She silently said a different name for every step.

Clayton Morrow. Jack Stilton. Bernard Fontaine. Eric Blakely. Dean Wexler.

One was in prison. One was a cop. One looked like an asshole. One had a sister who worked in a diner. One had left his teaching job without managing to make it onto the school's *Where Are They Now?* webpage.

Clayton Morrow. Bernard Fontaine. Eric Blakely. Dean Wexler. Jack Stilton.

Andrea could feel her muscles finally picking up the memory of exercise. Eventually, thankfully, the pain started to burn off. The endorphins finally flowed. She was able to raise her head without wincing.

Bible was ten feet in front of her. Andrea's eyes started to focus, to gather the details. He was wearing a dark blue USMS T-shirt and black running shorts. His sneakers were worn at the heel. The muscles in his legs had the sharp definition that came from working out at the gym. She could've spent the next hour wondering why Bible had asked her to tag along on what was clearly a reconnaissance mission when what she should've done back at the motel was call Mike. He could've filled her in all the *gnus* about Leonard Catfish Bible.

"You good?" Bible glanced at her over his shoulder. The guy wasn't even sweating.

"I'm good," Andrea huffed back.

Out of habit, her tongue felt for the ridge in her cheek that came from clenching her teeth. Her stomach was surprisingly fine. Bible was holding himself back, keeping the run light for her sake. She realized he was waiting for her to catch up with him. When the trail widened, she picked up his pace.

They ran in unison, their feet hitting the ground at the same time, though his stride was about a foot wider than hers. Andrea was trying to think of a way to offer him an opening when he beat her to the punch.

"Gotta confession," he said.

Andrea listened to her breath heaving out of her lungs.

"Might be something going on at the farm we need to take a look at."

Andrea looked up at him. Exercise had turned the scars on his face bright pink.

"Heard from the lady who owns the diner that there was a body found in the field." Bible glanced down at her. "Looks like a suicide."

Andrea nearly stumbled. That was a fucking coincidence. "Why did you hear it at the diner? Didn't the chief call you?"

"Well that's the nutty part, ain't it?" He leapt over a root sticking out of the ground. "Not a peep from ol' Cheese, even though I specifically asked him to let me know if any suicides hit his radar. That field is smack in the middle of his jurisdiction. He give you a buzz?"

Andrea shook her head, though she hadn't checked her work phone. The Android was back in her motel room. Out of habit, she'd tucked her iPhone into her pocket on the way out the door.

"The victim is female," Bible said. "On the younger side. Doesn't fit our profile, but it sticks in my craw that Cheese didn't flag it for us. Makes me wonder what else the crafty fella is hiding."

Andrea thought Cheese might be hiding a hell of a lot. "What do you know about the farm?"

"Other than it's hippie-dippie?"

Andrea shot him a look. They could only play pretend for so long.

"Started in the mid-eighties," he said. "Organic back before anybody cared. They grow fava beans. Bake 'em, season 'em and package 'em as snacks. They're called Dean's Magic Beans. You ever heard of 'em?"

"No," Andrea said, though she had heard of a man named Dean.

At approximately 4:50 p.m. on April 17, 1982, I, Dean Constantine Wexler, was driving my car down Richter Street on my way to chaperone the prom. I had to swerve to miss her. She was completely out of it. I don't know if she was using drugs. I don't know her well enough to make a distinction. She was only my student for a year. Still, I felt some responsibility as an adult and teacher. I parked my car and got out to check on her. It's my duty as a teacher to report kids who are not doing well. Emily was wearing a prom dress and said she was going to prom. I only point that out because she was expelled from school months ago for disturbing class. She wasn't wearing shoes. I didn't notice a purse. Her hair was disheveled. I told her to go home immediately. She argued with me, and I admit I let my temper get the better of me. I did not want to be around this girl. You have to understand she's been going around for months accusing complete strangers of impregnating her. If Melody Brickel is saying I pushed Emily against my car, I would say consider the source.

There was yelling. I will admit that. It mostly came from Emily. She started accusing me of all manner of crimes, to which I said something along the lines of, "Watch what you're saying," or "There's nothing for you to say." I don't remember exactly because at the time all I wanted to do was get away from her. You'll have to ask Melody Brickel for her scholarly opinion based on something she claims she witnessed from 200 feet away. They are both very obnoxious and uncontrollable girls. I know that everyone says Emily comes from a good family, but this proves the nature/nurture thing in my opinion. Those kids who live in

*ultra-conservative bubbles always crack when the real world
hits them. I am aware that Emily is in a coma but that has
nothing to do with me. I have no idea who the father of her
bastard is. I can state emphatically that there is no possible way
it's me. I want them all out of my life. If I could afford to quit
my job, I would be helping people who really need it instead of
wasting my talents in this godforsaken town. I've been instructed
to specify what I was wearing that night and it was a black suit
and tie, but everyone was wearing black. I swear the contents
of this amended statement are true under penalty of law.*

Bible asked, "How'd it go with the judge last night?"

"We'll see if she lets me back in the house." Andrea wondered
why he wasn't talking about the body in the field. "I made an
off-color joke about being glad that Reagan is dead, and she went
up to her room."

He laughed. "You're all good, Oliver. She's mellowed in her
old age."

Andrea hated to think what an unmellowed judge would be
like. But the judge was not the reason Andrea was running through
the forest in her sleep shirt.

"When you say the owner of the diner told you about the
suicide, do you mean Ricky Fontaine? The curly-haired older
woman who served us last night?"

"Yep." He shot her the same knowing look that Andrea had
given him before. "One of the drivers from the warehouse got to
talkin' at the diner. Said a girl didn't show up for her shift this
morning. Farmhands found her in the field around nine thirty.
Might'a took a bunch of pills. They called it into the chief, but
the chief did not call your friendly US Marshals."

Andrea muttered a non-word, because she was afraid a real
word might give her away.

"Thissaway." Bible led her down yet another fork in the trail.
He had clearly been out here before. The fact that he'd brought
Andrea for a second look had to mean something. He certainly
hadn't brought her for back-up. Neither one of them was armed.
Andrea's ID and Silver Star were inside the motel safe along with
her Glock.

The trail dog-legged, then turned back on itself before suddenly opening onto a large rolling field. Sunlight turned the rows of green, spindly plants into a lush carpet. Andrea had never seen fava beans before. She would've guessed by the long, waxy pods that she was looking at sugar snap peas or green beans. A greenhouse dipped below the next rise. Glass gleamed in the sunlight. The rainbow-colored buildings in the distance and the festive streamers hanging from the farmhouse's wraparound porch told her they had arrived at the hippie-dippie farm.

The vibe was considerably harshed by the bright white police tent in the middle of the field. Yellow tape cordoned off the scene, boxing in ten rows of plants, each with about three feet of space between them. An old blue farm truck with oversized tires to clear the plants straddled one of the rows.

As they got closer, Andrea could feel a chill come over her. She had learned two years ago that death had a stillness that reached into your soul. Her heartbeat slowed. Her breathing turned deeper. The sweat on her skin seemed to fade away.

Someone had covered the body with a white sheet. The bright white cotton draped along a curvy hip. The woman had died while lying on her side. From the sweet smell, Andrea assumed she hadn't been there for more than a few hours, which lined up with what the warehouse driver had said. The body had been found around 9:30.

Bible lifted the police tape and held it up for Andrea. He nodded at the two farmhands. Or at least Andrea assumed the men were farmhands by their overalls and the fact they were both leaning against the beat-up Ford truck. They seemed tense, unlike the three uniformed cops milling around the tent's perimeter. Two were reading their phones, one had his hands in his pockets; nothing much happening as far as any of them were concerned. She recognized Chief Jack Stilton by his shape. He was leaning into his squad car, radio to his mouth. He had clearly seen Andrea and Bible at the trailhead. His displeasure had traversed the distance like Washington Crossing the Delaware.

"Chief Cheese!" Bible waved his hands in the air. "How ya doin', buddy?"

Andrea watched Stilton take his time extricating himself from his car. The crowd had perked up. Hands came out of pockets. Phones were tucked away. The farm workers gave each other a wary glance. They were both white males, one approximately late fifties, the other probably mid-sixties. The older guy had long, scraggly hair and a tie-dyed T-shirt that put him squarely in the hippie category.

The younger guy had a cigarette dangling from his lips and a snarl that reminded Andrea of a photo she had seen the night before.

Delaware's own Billy Idol.

Bernard Fontaine had the audacity to wink at Andrea. She kept her expression fixed. There was a dead young woman on the ground between them. There was another young woman who'd been tossed into a Dumpster forty years ago. Nardo had known them both.

"Chief, you must'a forgot our conversation from last night." Bible clamped his hand on Stilton's shoulder. "I thought I asked you to call me about any suicides."

Stilton's eyes shifted back and forth between Bible and the covered body. "Well, Marshal, it's early days. We don't really know that this is a suicide."

Andrea gave him marks for brazenness. The tent had been set up to block the public's prying eyes, but no one was wearing protective clothing. No one was taking photos. There were no markers identifying possible evidence on the ground.

She asked Stilton, "Has the coroner been called?"

"What do you think I was just doing, sweetheart?"

"Why don't you tell me, sweetheart?"

Andrea heard snickers, which made the situation even more infuriating. No one seemed to be taking this seriously. She'd worked in a 911 call center. She knew the procedure when a dead body was found. The responding officers didn't put up a tent, call in back-up and tape off the scene before alerting the coroner. At the very least, there should already be a couple of fire trucks on the road, and definitely an ambulance.

And no one—ever—should assume that just because it looked like a suicide the victim had committed suicide.

"She's just poking at ya, Chief." Bible rested his hand on one of the tent poles. "I'm guessing this is the hippie-dippie farm you were talking about. No offense."

The last part was addressed to the old hippie, who said, "None taken."

Bible looked at the body. The sheet was stirred by a breeze. He reached down, asking Stilton, "Mind if I take a peep?"

"Yeah, I do." Stilton crossed his arms over his chest. "I don't want to be difficult here, but the Marshals don't have jurisdiction over these types of cases."

Bible asked, "What types of cases are those?"

Stilton's eyes couldn't stay in one place. They moved from the hippie to Nardo to his deputies then back to Bible. Clearly, he didn't want any Marshals here. Which was strange. Cops were usually like greyhounds. They got excited when there were other cops around.

Andrea tried to figure out why everything felt so off. This was her first real crime scene, but only Bible and Andrea seemed to appreciate the solemnity of the situation. The chief wanted them out of here. His officers were clueless. Nardo was clearly bored. The old hippie was focusing all of his attention on hand-rolling a cigarette. He was the right age for another person on Andrea's list of suspects: Dean Wexler. The fact that he was here with Bernard Fontaine said something she didn't quite yet understand.

She asked the old hippie, "Are you Dean Wexler?"

His tongue flicked out to wet the rolling paper. "That's me."

Andrea couldn't take a victory lap. Nor could she turn herself into a thermometer, because Wexler's temperature was barely registering. Neither he nor Nardo seemed concerned about the circumstances, which again was saying something that Andrea didn't yet understand.

She asked Wexler, "What are you growing out here?"

He flipped the cigarette up to his lips. "Vicia faba."

Andrea laughed, but only because Dean Wexler seemed like the kind of man who didn't like young women laughing at him. "That's a fancy way to say fava beans."

His jaw tightened. His hooded eyes flashed with a silent threat.

"Marshal," Stilton intervened, speaking to Bible. "I appreciate your help, but you can run along now. We got this."

"What's *this*?" Bible asked.

Stilton huffed air between his lips, exaggerating patience. "We got a girl—a young girl—who probably took a drug overdose. She's had problems for a while. This isn't the first time she's tried it."

"Oh, then," Bible said. "She the one you pulled out of the ocean last Christmas or the one who cut her wrists a year and a half ago?"

Andrea felt the tension pull tight like a string.

At Glynco, they'd trained it into all the cadets to listen to their bodies. The fight-or-flight impulse was a hell of a lot more perceptive than any of your other senses. She kept her attention on Nardo and the hippie. There was something about them that felt dangerous. For the first time in her entire life, she wished that she was armed.

"Marshal," Stilton said. "Correct me if I'm wrong, but this situation doesn't seem like it has a damn thing to do with the assignment that brought you and your partner into my town."

Bible looked down at Stilton. "Funny thing about being a United States Marshal is, we're one of only two law enforcement divisions in the United States that's charged with the blanket task of enforcing federal law. We're not limited to Customs and Borders. Or Alcohol, Tobacco and Firearms. Or Internal Revenue. We get all the laws, big and small, hot off the presses or going back to March 4, 1789, the effective date of the US Constitution."

Stilton looked uncomfortable, but he shrugged. "So?"

"USC 482-930.1 holds that it is a violation of federal law for any person to take their life by their own hand. It's an oldie but a goodie. Dates back to English common law." Bible winked at Andrea, because they both knew he was bluffing. "What do you think, partner?"

Andrea said, "Sounds like jurisdiction to me."

Stilton adjusted his approach. "Now I told you first thing that we're not sure about whether or not it's suicide."

Bible didn't point out that his story was a bit slippery. Instead, he pulled a pair of nitrile gloves out of the pocket of his running shorts. He winked at Andrea again, finally acknowledging that he'd come prepared.

Stilton said, "This is a crime scene, Marshal. You need to wait for the coroner. We can't disturb—"

Andrea asked, "Who put the sheet over the body?"

Wexler cleared his throat. "Guy who found her."

Ricky had said that a farmhand had found the body. Andrea could see only two men in the field. "Then the scene has already been disturbed."

Bible was all business now. He didn't speak. He just knelt down and gently pulled away the sheet.

Someone gasped. Andrea was so damn proud that it wasn't her.

Still, her stomach tightened like a fist.

She had seen corpses at the Glynco morgue, but she'd been given ample time to prepare for the experience. The decedents had all donated their bodies to science, so it had felt like there was an understanding between you and the dead. Everything had been solemn and predictable. You were there to learn. They were there to give you that opportunity.

Now, Andrea felt the shock of sudden death wash over her.

As with Judith's collages, at first she could only process the emotion, which bordered on overwhelming. Andrea forced herself to see the details. An empty prescription bottle on the ground. Dried pink foam around the mouth. Dirty blonde hair. Deathly pale skin. Blue fingertips curled into the palm of a red-stained hand. The woman had lain in the field for hours. Gravity had settled her blood into the parts of her body that touched the earth. The sheet had bunched up around her feet, but there was no mistaking her for sleeping. She was very clearly dead.

"Jesus," someone whispered.

Andrea breathed through her mouth as the smell hit her. She reminded herself that she was a cop. She knew what to do.

Analyze, understand, report.

The nude woman was lying on her side.

That was wrong.

The victim was not a woman. She looked like a girl, maybe sixteen or seventeen years old. The sharp angle of her left hip jutted into the air. Her pubis was shaved bare. The dark aureoles of her breasts were almost blackened by the early stages of decay.

A yellow dress was folded up like a pillow under her head. One arm was reaching out. The other was wrapped around her tiny waist.

The most startling part was the state of her emaciated body. Andrea had taken an anatomy class for figurative drawing during her first year of art school. She was reminded of the diagrams that illustrated a three-dimensional view into the body. The girl's bones were visible beneath her skin. Her joints were like doorknobs. An outline of her teeth showed in her sunken cheek. Her hair was filthy. There was a bruise underneath her right eye. Her lips were light blue. Starbursts of broken blood vessels spotted waxy, paper-thin skin. Pink scars crisscrossed her wrists.

She had tried this before.

"Oliver." Bible's tone was sharp. "Get some pictures."

Andrea knelt beside the girl. She took her iPhone out of her pocket. Her thumb moved to select the camera. She used the tips of her fingers to pull the sheet away from the girl's feet.

The fact that her feet were bare was not the most shocking discovery.

There was a metal band around her left ankle, the circumference so tight that the skin had rubbed away from the ankle bone. Three gemstones were at the center—an aquamarine flanked by two blue sapphires. The bracelet was almost like a piece of jewelry but for the smoldering line where it had been permanently welded around her ankle.

Andrea saw an inscription etched into the silver band.

Bible saw it, too. He asked, "Who is Alice Poulsen?"

OCTOBER 20, 1981

Emily picked at her breakfast with her fork. Across from her, Gram did the same, not quite understanding why there was so much tension in the room but instinctively knowing to keep silent. Esther and Franklin were at opposite ends of the table, both dressed for work as if this was a perfectly normal day in their normal lives. He was reading the newspaper. She was marking up a draft opinion, her lips pursed in concentration. They both wore their reading glasses. Eventually, they would take them off, stuff their papers into their respective briefcases, then go to work in separate cars.

Emily had seen her parents weather countless upheavals this way before. How they got through was to pretend that the terrible things weren't happening. Maybe Emily had a little bit of that ability inside of herself because she, too, was trying to pretend that last night hadn't happened. And that yesterday morning at Dr. Schroeder's office hadn't happened. And that The Party hadn't happened.

She was especially trying to pretend that her memories of Mr. Wexler driving her home that night were either figments of her imagination or vestiges of a bad acid trip.

As if by design, a sudden wave of nausea washed over her. The eggs on her plate had gelled into a yellow glob. The bacon grease congealed into a ridge around the toast. She had no idea how long she stared at her plate, but when she looked up, her parents were gone and only Gram was there.

"Do you have any plans for the day?" Gram asked. "I had thought that I would work a bit in the garden."

Emily felt tears threaten to fall. "I'm going to school, Gram."

Gram looked confused. She gathered up her silverware and plate before leaving.

Emily used the tips of her fingers to blot away tears. Putting on make-up this morning had felt like dragging sandpaper across her face. Her eyelids were chapped from crying all night. She hadn't slept. The person who peered back at her in the mirror had looked like an alien.

She was not *intact*.

Why didn't Emily feel anything other than shame? Sex was supposed to be a special, romantic time where she bonded with her soulmate, where she gave herself to a man who was worthy of her love.

Instead, it had happened in the back of her teacher's grimy, cheap clown car.

Maybe.

Emily was wary of relying on the flashes of memories she kept having, an almost strobe-lighted horror show of things that could or could not be true. She'd been so certain—even while she told herself that she was uncertain—that it had been one of the boys. And now, she was not allowing herself to believe that Dean Wexler with his bushy, sweaty mustache and clumsy, fumbling hands had taken from her something that she was not willing to give.

Because that was rape, wasn't it?

Or maybe it wasn't. Maybe her mother was right. And her father. If you drank too much, if you took drugs, you were accepting the inherent risk that a boy would do what boys do.

But Mr. Wexler was a man.

That made it different, right? If Emily told her father that it hadn't been one of the boys, that she had been taken advantage of by a grown man, her father would look at the situation differently. Or maybe he would just look at her, because, since last night, he'd completely erased Emily from his line of sight. Walking through the room, sitting at the table, reaching for the coffee pot, reading his newspaper—not once did he actually acknowledge that he saw his daughter sitting a few feet away from him.

Emily looked down at her hands. Her vision blurred with tears. She wondered if she was disappearing all together. Would no one ever see her as the same person again?

"Emily." Esther was standing in the doorway. She rested her hand against the jamb as she straightened the toe of her panty-hose. "Don't be late for school."

Emily looked not at her mother but out the window. She'd felt her heart rattle at the normal sound of her mother's tone. Esther wouldn't be angry about this again. There would be no more arguments or recriminations. She was a judge in every sense of the word. Once her decision had been rendered, she never questioned herself on the matter again.

When Emily looked back at the doorway, her mother was gone.

She let out a slow breath. She placed her knife and fork on her plate and took it to the kitchen. She scraped off the food into the trash. She put the plate and utensils in the sink for the house-keeper. She found her book bag and purse beside the garage door. Emily couldn't remember dropping them there last night, but then she couldn't remember a lot of things that were vastly more important than last night.

This was all she could come up with: The dark interior of Mr. Wexler's car. The dashboard lights glowing. A song playing softly on the radio. Emily's hands nervously working a tear in the hem of Ricky's green dress. Mr. Wexler's hand on her knee.

Emily blinked. Had that last part happened, or was she making herself believe something that was untrue?

The only thing she knew for certain was that she could not stand in the hallway thinking about this for the rest of her life. She had already missed an entire day of school—a scheduled meeting with her art teacher, a chemistry test, band practice, five minutes before PE to talk to Ricky about something that had seemed very important two days ago.

She opened the door. Her father's Mercedes was already gone. She walked through the garage. Her mother's driver was idling in front of the house.

"Em?"

She turned, surprised to find Cheese leaning against a tree smoking a cigarette.

"Oh, no, Cheese, I'm so sorry." Her heart sank. She had told him he could sleep in the shed. "I forgot to put out the pillow and blanket."

"It's cool." He stubbed out his cigarette on the bottom of his shoe and pocketed the butt. "You know I don't need much. I'm fine."

He didn't look fine, which made her feel worse. "I'm sorry."

"Looks like you had a rough night, too."

Emily couldn't think about her appearance right now. The shed was on the opposite side of the house, but Cheese could've heard what happened in the kitchen last night if he'd stood outside the garage. "What time did you get here?"

"Dunno." He shrugged. "Started out at home, but Mom was off the rails. Dad went to the station and I just . . ."

She watched his lower lip start to tremble. He hadn't heard anything. He had his own problems.

"Anyway," he said. "I'll walk you to school."

Emily let him take her book bag. They had to wait for her mother's car to circle round. Esther looked out the back window, then looked again. For a split second, her poker face melted away. Emily could hear her mother's thoughts—*Was it the Stilton boy?*

By the time the car made it to the driveway, Esther had regained her composure.

Cheese remained oblivious. He shook another cigarette out of his pack. They walked down the winding driveway in a companionable silence. Emily tried to remember the first time she'd met Cheese. Like most of her casual school friends, he had been a part of her life for as long as she could remember. They had probably been thrown together in pre-school or kindergarten. If she tried to think of her first memory of him, it was of a shy boy sitting in the corner watching everyone else have fun. He had never quite belonged, which was why Emily had always gone out of her way to talk to him. Even within the clique, she had often felt like she was on the outside looking in.

Especially now.

"Okey-dokey," Cheese said. "You gonna tell me what's up?"

Emily smiled. "I'm okay. Really."

Cheese smoked in silence, clearly disbelieving.

Emily thought of something. "Were you in the shed this time last month?"

He looked concerned. "If your parents got mad because—"

"No, no," she assured him. "They don't care about that. I just wondered because I came home really late that night—the night of the twenty-sixth. And they were very angry at me for busting curfew. I wondered if you'd heard anything or if you remembered anything."

"Jeesh," he said. "I'm sorry, Emily. If I was in the back, I didn't hear a peep. Did you get in a lot of trouble? Is that why you look so upset?"

She shook her head. Cheese was not inscrutable. If he'd been there that night, he would've said something already. She was asking him the wrong questions.

She tried, "Do you know much about investigations? I mean, from your dad?"

"I guess so." Cheese shrugged. "Maybe I know more from watching *Columbo* reruns."

She smiled because he smiled. The show was something her father had watched back when it was on. Emily had never seen it, but of course she knew that it was about a clever detective. "Let's say that Columbo had a case where someone did something bad."

"Emily, that's every Columbo case." He smiled playfully. "That's kind of the point."

"Right." Emily gave herself a moment to think. "Let's say there's a case where a woman was at a cocktail party where her—her diamond necklace was stolen."

"Okay."

"Only, she can't remember anything about the party because she'd had too much to drink." Emily waited for him to nod. "She has these memories, though. Flashes where she recalls talking to different people or being in certain places. But she can't tell if they're real memories or not."

"Sounds like she was drugged," Cheese said. "Booze doesn't really do that unless you're blackout drunk. At least that's what I've seen with my mom."

Emily guessed he would know. "How would the woman get the necklace back?"

He smiled again. "She'd call Columbo."

Emily mirrored his smile again. "But how would Columbo solve the case?"

He didn't take long to come up with an answer. "He would talk to the people at the party. Compare notes on them, such as, does what this one guy is saying match up with what this other guy is saying? Because if they don't match up, that means somebody is lying, and if somebody is lying, then you know that they're hiding something."

For the first time in days, Emily felt a lightness in her chest. That made perfect sense. Why hadn't she thought to talk to anyone? She could get them to confess.

There was just one problem.

She asked, "How does Columbo do it, though? If people are guilty, they're not going to talk, especially to the police."

"That's what my dad says." Cheese shrugged. "But if you watch TV, guilty people always talk. Sometimes, they make up lies to throw the heat onto somebody else. Or they wanna know if they're going to get caught, so they ask lots of questions about the investigation. And Columbo, he's the best at tricking them up. He doesn't go into it accusing people. He'll say, 'Sir, I see you were at the party. If you'll excuse me for asking, could you tell me if you saw anything suspicious or anyone behaving out of character?' He never points his finger at the guy and says 'You did it.' He lets them talk themselves into trouble."

Emily had to admit he did a very good Columbo voice. "What else?"

"Well, he writes everything down, which is what you're supposed to do when you're a cop. My dad says it's because you get a lot of information when you interview people, but only some of it is important, so you write it all down, then go back through and pick out the good stuff."

Emily nodded, because that made a lot of sense, too. She got overwhelmed with details in class sometimes, but then she looked back at her notes and found the sense.

"The best part is at the end of the episode," Cheese said. "Right before the commercial, Columbo will be talking to a suspect, and he'll act like he's finished with the questions, but then he'll turn around and say, 'Sir, I'm sorry. There's just one more thing.'"

"One more thing?"

"Yeah, that's when you save your biggest question, for the end when their guard is down." Cheese pinched the end off his cigarette before slipping the butt into his pocket. "You say, 'That's great, thanks for answering my questions,' and act like you're going to leave. And then you pack up your notebook or whatever, and the suspect is relieved, right, because they think it's over. And then you go back and say—"

"There's just one more thing."

"Correctamundo." Cheese's Fonz wasn't bad, either. "That's how you get your diamond necklace back."

"What?"

"The lady—the one that had her necklace stolen."

"Oh, right." Emily felt her heart tremble in her chest. She felt anxious now that there seemed to be a way forward. "You'll make a good cop one day, Cheese."

"Oh hell no." He shook out another cigarette. "If I'm still living in this shithole town ten years from now, remind me to put a bullet in my head."

"That's awful. Don't say that."

He handed over her book bag. They were close to school. Without another word, Cheese quickly walked away from her. A few years ago, Nardo had teased him about having a crush on Emily and he still went to great lengths to disabuse anyone of the notion.

Emily swung her purse at her side. She considered Cheese's advice. She should look at this as an investigation. The answer might not change anything, but it would at least bring her some peace. No matter what her father and mother said, someone had hurt her. That person had taken advantage of Emily at her most vulnerable. She wasn't foolish enough to think he would pay a price, but she had to know who'd done it for the sake of her own sanity.

"Whatcha doing?" Ricky bumped her shoulder. "You cut the Cheese?"

Emily rolled her eyes, but she gave Ricky a shoulder bump in response.

"I don't know why you bother with those broken toys."

Emily tried not to rise to the bait. The clique could be so vicious to outsiders. What would they do to Emily when they found out?

"Where were you yesterday?" Ricky demanded. "I called your house twice and your mom told me you were asleep both times."

"I had a stomach bug," Emily said. "I told you that on Saturday."

"Oh, right!" Ricky bumped her again. "I thought we were going to talk yesterday."

"About what?"

"I—oh, shit. There's Nardo." Ricky bolted across the quad without looking back.

Emily didn't follow. Instead, she kept an eye on the clique as they assembled outside the front doors of the gym. Nardo was smoking even though he'd been caught three times already. Blake had his back against the wall and a book in his hands. Only Clay was turned toward Emily. His eyes followed her as she walked up the steps to school. For the first time in her life, she didn't respond to him. She didn't raise her hand to wave. She didn't feel the tractor beam of his gaze pulling her to his side.

She turned away from him as she opened the door. The heat of his stare was still on her back even when the door closed behind her. She squinted in the bright overhead lights of the lobby. Kids were rushing past. She felt her body tense up the same way it always did when she was in school. Only this time, the anxiety wasn't from the silent will of Esther pushing her to succeed. She felt anxious because she had started to form a plan.

She would talk to Mr. Wexler. She would approach him casually, as if nothing was wrong. She would ask him some questions. Then, she would act like she was going to leave before she dropped the *one more thing*.

Emily felt her confidence start to falter. Could she really ask Mr. Wexler if he'd taken advantage of her? He would be outraged. Of course he would be outraged. But would that be because he was innocent or because he was guilty?

"Emily!" Melody Brickel was literally galloping up the hallway. She had a thing for horses, which was only one of the reasons she wasn't very popular. "You missed band practice yesterday!"

Emily resisted the urge to curl herself into a ball. Mrs. Brickel knew everything. Hadn't she told her daughter?

"Em?" Melody grabbed her hand and pulled her into Mr. Wexler's empty classroom. "What's wrong? You look awful. Have you been crying? But I love your hair."

"I'm—" Emily's brain seized. She was in Mr. Wexler's room. He would be here soon. She wasn't ready. There was no way she could confront him. She'd meant to write down a list of questions but now all she could think was that she had to get out of here before he showed up.

"Emily?" Melody asked. "What's wrong?"

"I—" Emily gulped. "Didn't your mom tell you?"

"Tell me what?" Melody asked. "Were you at Dr. Schroeder's yesterday? Mom's not allowed to say anything about what happens there. There's some kind of rule or something? I don't know. But you told me you were there so what's wrong, are you okay?"

"Yes, I—" Emily cast about for a lie. "It's my period. It started a few days ago and it's been really bad."

"Oh, no, poor you." Melody gripped her hand. "You're too old to still be seeing that stupid mean goat. You should talk to a proper gynecologist. My mom got me on the pill two years ago and I barely notice my periods anymore."

Emily didn't know which was more startling—that Melody had seen a gynecologist or that she was on the pill.

"Don't look so outraged, silly. The pill isn't just for sex. Though I live in hope!" She reached into her book bag and presented a cassette tape. "Here, I brought you this but you gotta promise to give it back."

Emily didn't know what to do but take the cassette. On the cover, five girls were sitting around in towels with cold cream covering their faces. The Go-Go's. *Beauty and the Beat.*

"I told you about it last week." Melody sounded excited. She was obsessed with music. "Listen to how the vocals slow down in the middle of 'Our Lips Are Sealed', okay? It's not exactly a time signature shift but it kind of reminds me of what the Beatles did in 'We Can Work It Out' where they dip from a 4/4 into a 3/4. Or 'Under My Thumb' where the Stones—"

Emily's hearing left her. Mr. Wexler had come into the room. In the periphery, she could see him dropping a stack of papers on his desk. She kept her gaze on Melody playing imaginary drums and tapping her foot to a beat only Melody could hear.

"Listen for it, okay?" Melody said. "It's so cool. And they wrote the music themselves, which is awesome, right?"

Emily nodded, though she had no idea what she was agreeing with. All she knew was it was enough to make Melody lope out of the room.

Mr. Wexler asked, "What's got her so excited this time?"

Emily had to swallow before she could speak. "The Go-Go's."

He guffawed. "She's comparing a bunch of chubby little girls to the Stones? Give me a break. They're just playacting so they can meet guys."

Last week, Emily would've taken him at his word, maybe even laughed along with him, but now she asked, "Don't guys join bands so they can meet girls?"

"Maybe the hairballs you listen to," Mr. Wexler said. "The Stones are actual musicians. They've got real talent."

Emily clasped her hands together. She had started sweating again. She had no plan. She couldn't do this. She wasn't Columbo.

"What do you need, Em?" Mr. Wexler ate a handful of trail mix from the bag in his desk. "I got so wasted last night. I dragged through my morning run like the ground was quicksand. I need to prep for class."

"I—" Emily remembered what Cheese had said. She needed to write things down. She couldn't use her class notebooks. She reached randomly in her purse for something to write on, then clicked her pen. She looked up at Mr. Wexler, but she didn't know what to say.

"Emily?" he asked. "Come on, what is it?"

"I—" She lost her nerve. "I missed class yesterday. I need to know my make-up work."

He laughed. "Uh, I think we're good. You've got your A. Don't worry."

"But I—"

"Emily, I can't remember what we did in class yesterday, all right? I marked you as present. You were here as far as I'm concerned. Take the win."

She watched him turn his back as he wiped the chalkboard clean. He was in great shape because he ran all the time, but that was where the discipline ended. His pants were wrinkled. His shirt was sweat-stained under the arms. His hair was unbrushed. When he turned back around, his eyes were bloodshot because he hadn't used the bottle of Visine on his desk.

The low lights of the dashboard. The song on the radio. The tear in Ricky's green dress.

"Em?" He leaned his hands on his desk. "For the love of God, what's up with you today? No offense, but you look like I feel, which is pure shit."

"I—" She tried to recall what Cheese had said. Ease into it. Don't be accusatory. She sat down in the front row of desks, trying to appear casual. "Do you remember when you picked me up from Nardo's last month?"

Immediately, he looked and acted guilty. His eyes narrowed. He walked over to the door and closed it. He turned to face her. "I thought I told you that we weren't going to talk about that."

Emily pressed her pen to paper. Her hand started moving.

"What are you writing?" Mr. Wexler snapped. "Jesus, why are you—"

She recoiled as he ripped the pen out of her hand.

He demanded, "What the hell is going on?"

"You—" She felt like she was spinning out of control. This wasn't how it was supposed to go. Don't confront. Don't accuse. "My grandmother saw you. That night. She recognized your car."

He looked crestfallen as he sank down into the desk beside her. "Fuck."

"She—she asked me about it last night. She asked why I was in your car that late because she knows you're a teacher."

He put his head in his hands. His voice was strained when he asked, "Did she tell your parents?"

Emily could see that he was afraid, which meant the power had shifted slightly in her direction. She needed to keep him vulnerable, so she answered, "Not yet. I asked her not to tell them, but . . ."

Mr. Wexler sat back in the chair. "We need to get our story straight in case she does. *When* she does, because you know she'll tell eventually."

Emily could only nod.

Like that, the power shifted back in his direction.

"Okay." He turned toward her, leaning forward on his elbows. "What did your grandmother see exactly?"

"That I—" Emily knew she needed to strategize, but she was at a loss. "I got out of your car and it was late and I was upset."

Mr. Wexler nodded his head. She heard the rough scrape of his unshaven face as he scratched his cheek. "All right, well, that's not a lot."

Emily kept her mouth tightly shut. Cheese had told her that guilty people wanted to talk. She needed to wait for Mr. Wexler to talk.

"Okay," he repeated, picking up her pen and handing it back to her. "This is what we're going to tell them."

Emily pressed the ballpoint to a clean sheet of paper.

"Nardo called me for help. You were wigged out. They were all stoned. I drove over to get you and take you home. All that stuff that happened between me and Clay—" He waved his hand. "Forget about it. It's our word against his and no one is going to believe him."

Clay?

"And I drove you home," Mr. Wexler finished. "End of story. Okay?"

"But—" Emily cast around for a way to elicit more information. "It's not just Clay we have to worry about, right? Nardo and Blake were there. And Ricky. Ricky was there."

"Ricky was passed out on the front lawn when I drove up," Mr. Wexler said. "I don't know where Nardo and Blake were. Could they see us from inside the house? There's windows over-looking the pool area, right?"

"Uh—yes. Maybe." Emily felt her mouth fill with cotton. Ricky passed out in the front yard. Nardo and Blake in the house somewhere. Clay and Emily outside by the pool. They wouldn't have been swimming. The pool had been covered and the water was too cold anyway. Why were they alone outside? That had to mean something.

"All right, that's settled." Mr. Wexler tapped her notepad. "Write it down if it helps. You called me because you were arguing with Clay. I picked you up. I brought you home. End of story."

Emily started to write the words, but she had to ask, "What was I arguing with Clay about?"

"Fuck if I know. Just pick an earlier fight and say it was ongoing. You kids piss each other off all the time." Mr. Wexler stood up. "You should get to class. Don't talk to any of them about this, okay? You know they'll take Clay's side and I don't want you to lose your friends over something stupid."

The cotton in her mouth turned to concrete. She had worried about losing the clique, but now she could feel the loss in a very real way. They were going to abandon her. The friends she'd clung to, the pals she'd known since first grade, the people she'd hung around with for every free moment outside of school for the last decade, would abandon her when things got difficult.

Especially if the difficult thing involved Clay.

Mr. Wexler said, "If your parents confront you about it, just stick to the story and we'll be fine. I'll tell them the same thing."

Emily looked at her notebook. She had written one word—*Clay*.

"Emily." Mr. Wexler looked at his watch. "Come on, go to class. I can't write you guys any more late passes. Mr. Lampert already told me that some of the teachers are ratting me out for playing favorites. I bet it's Darla North. God, that stupid bitch can't keep her fat mouth shut."

Emily packed up her notebook and pen. She stood up. She walked toward the door.

And then she turned around.

"Mr. Wexler?" she asked. "There's just one more thing."

He looked at his watch again. "What is it?"

"My grandmother . . ." Emily had to stop strategizing. She needed to open up her mouth and talk. "That night you brought me home. She said that my dress was torn. And that it was on inside out."

Mr. Wexler's jaw clenched so hard it looked like a piece of glass was sticking out of his face.

Emily said, "That's what she noticed about me when I got out of your car."

He rubbed his scruffy cheek again. She could hear the bristle scrape against his fingers.

Emily dropped the hammer. "What should I say when my father asks about that?"

He was motionless at first, and then he moved so quickly that Emily found herself incapable of reacting until he'd pressed her back against the wall and slapped one sweaty hand over her mouth and grabbed her neck with the other.

She choked for air, clawing at the back of his hand. Her feet brushed against the ground. He had lifted her just enough so that she could do nothing but gasp for air.

"You listen to me, you little bitch." His breath was a foul mixture of coffee and whiskey. "You're not telling your father a goddamn thing. Do you understand me?"

She couldn't answer because his fingers were digging into her throat.

"I picked you up from Nardo's. You were having a bullshit fight with Clay. I took you home. That's it." His grip tightened. "Do you understand me?"

She couldn't speak. She couldn't move. Her eyelids started to flutter.

In an instant, he had let her go. Emily dropped to the floor. Her fingers went to her bruised neck. She could feel the arteries throbbing. Tears rolled down her cheeks.

Mr. Wexler squatted in front of her. His finger jammed in her face. "Tell me what you're going to say."

"It—" She coughed. Blood dribbled into her throat. "It wasn't you."

"It wasn't me," he repeated. "Nardo called me to pick you up. I went to his house. You were fighting with Clay. I drove you home. I never touched you, or ripped your dress, or . . ."

Emily watched his eyes narrow. His gaze traveled slowly down from her face to her belly. She could almost hear a bell go off inside of his head.

"Fuck," Mr. Wexler said. "You're pregnant."

Emily listened to the word travel around the cinder block room. No one had really said it out loud before. Even Dr. Schroeder hadn't used the actual word. Her father had called it *knocked up*. Her mother talked around it the same way you would if someone had cancer.

"Fuck!" Mr. Wexler pounded his fist into the wall. And then he screamed in pain, clutching his hand. His knuckles were bloody. "Fuck."

"Mr. Wex—"

"Shut the fuck up," he hissed. "Jesus Christ, you stupid bitch. Do you know what this means?"

Emily tried to stand, but her legs were too wobbly. "I'm—I'm sorry."

"You're damn right you are."

"Mr. Wexler, I—" She tried to calm him down. "Dean, I'm sorry. I shouldn't have said anything. I'm just—I'm scared, okay? I'm really scared because something bad happened and I can't remember."

He stared at her, but she couldn't read his expression.

"I'm sorry," she repeated, feeling like those two words were the only two words she ever said to anybody anymore. "My grandmother saw me get out of your car, so I thought—I thought that maybe you . . ."

Her voice trailed off.

Mr. Wexler was still unreadable. Emily thought that they were going to stay like this forever, and then he broke the trance by standing up. He walked stiff-legged across the room. When he turned, she could see that blood from his knuckles had stained his shirt.

"I had mumps when I was a kid." He tested his fingers to see if anything was broken. "It gave me orchitis."

Emily stared up at him. She didn't know what he was saying. "Look it up in the dictionary, you dumb cunt." He sat down at his desk. "It means I'm not the fucking father."

5

Bible looked up from the silver band that had been permanently clamped around the dead girl's ankle.

"That's what the inscription on the shackle says." He asked them again, "Who is Alice Poulsen?"

Nardo looked at Wexler, who offered, "She's a volunteer. I don't know her."

Bible stood up. He was clearly angry. "Volunteer for what, exactly? Being deprived of basic nutrition and banded like a damn test subject in a science lab?"

Nardo and Wexler stared, as if they were expecting the question to be rephrased.

"All right." Bible's jaw clenched. "How many *volunteers* you got working here?"

Again, Nardo let Wexler answer. "Ten, maybe fifteen or twenty in the high season."

"Ten or fifteen or twenty. Sure, that's a ton of people to keep up with." Bible turned to Stilton. "Chief, I believe you said Ms. Poulsen tried to kill herself a year and a half ago. Cut open her wrists. Right?"

Stilton nodded. "That's right."

"So she's been living here on this farm for at least that long, maybe longer." Bible pointed his remarks back to Wexler. "How old is she?"

"Legal age," Wexler said. "We only take legal adults here. Make them show their passports or ID."

"But you don't know this particular adult who's been living and working on your property for eighteen months?"

Wexler picked a piece of tobacco off of his tongue, but said nothing.

Andrea could feel the tension hitting the triangle of Bible, Stilton and Dean Wexler. None of them were looking at the dead body on the ground, though two of them were clearly affected by the sight of the emaciated young woman.

Bible's response was fury. Andrea's was unfathomable horror. She felt overwhelmed by the darkness in front of her. This woman had been someone's daughter, or classmate, or friend, or maybe even sister. And now she was dead.

All Andrea could do was follow Bible's instructions. She documented the malice perpetrated on Alice Poulsen's body. The sunken cheeks. The painfully thin limbs. The fingerprint bruises that circled her wrists. The whalebone of her ribcage sticking out like the carcass of a decayed animal. To say the young girl was malnourished told only half the story. There were open wounds at her elbows and hip bones that looked like bedsores. Patches of hair had fallen to the ground like silk from a corn stalk. Her fingernails curled from stomach acids where she'd clearly gagged herself into vomiting.

Had she willingly submitted to this torture?

Andrea focused the camera on the prescription bottle. The label had been removed. The cap was overturned. Her hands were shaking as she took the last photos of the ankle band, which might as well have been a shackle. She wiped her palms on her shorts as she stood up. Everything felt so wrong. This girl had been starved into a skeleton and tagged like a farm animal. Even if Alice Poulsen had committed suicide, someone had pushed her toward that end.

She looked at Nardo, knowing instinctively that he was the more sadistic of the two. "Who welded this onto her ankle? She didn't do that to herself."

"Hold on, girl," Wexler said. "We don't know anything about that."

Andrea bit back the invectives that flooded into her mouth. He hadn't been shocked to see the band, and he clearly knew who the girl was. Alice had been living on his property for over a year. None of this had happened without Wexler's knowledge and approval. Andrea was so angry that she was shaking. The girl was barely out of high school. She had come here as a volunteer and she would leave in a body bag.

She pointed to the body. "She's flesh and bone. How could you let her get this way? You had to have seen her. She's must've been a walking corpse."

Wexler shrugged. "Not my department."

Andrea repeated Bible's earlier question. "Who is Alice Poulsen?"

"Dunno." Wexler shrugged again. "We got a couple of girls from Denmark last year. Could be she's one of them."

Of course he knew where she was from. "Who's the other girl? You said a couple, that's two, right?"

Wexler shrugged one more time. "Like I said, I don't know them well."

"All right." Bible took back over. "So who knows them well? Who let her get this way and didn't say anything?"

There was silence, then another infuriating shrug.

Andrea realized that her heart was beating so hard she could feel it inside of her mouth. She parted her lips. Took a deep breath. Worked to exert some control over the emotions vibrating through her body.

At the academy, she had learned how stress and anger could screw up your senses. Andrea forced herself to tamp down her fury and focus on what was happening right in front of her. The three uniformed cops were clearly interested in the conversation, but not on alert. They also weren't taking any cues from their boss. Stilton looked as if every muscle in his body was contracted. Nardo, meanwhile, had taken a few steps away from Wexler. Andrea couldn't tell if he was trying to put distance between them or inching toward the truck.

She didn't inch. She took several quick strides toward the truck, making it clear that she'd pull him out by the back of his collar if he tried to get in.

"You gotta gun on you, Slim?" Bible was talking to Nardo but he was looking at Andrea.

She felt a giant bead of sweat roll down the back of her neck. She had missed the fact that Nardo's loose-fitting overalls had been altered to accommodate a holster at the small of his back. Only now could Andrea see the outline of what was likely a 9mm micro handgun. She had been so angry that she'd forgotten to look for weapons, which was the number one thing you were supposed to look for. America had roughly 330 million people and nearly 400 million guns. Most times, the only way to tell the good guys from the bad guys was when the bad guys started shooting.

"I've got a permit," Nardo said. "But that's really none of your business."

"Sure-sure." Bible clapped together his hands. He'd managed to quell his anger better than Andrea. "Gentlemen, I think we all need to get back to the house up there and have a conversation."

"Not me," Nardo said. "I don't talk to pigs without a lawyer."

Andrea could've predicted his response, which almost exactly matched his full written statement from forty years ago.

It's April 18, 1982, and I, Bernard Aston Fontaine, do not talk to pigs without my lawyer.

Bible said, "Can't blame you there, my man. My wife, Cussy, she's always saying she hates talking to cops. Chief, why don't we all climb into your cruiser and take this show up the hill?"

"Not me," Wexler said. "If you want to talk, you can follow me to the house in my truck."

Andrea said, "I'll go with you."

She didn't wait for Wexler's approval before she walked around the truck and opened the door. Andrea had to pull herself up into the tall cab. Her first impression was that the joint in the ashtray was not the first one that had been smoked in the old Ford. Every inch was permeated with weed. She didn't let herself get distracted. She wasn't going to make the same gun mistake twice. She leaned down, making sure the end of a rifle wasn't sticking out from under the seat. She checked the pockets in the doors for weapons. Then she opened the glove box.

Wexler got behind the wheel and slammed the door. "You got a warrant to search my vehicle?"

"I've got probable cause," she told him. "Your partner is

carrying a concealed weapon. I checked your vehicle for weapons in order to ensure my safety."

He grunted dismissively as he started the engine. Andrea reached back for the seatbelt but it was stuck on the reel. Wexler didn't even try his belt. He bumped the gear with the heel of his hand. The bench seat vibrated from the old engine's rumble. The wheels slowly moved forward, straddling the neatly tended rows. They would have to go to the end of the field and swing around to avoid crushing the plants.

Andrea glanced around, realizing there were no workers harvesting or tending or whatever they would need to do with the beans. She didn't know how farms operated, but she knew that crowd control was always a concern when you were processing a potential crime scene. It seemed like the ten or fifteen or twenty volunteers would be close at hand considering one of their own was lying dead within shouting distance of where they ostensibly all lived.

Unless someone had told them to stay out of sight.

"Who's in charge of the volunteers?" Andrea asked. "Is it Nardo?"

Wexler chewed at the inside of his mouth in silence. The needle on the speedometer was hanging below five. She assumed he drove like an old man because that's what he was. At this rate, it would take several minutes to reach the farmhouse. That gave Andrea a little time to get him talking. The thermometer trick was still worthless. Dean Wexler was clearly unconcerned by the dead young woman in his field. He was used to running his farm exactly how he saw fit. He wasn't accustomed to answering questions, especially ones posed by a woman.

Andrea started with something easy. "How long have you lived here, Mr. Wexler?"

"A while." Wexler stared straight ahead as the truck rolled forward. She was trying to think of another softball question when he surprised her with an observation of his own. "Guess that bitch judge told you all about me last night."

Andrea said nothing.

"You got in yesterday afternoon. Ate at the diner. Spent the night at the judge's house. Slept at the motel." Dean's lips twisted in something like pleasure. He thought he was making her squirm. "Small town, sweetheart. Everybody knows everybody's business."

Andrea stared at him. "Is that how it works?"

"I'll tell you what else," he said. "You guys are here to watch the judge, which means that somebody finally got tired of her holier-than-thou bullshit."

"You sound pretty tired of it yourself."

"If you're trying to figure out who's been threatening her, I've got to be number six hundred on your list." He gave Andrea a knowing glance. "Nardo's even farther down. He's never given a shit about that family. Especially what's her name—the girl. Hell, I don't even remember what she was called."

"Emily," Andrea said. "Emily Vaughn."

Wexler gave another grunt. They had reached the end of the field. He took a lazy swerve past the forest, then lined up the truck's tires along the planted rows.

Instead of continuing forward, Wexler slammed on the brakes.

A yelp came out of Andrea's mouth. Her quick reaction was the only thing that kept her face from pounding into the metal dashboard. Wexler chuckled, a sick kind of pleasure in the sound. Scaring Andrea had not been the only goal. He had wanted to hurt her. There was no way to call Wexler out without admitting that he had gotten to her. All she could do was sit in silence as the truck slowly resumed its trudge toward the farmhouse.

Wexler was still smiling when his tobacco pouch came out of his pocket. He used his knees to keep the steering wheel steady while he rolled another cigarette. They were approaching the crime scene tent. Someone had placed the sheet back over the body. Wexler didn't even turn his head when they passed. Nor did he turn when a loud bang announced Nardo jumping into the bed of the truck.

Nardo winked at Andrea as he opened the sliding window between them. Then he mocked a gun with his hand and pulled the trigger in her direction.

Andrea looked ahead at the farmhouse. They had another few minutes before they reached their destination. Thanks to the open windows, Nardo could probably hear everything they said. Andrea didn't think it was a coincidence that Wexler had tried to scare her within moments of bringing Emily Vaughn into the conversation. She could not let him distract her.

She said, "They've never conclusively proven who the father of Emily's child is."

"Judith," answered the man who said he couldn't remember anything. Wexler lit his cigarette from a box of matches, then gripped the steering wheel between his hands. "It wasn't me, sweetheart. Even Emily didn't know who knocked her up. The judge tell you that? The girl had no fucking idea."

Andrea struggled to keep her expression neutral. She had known that it was a secret, but not a secret that was unknown to Emily herself.

"The bitch got stoned at a party and woke up pregnant. For all I know, every guy there got a piece of her." He smiled at Andrea's appalled reaction. "Emily was a party girl. She knew exactly what would happen. Hell, she probably wanted it. Her parents turned her into a fucking angel when she died. Nobody ever talks about how Emily Vaughn would fuck anything that moved."

Andrea felt like he'd punched her in the face. What he was describing was rape. Whether Emily was stoned was immaterial if she hadn't been capable of giving consent.

Wexler looked pleased as he smoked his cigarette. This was clearly what got him out of bed in the morning—the opportunity to make women feel like shit.

Andrea tried desperately to fall back on her training. She'd just learned something shocking, but you couldn't be shocked when you talked to suspects. You had to store your emotions somewhere else while you did your job, then you could deal with the fall-out later.

She told Dean, "I guess it'd be easy to get DNA from Emily's daughter. This isn't 1982. Paternity's easy to prove."

"I shoot blanks, baby doll." He had the same nasty grin on his face. "I was cleared forty years ago. You can ask Cheese about that. His daddy was the one who investigated the whole thing. If you can call it an investigation. We all knew who did it. Dumb fuck couldn't figure out how to lock him up before he skipped town."

Andrea said, "Clayton Morrow."

"Exactly." Wexler snorted smoke from his nose. "In other words, not me."

He shifted into second gear when they cleared the field. The needle on the speedometer bobbed past the ten. They were in wide-open space now, about fifty yards from the farmhouse. Grass and weeds competed for sunlight. There were outbuildings, chickens, goats.

Andrea ignored them all. She couldn't let Dean Wexler think he'd had the last word. She made an educated guess based on her earlier web searches. "Maybe you aren't the father, but you still lost your job over it."

Wexler was nonplussed. "Getting fired from that piece of shit school was the best thing that ever happened to me."

For the first time, Andrea felt like he was telling the unvarnished truth.

"This is my idea of heaven." Wexler spread out his hands, indicating the farm. "I can go out in the fields and work the soil if I feel like it, or I can swing in my hammock and smoke a joint. I've got food and shelter and all the money I need. Forty years ago, I walked out of that school and straight into freedom."

"And yet you still found a way to surround yourself with vulnerable young girls."

Wexler's foot jammed on the brake.

Andrea's head jerked forward. Again, her reflexes were the only thing that saved her. Nardo wasn't so fortunate. His shoulder slammed into the back window so hard that she felt the vibration in her teeth.

"Fuck, Dean!" Nardo banged his fist on the glass, but he was laughing. "What the hell, old man?"

Andrea's heart was pounding in her mouth again. She couldn't let it slide this time. "Mr. Wexler, if you try anything like that ever again, I will put you on the ground."

He barked a laugh. "I shit bigger than you, little girl."

"You should probably schedule a colonoscopy." Andrea reached for the door handle. "Maybe the doctor can get your head out of your ass."

Everything happened very fast but, for a split second, for just a tiny moment, Andrea's brain managed to slow it all down.

Nardo laughed from the back of the truck.

Andrea felt a sudden, sharp pain electrify her arm.

She looked down.

Dean's hand was clamped so tightly around her wrist that her ulnar nerve felt as if it was on fire.

US Marshal trainees had to practice anywhere from two to eight hours a day of army-style tactical combat training, Brazilian Jiujitsu and hand-to-hand combat in order to qualify for graduation. This wasn't a theoretical course with textbooks and pop quizzes. This was hands-on fighting in a flea-infested sandpit every single day, often twice a day, in the pounding rain or the scorching, tropical heat of Brunswick, South Georgia.

Sometimes, the instructors blasted you with a fire hose just to make it interesting.

For obvious reasons, or maybe to scare the shit out of them, an ambulance was always on standby. Washing out of the course because of a medical emergency was not unheard of. You didn't get to pick your sparring partner. That's not how it worked in real life and that wasn't how it worked in training. Women didn't only fight women and men weren't only paired with men. Everybody fought everybody, which meant that sometimes Andrea had to beat Paisley Spenser to the punch and sometimes she had to take on a six-three male cadet whose body looked like it was carved from a single block of granite.

She had learned very quickly that the main drawback to being a giant block of granite was that it took an enormous amount of physical energy to swing around your fist or sweep out your leg. Sure, the guy could break someone's spine once the blow landed, but landing the blow took a hell of a lot longer when all that muscle had to be activated.

Andrea didn't have that problem. She was quick and she was mean and she didn't mind fighting dirty.

That was why everything happened very fast inside of Dean Wexler's old Ford truck.

She grabbed his wrist with her right hand. Her thumb was pressed against the base of his palm and her fingers secured the back of his hand. Then she twisted his arm behind his back, pinned down his elbow, and drove him face first into the steering wheel in a perfectly executed rear wrist lock.

Andrea didn't even realize it was happening until she was on her knees pressing the full weight of her body into Wexler's back.

"Fuck a duck," Nardo said. "That's you finished by a little girl, old man."

Wexler was grunting, but this time it was from pain.

"I'm going to let you go," Andrea told Wexler. "Don't test me again."

Slowly, Andrea released her hold. She sat back with her hands at the ready, prepared to pin him again if he did something stupid.

Dean Wexler wasn't going to do anything stupid. He pushed open the door, mumbling, "Fucking cunt."

Andrea got out of the truck, but she kept her distance, giving Wexler some space. He moved like he drove—slowly, all stiff joints and arthritis. She found herself questioning her response. Had she been too forceful? Was there another way to de-escalate? Had her first real-world altercation turned her into one of those asshole cops on a power trip?

"Well done, old gal." Nardo was leaning against the back of the truck. He slipped a cigarette out of his pack of Camels. He offered one to Andrea.

She shook her head. Her fists were still clenched. Her heart was still racing. She reminded herself that this was her training. She had let the first time go. Then she had given him a warning. Wexler had escalated the situation by grabbing her wrist. She had reacted. And, most importantly, when Wexler had complied, she had released him.

"I imagine you could make a pile of money taking that show on the road." Nardo laughed, coughing out smoke. "How do you feel about wrestling in Jell-O?"

Andrea waved away the smoke. He reeked of stale beer and rancor. "I met your wife at the diner. What does she think about you running around out here with all these young girls?"

"Ex-wife, thank God." He took a long drag on the cigarette. "And you'd have to ask her."

Andrea tried, "What about her brother?"

"Dead as a doornail, poor old thing."

Andrea felt her breath catch. By Eric Blakely's own witness statement, he was the last of Emily's group who had spoken to her before the attack.

At approximately 6:00 p.m. on April 17, 1982, I, Eric Alan Blakely, witnessed Emily Vaughn heading toward Beach Drive from the vicinity of the gymnasium. I didn't notice how she was dressed because I did not care. Nor did I notice if she was high or intoxicated, though both seem likely given her storied past. She tried to speak to me. I spurned her attention. Then she shouted invectives, which caused me to try to calm her. She cussed at me, then walked into the alley. I walked away myself, heading toward the gym, which is what my other classmates have told you. The altercation frankly left a bad taste in my mouth, so I decided to return home where I watched videos with my sister, Erica Blakely. I do not know who the father of Emily's baby is. I was wearing a black tux that night but so was everyone else. I swear the contents of my statement are true under penalty of law.

Nardo took a drag on his cigarette. "Being dead is a bit like being stupid, isn't it? Easy for you, but hard for the people around you."

Andrea could only look at him. He was actually expecting her to laugh.

"Ah, well." He winced at her through the smoke. "You know, you'd be good-looking if you lost a few pounds. You're staying over at the motel, right?"

She recited the only prayer Laura had ever taught her. "God grant me the confidence of a mediocre white man."

"Very good." He looked impressed. "You southern ladies come out swinging."

"You mean like the person who swung a piece of wood at Emily Vaughn's head?"

Nardo's expression twisted into a familiar snarl. "Dyke."

Andrea supposed his generation thought that was an insult. She watched him stomp off toward the barn. She waited until he was inside to take a deep breath and hiss it out.

She looked down at her left hand. Her wrist was throbbing where Wexler had grabbed it. She would have a bruise, probably the same type of bruise she had seen on Alice Poulsen's wrist.

Andrea took another breath. She had to concentrate on the crime that was in front of her. Dean Wexler and Nardo Fontaine's storied past with Emily Vaughn was not the reason that she and Bible were at the farm. There was another young girl who'd lost her life only hours ago. She was lying in the field under a white sheet while a group of officers milled around checking their phones and tucking their hands into their pockets.

Andrea's own phone had documented the ravages of Alice Poulsen's daily existence. The young woman's parents were thousands of miles away, probably thinking their daughter was having an adventure in the States. Soon, someone would knock on their door and tell them otherwise. They would want to know what had happened to their child. Andrea and Bible might be the only reason why they got any answers.

Analyze, understand, report.

She took in her surroundings. Like the barn and three outbuildings, the one-story farmhouse was painted in bright, rainbow hues. Streamers hung from the wraparound front porch. Candles had been placed in the windows. There was a chicken coop filled with round hens. Three goats grazed under a beautiful willow oak. Wheelbarrows and farm tools were over by the large Day-Glo barn that housed a tractor that was probably worth more than a Lamborghini. In the distance, silos fed into what she assumed from the DEAN'S MAGIC BEANS sign outside was the warehouse. The logo colors were blue sapphire and aquamarine, the same as the gemstones in Alice Poulsen's ankle band.

"Fucking asshole," she muttered. Dean Wexler knew exactly who that girl was.

The crunch of gravel pulled her attention away from the sign. The chief's cruiser crawled up the road. They had taken their time, probably so Andrea could work Dean Wexler. Bible had thrown her in the deep end again. The jury was still out on whether she had managed to swim a few laps or tread water.

The cruiser took a sharp turn around a bend. Andrea noticed two low-lying metal buildings in the distance. The festive paintjob had stopped at the gravel road. The bare metal structures were dark with patches of rust. The roofs were caked with leaves. A stencil over the door on the larger building read BUNKHOUSE. The smaller one was marked CHOW HALL. All of the windows in both buildings were open to fight the coming heat.

Since Andrea had grown up in the south, she had to remind herself that it wasn't cruel and unusual up here to forgo air conditioning. The same could not be said for the line of five blue porta-potties standing thirty feet away from the chow hall.

The farm looked successful enough to have indoor plumbing. Especially given that the labor seemed to be supplied by volunteers, which Andrea assumed was a euphemism for unpaid help. Having read about her share of internships, she could imagine the ad touting the *lived experience* of the organic farmer's world: housing and Wi-Fi available. The accompanying photos would skip the primitive bunkhouse and showcase the multi-colored main buildings.

As a point of interest, the farmhouse had air conditioning.

Chief Stilton's cruiser parked behind the blue Ford truck. If he'd had a deep conversation with Bible on the ride over, neither one of them looked happy about it. Stilton slammed the car door almost as hard as Wexler had.

Andrea stepped back as he pounded his way toward the farmhouse.

"Not sure what's goin' on with Chief Cheese," Bible said. "How's the old guy?"

"Pissed off," Andrea said. "He grabbed my wrist. I put his face in the steering wheel."

"That's exactly right." Bible sounded very serious. "Marshal rule number one: don't ever let nobody lay hands on you."

Andrea was glad for the support, but she had to admit, "It's going to make things harder when we try to talk to him about Alice Poulsen."

"That ain't even part of the equation as far as I'm concerned." Bible looked back at the farmhouse. "Partner, I don't know about you, but I regret my sartorial choices."

"Same." At least he had on an official-looking T-shirt with his running shorts. Andrea's lavender pajama shirt had a ring of cartoon 'Z's floating around the collar.

The screen door opened. Wexler shouted, "I don't have all damn day."

"Curiouser and curiouser," Bible said.

Andrea was following him up the walkway when she saw two women leaving the barn. They were heading in the direction of the bunkhouse. Their matching gaits were slow and deliberate. Both were wearing long, yellow sleeveless dresses identical to the makeshift pillow that Alice Poulsen's head rested on. That wasn't the only similarity. Their feet were bare. Their stringy, dark hair was almost down to their waists. They were both so emaciated that their arms and legs looked like strings hanging down from their dresses. Either or both could've passed for Alice Poulsen's twin.

They both had silver bands clamped tightly around their left ankles.

"Oliver?" Bible was holding open the door. She could see Dean Wexler and Chief Stilton standing inside. Neither man was looking at the other, but the hostility between them was like a third person. Clearly they had a history. People always talked about how quaint small towns were, but the fact was that blood feuds lurked around almost every corner.

Andrea caught the screen door before it slammed shut. She had been expecting a depressingly grungy house, but what she found was surprisingly bright and modern. The open-concept living room and kitchen were painted in soft variations of gray and white. The leather couch and matching club chair were black. The kitchen appliances were not just stainless steel, but Sub-Zero and Wolf, probably topping out at her annual salary. All of the color had been saved for the floor. Each wide plank represented a hue from the twelve-point color wheel. Rabbits and foxes and birds swirled into the repeating patterns.

Everybody in this damn town was an artist.

"Mr. Wexler," Bible said. "Thanks for talking with us."

Wexler crossed his arms. "That bitch tell you what she did to me?"

"My partner told me that you tried to assault a federal law enforcement officer," Bible said. "So do you want me to arrest you or do you wanna sit down and have a chat like we planned?"

There was a moment of silence while Wexler weighed his options. He was saved a response by a woman appearing from the hallway. Clearly, she hadn't heard them. She was reaching back to pin up her hair. She froze at the sight of them, startled by the strangers in the room.

Andrea was startled to see the woman.

She was older than the others, possibly in her late twenties. Same yellow dress. Same long, dark hair. Same bare feet. Same heartbreaking thinness. The contours of her skull were visible under her skin. Her eyes were two round orbs pressing against her bruised-looking eyelids. The band around her ankle was so tight that the skin had been rubbed raw.

"Dean?" she asked, her voice trilling up in fear.

"It's all right, Star." Wexler had taken some of the gruffness out of his tone. "Keep working. None of this has anything to do with you."

Star didn't press for an explanation. She looked at no one, spoke to no one, as she slowly walked into the kitchen. Her movements were robotic as she reached up to open a cabinet door. Andrea realized that there was a slight pause after every action. Take out the flour. Stop. Place it on the counter. Stop. Take out the granulated sugar. Stop. Set it down. Stop. Then yeast. Stop.

"Dean?" Stilton unsnapped his shirt pocket and found his spiral notebook and pen. "Are we going to do this or what?"

"Sit down," Wexler said. "Let's get this the hell over with."

There was only the couch and the chair. Bible and Stilton were both big guys and Wexler was clearly going to take the chair. Andrea spared them any notions of chivalry and walked over to the kitchen. She pushed herself up on the single leather stool under the island. She could hear Star working behind her, but Andrea didn't turn around or acknowledge her presence. She gathered by the way Wexler was staring at her that this was exactly what he wanted.

"All right." Bible nodded to Stilton as they took their separate corners on the couch. They had clearly worked out who was going to take the lead. "Chief?"

Stilton said, "Dean, tell me about this poor girl in the field."

Andrea heard a glass being set down heavily behind her.

"I've told you all I know," Wexler said. "And that's not even what I really know because I told you I don't recall ever having met her."

"Alice Poulsen," Bible supplied.

Star stopped moving. Andrea could feel the tension building behind her, but she still did not turn around.

"That appears to be the victim's name," Bible said. "Alice Poulsen."

"Victim?" Wexler gave a familiar dismissive grunt. "She killed herself. That has nothing to do with me."

"And the state of her?" Bible was mindful that Star was in the same bad way. "What about that?"

"What state of her? She was a beautiful young woman, from what I could see." Wexler showed his teeth. "They're all adults. They can do whatever they like. I'm not even their employer. I've got no idea what the volunteers get up to when they're on their own time."

Bible adjusted his approach. "How does the volunteer system work? I guess you have a website or something?"

Wexler seemed to gauge whether or not to answer before finally nodding. "We get applications through the site. Most of them are international. America's gen X-Y-Z, whatever they're calling themselves, they're all too lazy to do this kind of work."

"I hear ya," Bible said. "Must've been hard starting a place like this from scratch."

"I inherited some money from a distant relative. I used it to buy the land." Wexler rubbed his mouth with his fingers. His eyes kept nervously finding Star. "Actually, I started the entire organic-hydroponic movement right here in Delaware. We've been using microbial activity to create nutrients from the beginning. No one else was doing it. Not even on the West Coast."

"Hydroponic." Bible seemed to let the word rest in his mouth. He was trying to get Wexler's guard down. "I thought that used water and—"

"Yes, in the beginning. Thanks to global warming we can cultivate in the fields. Hell, give it another ten years and we could probably grow oranges here." His hands gripped the arms of his chair. He stopped looking at Star. "When I started out, the whole town thought I was crazy. They said I couldn't get the beans to grow or find the workers to make it succeed. It took me twenty years before this place turned a real profit. Look at it now."

Andrea noticed that the grunting had fallen away. Dean Wexler was a hell of a lot more articulate when he was talking about how smart he was.

"Alice," Bible said. "She might've come from Denmark, you think?"

"Probably, but as I said I don't know. Europe has always been leaps and bounds ahead of us in the environmental arena. Particularly the Scandinavian countries." Wexler leaned forward, elbows on his knees. "I started during the eighties. Might as well have been the Stone Age. Carter had his faults, but he understood the environment was in danger. He asked Americans to make sacrifices and, as usual, they chose color televisions and micro-waves."

Bible noticed, "I see you don't have a television in here."

"Useless pabulum for the masses."

"You got that right." Bible slapped his knee. He was so damn good at this. "Now, fava beans. Are those the same as broad beans? I thought they had some kind'a toxin."

"Yes, phytohemagglutinin is a naturally occurring lectin." Wexler paused, but only to take in a breath. "There are low concentrations of the toxin in the bean. What you do is you boil them down for ten minutes. But that's where the process gets interesting."

Andrea waited for Dean Wexler to hit his stride. She slid out her iPhone. She wanted a photograph of Star. The girl had parents somewhere. They would want to know that she was still alive.

Wexler droned, "In their wild state, they're around the size of a fingernail, which is too small for the consumer market."

Andrea wondered how she could track down Star's parents. Or if it would even matter. The woman was standing in a room with three law enforcement officers. If she wanted help, all she had to do was open her mouth.

Unless she was too afraid.

"Favism," Wexler continued, "is an inborn error of metabolism.

Fava can break down the red blood cells, which can be very dangerous, particularly in newborns."

Andrea guessed that Wexler had been the type of teacher that kids found cool but adults found stupefying. She turned her head. Star openly stared back at her. The woman's eyes were like glowing crystal balls in her sunken face. Her lips were parted. The sickly sweetness of her breath smelled like cough medicine and rot.

She was looking at Andrea's phone.

"Star," Wexler commanded. "Bring me a glass of water."

Again, Star moved robotically, as if following a sub-routine. Walk to the cabinet. Stop. Take out a glass. Stop. Walk to the sink.

Andrea turned her back to the woman, which was exactly what Wexler seemed to have been waiting for.

He told Bible, "Let's get to the point. I have work to do."

"Sure," Bible said. "So, tell me about the application process for your volunteers."

"It's not very complicated. Entrants write an essay. They must have an interest in organic farming, preferably some studies already completed in the field. You might have gathered we've got a stellar international reputation. We get the cream of the crop."

"Must be hard to winnow it down to a dozen or so every year."

Wexler saw where this was going. "Bernard, the farm manager, goes through the applications. He's the one who chooses the volunteers."

Bible asked, "They all women?"

"What's that?"

"All the applicants," Bible said. "Are they all women, or does Bernard weed out the men?"

"You'd have to ask him that." The smug look was back on Wexler's face. He clearly accepted all of the credit and none of the blame. "For the last thirty-five years, Nardo has been completely in charge of the selection process. I helped set up the parameters in the very beginning, but I can't tell you the last time I read an application, let alone performed an interview."

"Nardo interviews 'em?" Bible asked. "What, he flies over to Europe and—"

"No, no. It's all through the computer. FaceTime or Zoom. I don't know the particulars. Where the ads are placed. What questions are asked. Why some people stick around for another year, why some decide to go home." Wexler looked up at Star. She stood beside him with a glass of water. He pointed at the side table and waited for her to place it on a coaster. "Once Nardo chooses the lucky few, he sends them the details and they book their tickets and fly over. I barely even meet them anymore."

Star walked back toward the kitchen. Flour dabbed her shallow cheek. Her skin was so white that it barely left a shadow. Andrea heard the swish of her bare feet across the floorboards. She moved like a ghost. Again, her eyes went to Andrea's phone.

Bible asked, "The volunteers have to pay their own way?"

"Of course. We're not their employers. We provide them with the opportunity to learn a high-level skill that has practical applications to their ongoing coursework when they return to university."

Andrea leaned back against the counter. She unlocked her phone. She placed it on the counter with the screen side up, then pushed it back with her elbow so that Star could take it.

"Is it all farming?" Bible asked. "Or do they work in that factory up the road, too?"

"That's where the beans are processed," Wexler told him. "It's mostly automated, but there are still things that have to be done by hand such as packing and taping boxes. Logging them in for shipping. Loading them into the trucks."

"High-level skills with practical applications,'" Bible quoted.

"Precisely," Wexler said, not picking up on the sarcasm. "We give them valuable skills before they are released back into the world. Anyone can sit behind a desk and read a textbook. This was the problem I saw every day when I was teaching. Why make someone read about a subject when they can put their hands in the soil and understand the earth in a metaphysical way?"

Andrea heard a rolling pin squeaking behind her. The smell of yeast filled the kitchen. She glanced down at her phone. It was exactly where she had left it. The screen had gone black. The phone was programmed to lock after thirty seconds.

"Funny how you said that," Bible told him. "'Released back into the world'. Does that mean you cut off those ankle bracelets before you let them go?"

"I've told you all that I know," Wexler said. "Cheese, when will I get my field back? We have work to do."

Stilton clearly didn't like the nickname any more when Wexler used it. "When I'm damn good and ready."

"What about Alice's parents?" Bible asked Wexler. "I assume you're going to notify them."

"I wouldn't know how."

"Nardo, then?"

"I wouldn't know."

Andrea debated about whether to unlock her phone again. Was Star trying to send her a different message? Andrea looked at her hands, her shorts. What had Star been trying to signal?

"We could take notifying her parents off your hands for you," Bible said. "Maybe there's some letters or a phone in Ms. Poulsen's personal belongings. People have all kinds of information on their phones."

"Don't you need a warrant for that?" The corners of Wexler's mouth twitched with his familiar smugness. "Probably not the best idea to ask for legal advice from a cop."

"I prefer to be called either Marshal or Deputy," Bible said. "Cops are generally like Chief Stilton here. They handle state-level issues like traffic tickets and DUIs. I'm at the federal level, so that covers things like wage theft, conspiracy to commit forced labor, sexual coercion and sex trafficking."

The room went so silent that Andrea could hear the oven ticking as it warmed up.

She tried not to startle when something small and solid pressed against her elbow. She waited until the rolling pin started to squeak again to look down. Star had pushed Andrea's iPhone away.

"Did Ms. Poulsen live over there in the bunkhouse?" Bible asked. "We can just pop over and—"

"Not without a warrant." Nardo was standing on the other side of the screen door. A fresh cigarette dangled from his lips. "There's no imminent danger. The girl is dead. You can't walk into any of these buildings without express permission. We have a reasonable expectation that our Fourth Amendment rights will be honored."

Bible laughed. "You sound like somebody who knows enough lawyers to try to sound like he's a lawyer."

"Right." Nardo pushed open the screen door, but didn't come in. "Dean, I need your help in the barn. You pigs will either have to leave the property or keep to the area around the body."

Wexler groaned as he pushed himself up from the chair. "That means now."

Stilton and Bible made to leave. Andrea turned back to Star, but the woman was busy kneading her hands into dough. She was making bread. The pan was already oiled on the stove top.

"Smells good," Andrea tried. "My grandmother used to make bread like that."

Star didn't look up. Maybe she could tell Andrea was lying. Or maybe she was terrified that Wexler or Nardo would punish her for speaking. She had not said one word beyond *Dean* since she'd entered the room.

"Out you go, old boys." Nardo held open the door as the law enforcement contingent passed through.

Andrea was glad for the fresh air. The house had felt stifling. Bible didn't head back toward the field, so neither did Andrea. He took his place in the chief's cruiser. Andrea climbed into the back. She could see Stilton walking around the front of the car through the wire mesh divider.

Bible asked, "What's that you had going on with Star?"

"She kept looking at—"

The door opened. Stilton got into the cruiser.

Andrea looked at her phone in case Star had somehow managed to do something while the screen was unlocked. She checked her email. Messages. Texts. Notes. Missed calls. Calendar. Thirty seconds wasn't that long. She had looked down at the phone and seen it exactly where she had left it. Maybe Star had pushed it away as a kind of *fuck off*.

Stilton cranked the engine. He turned to Bible. "Told you so."

"You sure did, Chief. That was a big waste of time." Bible sounded agreeable, but Andrea knew better. "Now riddle me this, what's the history with you three fellas? Seems like I caught some attitude between you and them."

"We went to high school together." Stilton seemed to think that was the end of it, but then he changed his mind. "They're bad people."

"That sounds accurate."

"They lie and cheat, but they're smart enough to never get caught. Nardo learned from his father. The guy spent five years in federal prison."

Andrea felt a bell go off in her head. She had found a Reginald Fontaine of Delaware during one of her aimless internet searches. There was no mention of family, but the man had been arrested in the Savings and Loan Scandal. He'd spent five years at Club Fed. The timing was around the same time that Bernard Fontaine had become the Junior Bean King to his former high school PE teacher.

Bible said, "Chief, I'm gonna be real honest with you here. I feel like you left out some details about the hippie-dippie farm."

Stilton swung the cruiser around the chicken coop.

Bible said, "We got some ladies wearing the same uniform, I guess you'd call it. All got the same long hair. All, and you'll excuse me for saying this, my wife's got me trained better than to comment on a woman's figure, but they ain't just skipped a few meals."

"Nope," Stilton said.

"They look like they're being starved."

"Yep," Stilton said.

"You got a theory on this?"

"My theory is the same as yours," Stilton said. "They're running some kind of cult. But you know as well as I do, Marshal, that being in a cult isn't against the law."

Andrea had felt a shiver at the word *cult*. She clenched her teeth to keep them from chattering. Of course it was a cult. The signs were all there. A bunch of lost, hopeless young women looking for meaning. A couple of dirty old men willing to supply it at a cost.

"Well," Bible said. "Can't disagree with you there, Chief. *Cult* seems about the right way to describe it."

Andrea unlocked her phone. She opened the photos. She found the close-ups she had taken of Alice Poulsen. The sharp bones. The bedsores. The chapped, split lips. The painfully tight ankle bracelet that had cut into her flesh.

Cult.

Alice had chosen to wear the yellow dress. She had chosen to grow out her hair. She had submitted, most likely, to the band being clamped around her ankle. She had starved herself nearly into oblivion.

And then she had walked into the field and swallowed a bunch of pills and died.

Bible told Stilton, "Seemed to me like you knew that girl in the house. Star, was it?"

Andrea looked up from the photos. She had totally missed this.

"Star Bonaire," Stilton provided. "Her mother's been trying for years to get her out."

"And?"

"Does she look out to you?" Stilton finally sounded angry. "Tell me what to do, Marshal. They may look like girls, but they're all adults. You can't go in and kidnap a bunch of grown women. They want to be there."

Bible asked, "Where does Star's mom live?"

"Couple of miles from downtown. But she's crazy," Stilton warned. "She tried to abduct her daughter last year. Drove her Prius right up to the bunkhouse and dragged her out by her arm. Had a cult deprogrammer waiting at the motel."

"And?" Bible asked.

"And next thing I know, I'm being called out to the farm to arrest her for trespassing and attempted kidnapping." Stilton shook his head. "She ended up having to do community service, which is damn lucky because she could've wound up in prison. They've got a restraining order against her. She's not allowed to attempt to contact or approach her daughter."

"Shit," Bible said. "That's one tough mother."

"Yeah, *shit* is right," Stilton shot back. "As in *batshit*. You get tangled up with the mom, you'll find out real quick how her daughter ended up at that place."

Andrea wasn't sure that qualified for batshit. If Andrea had gotten caught up in something like the farm, Laura would've tried the same thing. Except she would've succeeded.

Bible asked, "You ever had any other parents try to get their children out?"

"Not that I've heard of, and they've made it clear they don't give a shit about working through me." Stilton's anger had given way to self-pity. "Trust me, Wexler's got a shit ton of lawyers on speed dial. You don't wanna mess with those people. I sure as hell don't. They could bankrupt the town."

Andrea couldn't listen to his excuses anymore. She turned her attention back to the photos of Alice Poulsen. Alice had a mother, too. What would the woman do when she found out that her daughter had been driven to suicide? Because it was clear to anyone who saw Alice's body that the girl had found her only means of escape. Each close-up offered insight into the agony that Alice had endured. What kind of motivation did it take to starve yourself like that? Alice had worked on a farm. She had been surrounded by food. The deprivation was almost unbelievable. Andrea couldn't stop torturing herself with the photos. She swiped to the next one. Then the next.

And then she stopped.

Star hadn't needed the phone to be unlocked. There were two apps on the iPhone's lock screen that could be accessed without the password. One was for the flashlight. The other was for the camera.

Andrea zoomed in on the photograph that Star had taken with the phone. The woman had sprinkled white flour onto the black countertop and used her finger to carve out a single word—

Help.

OCTOBER 20, 1981

Emily had looked up orchitis in one of the Encyclopedia Britannicas that took up an entire section in the school library. *Inflammation of one or both testicles, usually caused by a virus or bacteria; often resulting in sterility.*

And then she had looked at the notes she had recorded after leaving Dean Wexler's classroom—

Says that he's "not the fucking father." Admitted he picked me up at The Party. Said Nardo called him to take me home. Said I was fighting with Clay by the pool when he got there. He promised he would hurt me if I ever publicly accused him. He grabbed my wrist. It really hurt.

Emily had sat in the library staring at the lines, trying to divine a meaning. Her normally good handwriting was almost illegible in parts because her entire body had been trembling when she transcribed the conversation. One thing had become immediately clear. Cheese had been right. She had missed an important detail.

She had written a question at the bottom—

He could be telling the truth about not being the father but that doesn't mean he didn't do something, right?

For the rest of the school day, Emily had been haunted not only by the conversation with Dean, but by what Dr. Schroeder had called a *looseness* that he would expect to find in a married woman. Mrs. Brickel had said he was lying, but she was only a nurse. Surely, a doctor would know better. Surely, there were rules against lying.

Emily closed her notebook and slipped it back into her purse.

She looked up at the sky as she walked down a lonely stretch of road. She had no idea what time it was or how long she'd been outside. Since yesterday morning, she had been losing time. The rest of the school day had passed in a fog. Art, band, chemistry, English. She'd talked to Ricky at PE and learned the important thing Ricky was going to share was that she was over Nardo. Which had lasted until the end of PE when Ricky saw Nardo in the hallway and completely forgot that Emily was standing beside her.

Could she tell Ricky what had happened?

Did she even want to?

Emily was fairly certain that Mr. Wexler would keep his mouth shut. She imagined he assumed that she would do the same. Her hand went to her neck where he had grabbed her. Choked her, really, because she hadn't been able to breathe. She still winced when she swallowed, though hours had passed since the confrontation.

Confrontation?

Had it really been that bad?

Before Emily had left school, a quick look in her locker mirror had shown a thin red mark on the side of her neck, not the handprint she had been expecting to see. What lingered more was the memory of his anger. Not angry like when he talked about Reagan exploiting his assassination attempt to help him gut the social safety net. Angry like his life was on the line.

Dean Wexler acted like his world travels had turned him into an iconoclast but, progressive politics aside, he was still the same hateful type as her father. He catalogued women as either attractive or fat, intelligent or stupid, worth his time or completely useless. It was easy to see the world in black and white when you controlled everything. Emily should've known better than to believe Wexler was something that he was not.

She retrieved her impromptu detective's journal in her purse. Emily selected the correct page for what she had titled her COLUMBO INVESTIGATION. She reviewed the summaries of her interviews for the hundredth time.

Nardo had called Mr. Wexler to pick her up. That sort of made sense as Nardo was the captain of the running team, so he had

Mr. Wexler's phone number. Everyone at The Party had all been high. Mr. Wexler wouldn't penalize them, let alone report them. He had a car. He could get Emily out of there, especially if she was arguing with Clay.

The alleged argument with Clay was another lost memory.

While there were constant spats among the clique, Emily was seldom at the center of them. She was generally the peacemaker, the one who smoothed things over. Especially where Clay was involved. Emily could count on one hand the number of times she'd challenged him, and only about something very important. Her refusal to continue stealing from out-of-state cars. Her insistence that they treat Cheese better or at least ignore him. The time she got furious at Clay for pushing her into the swimming pool.

Emily tried to force memories of The Party into her consciousness. Had Clay pushed her into the pool again? Emily was a good swimmer, but she hated feeling as if she had no control over her own body. The sensation of walking along the coping one moment, then flying through the air the next, had been terrifying.

Her head started to shake back and forth, because Ricky's green dress had not been wet. But maybe Emily had stuck it in the dryer? And maybe, possibly, she had taken it out of the dryer and been in such a rush that she'd accidentally put the dress on inside out?

And forgotten to put her underwear back on?

It was her panties that were missing, not her bra.

And her thighs had felt sticky. If she thought about it long enough, she could feel the same chafing sensation as she walked.

Emily's stomach stirred. She looked down at her notebook again. The first word she'd written was at the top of the page.

Clay.

Columbo would be heading to the Morrow house at this very moment, but even at school that day, Emily had found herself incapable of talking to Clay about anything, let alone something this crucial. If her plan was to trick someone into confessing, she would be better served doing what Cheese had advised: talk to the people who were there. If their stories didn't match up, someone was lying, and if someone was lying, that meant they were hiding something.

Ricky was the obvious starting point. Blake was always teasing her about having no filter. Whatever came into her mind came out of her mouth. This time last week, Emily would've said that Ricky was her best friend in the world. Now, she knew instinctively that Ricky would do everything in her power to protect her brother and Nardo, but maybe not in that order.

A car horn beeped behind her. Emily was surprised to see Big Al behind the wheel. Her watch told her it was nearly five o'clock. Al was late for the dinner rush. And Emily had been so distracted by her own thoughts that she had walked right past the Blakely house.

She turned around and headed back up the street. Her feet felt heavier as she got closer to the dark brown split-level that had belonged to Ricky and Blake's parents. Big Al had moved in after the boating accident that had killed his son and daughter-in-law. He hadn't been close to either, and the transition had been difficult. Emily was always struck by the fact that they acted more like reluctant roommates than a family.

Not that her own family was a shining example.

The Blakely house was at the top of a steep hill. The climb had never bothered Emily before, but now she found herself winded when she got to the garage. Then she made the turn and started the climb up the crazy steep stairs and had to stop on the second landing. She realized her hand was pressed to her back like an old woman. Or like a young pregnant woman. She hadn't yet felt a connection to what was going on inside her body. Before Dr. Schroeder's diagnosis, Emily had thought she'd had a stomach bug or eaten something that was off. She had made up all kinds of excuses.

There would be no more excuses now.

She looked down at her stomach. There was a baby growing inside of her. An actual human being. What in God's name was she going to do?

"Em?" Ricky held the screen door open. She looked as horrible as Emily felt. Tears formed a river down her face. Snot dripped from her nose. Her cheeks were splotchy red.

Emily felt ashamed that her initial reaction was anger. The thought of listening to Ricky sob over something inconsequential

Nardo had done to hurt her feelings while Emily's life was crashing down around her was too much.

It was also incredibly selfish.

"Ricky," she said. "What's wrong?"

"Al—" Ricky's voice choked. She grabbed Emily's hand and pulled her into the house. "Al just told us—he said—oh, God, Em, what are we going to do?"

Emily guided her to the overstuffed couch under the bay window. "Ricky, slow down. What's going on? What happened?"

Ricky fell into Emily. Her head ended up in Emily's lap. She was shaking.

"Rick." Emily looked up the stairs into the kitchen, wondering where Blake was. "It's going to be okay. Whatever it is, we'll—"

"It won't be okay," Ricky muttered. Her head turned to look up at Emily. "The money is gone."

"What money?"

"From the lawsuit," Ricky said. "It was supposed to be held in a trust for us to go to college, but Al spent it."

Emily shook her head, disbelieving. Al was blunt and often rude, but he wouldn't steal from his own grandchildren.

"We're going to be stuck here," Ricky said. "Forever."

"I don't . . ." Emily tried to understand what had happened. It didn't make sense. She was a judge's daughter. She knew that trusts were very structured. You couldn't raid them on a whim. And also, not to be rude, but the house the Blakelys lived in was hardly grand. Al drove a truck that was older than the twins.

She asked Ricky, "What did he spend it on?"

"The restaurant."

Emily leaned back into the couch. The restaurant had nearly burned to the ground a few years ago. Al had managed to rebuild. Now, she understood how.

Ricky said, "Al told us that the restaurant was our—our legacy. He thinks we want to work at that stupid place, Em. That's all he thinks we're good for is slinging milkshakes for fat, rich assholes from Baltimore."

Emily chewed her lip. Maybe she would've agreed with Ricky's disgust last week, but now, she understood what it meant to have someone else depending on you. Every choice Emily made for the rest of her life would be either to the benefit or the detriment of the child growing inside of her. The diner was a viable business, even successful. College was important, but so was having money for food and a roof over your head.

"It's too late to apply for scholarships," Ricky said. "We can't get financial aid because Al makes too much money. At least on paper."

"I'm—" Emily didn't know what to say. She was slightly horrified to find herself siding with Al. "I'm sorry, Ricky."

"He loves that stupid restaurant more than us."

Emily tried, "You could work for a year and save up?"

Ricky looked aghast as she sat up. "Work at what, Em? Are you kidding me?"

"I'm sorry," Emily apologized instinctively. Ricky had always been mercurial, but her fury was head-turning. "You want to go into journalism. You could find an internship at a newspaper or—"

"Shut up!" Ricky screamed. "You're worse than Al. Do you know that?"

"I—"

"You want me to fetch coffee for a bunch of cranky old jerks who look at me like I'm a child?" Ricky demanded. "I need a journalism degree, Emily. No one will respect me if I'm just the errand girl. I have to have an education."

Emily didn't know what journalism schools taught, but she couldn't see that it was a bad idea to have some experience at an actual newspaper. "But you could work your way up to—"

"Work my way up?" Ricky's voice was shrill. "My parents died, Emily! They were killed because some fucking charter service broke the law."

"I know that, Ricky, but—"

"There's no *but* about it!" Ricky screamed. "Jesus Christ, Em. They didn't die so that I would be forced to choose between taking shit from old farts and taking shit from tourists."

"But you'll take shit no matter what!" Emily was surprised to find herself screaming. "They won't respect you either way, Ricky. They just won't."

Ricky had been shocked into silence.

"No one will respect you." Emily heard her mother's sanguine warning echoing in her head. "You're a townie from a beach resort with okay grades and a big pair of breasts. None of those things command respect."

Ricky's shock did not abate. She looked at Emily as if she'd turned into a stranger. "Who the fuck do you think you are?"

"I'm your friend," Emily tried. "I'm just saying that you can get through this. It's going to take hard work, but—"

"Hard work?" Ricky laughed in her face. "Like the hard work you do, judge's daughter? Is that silver spoon gagging you?"

"I'm not—"

"Spoiled fucking bitch, that's what you are." Ricky had her arms crossed. "Everything comes so fucking easy for you. You don't know a damn thing about living in the real world."

Emily felt her throat work. "I'm pregnant."

Ricky's mouth dropped open but, for once, she was silent.

"I'm not going to college, either. I'll be lucky if I'm able to finish my senior year." Emily had thought the words before, but hearing them out loud, even in her own voice, sounded like a death sentence. "I won't be able to get a congressional internship. I probably won't be able to find a job because I'll be home changing diapers and taking care of a baby. And even when the baby is old enough to go to school, who's going to hire an unmarried mother?"

Ricky's mouth closed, then opened again.

"Do you remember The Party last month?" Emily asked. "Someone did something to me. Took advantage of me. And now I'm going to pay for it for the rest of my life."

Ricky's head started shaking back and forth. She was having the same initial reaction as Emily. "The boys wouldn't do that. You're lying."

"Then who was it?" Emily asked. "Honestly, Ricky, tell me who else it could be."

Ricky kept shaking her head. "Not the boys."

Emily could only repeat herself. "Then who else?"

"Who else?" Ricky's head stopped shaking. She looked Emily in the eye. "Anybody, Em. It could literally be anybody."

Now it was Emily's turn to be without words.

"You don't know that you got pregnant at The Party." Ricky's hands went to her hips. "You're just saying that because you want to trap one of them."

Emily was stunned that Ricky would even think such a thing, let alone say it out loud. "I never—"

"You talk to other guys all the time," Ricky said. "You and your broken toys. You went to band camp with Melody two summers in a row. Debate club. Art shows. You disappeared all day yesterday. You could be screwing half the town for all I know. I saw you with Cheese this morning and he ran off like a scared rat."

"You think Cheese and I—"

"You act all high and mighty but who knows what you've been doing when we're not around?"

"Nothing," Emily whispered. "I haven't done anything."

Ricky got up and started pacing the room, working herself up more and more with each step. "You think you can make Nardo or Blake take the fall for this? Or Clay? God knows you'd love that, wouldn't you? Clay's ignored you for ten years and now you've figured out a way to trap him."

"Stop saying I'm trying to trap someone." Emily stood up, too. "You know that's not true."

"I'm not going to lie for you," Ricky said. "If your plan is to drag Clay down with you, then you're on your own. And the boys won't support you, either."

"I don't—" Emily had to stop to swallow. "I don't want to marry Clay. That's not why—"

"Bitch," Ricky spat out the word. And then something like recognition flashed in her eyes. She'd thought she'd figured it out. "You're going after Nardo, aren't you?"

"What?"

"You always take the easy path, Emily. You don't give a shit who gets hurt so long as it's easy."

"What?"

"I said you're fucking easy!" Ricky was so mad that spit came out of her mouth. "I bet your dad's already worked out a deal with them. Rich people always bail each other out. How much money changed hands, Emily? Or was it entrée into DC society?

Maybe your mom will throw a case his way? What kind of bribe did your dad give to ruin Nardo's life?"

Emily couldn't believe what she was hearing. "That's not—no. That's not going to happen. My parents wouldn't—"

"You're such a fucking Pollyanna! Of course they would! You just float along through life with fucking bluebirds on your shoulder, completely oblivious to all the people your parents screw over to keep everything nice and easy for their precious, good little girl!" Ricky looked maniacal. "What'd they say when they found out you're not their virginal angel anymore?"

Emily opened her mouth to answer, but Ricky beat her to it.

"Let me guess. Daddy glowered and grumbled and Mommy came up with a plan."

Emily felt the sting of betrayal. Ricky's guess was only accurate because Emily had shared with her the many times it had happened before.

"You can't get rid of it, right? Not with your mom on Reagan's shortlist. That'd give the game away, wouldn't it?" Ricky gave a bitter laugh. "They'll probably use you as an example, right? Like some poor, pregnant black girl in the projects should follow the Vaughns' righteous lead because their spoiled whore of a daughter is in the exact same situation."

The words stung because they were so close to the truth.

"Brave Emily is pro-life." Ricky was using the tone they used to mock Franklin's country club friends. "That's easy to say when your life comes with a nanny in a million-dollar estate two miles from the beach."

Emily found her voice. "That's not fair."

"You think what's happening to me and Blake is fair? And now you come along with even worse news?" Ricky demanded. "I've got the solution, Emily. This will fix everything! Just find an internship in *go fuck yourself!*"

The last words echoed in Emily's ears like a siren. She had seen Ricky furious before. She knew how cold her friend could be. Ricky cut people out of her life like a cancer. And she was doing the same thing to Emily now.

"You stupid bitch," Ricky muttered. "You've destroyed every-thing."

"Ricky . . ." Emily tried, but she could feel the finality of her words. It was over. The clique was gone. Emily's best friend was gone. She had no one. Nothing.

Except for this *thing* that was growing inside of her.

"Get out." Ricky pointed to the door. "Get the fuck out of my house, you stupid slut."

Emily touched her cheek. She expected to feel tears, but what she felt instead was the heat of shame. She had done this to herself. Ricky was right. She had ruined all of their lives. The clique was over. All she could do now was try not to drag them down alongside her.

"Go!" Ricky screamed.

Emily ran toward the door. She stumbled down the steep stairs. And then she stopped.

Blake was sitting on the bottom stair. He held a cigarette between his fingers. He glanced back at Emily. "I'll marry you."

Emily didn't know what to say.

"It won't be so bad, right?" He stood up and looked at her. "We've always gotten along."

Emily couldn't read his expression. Was he joking? Was he making an admission?

Blake read her mind. "It wasn't me, Emmie. Not if it happened at The Party. Or any time else. I think I'd remember where my dick has been. I'm really quite attached to it."

She watched a bird land in one of the trees across the driveway. This was what she had lost with her chastity. Before, no one directed rough language at her. Now, everyone seemed to.

"Anyway, I was completely wasted at The Party," Blake said. "I zonked out in the upstairs bathroom. Nardo had to break the lock to get to me. I'd pissed myself like a baby. Can't for the life of me remember why. The john was right there."

Emily pursed her lips. She thought about her Columbo Investigation. Mr. Wexler had said that Blake and Nardo were still inside the house when he'd arrived. Blake was saying the same thing. If their stories matched, then they were likely telling the truth.

Which meant that Clay was the only boy left alone with Emily.

"Come on." Blake dropped his cigarette into a coffee can. He nodded toward the garage. Emily felt powerless to do anything

but follow him inside. Rock posters hung on the unfinished walls.
There was a ping-pong table and an old couch and a giant hi-fi
system that had belonged to Blake and Ricky's parents. The clique
had spent countless hours in the garage smoking and drinking
and listening to music and talking about how they were going to
change the world.

Now, Emily was going to be trapped in Longbill Beach forever.
Thanks to Al, Blake and Ricky weren't even going to college.
Nardo wouldn't last a year at Penn. Only Clay would get away
from this claustrophobic town. Which seemed as predestined as
the sun rising in the east and setting in the west.

She told Blake, "I can't marry you. We're not in love. And if
you're not the—"

"I'm not." He sat down on the couch. "You know I've never
thought about you that way."

Emily knew the opposite to be true. He had kissed her two
years ago in the alley downtown. She still caught him looking at
her sometimes in a way that made her uncomfortable.

"Sit down, okay?" Blake waited for her to perch beside him
on the couch. "Think about it, Em. It's a solution for both of
us."

She shook her head. She couldn't think about it.

"You get respectability, and . . ." He held out his arms in an
open shrug. "I assume your parents will want their son-in-law to
go to college."

Emily felt the hairs on the back of her neck go up. Nardo's
father was the banker, but Blake had always been the one who
was the most transactional. He kept a running score in his head.
*I'll do this for you, but you're going to do something for me in
return.*

She asked, "What about me? Do I just stay home and bake
cookies?"

"It's not a bad life."

Emily laughed. It wasn't the life she had planned. She was
going to live at Foggy Bottom. She was going to intern for a
senator. She was going to become a lawyer. If she made cookies
for her husband and child, the baking would take place between
arguing in a courtroom and preparing a motion for the next day.

"Be reasonable," Blake said. "I mean, you can go to college. Of course you can go to college. But you can't really have a career. Not with the kind of future your folks will expect me to have."

Emily was struck by his cold calculations. "What kind of future is that?"

"Politics, of course." He shrugged. "Your mom's going to be tapped for something in the administration. Why not ride her coattails into a better life for both of us?"

Emily looked down at the ground. He had clearly thought about this before. Her pregnancy was nothing but an opportunity. "You're forgetting my parents are Republicans."

"Does it matter?" He shrugged again when she looked at him. "Political ideology is nothing more than a fulcrum to pry open the levers of power."

Emily had to sit back on the couch. She couldn't take this in. "So I'm one of those fulcrums you're manipulating?"

"Don't be melodramatic."

"Blake, you're literally talking about marrying me, being a father to my child, as a way to launch your political future."

"You're missing the upside," Blake said. "We're both in a bad way. We both want better lives for ourselves. And I don't find you entirely repulsive."

"That's romantic."

"Come on, Emmie." Blake stroked back her hair. "We can make this work. No one has to get hurt. We can all stay friends."

The word *friends* gave her tears permission to fall. What he was offering was actually a solution. They would keep it in the clique. Ricky's anger would burn out easily against Blake's logical explanation. Nardo would make a joke about dodging a bullet. Clay would slink off to his new, exciting life far away from all of them. And Emily would be married to a boy she didn't love. A boy who saw her as nothing but a means to an end.

"Emily." Blake moved closer. His breath was in her ear. "Come on, would it be so bad?"

Emily closed her eyes. Tears seeped out. She saw the next year, the next few years, open up like a flower. She could go back to being the good girl everyone admired. Blake would get his college and his career and access to a political future. It would be just as Ricky had predicted—the Vaughn family money buying Emily's way out of a bad spot.

Easy.

"Emmie." Blake's lips brushed her ears. He took her hand and placed it on his *thing*.

Emily was paralyzed. She could feel the hard shape of him.

"That's good." He moved her hand. His tongue was in her ear.

"Blake!" She screamed his name as she pulled away. "What are you doing?"

"Jesus." He sat back on the couch. His legs were wide. The front of his pants stuck up like a tent. "What is wrong with you?"

"What is wrong with *you*?" she demanded. "What were you doing?"

"I think it's pretty clear what I was doing." He found his cigarettes in his pocket. "Come on, it's not like you can get pregnant twice."

She put her hand to her throat. She could feel her heart pounding.

He flicked his lighter open. "Let me be clear about this, my girl. I'll buy the cow, but I expect to get more than my fair share of milk."

Emily watched him light the end of his cigarette. She had given him the Zippo lighter for his sixteenth birthday. She had paid extra to have his initials etched into the side so that Ricky wouldn't steal it.

She said, "You're a monster."

"What I am is your second-best option." He saw her confused expression and coughed out a laugh. "Don't be obtuse, Emily. Your best option is to flush it down the toilet."

6

Andrea sat on the edge of the bed in her motel room staring down at the photograph that Star Bonaire had taken. The woman had used her finger to carve a single word in the white flour.

Help.

Andrea had waited until she was alone with Bible to show him the photo. He hadn't said much beyond telling Andrea to get showered and be ready when he called. That was well over an hour ago. Andrea was showered. She was ready. Bible still had not called.

Help.

How terrified would a woman have to be to do something like that?

Andrea swiped back to the photos of Alice Poulsen. Her throat tightened over the ravages by starvation. Anorexia was about control, but then, to some degree, so was suicide. You were literally taking your own life into your hands. Alice Poulsen had walked into that field and known that she would not turn back. What kind of nerve did that take? What kind of desperation?

The same type of desperation Star Bonaire had probably been feeling when she photographed her cry for help.

Andrea couldn't look at the photos anymore. She tossed her phone on the desk. She stared all of her helplessness into the black television screen across from her bed. The curtains were drawn. The lights were off. Her left wrist ached where Wexler had grabbed her. Stray memories flashed through her mind— Wexler's face pressed against the steering wheel; Nardo lighting a cigarette; Star's ghostly presence as she moved around the kitchen; the two women who'd walked out of the barn. The yellow dresses. The long hair. The bare feet. The attenuated limbs. The matching ankle bracelets.

Victimized. Tagged. Degraded.

Cult. Cult. Cult.

Stilton was right. There was no federal or state law that said you couldn't be in a cult. Nothing could be done to save those women. Star Bonaire's mother had already tried the most extreme version of a rescue. She'd ended up arrested and hit with a restraining order barring her from seeing her own child.

Andrea stood up. She started pacing. She felt so fucking powerless. She had all this training and none of it, not one piece, could help Star Bonaire. Or anyone else, for that matter. She looked at her phone, willing Bible to call her. He was probably hitting the same dead ends that she was. Her eyes darted to the notebook and pen she'd placed on the desk. She'd been so filled with purpose when she'd started an internet trawl for all the dirty laundry on Dean's Magic Beans.

An hour later, the notebook pages were still blank.

She mentally reviewed what little she had learned about the operation. Dean's Magic Beans had been a registered Delaware corporation since 1983. Andrea had found the original articles of incorporation. Dean Wexler was listed as the president. Bernard Fontaine was vice president. Which was interesting given the fact that Nardo was only nineteen in 1983, around the same time that his father had been arrested for bank fraud, but not interesting in any way that could move an investigation forward.

Also interesting but ultimately useless was that Bernard Fontaine was listed as secretary of BFL Trust, a charitable organization established in Delaware in the fall of 2003. The IRS listed the non-profit as a 501(c)3 in good standing, though Charity Navigator, a ratings agency that collected information about how donated dollars were used, had no information on the organization.

Googling "Dean's Magic Beans+cult" had brought back an avalanche of fan pages curated by health nuts and fava bean lovers but nothing, not one site, mentioned the fact that the women who processed the beans were literally starving. The intern sites, the college board postings, the Facebook pages dedicated to finding fun summer work, all talked about Dean's in glowing terms. Even the one-star reviews on Amazon had been overshadowed by glowing recommendations.

Not one post or page mentioned Dean Wexler by name.

Nor did they mention Nardo Fontaine.

Stilton had said Wexler had a lot of lawyers on speed dial. It made sense that an overly litigious cult would be very good at keeping negative shit at the low end of the search results. Barring that, Dean had up to twenty volunteers who could sit at their respective laptops all day scrubbing the internet.

It's not like the women were stopping for lunch breaks.

One of the few sites that you couldn't scrub or buy your way out of was PACER, the Public Access to Court Electronic Records, which provided a searchable database of legal filings, motions and transcripts. Fortunately, she had Gordon's log-in credentials. Desperation hadn't led Andrea to the webpage. She'd had a hunch. Back at the farm, she had flagged it as unusual that Wexler kept referring to the women as *volunteers* instead of *interns*. A court case from twenty years ago had provided an explanation.

In 2002, the Department of Justice had sued Dean's Magic Beans under the Fair Labor Standards Act for failing what was called the Primary Beneficiary Test. There were seven criteria for judging the legality of an unpaid internship, most of them having to do with furthering academic coursework, offering college credits and following the academic calendar. In other words, the internship had to benefit the intern, not just the sponsor.

If they were going to be exploited, they had to volunteer for that.

Everything had gone downhill after the PACER hit. Andrea had forced herself to take a break when the motel room had started to feel like a prison cell. She'd ended up buying an egg salad sandwich from the vending machine, then gone back to her room where she'd wasted half an hour scrolling through the Sussex County register for marriages, divorces and deaths.

She had found records of Ricky and Nardo's marriage and divorce, but nothing returned on Eric Blakely when she searched death certificates. If Bible took much longer, she'd probably end up scrolling through rabies tag registrations for domestic house-hold animals.

Her phone pinged. She reluctantly dragged it off the desk. Mike had texted her again. She recognized the animal in the photo this time. The dik-dik was a tiny antelope that stood about a foot high.

Andrea didn't have it in her to find a clever response to the dik-pic.

Instead, she let her thumb hover over the *call* button. Mike could be an incredibly good listener once you cut through the bullshit. But he'd also been an adult when she had ghosted him exactly one year and eight months ago. The least Andrea could do now was be an adult and stand by her decision. No matter how much she wanted to hear his voice.

She was swiping away his info when her phone rang.

Andrea closed her eyes. This was the last thing she needed. She tapped to answer. "Hey, Mom."

"Sweetheart," Laura said. "I won't keep you long, I know you're busy, but I was just thinking I could help you find a place."

"A what?"

"You'll need a place to live, my darling. I can go online and set up some appointments for you to look at apartments."

A curse bubbled its way to Andrea's lips. That would actually be a really helpful thing if not for the fact that she needed a place in Baltimore, not Portland, Oregon.

"You don't want to make a quick decision and regret it," Laura said. "Tell me a neighborhood and I'll go online. It's better to go through a broker up there, that way you have some protections."

"I don't know." Andrea was desperate to get off the phone. "Laurelhurst?"

"Laurelhurst? How did you hear about it? Do other Marshals live there?"

Andrea knew about it because she'd read in *Rolling Stone* that Sleater-Kinney had played at a bar there. "Someone mentioned it at the office. They said it's nice."

"My God, I should hope so. You should see these prices." Laura was clearly using the desktop computer in her office. Andrea could hear her typing on the clunky keyboard. "Oh, here's one but—oh, no, it says you have to have a pet. What sort of landlord *wants* you to have a pet? I don't understand Portland. Oh, here's another one, but—"

Andrea listened to Laura's streaming commentary about a one-bedroom basement apartment that was clearly a studio and perhaps had a Wiccan altar in the bathroom but, either way, was overpriced.

"Okay," Laura continued. "Laurelhurst spans the northeast and southeast part of Portland. Oh, one of the parks has a statue of Joan of Arc. But these listings are so expensive, darling. You can't just pop next door and steal peanut butter out of my pantry."

Andrea sat on the edge of the bed as Laura started looking for cheaper areas.

"Concordia? Hosford-Abernathy? Buckman Neighborhood?"

Andrea put her head in her hand. The worst hood she had ever lived in was adulthood.

She had to stop this. "Hey, Mom, I need to go."

"Okay, but—"

"I'll call you later. Love you."

Andrea ended the call. She fell back onto the bed and stared up at the popcorn ceiling. A water stain had left a brown cloud. She felt disgusted with herself for carrying on this stupid Portland charade with her mother. For two solid years, Andrea had punished Laura for being such a damn good liar. The apple had fallen right on top of the tree.

"Oliver!" Bible banged on her door. "It's me, partner. You decent?"

"Finally." Andrea pushed herself up. She opened the door. Bible had changed into jeans and a USMS T-shirt, identical to what Andrea was wearing. They both had their guns on their belts. Which made the tiny woman standing behind him in a navy power suit and very high heels look even more out of place.

"I gotta confession," Bible said. "I made an executive decision to bring in the boss. Deputy Chief Cecelia Compton, this is Deputy Andrea Oliver."

"Uh—" Andrea tucked in her shirt. "Ma'am, I thought you were in Baltimore?"

"My husband works in the area. Mind if I come in?" Compton didn't wait for an invitation. She walked into the room. She looked around, taking in all the things that Andrea did not want anyone to see, let alone her boss. Her duffel hanging open, all of her underwear disgorged onto the floor. Her running clothes wadded up beside the mini fridge. Her backpack tossed onto the bed. Thank God her mind had been too consumed by Alice Poulsen and Star Bonaire to take out Emily Vaughn's case file.

"All right." Compton sat on the edge of the desk where Andrea's half-finished egg salad sandwich was molting. "Bible told me about the farm. What were your impressions?"

Andrea hadn't prepared for this. The fact that Cecelia Compton was one of those scary, intimidating women who clearly had her shit together did not help matters.

"Take a breath, Oliver." Bible was leaning against the closed door. "Start with Star."

"Star," Andrea said. "She was really thin like the rest of them, but older, maybe late twenties. Barefoot. Long hair. Wearing the same yellow shift as the rest of them."

"Do you think she's been there a while?"

"Chief Stilton made it seem like it's been at least two years. I guess you could infer something from the fact that she was in the house rather than doing manual labor on the farm. She was on a first-name basis with Wexler. Stilton says her mother lives in town."

"I heard about the mother. Can't fault her for the kidnapping, though her execution was flawed," Compton said. "What about Alice Poulsen? Did it look like suicide to you?"

Andrea felt ill-equipped to answer her questions. She decided to be honest. "I've only ever evaluated two dead bodies as an investigator, ma'am. Both of them were at the morgue back at Glynco. So to answer your question, yes, based on my limited experience, it appeared to me that Alice Poulsen committed suicide."

Compton wanted more. "Go on."

Andrea tried to gather her thoughts. "She had newer-looking scars on her wrists where she'd tried to kill herself before, which is backed up by Chief Stilton. There was an empty bottle of pills at the scene. She had dried foam around her mouth. There was no petechiae in her eyes indicating strangulation. She didn't have defensive wounds or ligature marks. There was some bruising, particularly around her wrist, but nothing that looked like an attack."

"It sounds like you made a very thorough assessment," Compton said. "May I see the photographs?"

Andrea unlocked her iPhone and handed it over.

Compton took her time with the pictures. She studied each one, zooming in and out. Going back and forth to make comparisons. She even studied Star Bonaire's photo asking for help. She didn't speak until she had examined them all.

"Alice Poulsen is a Danish citizen. The State Department will coordinate with their embassy. I'm here to handhold with the locals. We don't want the Danes to think we're not taking this seriously." She handed the phone back to Andrea. "We've scheduled an autopsy, but based on what I've seen in these images, I concur with your opinion."

"What about the last image?" Andrea asked. "Star Bonaire asked for help."

"She's asked before," Compton said. "I visited Chief Stilton before I came here. He was very candid with me."

Andrea felt her teeth set. She doubted Stilton had called Cecelia Compton *sweetheart*.

Compton said, "Two years ago, Star Bonaire slipped a note to a delivery driver at the warehouse. She wrote the same thing she wrote today—*help*. Stilton went out to talk to her. He got her alone. She denied writing the note. There was nothing else he could do but leave."

Andrea felt her head shaking. There was always something more you could do.

"The second time was more of the same," Compton continued. "Star telephoned her mother in the middle of the night. She asked for help. Stilton went out to the farm again. Star denied making the call."

Andrea kept shaking her head. She had seen first-hand how Jack Stilton talked to women. He was the exact wrong person for the job.

"Hey, partner." Bible seemed to sense her frustration. "It's not illegal to slip somebody a note, then deny you did it. Hell, it's not even illegal to call your mama one day, then the next day tell her to go away."

"She didn't ask her mother for help," Andrea insisted. "She asked *me* for help. She used *my* phone to take the photo."

"Play that out for me, though," Bible said. "We go back to the farm. We ask to talk to Star. Then what?"

Andrea said, "We talk to Star."

"Okay, but what do we do when she denies taking the picture?"

Andrea's mouth opened. Then closed.

"What if Bernard Fontaine jumps back in with his Twitter Law degree and tells us to leave? Or they sic the lawyers on us for harassment?" Bible held up his hands. "We're the po-po, Oliver. We gotta play by constitutional rules."

"If I could get Star alone—"

"How?" he asked. "Not like we can catch her out at the grocery store. Stilton says Star is the only girl who's ever off the farm, but she's always got Nardo or Dean with her. And don't forget her own mother tried to break her out already. She landed in the shit. It's only luck and lawyering that kept her out of the pokey."

Andrea couldn't accept what they were saying. They were United States Marshals. There had to be other options.

"Deputy Oliver." Compton reached into her purse and took out her phone. "Tell me how to legally help Star Bonaire and we'll do it right now."

Andrea felt like her brain was spinning inside of her head. She'd already tried to find a solution. They were the experienced ones. They should be coming up with a plan.

"Oliver?" Bible prompted.

All that Andrea could come up with was the truth. "This just sucks."

"It does, partner. It really and truly does." Bible let out a long sigh. "Times like this, I usually ask my wife, Cussy, for help. She's a pretty smart lady. She understands the politics behind these types of tricky situations."

Compton huffed out an exasperated breath. "Go fuck yourself, Leonard."

"Now, Cussy—"

"Fuck off." Compton crossed her arms. "I'm not gonna flush everything I just told you down the shitter. Your wife agrees with your goddamn boss."

Andrea sat down on the bed. "You're married? To each other?"

"We keep it separate from work," Compton said. "Leonard, you've had barely more than one goddamn day with this woman and you're already coaching her up on breaking the rules?"

"You sound a lot like my boss."

"Fuck you." Compton leaned down and slipped off her heels. "You're making life pretty shitty for both of us right now."

"I'm sorry for that, darling." Bible patted his hands in the air to calm her down. "But tell me now, if you were in my boots, what would you do?"

"Well first, I'd transfer myself the hell away from this girl. She's obviously got a bright career if you don't fuck it up."

Andrea tried to disappear into the pattern on the bedspread.

"Good note," Bible said. "Appreciate it. Then what would you do?"

Compton looked at her watch. "You've got two and a half hours before you're due at the Vaughn estate. Did you forget you've got an actual assignment, Marshal? Esther's received credible death threats. I didn't send you out here for a beach vacation."

"Understood, Boss." He smiled. "But I was asking my wife."

"Fuck." She seamlessly switched back into the role. "Okay, but just humoring your stupid ass here, what you need is somebody who's willing to feed you information. Someone on the inside who will make them nervous enough to make a mistake."

"I hear ya," Bible said. "But none of those girls has ever squeaked a peep, and my boss just made it clear we gotta stay away from Star Bonaire."

"We need someone who's left the group. Someone who's willing to talk."

Bible shook his head. "I'm not betting on them keeping a list of ex-volunteers around."

"I know somebody who might talk." Andrea was as surprised as anyone that the words had come out of her mouth. And that her twenty minutes of scrolling Sussex County public records had paid off. "The woman who owns the diner, Ricky Fontaine. She was married to Bernard Fontaine. I'm assuming the divorce was acrimonious."

"And?" Compton prompted.

"And—" Andrea wondered if they could see the lightbulbs popping on over her head. Nardo had told her that Ricky was his ex, but the county records had provided the date their divorce was finalized—August 4, 2002—which was very close to another important date in the farm's history.

She told Compton, "I'm not sure one has anything to do with the other, but in 2002, around the same time as the Fontaines' divorce, the farm was sued by the Department of Justice for internship violations. According to the DOJ's affidavit of facts, the tip came from an anonymous female using a payphone located on Beach Street in Longbill Beach, Delaware."

Bible said nothing, but his jaw had clenched.

"Well, damn," Compton said. "Bible, you should talk to your partner more and leave your wife out of it. *A woman scorned* is the easiest play in the book. What's this Ricky person doing now?"

Bible's attention was on Andrea. "How is it that you know all that?"

Andrea shrugged. "How is it that anybody knows anything?"

"Great, Bible, she sounds just like you." Compton was done with the teasing. She asked Andrea, "Tell me about Ricky. Do you think you can get her to turn on her ex?"

Andrea couldn't help the panicked look she gave Bible. This wasn't the deep end. This was the middle of the ocean. "I'm not sure Ricky is the woman who made the phone call. I mean, when I read about it on PACER, I thought maybe one of the girls on the farm called in the tip. Either way, maybe Bible should—"

"The smeller is the feller." Bible looked at his watch. "The lunch rush should be over. I'll call down at the diner and make sure Ricky's there."

Andrea didn't get a chance to equivocate.

The door rattled from two hard knocks.

Bible's hand rested on the butt of his gun. "You expecting company?"

Andrea's hand had gone to her weapon, too. "No."

"Probably the goddamn maid." Still, Compton slipped back into boss mode, silently checking with Bible before swinging open the door.

Andrea wanted to scream when she saw who was standing outside.

"Hey, baby!" Mike flashed his big, stupid grin. "Surprise!"

Andrea waited until she and Mike had walked around to the backside of the motel before she threw her hands into the air. "What the fuck are you doing here?"

"Whoa," he said, like he was soothing a wild horse. "How about we—"

"Don't you dare try to de-escalate me. You're not my fucking boyfriend. And you're sure as hell not my fiancé."

"Fiancé?" Mike laughed. "Who told you that?"

"Bible, Compton, Harri, Krump—" She threw her hands into the air again. "What the fuck, Mike?"

He was still laughing. "Ah, honey, they're just messing with you. I never said we were engaged. Did they bring up the rumors? Because those are true."

"Stop laughing, dammit." Andrea realized that she had stamped her foot just like her mother did. "This isn't funny. I'm not kidding around."

"Look—"

"Don't *look* me, asshole. What the hell are you doing here? This stalking shit with all the texts and just showing up at my door—in front of my boss—is not okay. I have a job to do."

"All right. That's a lot to unload." His voice had gone soft. He was doing the fucking thermometer. "Do you remember that I have a job to do, too? I'm an inspector in Witness Security, which means that the entire purpose of my being is to assess and prevent threats against my witnesses."

"I know the job description, Mike. I just spent four months of my life learning all about it."

"Then answer your own goddamn questions." Mike's thermometer broke. "Why did I text you? To get your fucking attention. Why did I tell everybody we're together? So they would keep a fucking eye on you. Why did I end up knocking on your door? I've got a volatile witness whose ex is a psychopath and now her daughter is in his hometown kicking every hornets' nest she can find."

Andrea pressed together her lips.

"What's the threat assessment here, Deputy? You've got four months of school under your belt. Tell me, is my witness safe?"

"Of course she is." Andrea didn't remind him that Laura had never needed his help before. "She's fine. She thinks I'm in Oregon."

"Oh, that makes it all better," Mike said. "Here I was all worried that some local jackass would call up Clayton Morrow and tell him you're in town asking questions, but that's cool. Laura thinks you're in Oregon, so it's all fine."

"He's an inmate in a federal prison," Andrea reminded him. "You're supposed to be monitoring his correspondences."

"I hate to break this to you, baby, but cons get their hands on cell phones all the time. They spoof the caller ID and reach out to witnesses and drug dealers and, sometimes, they put out hits on people they want to shut up." He repeated the question. "Is my witness safe?"

Andrea's flash of anger had melted into a burning anxiety. Her father could be a very dangerous man. "Why didn't you say all this two days ago? You set up the meeting with Jasper. What did you expect?"

"Not this shitshow," Mike countered. "Jasper told me he was going to put you in Baltimore so you'd be close to the action in DC. Compton's a rock star. Bible is a legend. I didn't find out you were in Longbill until Mitt Harri hit me up on Slack at ten this morning."

Andrea didn't ask why Mitt Harri was talking to Mike about her. They were like a bunch of high school girls. "You thought Jasper was trying to help me?"

"Why wouldn't I? He's your uncle."

Her uncle was a duplicitous cocksucker, but Mike had a weird blindness when it came to family. She asked him, "What do you want me to do? You clearly came here with an agenda."

"Transfer the hell out of here. Go out west like you wanted. Compton won't ask questions. She knows I'm in WitSec. It won't take her long to put together the pieces."

"Are you kidding me?" Andrea was incredulous. "You're literally telling me to run away."

"Andy—"

"Listen to me, okay? Because you really need to hear this. I'm not the same helpless little girl I was two years ago. I'm Laura Oliver's fucking daughter. I don't run away from things, and I don't need you to rescue me."

Mike looked like he didn't know where to start. "Helpless little girl?"

"That's right," she said. "I'm not the same person. The sooner you realize that, the better it'll be for both of us."

Mike looked confused. "Andy, I'm not here to save you. I'm here because your mom will rip apart the world with her teeth if Clayton Morrow comes near you."

Andrea shook her head, though she knew that Mike wasn't exaggerating. "He won't hurt me."

"He's not Hannibal Lecter, Clarice. He doesn't have a code."

Andrea didn't have a comeback for him. She was suddenly so damn tired. Every step forward felt like it was followed by two steps back. She couldn't help Star. She couldn't find Emily Vaughn's killer. If Compton sent Andrea to get details from Ricky about the farm, she would probably fail at that, too.

"Andy."

She shook her head, silently begging herself not to cry. Tears would cancel out everything she had just said. The last two years would have been for nothing. Pushing Mike away would have been for nothing.

"Baby, talk to me."

"No." She shook her head. "I can't do this with you. I need to do my job."

He reached for her hand.

Andrea flinched when he accidentally tweaked her wrist.

"Andy?"

She turned away from him, silently running through a string of expletives. Fucking job. Fucking farm. Fucking Wexler. She should've punched him in the fucking throat. Broken his fucking hyoid and sent him to the fucking hospital.

"Andrea." Mike was standing in front of her. His chest was puffed out, fists clenched. "Did somebody hurt you?"

She couldn't stop herself. She pressed her forehead to his chest. The relief was immediate, an almost weightlessness as she let him take on some of the load. His hands lightly cupped the back of her head. She could feel his heart pounding. He was waiting for a sign that it was okay to hold her.

Andrea would not let herself give him the sign.

"I'm okay. Really." She lifted her head. "I took care of it. I don't need you to save me."

His hands fell away. "Why do you keep saying that?"

"Because I need it to be true." Andrea felt tears well into her eyes. She wiped them away with her fist, furious with her body for betraying her. "I'm not your bossy older sisters who constantly need you to bail them out, or your mom who expects you to wait on her hand and foot. I'm a thirty-three-goddamn-year-old woman. I can take care of myself."

"Sure." He stepped away from her. Her shitty words had the intended effect. He took another step, then another. His head was nodding. His arms were crossed. "I get it. Loud and clear."

Andrea swallowed down the apology that rushed into her mouth. She could say just about anything to him, but his sisters and mom were way too far over the line.

There was nothing to do but twist the knife. "I'll see you around."

"You bet."

Andrea walked away. Her back could feel the heat of his glare until she turned the corner. She couldn't imagine what Mike was thinking right now but, for her part, Andrea's only thought was that she was turning into her mother.

For all of Laura's *darlings* and *my loves*, she could sometimes be a stone-cold bitch. It made sense considering how she'd grown up, and especially considering how Clayton Morrow had damaged her. Over the years, Andrea had watched her mother switch the coldness on and off like a freeze ray—one day celebrating Christmas with the family, the next day telling Gordon it was over. This was how her mother protected herself. When people got too close, she pushed them away. If Andrea was going to keep claiming her mother's steely resolve, she had to claim the damage it left in its wake. Two years of fighting to become a stronger person wasn't going to change the basics.

Wherever you go, there you are.

Mike's rental car was parked in front of her motel room door. She knew it was Mike's because he drove so many different rentals that he always hung a rabbit's foot from the rearview mirror to help him remember which car was his.

"We good?" Bible was leaning against his SUV. He'd brought Andrea's backpack out for her.

"We're good." She grabbed the bag as she climbed into the Explorer. It took all of her willpower not to look back for Mike.

"I called the diner." Bible kept it professional as he pulled out of the space. "Ricky's at home right now, lives a hop and a skip away. It's always good to talk to somebody on their home turf. She'll be relaxed and comfortable. Me, I'd approach it like, hey lady, I'm trying to help you here. Tell me what you know about your ex so we can lock up that fella and throw away the key."

Andrea doubted it would be that simple, but she said, "Easy peasy."

"Lemon squeezy," Bible finished. "Excellent, partner. I know you're gonna knock it outta the park."

Andrea appreciated the sentiment, but she wasn't so sure. Mike had shaken her.

He had also lied to her.

He'd told Andrea that Mitt Harri had sent him a message through Slack at ten this morning. That was the first time Mike had learned that Andrea was in Longbill Beach. Yet the timestamp on his *gnus* text was 8:32 this morning, which meant that Mike had not been reaching out to Andrea for work. He was reaching out to her because he'd wanted to reach out to her. The dik-dik picture had been sent when he was fifteen minutes out from the motel.

The timing didn't add up for the relationship gossip, either. Andrea had known Bible less than five minutes when he'd congratulated her on the engagement. Mike had no reason to worry about Clayton Morrow yesterday afternoon. As far as he knew then, Andrea was in Baltimore. He hadn't started the rumor to mark her like a fire hydrant or make her life difficult. He had started it because he wanted his name in Andrea's mouth.

She had hurt him.

Why had she hurt him?

"You know," Bible said. "My son's about Mike's age."

Andrea took the opening, though it felt strange that he was choosing now to tell her about his personal life. "I didn't know you had a kid."

"Two. My girl's a doctor over in Bethesda. Super smart like her mama." Bible's smile was filled with pride. "My boy, well, don't get me wrong. He's a good kid. Got a full ride to West Point. Ended up getting his law degree from Georgetown."

Andrea sensed a *but* coming.

"Me and Cussy, we don't tell many people this, but he came out to us his second year at G-Town. Told us he wanted to work in criminal defense."

Andrea reluctantly smiled. Cops despised criminal defense attorneys. Until they needed one. "Don't worry. I'm good at keeping secrets."

"I picked up on that." As usual, Bible's words had an alternate meaning. He was giving Andrea the opportunity to explain why she knew so much about Dean Wexler, Nardo Fontaine and Ricky Fontaine.

She couldn't explain it. Alice Poulsen and Star Bonaire had to be the focus right now. If she let herself get caught up in Emily Vaughn, she would lose any chance she had of talking Ricky Fontaine into turning on her ex-husband. Compton had made it clear this was their only opportunity to stop the madness at the farm.

Bible said, "I started out in drug enforcement. Mike tell you that?"

Andrea guessed Bible was going to tell her another story to try to get her to open up. She only half played along, staring out the window as she said, "Mike hasn't told me anything."

"Well, them WitSec guys are squirrelly." Bible cleared his throat before continuing. "What happened was, I was sitting at my desk one day. Gotta call from the Big, Big Boss in DC. He tells me that the DEA needs a fresh face down in El Paso to drive a truck back and forth across the border. Little hokey pokey—you put the heroin in, you take the money out, and that's what it's all about."

Andrea knew the Marshals were often pulled onto various task forces. Bible would've easily blended in with his military tattoos and thick Tex-Arkana accent.

"So, I report to El Paso, and we're trying to nab some Narcos bringing coke up from Sinaloa. You ever been there?" He waited for Andrea to shake her head. "Damn beautiful state—you got the Sierra Madres, the Baja California Sur. Salt-of-the-earth people down there. Friendly as all get out. And the food—"

Bible did a chef's kiss as he slowed for a turn. Beach Road disappeared in the rearview mirror. There were no McMansions at this end of town, just a blue-collar residential area with small houses and older cars.

"Anyways," Bible said. "I get the official invite down to Culiacán, which is a very big deal. I play it cool—drink some beers, talk up my bad boy bona fides, make it clear I'm easy like Sunday morning."

Andrea felt a shift in the air.

Bible wasn't spooling out a story. He was telling her that he had infiltrated the higher echelons of a Mexican drug cartel. She looked at the long, thin lines that scarred his face. She had never noticed before, but they skipped down his neck and disappeared under his shirt collar.

She turned to face him, to let him know that she understood he was telling her something that he didn't usually share.

He nodded, acknowledging the stakes. Then he took a deep breath and said, "Couple'a months go by, I start working this informant on the inside. At least I thought I was working him. Let's just say the fella was not my *amigo*. Shit goes down. Next thing I know, I'm tied up to a chair and they're playing pin the tail on the Marshal."

Andrea couldn't take her eyes off the scars.

"Yeah, it's everywhere." Bible rubbed his face. She had never seen him look unsure of himself before. Even the tenor of his voice had changed. "That fella who went after me, they called him *el Cirujano*. You speak Spanish?"

Andrea shook her head.

"'The Surgeon,'" Bible said. "Only I don't think that dude learned how to slice up people like that in medical school."

Andrea felt a tightness in her chest. She had an oblique reference to that kind of fear, but she had fortunately been spared the excruciating pain. "He tortured you?"

"Oh, hell no. With torture, you want information. I told 'em everything they wanted to know right off the bat. This guy just wanted me to hurt."

Andrea didn't know what to say.

"So, this was six years ago," Bible said. "I know it don't seem that way, but I was still a young man back then. Still wanted to be a Marshal. But my wife, Cussy, she put her foot down. Wanted me to take retirement. Can you see me fishing off a pier for the rest of my life? Taking up macramé? Learning how to craft?"

Andrea still couldn't speak, so she shook her head.

"Damn straight," Bible said. "But then Judge Vaughn walked into the hospital. Did I mention I was in rehab a couple'a six months?"

Again, Andrea shook her head. She knew from Laura's work what rehab looked like. They didn't keep you there for six months unless you needed a hell of a lot of help.

"So, there's Esther Vaughn walking into my hospital room like she owns the place. I'm not ashamed to say I was feeling awful sorry for myself. That lady, she struts right up to my bed and doesn't say *hello* or *nice to meet you* or *sorry you're shitting in a bag*. She says, 'I don't like the Marshal they assigned to my courtroom. When can you start?'"

Andrea asked, "Did she know you?"

"Never met her before in my life. Nodded to her in the hallway once, maybe twice."

Andrea knew the Marshals worked out of the federal courthouse. "Did your wife—I mean your boss—"

"Nope. The Judge showed up on her own. Trust me, no one tells Esther Vaughn what to do." Bible shrugged it off, but clearly the meeting had made an impact. "Took me another two months to get back on my feet. And I spent the next four years sitting in her courtroom. Some of the judges like having a Marshal there, especially the older ones. Lifetime appointment. They tend to piss people off."

Every time Andrea thought she'd figured out who Esther Vaughn really was, someone came along and changed her mind.

"Esther's not well," Bible said. "Her throat cancer is back. She's not gonna beat it this time. The lady is tired of fighting."

Andrea could only think of Judith and Guinevere. They were going to lose someone else.

"Esther Vaughn saved my life. I want to find out who killed her daughter before she dies. That's why I know so much about the case."

Andrea tried to deflect. "Does the judge know you're looking into it?"

"We keep the professional stuff professional and the personal stuff personal," Bible said. "The judge knows how much power she has. She'd never use it to ask for a personal favor. The lady's mindful of appearances."

Andrea wondered if pride had more to do with it. "Have you interviewed suspects or—"

"Not yet, but I'll get to it. You don't start knockin' down doors unless you know what's on the other side." He paused a beat. "Now this is the part where you explain how I been looking into this thing for two days and you just got here a hot second ago, but you know about as much as I do about the case."

Andrea felt caught out, which was exactly where Bible wanted her. She desperately wanted to tell him the truth, but she knew that she could not. Mike had made fun of Andrea's four months at Glynco, but the first rule of Witness Security was that you never, ever talked about Witness Security. Even with another Marshal. Even when that Marshal had somehow in one day made you think that he was the most trustworthy person you had ever met in your life.

She hated herself for saying, "What makes you think I know anything?"

"You gotta work on your deadpan, partner. I near about saw the brick drop outta your shorts when you realized you were talking to Dean Wexler and Nardo Fontaine at the farm a while ago." He paused a beat. "And then outta nowhere you throw out the date of Ricky Fontaine's divorce alongside details from a twenty-year-old court case nobody's ever heard about?"

Andrea's throat felt very dry. If her expression couldn't lie, her mouth could. "I found it on the internet. About Emily being murdered. My flight got delayed so I had a lot of time on my hands."

"And Mike knocking on your door has nothing to do with it?"

The Mike of it all felt too close. Instinctively, Andrea pushed back. "My thing with Mike is complicated."

"That's what my children say when they don't want to talk about it."

Andrea let her silence be his answer.

"All right," Bible finally said, using the now-familiar tone that said it wasn't all right. He pulled the SUV to the curb. Put the gear in park. "Here we are."

Andrea looked up. A split-level house was perched at the top of a steep hill. The steps to the front porch zigzagged up three flights because the pitch was so severe. The garage door was open. Cardboard boxes and storage racks filled both bays. Ricky was clearly using the area as overflow for the diner. Piles of dirty aprons and bar towels were stacked around an ancient-looking washer and dryer.

Bible said, "I'll stay down here in the car. Before you go, I'll give you Marshal rule number five: you can't ride two horses with one ass."

That sounded more like one of his Foghorn Leghorn homilies, but Andrea had already figured it out on her own. He was telling her to put Emily Vaughn out of her mind.

"We need Ricky to give us some actionable information on Wexler, Nardo or the farm. That's how we help Star Bonaire."

"Exactly."

Andrea opened the car door. She rubbed her sore wrist as she started the vertical ascent to the house. A bruise was starting to come up. She had no idea why she was being so precious about the injury. After a kidney punch at Glynco, she had literally pissed blood. She'd gotten a black eye and a split lip, both of which had felt like badges of honor.

She supposed the thing that made her wrist different was Dean Wexler. He had meant to hurt her. He'd wanted to put Andrea in her place, the same way he had put Star, Alice and all of the other women at the farm in their place.

Though Marshals didn't generally investigate, several hours of Andrea's training had been devoted to interviewing, questioning and interrogating. Ricky Fontaine wasn't a suspect, but she was a possible witness to whatever was happening at the farm. Barring that, she might know some women who had gotten away. Andrea would need to establish a rapport to make Ricky feel comfortable, all while projecting competence so that Ricky felt that any information she provided would be thoroughly investigated and, if criminal violations were found, acted upon.

Andrea let go of her wrist as she walked past the green Honda Civic parked in the driveway. She glanced inside. The car was a mess, papers and trash scattered everywhere. She looked up at the house, which was probably the same house Eric and Erica Blakely had grown up in. Andrea couldn't help but wonder if Clayton Morrow had ever made this same arduous climb up the three flights of concrete stairs. She could be about to place her feet in the same footsteps that her father had made forty years ago.

"Hey, hon. Sorry about the stairs. They're murder on your calves." Ricky had thrown open the screen door. She was in shorts and T-shirt. Her ankles were bare, but her Madonna bangles were on full display. She had added a few ribbons to break up the color of the black and silver bracelets.

Andrea took a turn on the second landing and climbed the last flight of stairs. Her first impression was that Ricky's efficient, maternal vibe was gone. This was the exact opposite of an Esther Vaughn-like transformation. The woman looked completely drained of energy, which made sense considering the restaurant was open seven days a week, from six until midnight.

Ricky said, "They called from the diner to tell me you were looking for me. Do you want some soda?"

"That'd be great." Andrea's instructors had taught her that the easiest way to put someone at ease was to let them serve you. "Thanks for talking to me. I'll try not to take up too much of your time."

"Hope you don't mind me working while we talk. I've got my timer set for the dryer. If I don't keep the laundry going, I'll never get it done. This way."

Ricky led her through the living room. Clean towels and aprons filled three baskets on the floor. The couch and chairs looked new, but the tan carpet had to be original. The art on the pastel walls had probably been advertised as "couch-sized" on the banners inside the flea market. Andrea saw a bunch of framed photographs on a console table near the hallway. Two narrow drawers were under the wooden top. Ricky had stacked oversized books into the open space below, using the cross-bracing between the spindly legs as a platform. There was no way to get a closer look. Ricky was already walking up a single flight of open-backed stairs.

Andrea could smell a mustiness in the kitchen, probably because of the clutter. An oval table was piled with yellowing bills and paperwork that probably dated back to Andrea's birth. A small, sad section was carved out where Ricky clearly ate her meals alone. Andrea guessed at some point the woman had taken an interest in decorating. A light blue pendant lamp hung over the sink. The countertops were black quartz. The cabinets had been painted bright blue. All of the appliances were white except for the fridge, which was black. Postcards and Save the Dates and photographs and the usual kinds of crap peppered the doors.

"Don't get old, hon." Ricky was twisting the cap off a prescription bottle.

Andrea recognized the red ClearRx bottle from Target. Ricky tossed back two pills while Andrea watched. There were at least a dozen more pill bottles on the counter.

Ricky called them out. "Blood pressure, cholesterol, anti-inflammatories, shit for my thyroid, my acid reflux, my back pain, my nerves. Pepsi okay?"

Andrea took a second to realize she was talking about the soda. "Yes, thank you."

Ricky opened the fridge. A faded Polaroid of a teenage boy in cut-off shorts caught Andrea's eye. His hair was shaggy in a distinctive late-seventies style. He was shirtless, his skinny chest and awkward elbows putting him on the cusp of puberty.

Eric Blakely.

Andrea remembered what Nardo had said about Ricky's brother back at the farm—

Dead as a doornail, poor old thing.

"Okay." Ricky had filled a glass with ice. She popped the top on the can of Pepsi and poured it with an expert flick of her wrist. "I'm guessing you're here because of the judge."

Andrea was mindful that her deadpan needed practice. She worked to keep her expression neutral. "Why do you say that?"

Ricky took the chewing gum out of her mouth and wadded it up in a napkin. "Judith hasn't said a word, but it's gotten around town that the judge's cancer is back for real this time. Poor thing probably won't make it to the end of the year. If it was me, I would want to know what happened to Emily before I died."

Andrea took a sip of Pepsi as she thought about how to handle this. She had explicitly told herself that she wasn't going to talk about Emily, but she was also mindful that showing empathy in front of a witness was the quickest way to build trust.

She told Ricky, "I think it would give the judge some peace to know the truth."

Ricky nodded, like the confirmation was all that she needed. "Follow me."

Andrea left the glass on the counter as she trailed Ricky back down the stairs. Ricky stopped in front of the console table by the hallway. She picked up one of the framed photographs.

The picture was familiar. Andrea had seen a copy in Judith's collage last night. Except this one was folded accordion-style to crop Emily out of the group.

"Sorry. It's still hard for me to see her face. Brings it all back." Ricky flipped the frame over and opened the back. She unfolded the photograph and showed it to Andrea. "She was pretty, right?"

Andrea nodded, trying to pretend like she had never seen the picture before. She randomly pointed to Nardo. "Who is this?"

"My asshole ex," Ricky muttered, but she didn't sound bitter. She pointed to Clay in the photo. "That's Clayton Morrow. You're a cop, so you probably know more about him than I do. That's me, of course, back before my tits dropped and my hair turned gray. And that's my brother Eric. We called him Blake."

Andrea saw an opening. "Called?"

Ricky carefully refolded the picture. "He died two weeks after Emily did."

Andrea watched Ricky put the frame back together. There were more photographs on the table, a kind of shrine to Ricky's youth. Clay and Nardo smoking in the front seat of a convertible. Blake and Nardo dressed up as Al Capone-era gangsters. Blake and Ricky in matching tuxes. If you didn't know Emily Vaughn was part of the group, you would never miss her.

Ricky said, "About a week after Emily was attacked, Clay told us he had enough credits to graduate early. He was going to head out to New Mexico to find a job before college started."

Andrea looked down at the oversized books stacked under the two wide drawers. Yearbooks. Dozier Elementary. Milton Junior High. Longbill Beach Senior High.

"Blake offered to help Clay with the drive. Two thousand miles was a lot different back then. No cell phones if you broke down. Long-distance calls were astronomical. We didn't even own our phone. We rented it from C&P."

Ricky carefully placed the framed group photo back beside the others. She touched her finger to her brother's chest.

"I can't blame him for wanting to get away," Ricky said. "Things were so tense between all of us. Even me and Blake. He was my twin, you know?"

Andrea shook her head, though she knew. "Did Emily ever tell you who the father of her baby was?"

"No." Ricky's voice had filled with regret. "Emily wasn't talking to me at all by the end. I had no idea."

Andrea considered what Wexler had told her in the truck. Emily had been raped at a party. Andrea had to assume Ricky had been in attendance. And Eric. And Nardo. And Clay. And maybe Jack Stilton and Dean Wexler. There was a psychiatric syndrome called *folie à plusieurs*—a shared psychosis where a group of people together commit bad acts that they wouldn't otherwise commit on their own. Andrea had no problem buying that her father had taken this otherwise disparate group of people and given them permission to let the worst of themselves come out. Then he had left town and Dean Wexler had stepped in to fill the role.

She tried another avenue. "Did you have a theory about who could've killed Emily?"

Ricky shrugged, but said, "From the beginning, the cops were laser-focused on Clay. That's why he wanted to get out of town so badly. And Blake—well, he wanted to leave for his own reasons. Things weren't good with my grandfather. There was a blow-up about money. It was a really bad time for both of us. We weren't really talking."

Andrea cleared her throat. She knew that she had to be careful. Ricky didn't keep a shrine to her friend circle because she thought they were terrible people. "Why were the police focusing on Clay?"

"Stilton despised him," Ricky said. "Both Stiltons, actually. Clay was different. He was brilliant. Sarcastic. Good-looking. He was too much for their little brains to understand, and they hated him for it."

Andrea didn't remind her that Clayton Morrow was also a psychopath and a convicted criminal.

"I shouldn't say this, but we were all a little in love with Clay. Emily adored him. Nardo wanted to be him. Blake thought he hung the moon. We were such a special little clique." Ricky looked down at the photograph of Clay and her brother. "They were hiking in the Sandia Mountains just outside of Albuquerque. They went for a swim near Tijeras. Blake ducked under the falls, but he didn't come back up. He was never a strong swimmer. They found his body two days later."

At least that explained why Eric Blakely's death certificate wasn't registered in Sussex County. He had died in another state.

Ricky turned away from the photo. Her arms were crossed. "Clay must've been the one who killed her, right? I mean, that's what makes sense."

Andrea thought it had made more sense before she'd witnessed for herself the cruelty that Nardo Fontaine and Dean Wexler were capable of.

"I was so horrible to Emily when she told me she was pregnant." Ricky's gaze went to the couch under the window. "We were both right here in this room, and I said so many nasty things to her. I don't know why I was so angry. I guess I knew that it was over, you know? Our little clique. Nothing would be the same ever again."

Andrea had let Ricky get comfortable enough. She tried to gently take back control. "The way you talk about her is so different from the picture Dean Wexler painted."

"Dean?" Ricky looked surprised. "Why would he be talking about Emily?"

Andrea shrugged. "He told me she had some problems with drugs and alcohol."

"That's not true. Emily didn't even smoke." Ricky was suddenly agitated. "If you talked to Dean, then you talked to Nardo. What did he have to say about Emily?"

"He didn't mention her," Andrea said. "Marshal Bible and I were at the farm because of the body in the field. But you knew that already, right? You're the one who told Bible about the girl."

Ricky tucked her chin into her chest. "It's what I said before, Cheese is a worthless drunk. Sometimes I wonder if Dean has something on him. All that craziness going on at the farm for years—decades. And Cheese sticks his thumb up his ass and looks the other way."

"What kind of craziness?"

"The volunteers?" Ricky's agitation was ramping up. "You want to know the history on that, you should look up the court case from twenty years ago. They're exploiting the hell out of those girls."

"I've read the court case." Andrea kept her voice calm because Ricky's was not. "An anonymous caller tipped off the feds. She made the call from a public payphone on Beach Road."

Guilt flashed across Ricky's face. She took her phone out of her back pocket. She checked her timer, which showed another four minutes. "My dryer's about to go off."

Andrea wasn't going to let her go. "The girl in the field probably killed herself."

"I heard."

"She was gaunt, almost starved to death." Andrea watched Ricky check the timer again. "All of the women on the farm are

starving themselves. They look like they're living in a concentration camp."

"I pray for them." Ricky used the tail of her shirt to wipe the
screen. "I pray for their parents. Dean has a battalion of lawyers
on standby. They're not going to get anything out of him. He
always wins."

Andrea could tell she was losing Ricky. "Do you know any
girls who aren't there anymore? Maybe they'd be willing to talk."

"I barely have time to do laundry. Do you really think I've
kept up with anyone from that period of my life?"

Andrea tried again. "If you had any information, it could be
an anonymous tip or—"

"Hon, get the wax out of your ears, okay? I don't know anyone.
I haven't stepped foot near the farm in twenty years." Ricky was
finally satisfied that the phone was clean. "I've got a permanent
restraining order against me that says I can't go within twenty
feet of Nardo without being arrested. During the divorce, Dean
came after me so hard that I barely held onto the diner. Thank
God the house was in a trust or I would've been homeless."

Andrea could see that she was scared. "Dean helped Nardo
finance the divorce?"

"Dean helps Nardo with everything. He lives on the farm rent-
free. Nardo doesn't even get a paycheck which, believe me, fucked
me over real good during the divorce." Ricky sounded more bitter
about Wexler than she did about her ex-husband. "That farm is
a goldmine, and all Dean does with the money is use it to buy
people or to fuck them over. He runs it like a dictatorship. No
one tells him what to do."

Andrea could tell Ricky was just getting started.

"What Dean is doing to those girls—I promise you on my life
it wasn't like that when I was there. Nardo's a sick fuck, but he's
not that sick. And I never saw anything beyond exploited labor.
I assumed that ended when Dean negotiated a settlement with
the government." Ricky used her sleeve to wipe her eyes. She had
started to cry. "I know I said I'm a coward because of how I
treated Emily, but if I had seen something so—so disgusting? Evil?
Whatever you want to call what they're doing over there. There's
no way I would've kept my mouth shut."

"I believe you," Andrea said, but only because that was what Ricky needed to hear. "As a woman, I'm outraged, but, as a Marshal, I need a legal justification to open an investigation."

Ricky wiped her eyes again. "Jesus, I really wish I could help you."

Andrea could feel the woman's helplessness. "I heard the mother of one of the girls attempted a rescue."

"Crazy bitch tried to kidnap her own daughter." Ricky forced out a laugh. "I don't know what I'd do if my kid was living at that place. Not that we ever had kids, thank God. The only reason I married that asshole was because he had money. And then a year later, his father lost it all and he's wrapped up in the Cult of Dean. Jesus, if I didn't have bad luck, I wouldn't have any at all."

Madonna's "Holiday" started playing on Ricky's phone. She tapped off the alarm, but she didn't move. Instead, she wiped her eyes again. Her jaw worked. She was weighing her options, trying to decide how much was too much to say.

Finally, she told Andrea, "I've never really thought about it before, but maybe because you brought up Emily, and then we started talking about Dean and . . ."

In the silence, Andrea could hear the dryer beeping to signal the end of the cycle. Ricky must have heard it too, but she was clearly still debating the risks. The woman was twenty years out from her divorce, and yet part of her was still afraid of what Dean Wexler could do to her.

Ricky wiped her eyes again. She cleared her throat.

"I never looked at it this way before," she said. "But the shit that's happening at the farm is the same shit that happened to Emily Vaughn forty years ago."

OCTOBER 21, 1981

Emily sat on the floor in the very back of the school library with her forehead resting on her knees. She could not stop crying. She had a pounding headache. She hadn't been able to sleep the night before. Her legs kept cramping. Her stomach kept turning. Her thoughts kept ricocheting between Ricky telling her that their friendship was over and Blake placing Emily's hand on his *thing*.

Had the twins always been that cruel, or was Emily simply stupid?

She found a tissue in her book bag and blew her nose. Laughter filled the front of the library. She hunched down against the wall. She didn't want anyone to find her back here. She'd skipped chemistry. She never skipped class. Not until this week. Not until her entire life had been thrown into turmoil.

It was the stares of her classmates that Emily could not abide. In the hallway. From the back of the chemistry lab. Some of them had been pointing and giggling. Others had looked at her as if she was the most disgusting creature they had ever laid eyes on. Ricky had a big mouth, but Emily knew it was Blake who had started the rumor that she was pregnant, because the pointers and gigglers and most of the blatantly hostile stares had come from the boys. Not that Emily's current state was a rumor, because the word *rumor* implied an uncertainty or lack of truth.

No matter the source of the salacious information, whether it was Blake or Ricky or even Dean Wexler, Clay clearly knew that she was pregnant. Emily had seen him this morning as she was walking past the row of downtown shops. Clay was alone, smoking one last cigarette before heading across the road to school. Their eyes had met. There was no mistaking that he had seen her. Even from a distance, there was the flash of recognition in his features, the twist of his mouth into a quick grin. Emily had started to wave her hand, but his grin had melted away. He'd tossed the cigarette into the gutter, then turned on his heel like a soldier on the parade field and walked in the opposite direction.

So much for Clayton Morrow styling himself as a rebel who shirked the norms of the religiously bankrupt modern American society. He might as well have traded his Marlboro for a pitchfork. Or maybe he was running away from his own mistake.

Clay?

That was the first word she had written down in her Columbo notes. The more Emily talked to people, the more she thought that it really might be him.

Would that be so bad?

Emily had always liked Clay. She'd had embarrassingly sweaty dreams about him before. And sometimes when he was close, or he looked at her a certain way, she'd felt a rush of what could only be called desire. Clay had told her that nothing was going to happen, and she had accepted that, but maybe Emily had come onto him the night of The Party. And maybe Clay had been so stoned that he'd given in against his better judgment. Her father had said that teenage boys had a hard time controlling themselves. Emily had been thinking all along that she was somehow the victim, but maybe she was the aggressor.

Was that possible?

Emily used the back of her arm to wipe her tears. Her skin felt raw. The bruise on her neck where Dean Wexler had grabbed her had started to turn an angry, dark blue. She took a deep breath. She found her Columbo Investigation tucked deep inside her purse.

The notes she had recorded from her interaction with Ricky and Blake yesterday were smeared by her own tears. They had both been equally disgusting in their own unique ways. Emily shuddered when she thought about Blake moving her hand to his lap. His slick tongue in her ear. She shuddered a second time, her hand going to her ear as if his gross tongue was still there.

Emily closed her notebook. She had practically memorized the three different transcriptions. Dean Wexler had said that Nardo and Blake were inside the house that night. Blake had also told her that he and Nardo were in the house. Using Cheese's Columbo logic, she had two people telling the same story, which likely meant that they were both telling the truth, which meant she could eliminate Dean and Blake.

Right?

She wasn't certain. Dean and Blake could be telling the same story because they had previously agreed to a story. Seeking out a third confirmation from Nardo was a non-starter. In fact, his response to Emily's pregnancy was the only one that she did not find surprising.

Yesterday, Ricky had railed against Esther and Franklin Vaughn for being rich assholes who bought their way out of trouble, but this time, the Fontaines had beaten her parents to the punch. A hand-delivered letter had arrived before breakfast this morning. Gerald Fontaine was putting the Vaughns on notice that Emily was not to speak to—or more importantly, speak about—Bernard Fontaine in any false, negative or inflammatory manner unless they wanted to be staring down a very expensive lawsuit for libel.

"What a ridiculous buffoon," Esther had pronounced when she'd read the letter. "Libel pertains to written or printed statements that are found to be either false or defamatory. Slander is oral or spoken defamation."

Her mother had seemed to triumph in scoring a rhetorical point, but Emily was the one who was paying the price.

"Em?"

She looked up. Cheese was leaning his shoulder against one of the long bookshelves. She had chosen to hide in Biblical References because she knew that no one would accidentally wander by.

Except for the people who knew that Emily always hid in Biblical References.

He asked, "Are you okay?"

She shook her head and shrugged at the same time, but the response that came out of her mouth was the God's honest truth. "No. I'm really not okay."

Cheese glanced over his shoulder before joining her against the wall. He slid down beside her, their knees almost touching.

He asked, "Anything new going on?"

She laughed. And then she started to cry. Her head went into her hands again.

"Aw, Em." His arm wrapped around her shoulders. "I'm so sorry."

She leaned into him. He smelled of Old Spice and Camels.

"It's gonna be okay." He rubbed her arm, holding her tight. "Do your—will your parents let you—you know?"

She shook her head. Her parents had already decided this was going to happen.

"Okay." His chest rose as he took a deep breath. "I could—well, if you wanted me to, I could—"

"Thank you, but no." Emily looked into his big cow eyes. "Blake already asked me to marry him."

"Oh, Jesus." Cheese pulled away from her. "No, Emily. I wasn't gonna ask you that. I was—well, I was gonna offer to beat up whoever did this to you."

Emily wasn't sure she believed him, but she chose to take him at face value. "That's all I need is for you to get suspended."

"You're not going to marry Blake, are you?" Cheese looked concerned. "Em, he's the worst of all of them."

She almost laughed. "Why would you say that?"

"He's devious," Cheese said. "Not like Nardo, who's just mean. Or Clay, who's just bored. When Blake takes against you, he really takes against you."

Emily felt her own concern bubble up. "Blake hasn't done something to you?"

Cheese shook his head, but she didn't believe him. "You know, you could do something for me, if you want. I know I have no right to ask, but—"

"What is it?" Emily couldn't recall him ever asking her for anything.

"I don't want you to call me Cheese anymore." He saw her face. "It doesn't bother me when you say it, but it's what they say, so—"

"Okay, Jack." The name sounded funny. She had known him

since he'd eaten one of her crayons in kindergarten. "Nice to meet you, Jack."

He didn't smile. "You're not alone, Em. I'm here. Your parents are probably mad, but they'll get over it. And people at school, well, they're all a bunch of rejects anyway. What do you care about what they're saying? This time next year, we're all gonna be out of this insane asylum anyway, right? Who cares?"

Emily had to swallow before she could speak. "Tell me what they're saying."

"That you're a dirty, dirty girl," Nardo said.

They both flinched at the sound of his snarky voice.

"What are you two lovebirds doing over here in the corner?" Nardo was leaning against the bookshelves. "Is this where you made your illicit love child?"

"Fuck off." Jack struggled to stand up. His fists were clenched. He was bigger than Nardo, but Nardo was far too cruel. Jack barely glanced back at Emily before stomping away.

"Well," Nardo said. "Such a drama queen, our Cheese."

"He wants to be called Jack now."

"I want to be called Sir Dicks-a-Lot of Cuntfuckery." Nardo sat on the floor with a flourish. "Alas, we can't always get what we want."

The only consolation in this entire ordeal was that she would never have to pretend to ignore his snide remarks again. "Your parents made it clear that I'm not supposed to talk to you."

"Where's the fun in that, Emmie-Em?" Nardo knocked some books off the bottom shelf. "I hear you've been searching for the baker who put that bun in your oven."

Emily wiped her eyes. She no longer cared about her Columbo Investigation. She wanted desperately for Nardo to leave. "It doesn't matter."

"Doesn't it?" Nardo asked. "You could do worse than Blake."

Emily didn't see how.

"It's always been his dream to marry a rich woman he can control." Nardo gave a sharp, sinister laugh. "Just like your father with your mother, right?"

Emily wiped her eyes again. She hated that he could see her crying. "That's not funny."

"Come on, kid. You know I'm just teasing you." Nardo paused, probably expecting Emily to say it was okay.

Emily did not.

It wasn't okay.

He said, "I guess you're going to get really fat and disgusting now. Dean says that's going to be the worst part. You'll blow up like a balloon."

Emily hadn't let herself think past a few hours at a time. She put her hand to her stomach. She had never been beautiful, but she had always passed for okay-looking. What would men think when they saw her eight months from now? Or a year from now when she had a screaming baby on her hip?

"You'd better plan on starving yourself the second you squeeze that thing out," Nardo advised. "You're lucky you've started out with a good figure. Look at Ricky. If she ever gets pregnant, she'll turn into a blimp and that will be that for the rest of her life. The same thing happened to my aunt Pauline. She's disgusting to look at."

Emily didn't think Nardo had any room to talk. He had always been plump, but boys could get away with that. "What do you want, Nardo?"

"Just making conversation." Nardo knocked another book onto the floor. "Ricky will come around, you know. She's got that weird sniveling rivalry with Blake, but she'll miss you eventually. She's not like you. She doesn't have any other friends."

Emily had never heard it put so succinctly, but of course he was right. The question was—did Emily want Ricky back? How could Emily ever forget all of the awful things that Ricky had said? She would never be able to trust her again.

"Unfortunately, Mummy and Daddy have made it clear that I can't do the gallant thing and fall on my sword for you." Nardo chuckled to himself. "Can you imagine us getting married? Ricky would slit both of our throats before we made it to the honeymoon."

Emily was so tired of useless boys talking uselessly about marriage.

"I can't say I haven't thought about it, though." Nardo knocked over another book. "You and me. There are worse things. Though of course that's not an option now. Spoiled goods and all that."

Another book hit the floor. He was trying to act casual, but Nardo always had an agenda.

He asked, "You're sure it was the night of The Party?"

Emily felt her body tense. "Yes."

"And you don't remember how it happened? Or who it happened with?"

Emily's throat strained as she tried to swallow. Ricky had really told him everything. "No, I can't remember."

"Jesus," Nardo said. "Well, I don't recall much from that night myself, so I suppose I should cut you some slack."

Emily looked at him for the first time since he'd shown up. The usual snide curl to his lips was gone. He seldom let his asshole persona slip away. This was the guy Ricky saw when she thought about how much she loved him. And in truth, it was the same guy Emily saw when she thought about Nardo Fontaine as one of her closest friends.

She asked, "It's all a blank?"

"Most of it. But Blake was absolutely out of his mind. I know that much." Nardo scooped up one of the books he'd let fall to the floor. He picked at the edge with his thumbnail. "I was face down on the couch watching two dustbunnies dance the opening scene from the Nutcracker, and then I heard this bleating upstairs. Like a sheep. It was Blake, if you can believe it."

Emily shook her head. She wasn't sure what she believed anymore.

"I go upstairs, and he's locked himself in my parents' bathroom, of all places. I had to break the lock to help the old boy." Nardo turned over the book and examined the spine. "He was on his knees, hands out like he was holding his pecker, but his pants were still zipped. And he was about three feet from the toilet. I have no idea what he was thinking, but for godsakes, what an idiot. His first acid trip is thinking he's taking a piss? The entire front of his jeans was soaked in it. And don't ask me about the bleating. What a loon."

Emily watched Nardo's toothy grin come out.

"At least I saw an actual unicorn," Nardo said. "What about you?"

Emily tried to swallow again. "I really don't remember."

"Anything?" Nardo asked the question for a second time. "Like, not even getting there?"

"Yes," Emily admitted. "I remember walking to your front door. Taking the tab of acid from Clay. And then the next thing I know, Mr. Wexler is driving me home."

"Yeah, well," Nardo rolled his eyes. "That part I remember. You were hysterical over something. I couldn't drive you home. I could barely see my hand in front of me. Blake was covered in piss. I had to bribe the old fuck with the rest of our acid just to get him to come get you."

Emily listened to the cadence of his voice. There was a practiced tone to it, all of his usual vitriol stripped away. "What about Clay?"

Nardo lifted one shoulder in a shrug. "Fuck if I know. You were screaming at him about something or the other. Then you ran into the house. You were actually a bit mad. I was afraid you'd break Mother's good china. And you were partaking of rather too much of Father's Scotch. They were going to be very pissed when they got home."

Emily had never seen Nardo's parents get pissed about anything.

"Well it sure as hell wasn't Dean who knocked you up. The man's balls got fried when he was a kid. He couldn't make a baby if he wanted to."

Emily looked down at her hands. That wasn't the kind of information that Dean Wexler would randomly throw around. Which meant that he had talked to Nardo already.

"Do you—" Nardo dropped the book back onto the floor. "Do you think it could've been Clay?"

"I—" Emily stopped herself. She silently ran through the list of questions Nardo had thrown at her. He was Columboing her. All that was missing was the *one more thing*.

She cleared her throat, trying to keep the shake out of her voice. It wasn't only Dean and Nardo. They had all strategized— Blake, Ricky, Clay, Nardo and Dean. They were all in this together. And they had all agreed that Nardo was their best hope of shutting this down.

She asked, "Do *you* think it was Clay?"

"I mean—" Nardo shrugged. "I don't want to hurt your feelings, old girl, but Clay has been very clear that he doesn't see you that way. Acid doesn't make you do shit you wouldn't do when you're sober. And frankly, he's got a better selection at his hands, doesn't he? No need to fish in the little pond."

Emily stared at her hands.

"Come now, old girl, you don't want to fall into wishful thinking, do you?" Nardo waited for her to look up. "An allegation like that could ruin Clay's life."

Yet again, they were circling the wagons around Clay. Emily wondered why no one ever really worried about her life being ruined. Even Ricky had focused only on the boys—what Emily's pregnancy would do to *them*, how it might ruin *their* lives.

"You need to be careful," Nardo said. "You've said yourself that you're not sure who did it. You might even have the wrong night. I mean, who knows? You certainly have an expanded group outside the clique, with all your practices and debates and whatnot."

She borrowed a line from Blake. "I know where my vagina has been, Nardo. I'm very attached to it."

He looked surprised by her coarseness.

She put it to him plainly. "You claim that you were in the bathroom with Blake. Mr. Wexler is sterile. Who else could it be?"

"What about Cheese?"

She laughed for the first time in days. "You can't be serious."

"Of course I'm serious."

"He wasn't even there."

"He was standing right in front of you when you walked into the house," Nardo countered. "Jesus, Emily. Who do you think sold us the acid?"

7

Andrea watched the screen door close behind Ricky Fontaine. The only way to access the laundry in the garage was via the outside stairs. Ricky's sandals slapped the concrete as she walked down the zigzagging flights to get the towels out of the dryer.

The shit that's happening at the farm is the same shit that happened to Emily Vaughn forty years ago.

As a parting line, it packed a punch, but it didn't hold up under scrutiny. Emily Vaughn hadn't been starved nearly to death. She was seven months pregnant on the night of her attack. She was wearing a turquoise or teal prom dress, according to the witness statements, not a yellow shift. Her shoulder-length hair had been permed, not long and stringy to her waist. She was barefooted, but maybe Andrea's southern roots were showing because she assumed that a lot of people on farms ran around barefoot.

So how was one like the other?

Andrea thought back to the beginning of the conversation. Ricky was the person who had told Bible about the dead body at the farm, but a US Marshal had knocked on her door four hours later and all Ricky wanted to talk about was Emily Vaughn. It was the same thing Wexler had done in the truck, but he'd been such an obvious asshole that Andrea had seen right through him.

"Fuck," Andrea muttered.

She went to the screen door. Ricky had made it to the first landing. Bible was still in his SUV on the street. Andrea found his contact info in her phone.

He answered on the first ring. "Yep?"

"Tell me when she's heading back up."

"Will do."

Andrea shoved her phone back into her pocket. Her nerves were jangling. Ricky had invited her into the house, which meant the woman had consented to entry and waived her Fourth Amendment rights.

The house was fair game.

Andrea's phone came back out of her pocket as she headed to the console table. She took photographs of the framed photos. Then she knelt down and found the 1981–82 Longbill Beach Senior High School yearbook. The printer had left the first few pages blank so that classmates could sign them. Ricky hadn't had a lot of friends, but Andrea took photographs of the signatures and short notes. There were lots of *K.I.T.*s for Keep In Touch and several *Go Longbills!*

She looked at the closed drawers. Her heart ticked like a stopwatch. The scope of Andrea's authority was limited to what a reasonable person would think they were consenting to. Was it reasonable for Ricky to believe Andrea would open the drawers where they had just been standing? Ricky had freely talked about the group, the photos, Emily Vaughn, her brother.

The justification felt shady, but it was still a justification.

The left-side drawer took some work to get open. Andrea found scraps of paper, old receipts, a snapshot of Ricky and Blake blowing out candles on a birthday cake, another of Nardo and Clay sitting at the counter at the diner. Andrea documented as much as she could. She clocked the time on her phone. She had no idea when Ricky had gone downstairs, but it didn't take hours to unload a dryer, load it back up with wet towels, fill up the washer and walk back up the stairs.

Andrea's hands were sweating when she jerked open the right-side drawer.

More memories. Some wedding snapshots showing a much younger Ricky and Nardo. A silver Zippo lighter with the initials EAB on them. A New Mexico death certificate for Eric Alan Blakely. A burial policy for Al Blakely. A $200 receipt from a Longbill Beach funeral home with *ashes* in the description. A receipt from Maggie's Formal Wear marked with a faded red PAID and the clerk's initials. Andrea reached into the back of the drawer and felt a flat metal box that was slightly larger than her hand. She pulled it out.

Andrea had no idea what she was looking at.

The metal case was around 4x6 and painted a cheap brown. She thought it might be meant to hold smaller cigars, but there was a thermometer-looking window cut out of the top. Instead of numbers, there were paired letters of the alphabet on a white background. A silver metal pointer slid up and down the window.

Andrea was still clueless. She turned the box over in her hand, trying to find a clasp or a button or a logo or even a serial number.

Her phone rang.

Bible said, "Heading back up the stairs."

"Fuck." Andrea took three quick photos from different angles before dropping the metal case back into the drawer. She had to use her hip to slam it shut. And then she sprinted across the room so she could meet Ricky at the front door.

"Let me help," Andrea offered to take the basket, but Ricky pulled away.

"I've got it, hon." She was chomping on a wad of chewing gum again. Her entire demeanor had changed. Andrea wondered if Ricky had made a call in the garage, or maybe she'd realized that she'd said too much. "Sorry, I need to ask you to leave. I'm already late for work."

Andrea wasn't going to leave. "What you said about the farm—that the same thing that happened to Emily is happening there. What did you mean?"

"Oh, I don't know." Ricky dumped the towels onto the couch and started folding in syncopation with the gum-popping and the clanging of her silver bangles. "Honestly, you caught me at a bad time. It's obvious that I can't stand Dean and Nardo. I'm not what you'd call a reliable witness, especially considering the restraining order."

Andrea watched her quick, practiced movements. Ricky was talking faster than before. Maybe she hadn't called someone. Maybe the two pills she had dry-swallowed in the kitchen had finally kicked in.

"I wish I could be more helpful." Ricky snapped out a towel and folded it in thirds. "What you said about Esther—you're right. She deserves some peace. I can only tell you what I told Bob Stilton forty years ago. I saw Clay in the gym dancing with some cheerleader most of the night. I can't even remember her name now."

Andrea pretended that she hadn't read the exact opposite in Ricky's witness statement. Emily's best friend had claimed that she'd skipped the prom altogether. "Who else do you think it could be?"

"I mean—" Ricky plucked another towel from the pile. "People will do anything to protect their children, right?"

Andrea felt a warning flag go up. "Right."

"You're not getting it, are you?" Ricky snapped out another towel. "Emily had a hard time being mean to people, even when they deserved it. Clay called them her collection of broken toys. And Cheese was the most broken of them all. He was always hanging around her, sort of like a sad little puppy. And she was nice to him, but not like that."

Andrea wanted to make sure she understood what Ricky was saying. "You're telling me that Jack Stilton, the current chief of police, killed Emily Vaughn?"

"I'm only saying it could explain why no one was ever charged. The old man was protecting his son." Ricky looked up from her folding. "Don't listen to me, hon. I watch too many murder shows on TV."

Andrea figured she'd heard enough. "Thank you for your time. Let me know if you think of anything else."

Ricky took a break from the gum-smacking. "I'll do that."

Andrea walked out the door. She felt her tongue finding the ridge inside of her cheek as she walked down the steps. She tried to wrap her brain around what had just happened, if only because Bible would have questions.

He waited until she had closed the car door and put on her seatbelt. "Whatcha got?"

"You ever hear the term goat-rope?"

"I certainly have, partner." Bible pulled away from the curb. "Generally that kind of animal clusterfuckery is marked by human error, and I have a hard time believing you made some kind of mistake in there."

He had no idea. "Ricky thinks Stilton killed Emily Vaughn."

Bible gave a surprised laugh. "Junior or Senior?"

"Junior. Senior covered it up."

"Well ain't that something." Bible didn't sound convinced. "But what I'm hearing is your ass kind'a straddled two horses in there."

Andrea felt the rebuke, but she continued the metaphor. "Ricky led me by the reins. Right out of the gate, she brought up Emily Vaughn. I didn't even get to drink my Pepsi. Dean Wexler did the same thing earlier in the truck. It's like they were both reading from identical scripts—first they bring up the judge, then they bring up Emily, then the goat-rope commences."

Bible frowned. "Be more specific about Ricky."

Andrea tried to bullet-point it. "She talked about how her brother drowned in New Mexico two weeks after Emily died. She told me that she was a shitty friend to Emily. And then when I finally pushed her onto the subject of the farm, she went after Dean Wexler."

"What about Nardo?"

"She says he's not into whatever Dean is doing but—I don't know. He has to know it's happening. Then again, he's clearly a sadist. Maybe he likes to watch?" Andrea felt like she needed to write all of this down in her notebook so she could keep it straight. "Ricky claims that none of the culty stuff was going on when she lived at the farm."

"Do you believe her?"

"I don't know." Andrea should get a tattoo of the words on her forehead. "She's scared of them, I think. Definitely more Wexler than Nardo."

"Makes sense. He controls the money. He's in charge," Bible said. "Keep going."

"Dean pushed through a permanent restraining order against Ricky. Can we look that up?"

"I'll get Leeta on it." Bible typed on his phone as he drove. He asked Andrea, "*Permanent* throw up a flag for you?"

"Yes," she said. "With a temporary order, the judge usually signs off on a sworn statement, and the order expires in a few months or a few years. To make it permanent, there's a hearing where you have to present a statement of danger, show evidence of violence or abuse, and give graphic details that persuade the judge to make the order indefinite."

"Correct," Bible said. "What else?"

"I guess the weirdest part was, Ricky told me that whatever is going on at the farm is the same shit that happened to Emily."

Bible considered the statement. "That don't make sense to me. You press her for an explanation?"

"I tried, but the buzzer went off for the dryer. When she came back upstairs, she brushed it off."

"Well," he said. "What about your little Fourth Amendment foray?"

Andrea slipped out her iPhone. She was going to have to organize her photographs into albums so that she didn't accidentally send her vacation photos to the USMS cloud. She swiped through the pictures as she talked. "There were a bunch of yearbooks going back to elementary school. A lot of group photos, but Emily was cropped out. A Zippo. Eric Blakely's New Mexico death certificate dated June 23, 1982. A death certificate for Al Blakely from 1994. I guess that's Big Al. There was a burial policy for him, too."

"Huh," Bible said.

Andrea had found the picture of the metal case. She showed it to Bible. "Is this a small cigar case or a business card holder or—"

He laughed. "That's a pocket index."

"I have no idea what that is."

"It's from the Stone Age, back before people carried their lives in their pockets." He pointed to the window with the letters. "The little slider there, you line it up to the corresponding letter, like for Bible, you'd point to A-B, or Oliver, you'd slide to—"

"O-P," Andrea said. "It's an address book."

"You got it, partner," Bible said. "So, if I wanted to look up your number, I'd slide the pointer to the O-P, then click a button at the bottom of the case, and the top pops open and shows you all the O-P pages."

Andrea zoomed in on the photo that captured the bottom edge. The button was nothing more than a sliver imbedded in the case. "How do you press it?"

"With your thumbnail. If you weren't careful, you'd end up

with a bruise under your nail. Very uncomfortable," Bible said. "You kids don't know how good you have it."

Andrea's life would be two thousand percent less stressful if she didn't have a phone. "The address book must've belonged to Ricky's brother or her grandfather. Everything else in the drawer had their names on it."

"Drawer?" The way Bible said the word felt different. "You have probable cause to look inside a drawer?"

Andrea's face turned red. "I've got a justification."

"Partner, for future reference, justifications don't work for me. I need it by the book. You don't do right by doing wrong." His tone was soft, but the rebuke was firm. "Understood?"

She forced herself to look him in the eye. "Understood."

"All right, lesson learned. You can put that away."

Andrea clicked off her phone. She hadn't realized how much she wanted to impress Bible until she had disappointed him. "It was for nothing. I didn't get any information that would help Star Bonaire or any of the girls at the farm. Ricky played me. I'm sorry."

"Lady, you need to stop running down my partner." Bible pulled the car over to the curb again. He unclipped his seatbelt and shifted to face her. "I wanna tell you something, partner. There's two kinds of types you'll meet during what I am certain will be your long and successful law enforcement career: people who want to talk to you and people who don't."

"Okay," Andrea said. Obviously, she needed more training.

"With each type, you gotta ask yourself—why? If he clams up, that don't always mean he's a bad fella. Maybe he's seen videos of people who look like you hurting people who look like him. Or maybe he just wants to go about his business and keep his dang mouth shut. And that's fine, because not talking to the police is your inalienable right as an American citizen. Hell, you ever read your employment contract? Every law enforcement union makes 'em put it in writing that you cannot interview an officer unless that officer has a lawyer present. That's some real goose/gander irony right there."

Andrea chewed the inside of her cheek. "Ricky definitely wanted to talk to me."

"That's the other type," Bible said. "Sometimes, straight up they just wanna be helpful. Sometimes, they don't know squat but they wanna be in on the action. Or maybe they're trying to bend your thinking in a direction that's better for them. Or maybe they're guilty as hell and wanna know what you know. Or maybe they're a spoon—always stirring up shit."

"Ricky could be any of those things," Andrea admitted. "I don't know what her agenda is but, by the end of the conversation, my gut was telling me that she's hiding something."

For once, Bible was the one with a phone in his hands. He squinted as he tapped, but he quickly found what he was looking for. He passed his phone to Andrea.

She didn't know what she was expecting to see, but it wasn't a scanned letter. Twelve point type. Times Roman. Black on white. One sentence, all caps—

HOW WOULD YOU LIKE THE WORLD TO KNOW THAT YOUR HUSBAND PHYSICALLY ABUSED YOU AND YOUR DAUGHTER, BUT YOU DID NOTHING TO PROTECT HER?

Andrea looked at Bible.

He said, "Keep going."

Andrea paged to the next scan—

YOU SACRIFICED YOUR CHILD FOR YOUR CAREER! YOU DESERVE YOUR CANCEROUS DEATH SENTENCE!

Again, Andrea looked at Bible. "Are these the threats that were mailed to the judge?"

"Yep."

She felt her eyes narrow. "Then the first one claimed that Franklin Vaughn abused his wife and kid."

"It did," Bible confirmed. "Keep going."

She paged again—

YOU'RE DYING OF CANCER AND YOUR HUSBAND IS A VEGETABLE, BUT ALL YOU CARE ABOUT IS YOUR SO-CALLED LEGACY!

Andrea remembered Bible telling her there were *particular details* about the judge's private life that had made the death threats credible. She told him, "Ricky said the judge's cancer is an open secret. Everyone knows it's terminal."

"Keep reading."

Andrea loaded the next scan—

YOU ARE GOING TO DIE, YOU ARROGANT, NEEDY, AND WORTHLESS BITCH! EVERYONE WILL KNOW WHAT A FRAUD YOU ARE. I WILL MAKE SURE YOU SUFFER!

Then the next—

YOU DESERVE TO DIE A SLOW, PAINFUL, AND TERRIFYING DEATH FOR WHAT YOU DID! NO ONE WILL CARE WHEN YOU ARE A ROTTING CORPSE IN YOUR GRAVE! I AM GOING TO KILL YOU SOON. WATCH YOUR BACK!

Bible provided, "Judicial Security screens every piece of mail that every judge receives at the courthouse. That first one didn't seem like anything, so it got filed. Then the second one came the next day, and it flagged the judge's cancer, so they talked to her about it, offered her security, and she said it was no big deal. Then number three and four came in on day three and four, and the judge waved them off, too. Which is her prerogative. We can't force her to take security. But then the rat got mailed to her personal residence in Baltimore along with letter number five, and that's when I came in."

"That sounds like manic behavior," Andrea said. "Sending them so close together."

"It does."

"Did Esther ask for you?"

"She didn't have to," Bible said. "The Boss, she kept me in the loop about the letters from the get-go. And my wife, Cussy, she keeps an eye on Esther because she's grateful for what she did for me a few years back."

Andrea was finally figuring out the code. "And both your boss and your wife agreed that you should work security until the threat was investigated and neutralized?"

"See, I told you you're smart."

Andrea didn't want a participation trophy. "Did the judge admit that she and Emily were abused by her husband?"

"The judge don't answer questions she don't want to answer."

That sounded like Esther Vaughn, but it was hard to say whether her silence was a confirmation of the abuse or a denial.

That's what being imperious got you.

Andrea paged through the scans, reading all five letters again. As death threats went, they were fairly tame. Andrea had faced more vitriol when she'd casually weighed in on the Philip Guston discussion on the SCAD Facebook page. She didn't know of any woman on the internet who hadn't been subjected to at least one violent rape threat for simply expressing her opinion.

The phone vibrated. Bible had gotten an email.

Andrea couldn't help but read the notification. "Leeta responded to your query about Ricky's restraining order."

"Take a look."

Andrea tapped open the email, then the attachment, which showed the actual judge's order against Ricky Jo Blakely Fontaine.

YOU, THE ADVERSE PARTY, ARE HERBY NOTIFIED THAT ANY INTENTIONAL VIOLATION OF THIS PERMANENT ORDER IS A CRIMINAL VIOLATION THAT WILL RESULT IN YOUR IMMINENT ARREST.

"Damn," Andrea muttered. That was crystal clear. She bypassed the legal boilerplate and located the original request for a restraining order. She scrolled down to the meat of Bernard Fontaine's complaint and read it aloud for Bible's benefit.

"'On several occasions over the last decade, my ex-wife, Ricky Jo Blakely (Fontaine), has shown up at my house and the house of my business partner, Dean Wexler, and verbally threatened me. On the last occasion, she was intoxicated and left a pile of vomit on my doorstep (photo attached). Throughout the previous six months, her attacks have escalated. She punctured all of the tires on my automobile (photo attached). She threw a rock through my bedroom window (photo attached). She threatened some of the workers at my place of employment (affidavits attached). She has written anonymous letters to various government agencies telling them that my business partner (Wexler) and I are operating outside the law (copies attached). She came to my place of employment last night brandishing a weapon (knife) and threatening to kill me. The police were called (report attached). During the process of her arrest, she verbally threatened to kill both me and Dean Wexler. She is currently in jail but I am in fear of my life should she be released.'"

"Well now, that ticks all the boxes for *permanent*," Bible said. "Sounds like ol' Ricky Jo's got a wild side. When did all this happen?"

"Shit, it was only four years ago." Andrea had nearly dropped his phone when she saw the date. This wasn't a goat-rope. It was a goat massacre.

At the house, Ricky had made it seem like she had been destroyed by the divorce and terrified of Nardo and Wexler. You didn't slash someone's tires and puke on their doorstep sixteen years later if you were terrified. You did those things because you wanted their attention.

Andrea looked at Bible. He was waiting for her to figure something out, and it had nothing to do with the restraining order.

She said, "I was talking about Ricky and you showed me the death threats that were mailed to the judge."

"That is an accurate sequence of events."

Andrea took an educated guess. "You think that Ricky wrote the death threats."

He looked very pleased. "Accurate again, partner."

"Shit," she whispered, because she hadn't been sure at all. In retrospect, that would explain the absence of sexual violence in the threats. And the rat. There were traps all along the boardwalk. Ricky wouldn't have to go far to find one. Not to mention that the stamped letters had been dropped in the blue mail collection box at the end of Beach Road.

She asked Bible, "Why? What did the judge ever do to Ricky?"

"Round about fifty years ago, the diner burned down."

Andrea remembered reading about the devastating fire on the RJ's Eats website but, unless Esther Vaughn was an arsonist, she didn't see the connection. "And?"

"Big Al raised the kids after Ricky and Eric's parents died in a boating accident." Bible was watching Andrea carefully, taking in her reaction. "There was a legal settlement with the boat operator of two hundred thousand dollars that was put in a trust to take care of the kids. Big Al was the trustee. The kids knew about the money. They thought they were set for college, maybe a new car and a down payment on a house. Used to be that kind of money, even split down the middle, could buy you a hell of a lot of things."

Two and a half years at SCAD had cost Andrea almost the entire amount. "But then the diner burned down."

"Right, and Big Al as trustee felt that it would be for the benefit of the kids to use the money to rebuild the diner. The restaurant had been in the family for years. He petitioned the court. The court was persuaded, and the money was spent."

"Petitioned the court?" Andrea echoed.

"The Delaware Court of Chancery adjudicates civil rights, real property, guardianships, trusts, that kind of thing. At the time, Esther was Chancellor. She granted Big Al's request to use the money to rebuild the diner. Even said something about how a college education was all well and good, but the diner would supply a reasonable income for both kids for the remainder of their lifetimes."

Andrea tried to think how she'd feel if the entire course of her adult life had been changed by one person. Actually, it didn't take a lot of imagination.

She told Bible, "I am assuming there's no proof, otherwise Ricky would be arrested. Has anyone interviewed her?"

"You don't go straight on at a rattlesnake, you grab that sucker by the tail."

Andrea had heard the phrase before. The best way to break a suspect was to surprise them with information they didn't know you had. That was where the inspector with Judicial Security probably came in. Andrea and Bible were babysitters, not investigators.

She asked, "Does the judge know Ricky wrote the threats?"

"Indeed she does," Bible said. "But it's a theory, not a provable fact. The Marshals are keeping the Vaughns safe on the outside chance I'm wrong. And I know this is hard to believe, partner, but I have been wrong before."

"Wait a minute." Andrea saw a gaping hole in his explanation. "You told me last night that the profile for a person who threatens a judge is a suicidal middle-aged white male."

"That's true, which would make Ricky an outlier. Marshal rule number—"

"Oh, come on."

"All right, you got me." His shit-eating grin reminded her of Mike. "I could've told you Ricky was on my radar straight outta

the gate. I was screwing with you, partner. You're hiding shit.
I'm hiding shit. We gotta build trust, right? We good?"

Andrea forced her molars to unclench. "We're good."

"Fantastic," Bible said. "So, here's something else you should
know: Ricky's only an outlier because she's female. That I know
about, she's attempted suicide at least three times over the years."

Andrea felt her lips part in surprise.

"First time was a single-car accident when she was in her
twenties. Second time she OD'd in the middle of the street on
her fortieth birthday. Pretty spectacular—she stopped traffic. Third
time was in custody at the jail. Tried to hang herself in Stilton's
holding cell after Dean had her arrested on the restraining order."

"You asked Stilton about suicides and he left Ricky completely
out."

"Yep, which means he was lying," Bible said. "The first two I
could see slipping his mind, but the last one was four years ago
and happened inside his own shop."

Andrea had to take a moment to think all of this through.
There was a glaringly obvious reason that Stilton was trying to
keep away two US Marshals. "You laughed when I told you Ricky
said Jack Stilton killed Emily."

"Not gonna say Jack ain't on my list, but there are much better
suspects."

*Clayton Morrow. Jack Stilton. Bernard Fontaine. Eric Blakely.
Dean Wexler.*

"This is a crazy question," Andrea warned. "But could the lost
trust fund money be a motive for the attack? Obviously, Ricky
is still pissed off about it. I can see where both she and her brother
would blame the judge for ruining their lives."

"Didn't witnesses place Eric in the gym during the time of the
attack?" Bible asked. "And nobody saw Ricky there."

"But witnesses aren't always reliable. Everybody in Emily's
friend group has some kind of alibi. They can't all be telling the
truth."

"That's true. And people generally only say what they think
you want to hear."

"I think I've answered my own crazy question," Andrea said.
"This wasn't about the judge and the trust fund. Whoever killed

Emily wasn't mad at Esther. They were mad at Emily. Her face was beaten to a pulp. Two vertebrae in her neck were broken. She was stripped out of her clothes. She was thrown away in a Dumpster. Why do all that instead of dropping her in the ocean, which was twenty yards away?"

"You do all that because it's personal," Bible said. "And you're not really good at murdering."

She said, "So, that brings us back to the motive everyone assumed from the beginning: Emily was going to publicly name the father and the father shut her up."

"Right." Bible had clearly reached the same conclusion as Andrea. "Forty years ago, Wexler took himself out of the running. Claimed he was sterile."

Andrea knew this from her reading. "Bob Stilton took him at his word, but there was no medical record or doctor's affidavit in the—"

"File?"

Bible was grinning again. He'd gotten her to admit that she had read the Emily Vaughn's investigation file.

He said, "You got anything else to tell me?"

Andrea had one more detail, but it hadn't come from Emily's file. "Dean Wexler told me that Emily was drugged at a party. That's how she got pregnant. He told me she never found who did it."

Bible didn't seem surprised by the news, but he had talked to more people than Andrea had, including Emily's own mother.

He said, "I'm guessing you've got a theory on what happened that night?"

Andrea guessed she did. "Emily Vaughn was attacked sometime between six to six thirty on April 17, 1982. The sun set around seven forty-two."

Bible started nodding, like this was what he wanted.

"The violence of the attack points to a known assailant. The weapon was already in the alley, so it was probably spur-of-the-moment. Some black threads were found on the pallet, but all of the boys were wearing black that night. After the attack, the assailant likely hid Emily behind a pile of trash bags and waited until it was dark to move her."

"What else?"

"The witness statements. Stilton said he left the prom early and watched TV with his mother. Clay was seen dancing with a cheerleader, but the times are spotty. Nardo's the same—people saw him, then they didn't. Ditto with Dean Wexler, who was there as a chaperone. He was seen and then not seen. Eric was at the prom. Witnesses saw him have an argument with Emily moments before the attack. Then they saw him walk away. In his statement, Eric claims he left early and spent the rest of the night watching movies with his sister."

Andrea had to stop for a breath. She also had a new detail. "At the time, Ricky's witness statement backed up Eric's story, but just now at her house, she told me that Clay couldn't be the killer because she saw him at the prom dancing with a cheerleader all night."

"Sandwich the before and after." Bible's poker face had cracked. "Take yourself back to Ricky's house. How was she acting when you first got there? What was she like by the time you left? Then drill down to the middle. Was she nervous? Was she looking you in the eye or—"

"She looked exhausted when she opened the door. Like she hadn't slept all night. And then when she returned from the garage, she was manic, and she stayed that way the rest of the time." Andrea had already guessed the probable explanation. "When I first got there, Ricky knocked back two pills from one of her prescription bottles. I think when she returned from the garage, the drugs had kicked in. She went off script. She accidentally put herself near the crime scene when she clearly wasn't there. Worse, she exonerated Clay Morrow."

"Why is that worse?"

"Well—" Andrea shrugged. For once, her personal relationship to Clay felt immaterial. "It's not smart. Everyone in town assumes Clay killed Emily. Why volunteer an alibi for him? If you're trying to pin a murder on somebody, pin it on the guy who's already in prison."

Bible didn't respond. He stared out the window, scratching his chin in thought.

Andrea let out a long breath. The tightness in her chest had

gone away. Giving herself permission to talk about Emily Vaughn
had lifted an anvil off her back. Though the relief was small
consolation considering she was no closer to finding out whether
Clay Morrow was already a sadistic murderer before he met Laura
or if that had come afterward.

"Partner, I'm gonna tell you something you won't often hear,"
Bible said. "I was wrong. We got us a *two asses, one horse* situation here."

Andrea laughed. "I'll agree to being one of the asses if you
drop the horse metaphor."

"Fair enough," he said. "We've got Stilton, Nardo, Dean and
Ricky. What do they have in common? They are all either directly
or indirectly connected to both the activities at the farm and
Emily Vaughn's murder."

Andrea nodded, because they were all somehow linked together.

He asked, "You ever hear of a SODDI defense?"

"Some Other Dude Did It," Andrea said. Most criminals were
gladly willing to turn on other criminals, especially if making a
deal kept them out of prison. "But how does that help us? We
don't have leverage against any of them. You can't pin the death
threats on Ricky. We don't have anyone inside the farm who will
flip on Nardo or Wexler. Eric Blakely is dead. Clay Morrow will
fuck around with us because he's bored and he can fuck with
anybody. Stilton can say he forgot about Ricky's suicide attempts
or that he was embarrassed to bring them up because she nearly
died in his custody. Which is fair, because he should be embarrassed."

Bible waited to make sure she was finished. "Ricky was so
shaky that she had to pop some pills when you showed up at her
door. Wexler tried to scare you off by assaulting a US Marshal.
Nardo invoked his right to silence, then he chased you down for
a chat. Stilton could be the worst cop in the world, or he could
be trying to keep us away from the farm because he's afraid we'll
find out something."

The car turned silent again, but this time it was Andrea who
was in thought.

"They're all freaking out," she realized. "Stilton didn't call you
about Alice Poulsen's suicide. Ricky gave you the details in the

diner, but only after she, Nardo and Wexler had time to get their stories straight."

"We've got 'em right where we want 'em," Bible said. "In my experience, people who freak out tend to make a lot of mistakes. That's when you ramp up the pressure."

Pressure sounded like something that happened very slowly.

Andrea felt like every second of time since she'd left Glynco had been spent trying to surf a wave that she couldn't quite catch. As good as it felt to talk out the Emily Vaughn case with Bible, they still hadn't reached a resolution. Meanwhile, Alice Poulsen was still dead and Star Bonaire was a walking corpse who for all intents and purposes was slowly digging her own grave.

The *why* of Andrea joining the Marshal Service didn't have a definitive answer, but she sure as hell hadn't gone through more than four months of absolute hell to end up sitting on her ass when a desperate young woman begged her for help.

She asked Bible, "What can we do?"

"It's five fifteen, partner. What do you think we're going to do?"

Andrea swallowed back her disappointment. What they had to do was relieve Mitt Harri and Bryan Krump. The two men had been patrolling the Vaughn estate since six this morning. Andrea and Bible were expected to report for duty in forty-five minutes.

"Marshal rule number three," Bible said. "Always do your job."

Andrea leaned against the wall as she waited for her order to be called at McDonald's. Both she and Bible had agreed the diner wasn't the best place for dinner tonight. He had driven to a fast-food joint just outside the town limits. And then he'd grinned at Andrea when they'd pulled into the parking lot, because the address put the restaurant in exactly the same spot that Skeeter's Grill had occupied forty years ago when Emily Vaughn's body was found inside their Dumpster.

She looked at her phone, mindlessly scrolling through Insta because there was literally nothing else she could do. The last twenty-four hours had finally hit her like twelve tons of bricks. Four hours of sleep was not enough for an adult woman. Every single nerve in her body felt raw. Every emotion felt drained. If she ran through the Emily Vaughn case again, her head would explode. If she thought about Alice Poulsen and Star Bonaire one more second, her heart would probably explode, too.

To punish herself, she opened her texts and reviewed Mike's attempts to get her attention. The gnus, the dik-pic. He might honestly believe that he'd taken the first plane to Delaware in pursuit of his job, but he could've made a phone call. He had wanted to see Andrea in person. He had wanted to know that she was safe. And she had kicked him in the teeth for his troubles.

She stared at the blinking cursor in the message panel. Mike was probably on a plane back to Atlanta by now. She needed to apologize to him. She *had* to apologize to him. She had been so damn shitty.

Why had she been so shitty?

A notification banner dipped into the screen. Laura had sent a link to crime statistics in the metropolitan Portland area broken down by neighborhood. She'd added—

Can do a deeper dive when you tell me in which areas you would like to live.

Andrea clicked off her phone. She wanted to live in a pineapple under the sea.

"Thirty-six?"

Andrea jumped like she'd won at bingo. She grabbed the bags and drinks off the counter. Bible was on the phone when she opened the door to his SUV.

"I hear ya, Boss." He winked at Andrea. "We're heading over to the judge's place now. Running a little late. Don't think I'm gonna have time to call my wife."

"I hope she understands." Compton ended the call.

Bible pulled out of the parking space, telling Andrea, "The boss figured our pressure campaign could stand the heat getting turned up a little."

Andrea couldn't do any more riddles. She jammed their Cokes into the cup holders and opened her Happy Meal.

Bible said, "She had the press office grant an interview with a couple of reporters from one of the largest newspapers in Denmark. Over half the country reads it. Granted, that's maybe two hundred people and some of the more socially engaged hedgehogs, but the story might stir up some interests elsewhere."

Andrea chewed her fries.

"The reporters are flying over first thing. Should be in Longbill Beach by late afternoon. I don't know about you, partner, but I'm guessing Ricky will start sweating when she sees two reporters poking around town. And Dean Wexler sure as shit won't like a couple of nosy Danes knocking on his door asking why something is rotten in the state of Delaware."

She appreciated the *Hamlet* reference, but Andrea could not follow him down the path of hopefulness again. "European libel laws are even tougher than ours. They're going to run into the same problem we have. The girls at the farm aren't talking. No one is talking."

"Marshal rule number sixteen: slow and steady wins the race."

Bible was smiling as he unwrapped his cheeseburger, but he seemed to pick up on her mood. He clicked on the radio. Yacht Rock trilled softly from the speakers. He drove with one hand as he took tiny bites of his burger.

Andrea finished her fries. She felt bad for her deflated mood in the face of Bible's relentless positivity. Given the fact that he had endured unspeakable torture at the hands of a Mexican drug cartel, she should've been impressed that he managed to get out of bed in the morning, let alone joke about hedgehogs. Now, she found herself content to listen to the sound of his chewing over Toto's 'Rosanna'. There was only a couple of hours of sunlight left in one of the longest days of her life. She was looking at twelve hours of walking the Vaughn estate because of a threat that wasn't exactly anonymous anymore.

To keep herself from spinning the magic dial of her thoughts from Mike to Emily to Alice to Star to Ricky to Clay to Jack to Nardo to Blake to Dean, Andrea stared out the window. They were in another residential neighborhood, this one not upscale but not blue-collar, either. The town of Longbill Beach was basically one giant circle with a state forest in the middle. Ricky's house, the downtown area, the Vaughn estate and the farm were spokes on the wheel. You could probably walk from one side to the other in twenty minutes.

"Hey partner?" Bible turned down the radio. "I gotta confession."

His confessions so far had been more like shocking revelations. She told him, "I don't think that word means what you think it means."

He laughed good-naturedly. "Don't tell the boss, but I cleared it with Harri and Krump that we're gonna be a little late. We're only about three minutes from the Judge's house as the crow flies. Figured you wouldn't mind if we made another stop."

He didn't wait for her opinion. The SUV slowed. Bible pulled to the side of the road.

Andrea looked at the small cottage they were parked in front of. Gray asbestos tiles. Black trim. Seashells had been glued all over the mailbox. A converted attic with an eyebrow dormer in the shingled roof. The yard was overgrown, but not with weeds. The natural, low-water consumption landscaping reminded her of Laura's yard.

Bible provided, "This is where Star Bonaire grew up. Her mom's living there now. Thought we'd drop in for a chat, see if Melody Brickel knows anything about her daughter's situation at the farm."

Andrea caught the sly look he gave her before opening the door. Bible knew that Andrea recognized the name. She should have been surprised by the revelation, but it made a certain kind of sense that Melody Brickel was Star Bonaire's mother.

She glanced around the street before following Bible up the walkway. The houses were tidier and farther apart than the ones in Ricky's neighborhood. A yellow Prius was in the drive. A long cord plugged into the car and snaked into an outlet inside the carport. There was a water collection tank to catch the run-off from the gutters. Solar panels stood proud on the sway-backed roof. Andrea's small-town experience told her that the copper rain chains alone could make the locals think that Melody was crazy.

Bible said, "Guess ol' Star gets her green thumb from her mom."

Andrea doubted that was something Melody was happy about. She stopped at the bottom of the steps and let Bible go ahead of her to the front door. She didn't think Melody Brickel would greet them with an AR-15, but it was better to be safe than sorry. Sometimes a crazy bitch was really a crazy bitch.

Bible gave two soft knocks. The door opened almost immediately.

An older woman with short, shaggy, dark hair peered at them from the other side of the screen. She had to be Ricky's age but she could've easily passed for ten years younger. She was also incredibly fit. Her tight black top showed sculpted arms and shoulders. A colorful tattoo of a butterfly was on the back of her right hand. Her left eyebrow was pierced with a small silver hoop.

Bible asked, "Melody Brickel?"

"The one and only." Melody looked at Bible's shirt. "USMS? If the M stands for Mormon, you're barking up the wrong tree."

"United States Marshal Service." Bible gave her one of his better smiles. "I'm Deputy Bible. This is Deputy Oliver."

"Well." Her arms crossed over her chest. She glanced back at Andrea. "Let me feed my cats before you take me in, please. I know I violated my restraining order. I'm not going to tack on lying to a police officer on top of everything else."

Bible asked, "What kind of cats you got?"

Melody's eyes narrowed, but she said, "A bushy little calico and a very talkative Siamese."

"I gotta Siamese called Hedy," Bible said. "My wife calls her my girlfriend because I love her so much."

Melody looked back at Andrea, then at Bible. "You'll have to forgive me. I thought Marshals spent their time guarding airplanes and tracking down fugitives."

"Well, you're only half right there, ma'am. Federal Air Marshals are part of the Transportation and Security Administration of the Department of Homeland Security. US Marshals are with the Department of Justice. Fugitive-tracking is only one of the many services we offer." Bible smiled again. "Right now, we're just here to talk."

She wasn't amused. "According to my lawyer, I shouldn't talk to the police without calling him first."

"Sounds like good advice."

"Well, you've clearly never had to pay a legal bill." She opened the door. "Come in. Let's get this over with."

As with Wexler's farmhouse, Andrea found herself surprised by the interior of the cottage. Based on the overgrown yard and rainwater collection, she'd assumed Melody Brickel's decorating style would lean toward quilts and spirit catchers. Instead, the woman seemed to prefer large floral patterns from the 1970s with a few anachronistic posters of the Eurythmics and the Go-Go's doing their best to complement the explosion of color.

"My mother's house," Melody explained. "I moved back here four years ago when I found out Star had lost her mind. Let's go to the back. It's more comfortable there."

Bible let Andrea take the lead as they followed Melody through the living room. Andrea looked down at the woman's left ankle. Her pants were cropped. There was no silver band.

"This is Star. My Star, at least." Melody had stopped at a series of photographs filling the short hallway. "I know what you're thinking, but I named her after Ringo Starr. She dropped the second *R* in middle school. I swear I wasn't setting her up to join a cult."

Andrea tried not to respond to the word *cult*. She leaned toward the photos. She barely recognized the young girl doing all the things that young girls did in photos. Star was ghostly now, nothing like the vibrant, healthy-looking teenager who smiled so openly at the camera.

Melody said what they were all thinking. "She's going to end up dead if she stays at that place."

Andrea followed her through into the kitchen, which was as cluttered as Ricky's, but in a warm and welcoming way. A large pot simmered on the stove. The smell of yeast filled the air. There was a loaf of bread baking in the oven, which made Star's bread-making feel even more poignant.

"Tell me something," Bible said to Melody. "I'm not asking as a Marshal, just out of curiosity. Why'd you violate your restraining order?"

"I heard about the dead girl in the field. I had to know whether or not it was Star." Melody stopped to stir the pot on the stove. "Now you tell me, Mr. Bible, not as a Marshal but as a human being. Did that girl kill herself or did she die on her own?"

Bible asked, "What's that mean—on her own?"

"What they're doing is a slow suicide," Melody said. "That I know of, two of them have already starved to death. Literally. Their bodies gave out and they died."

Bible asked, "When was this?"

She put down the spoon. "One was three years ago. The other was last May. I won't give you their names because there's nothing you can do, and it would be piling onto a tragedy for you to give their grieving parents any hope."

Bible nodded, but asked, "How do you know about the two deaths?"

"I'm part of a group of parents and family members who have lost their children to Dean Wexler. We had a website, but we were forced to take it down. Our Facebook page kept getting attacked. They even found us on the dark web. We were all doxed, sent death threats. Every penny that damn place makes is spent protecting Dean Wexler."

Melody's pain was so palpable that Andrea felt helpless all over again. "What about Nardo?"

"He's never been anything more than a sick opportunist. Dean is the Charles Manson of the place." Melody placed the lid back on the pot. "If there's any justice in the world, he'll die a miserable, excruciating death."

"Life usually makes you pay for your personality," Bible said. "Any chance you know the names of any girls who got away? Maybe they're willing to—"

"There's not a chance in hell," Melody said. "Mr. Bible, I have no retirement left. I'm coasting to social security, teaching the piccolo to kindergartners, because every dime I have ever earned has gone to lawyers who could not help get my daughter out of that place. As far as I'm concerned, any girl who has the strength or courage to pull away from Dean Wexler should be left in peace."

"I hear ya loud and clear," Bible said. "But going back to what you said about those girls who lost their lives, I'm wondering why no one took their stories to the press?"

"You mean the *New York Times*? The *Washington Post*? The *Baltimore Sun*?" She gave a rueful laugh. "Slow and deliberate starvation isn't very sexy compared to a worldwide pandemic, insane election conspiracies, whatever social upheaval is going on in the world and a mass shooting every single week. The few reporters who returned my calls told me to give it time."

"I understand," he said.

"Mr. Bible, forgive me, but I don't think you do. Time is the very thing that's going to kill my daughter." Melody had put her hands on her hips. "When Star first got wrapped up in this madness, I talked to an eating disorder specialist about what to expect. My mother was a nurse. I needed to understand the science. Anorexia nervosa has the highest mortality rate of all mental health disorders. Typically, the heart simply gives out. There's not enough potassium and calcium to generate the electricity required to maintain a normal heartbeat."

Andrea thought about Star's deliberate movements around the kitchen. The long pauses in between. She was so malnourished that the slightest expenditure of energy exhausted her.

Melody continued, "If their heart doesn't stop, there's the osteopenia from the loss of calcium. Their bones are more susceptible to breaks, and the breaks don't heal. Infections are more life-threatening because the immune system is compromised. The neurological problems range from seizures to cognitive deficits caused by structural changes in the brain. And don't forget anemia, gastrointestinal disorders, organ failure, hormonal fluctuations, infertility—though I suppose that part is very convenient for Dean and Nardo."

Bible asked, "How's that?"

"Mr. Bible, I'm not the hysterical, febrile woman Jack Stilton has made me out to be. Why else would they be starving and brutalizing my daughter if they weren't fucking her?"

She let them consider her words as she led them to the sunroom off the kitchen.

Again, Andrea was surprised by the décor. One entire wall was taken up by a massive vinyl album collection. A professional drum kit filled the corner, which explained the Ringo Starr affinity. The framed posters on the walls were clearly originals. Andrea recognized the festivals. Bonnaroo. Burning Man. Coachella. Lilith Fair. Lollapalooza. Signatures were scrawled across the band names.

"I mostly work as a session drummer now, but my husband and I toured for thirty years," Melody explained. "My mother watched Star while we were on the road. I never left her for more than two weeks at a time, but they were very close. Then, four and a half years ago Mother died. I think that's what triggered Star to start searching for meaning. She felt lost. I'm her mother so obviously I couldn't give her what she needed. For better or worse, the farm gave her something to believe in."

Bible sat on the futon, which was so low that his knees were at chest-level. "Is your husband still touring?"

"Denny passed away the year before my mother. Looking back, that's when Star began to go downhill. She was experimenting with drugs. Which was fine. I experimented with drugs—they were fabulous. But Star couldn't stop." Melody sat down cross-legged on the floor. A tubby calico appeared out of nowhere and crawled into her lap. "Dean Wexler aside, I was actually glad when she started volunteering at the farm. She stopped using. She was my little girl again. It's funny how easy it is to see all of your mistakes after the fact."

Bible expertly pulled her away from the self-recriminations. "What was that like? Touring around and such?"

"It was a fucking blast." She gave a deep belly laugh. "We weren't huge, but we were good enough to make a living, which is more than most can say. I went by Melody Bricks, short for Brickel, not to be confused with Edie Brickell. That's me in the corner, to quote R.E.M."

Andrea felt caught out. Her eyes had wandered to the alpha-betized vinyl collection. The Melody Bricks Experience was faced out in the B section. A younger version of Melody was on the front. She was screaming into a microphone from behind her drum kit. Andrea read some of the track names. "Everything Gone"; "Misery Loves Comity"; "Absent in Absentia." Very New Wave.

Melody told her, "There's a signed *Missundaztood* in there. I got to sit in with Pink on the Midwest swing of the Party Tour. Feel free to poke around."

Andrea wasn't here for the record collection, but Bible had established an easy tempo with the woman that she didn't want to break.

"Hold on before we get to the hard part." Melody leaned over and started cranking open the windows. A light breeze filled the room. "Menopause is not for sissies."

"Gotta agree with you there." Bible chuckled. "My wife, Cussy, I don't know how she does it."

Melody sat back on the floor. "As much fun as it is to talk about cats and menopause with you, Mr. Bible, let's please cut to the chase."

"My partner and I were out at the farm this morning." Bible paused. "We saw your daughter."

Andrea looked away from the albums. Tears had sprung into Melody's eyes.

"Is she—" Melody's voice caught. "Is she all right?"

"She's alive," Bible told her. "I didn't speak to her, but—"

His work phone started ringing. He checked the caller ID.

"Mr. Bible," Melody said. "Please don't answer that."

"It's just my boss. She can wait." Bible silenced the ringer. "Oliver, show her the photograph that Star took with your phone."

"What?" Melody stood up. "How did Star get your phone?"

"I left it for her on the counter." Andrea tucked the album she was holding under her arm so that she could retrieve her iPhone. "You can take a photo without the password."

"Yes," Melody said. "The button is on the lock screen. Can you hurry, please?"

Andrea tapped in her code and swiped through to the photo.

Melody gently took the phone away from Andrea. Her hands were trembling. She zoomed in on the word Star had drawn in the flour.

Help.

Melody's throat worked. She didn't wipe the tears streaming from her eyes. Andrea assumed that after everything Melody had survived over the last four years, she was no stranger to crying.

Melody asked, "Was she okay? Did she—did she speak or . . . ?"

Andrea looked at Bible. "No, ma'am. We didn't speak. She was very thin, but she was moving around. The flour was on the counter because she was baking bread."

Melody's tears kept flowing as she stared at what was probably her only recent proof that her daughter was still alive. "She's done something like this before. Once, she passed a note to a delivery driver. A few months ago, she called me in the middle of the night and told me that she wanted to come home."

"What did you do?" Andrea asked.

"I got Jack involved. To his credit, he went out both times and tried to make a stink. But Star wouldn't cooperate. She never cooperates. I think she likes it—the attention. My therapist says she must be getting something out of it. People don't do things unless there's a reward. Even if there's negative consequences. There is comfort in the familiar."

"What about—" Andrea didn't know how to frame the question, so she was blunt. "You tried to kidnap her and take her to a deprogrammer?"

"I did." Melody's smile was weak. She slid the album out from Andrea's arm and used that as an excuse to change the subject. "Jinx at Monterey Live. Stéphane Grappelli sat in for 'Daphne'. Are you a jazz fan?"

Andrea shook her head. "My father loves it."

"Sorry, ladies." Bible was looking at his personal phone. "That's my wife. Can't ignore her. If you don't mind, I'll take it outside."

"Help yourself." Melody placed the album on top of the shelves as Bible left through the kitchen. She stared down at Star's flour photo again. Before Andrea could stop her, she had swiped to the previous picture.

Alice Poulsen's concave face filled the screen.

Glassy eyes. Sunken cheeks. Dried foam around pale blue lips. There was no exclamation of horror.

Melody swiped back again, then again. She seemed impassive as she stared at the bright red bedsores on Alice Poulsen's shoulder blades. Her stark ribs. Her brittle fingernails. The light bruises ringing her wrists.

Melody asked, "Do you know that a bruised or sprained wrist is one of the most common signs of domestic violence?"

Andrea felt herself wanting to cradle her wrist again.

"My therapist told me that," Melody said. "There are so many nerves and ligaments and bones in that one small space. They grab you there, and you do whatever they want."

Andrea was familiar with pain compliance, but she hadn't considered it in the context of domestic violence.

"That's how it started with Star. She came home with her wrist wrapped in a bandage. She was so deep into her addiction. I didn't want to know how it happened. I was so caught up in Mother's estate and trying to figure out what to do with my life."

Andrea didn't try to make excuses because she knew that Melody wouldn't accept them.

"Dean is an animal—any man who abuses a woman is. They have an instinct that tells them to start off slowly. Grab her wrist and see if she lets you get away with it. Then her shoulder or her arm. Then, before too long, their hands are around her neck. They're so good at knowing who will keep their mouths shut and put up with it."

Melody's gaze was on the phone again. She had found the first photograph Andrea had taken of Alice Poulsen lying naked in the field. Melody's tears had never really stopped, but now they formed a river down her face, welling into the collar of her shirt.

She said, "This is going to be Star one day, and there's not a damn thing I can do about it."

Andrea gently made to take back the phone, but Melody finally let out a cry—not from horror, but from surprise. She'd swiped one last time and discovered the photograph of the mixtape liner notes Andrea had taken of Judith's collage.

"My God, I'd forgotten all about this!" She wiped her eyes. "Where did you find it?"

Andrea protected Judith by instinct. "In a box of Emily's things at the Vaughns'."

"Of course." Melody easily accepted the explanation. "I wasn't allowed to talk to Emily, but I put mixtapes in her mailbox every few weeks. This is the last one I made for her before she was murdered. Look at my silly handwriting. I was trying to disguise my identity in case my mother somehow found out I was disobeying her."

Andrea pretended to look at the text, but she already knew it by heart. "Did you know Emily well?"

"Not as well as I wanted to. She was an amazing girl, but she had her group. We shared a love of music. It's such a tragedy that she's gone and Dean Wexler is still walking the face of this earth."

Andrea said, "I've heard a lot about Emily's drug use."

"Oh, that's bullshit." Melody finally handed back the phone. "Don't get me wrong—none of us Just Said No to drugs, but Emily was never into the hard stuff. I hate to sound like my mother, but she hung around with a bad crowd."

Andrea couldn't agree more. "Do you have any theories about who killed her?"

"I mean—" Melody sputtered air between her lips. "Everybody seems to think it was Clay. And look at what he did after he left town. If that's not a pattern, I don't know what is."

"Ricky Fontaine had a theory." Andrea noted Melody's arched eyebrow when she'd heard Ricky's name. "She thinks that Jack Stilton did it."

"For fucksakes!" Melody's booming laugh filled the room. "Ricky is such a lying cunt. They always hated Jack. We're talking all the way back to kindergarten. Nardo in particular took a sick joy out of torturing him. Emily hated him for it. She always took up for Jack. There's no way he would've ever hurt her."

Andrea thought of the restraining order. "Ricky can be a very vindictive person."

"Understatement of the year. The only thing Ricky Blakely has ever cared about is Nardo Fontaine. She's obsessed with him, and he never misses an opportunity to screw with her." Melody's hands had gone to her hips again. "At least once a week Nardo shows up late at that stupid diner. He drags along Star so she can play his audience. It's all disgusting, really, but like I said— they must be getting something out of it. There's comfort in the familiar."

For the first time, Andrea questioned Melody's veracity. "Ricky has a permanent restraining order against her. She can't go within twenty feet of Nardo."

"I'm legally barred from the farm and I was there this morning," Melody pointed out. "The law doesn't matter if no one is going to enforce it."

Andrea could not say that she was wrong. "Can I ask your opinion on something else Ricky told me?"

"I'm clearly on a tear," Melody acknowledged. "Go ahead."

"She said that whatever is happening at the farm today is the same shit that happened to Emily forty years ago."

"Huh," Melody said.

Not *No way*, or *Ricky's full of shit* or another *For fucksakes*. And then Melody added, "Well, maybe?"

Andrea felt her heart start to shake in her chest. Melody had known Emily. She knew the group. She knew exactly what was happening at the farm.

"Okay—" Melody paused to gather her thoughts. "My mother told me some stuff before she died. I'm not supposed to know because there was a medical confidentiality, but surely that doesn't matter anymore."

Andrea held her breath.

"This is a little from Mom and a little from what I heard at school and a little from what Emily told me herself," Melody prefaced. "Emily was drugged and raped at a party. She literally had no memory of what happened. I don't think she ever found out who raped her. And it wasn't a party like what you're thinking. It was only ever her and the clique. That's Nardo, Blake, Ricky and Clay."

"The clique?" Andrea remembered Ricky using the same phrase.

"Oh, yes, *the clique*. Everyone thought they were so mysterious." Melody rolled her eyes. "The hilarious part was, they were all kind of pathetic—and I say this as a person who was pathetic myself. Emily and I were both band geeks. We wore *Mork & Mindy* rainbow suspenders and head gear for our braces."

Andrea almost laughed. She had assumed the exact opposite. "From her photos, Emily was very pretty."

"It doesn't matter how pretty you are if you don't know it," Melody said. "Ricky was wildly unpopular. She was volatile and dramatic, even for a teenage girl. And Blake was always calculating. Every conversation, he was looking for a way to exploit you. Then there's Nardo. Kids would literally take a different route to class so that they wouldn't run into him. He was and still is unbelievably cruel."

Andrea had never before heard anyone describe them all so clearly. "And Clay?"

"Well, he brought them together, didn't he? He made them feel special, part of *the clique*. They would've been nothing without him. All he demanded in return was their unquestioning devotion. And that extended to breaking into cars, taking drugs—whatever Clay wanted them to do." Her shrug belied everything the group had given up in return. "Clay was the only one of them who was genuinely popular. Everyone loved him. He had an uncanny ability to find out what you were missing and fill the void. He was a chameleon, even back then."

Andrea knew that he was still a chameleon now. "What about Dean Wexler?"

"He was the creepy gym teacher who kept *accidentally* walking into the girls' locker room when we were changing. And now, you could say that he's nothing but a cheap imitation of Clay Morrow. You'd think it was the opposite since Dean was older, but it's hard to convey how malicious Clay's influence was. Dean studied at the altar." Melody's tone changed at the mention of her daughter's tormentor. "At least Clay had charm. Dean is so primitive. He only cares about control. He is a wraith from the bowels of hell."

"Can we go back to something you said earlier?" Andrea gently steered her away from Wexler. "What was Emily's reaction when she realized she'd been raped? She must've been devastated."

"She was," Melody said. "My mother was there when Emily found out she was pregnant. She said it was one of the most painful moments of her life. Emily was in shock. Mother said it wasn't the pregnancy at that point so much as the betrayal that cut Emily to the bone. The clique was her life. To have one of them do such an unthinkable thing to her was unimaginable. She was obsessed with trying to find out who did it. She called it her *Columbo Investigation*."

"After the TV detective?"

"Peter Falk. Amazing actor," Melody said. "Emily approached the investigation very seriously. I told you she was a nerd. She did proper interviews with people. She wrote everything down. I would see her in class or in the hall poring over her notes, trying to see if she had missed anything. I suppose it was like a diary. She was never without it. I felt so sorry for her. Asking so many questions was probably what got her killed."

Andrea wondered if pieces of Emily's Columbo Investigation had made it into teenage Judith's collage. The stray lines felt like the sort of affirmations a geeky young girl might write to bolster herself—

Keep working it out! You will find the truth!!!

She asked Melody, "Which people did Emily investigate?"

Melody shrugged. "I'm assuming the same people Jack's dad investigated."

Clayton Morrow. Jack Stilton. Bernard Fontaine. Eric Blakely. Dean Wexler.

Andrea asked, "How does what happened to Emily at the party tie into what's happening at the farm? Is Dean drugging the girls?"

"They don't have to be drugged. Obviously, the girls will do whatever Dean wants." Melody shrugged again. "It's cunning, isn't it? The way they instinctively choose the girls who will be vulnerable to their manipulations. Nardo screens them. I remember Star being very excited about her interviews. I blame myself for not noticing that she was losing too much weight. I mean, you never say that to a woman, do you—you're too thin?"

Andrea shook her head, though she knew that Melody wasn't looking for validation.

"I stopped seeing her after she moved to the farm. That's part of the pattern. Dean isolates them from their families. First, there are no in-person visits, then only phone calls, then all you get is the occasional email, then nothing. Every parent I speak with tells the exact same story. And looking back, it's the same thing Clay did with the clique. They were completely isolated. All but Emily, but her life was incredibly narrow because of him."

Andrea had to ask, "Do you know about the ankle bracelets the girls wear at the farm?"

"Yes." Melody took a quick breath. The bracelet was clearly difficult for her to talk about. "I saw it a few days after Star stopped communicating with me. I drove over there and pounded on the door and demanded that they let me see her. She was so proud of the anklet, as if she'd been initiated into something special. You have to earn one, apparently. As if Dean's still a teacher handing out 'A's to his favorite students. I don't understand it."

Andrea couldn't understand it, either. "You said he acted creepy in school. Where does the weight thing come in?"

"He was always into health food and ultra-marathon running and all that stuff that everyone thought was crazy in the eighties. I remember him being particularly cruel to the overweight girl in class, but of course everyone was cruel to her. Groups of kids can be sadistic by nature. But he singled her out. He would leave diet plans on her desk. He would make noises with his mouth when she walked." Melody shook her head in disgust. "In any case, it's not hard to draw a direct line from past Dean to the current Dean's anorexia fetish. And of course sex is sex. It makes sense to blend his two passions."

"What about Star?" Andrea asked. "What's she getting out of this?"

"I asked her once, back when she would still speak to me, and she gave me some bullshit drivel about love," Melody said. "The thing that I learned from the eating disorder specialist is that with anorexia, starvation can become addictive, and it can act like a hallucinogenic on the system. At first, you go into dreamlike trances where you're highly suggestible. Then eventually, your brain will shut down to conserve energy. You lose—"

Melody's hand went to her mouth. Tears wept from her eyes again. She was clearly thinking about her own daughter.

"Take your time," Andrea said.

Several seconds passed before Melody slowly dropped away her hand. "You lose consciousness. That's what happens when you deprive your body of basic nutrition. You pass out. You're completely senseless."

Andrea repeated Ricky's words. "'The shit that's happening at the farm is the same shit that happened to Emily Vaughn forty years ago.'"

"Yes, you could say that Emily was senseless when she was raped," Melody said. "You know, when I first realized what was happening to Star, all I could think was, what kind of twisted fucker wants to have sex with a woman who's for all practical purposes in a coma?"

Clayton Morrow. Jack Stilton. Bernard Fontaine. Eric Blakely. Dean Wexler.

"It's almost a form of necrophilia, isn't it? The woman has no idea what the man is doing. She's completely helpless the entire time. She can't tell him to stop or even tell him to keep going if it feels good. She's an inanimate series of holes. She might as well be a mannequin. What kind of sadist gets off on that?"

Andrea looked down at her left hand. The bruise had started to show. There was a dark band around her wrist that had been left by Dean Wexler's thumb and fingers.

"Oliver!"

They both jumped when Bible slammed open the front door. He called, "I need you!"

The alarm in his voice set off a chain reaction inside of Andrea's body.

At the academy, they had spent hours talking about adrenaline, how it could save you or kill you. The hormone, also called epinephrine, flooded into your bloodstream, triggering your fight-or-flight response. Your senses became finely honed. Your nervous system lit up. At the microscopic level, air passages dilated and blood vessels contracted, redirecting energy toward the lungs and major muscle groups.

Andrea was unaware of any of this happening as she bolted toward the door. She was outside before she realized that she was even moving. Her foot hit the top of the stairs. She leapt into the air and landed hard on the walkway. Bible was already in his SUV. The window was down.

"Look!" He pointed to a plume of black smoke curling in the distance. "That's the judge's house. Call it in!"

Bible was so panicked that he didn't even wait for Andrea to get into the car. He was peeling away as she dialed 911. Dusk had turned the sky iridescent. She could barely see Bible taking a sharp left turn at the end of the street. Andrea didn't follow him. He'd told her earlier that the house was three minutes away as the crow flies. The smoke acted like a giant arrow pointing her in the right direction.

She dialed 911 as she darted into the yard across from Melody's cottage. Andrea was jumping over a chain-link fence when the emergency operator finally picked up.

"There's a fire at—"

"Judge Vaughn's," the woman said. "We've got units responding."

Andrea jammed her phone back into her pocket. She climbed over a wooden fence. She landed on a trashcan, then tumbled to the ground. She could smell the smoke now, thick and pungent. The dark color told her that man-made materials were burning. Wood and drywall and furniture. She pushed her legs to keep pumping. Her lungs were screaming. The wind shifted, sending smoke into her face. Her eyes were stinging so badly that she could barely keep them open.

She broke through a line of trees and found herself across the street from the judge's estate. Flames licked up from the back of the house. Andrea had walked the property for hours the night before. She mentally called up the interior of the house. Two wings, north and south. The main section with the library, office, formal living room and dining room. The kitchen in the back by the garage. She had never gone upstairs, but she knew that the judge and her husband slept on the second floor of the north wing. She had seen the lights on in their bedroom as she walked the rounds. Their balcony overlooked Judith's studio.

"Fuck!" she groaned, pushing herself back into a full run.

The studio.

Turpentine. Spray adhesive. Paints. Mordant. Acids. Canvas and wood and so many things that could either catch on fire or cause an explosion that could take out the rest of the house.

Bible's SUV caught up to her on the driveway. She banged her hand on the side panel as she ran alongside it.

"The studio!" she screamed.

"Go!" he yelled, speeding up to pass her.

She watched Bible's SUV slide to a stop in front of the garage. He jumped out of the car. A lumbering shape came out of the garage. Harri and Krump. They carried Franklin Vaughn between them. The judge trailed behind, clutching a large briefcase to her chest. The thing was so heavy that the old woman nearly stumbled before Bible grabbed her by the waist and carried her away from the flames.

Andrea was skirting around the side of the house when she caught sight of Guinevere running back into the garage. She hesitated, but then Bible chased after the girl. Andrea picked up her pace. None of it would matter if the studio caught fire. The house would be leveled before anyone could reach a safe distance.

Her foot slipped as she turned the corner. The roaring blaze illuminated the backyard. The English garden. The pool. The studio. Andrea coughed, strangled by the thick, acrid fumes. The fire had engulfed the judge's bedroom. Flames licked out of the windows, chewed away at the wood accents, reached like desperately searching hands toward the studio.

Andrea tripped.

She fell flat on her face. Her nose crunched against the stone path. Stars filled her vision. She squinted them away as she looked behind her, trying to see what she'd tripped on. Turpentine. Cans of paint. Varnishes. Judith had beaten her to the studio. She was running back and forth, tossing the flammable liquids into the swimming pool.

Andrea pushed herself up.

She ran into the studio and started grabbing anything that looked dangerous—spray cans, pots of liquid adhesive. She passed Judith on the way to the pool. Their eyes met for a second. They both knew how deadly the chemicals could be. The first class you took in art school started with all the ways you could poison or burn yourself alive.

Andrea tossed an armful of cans into the pool before heading back for more. The smoke thickened inside her chest. Her fight or flight was turning on her, telling her to back away. There was fresh air in the distance. Or she could lie down. She could staunch the blood that was rolling down her throat. She could close her eyes and rest.

She shook her head as hard as she could, knocking some sense into herself. She threw herself into a run toward the studio. Judith was dragging a five-gallon bucket behind her. Andrea recognized the markings on the label. Sulfuric acid wasn't flammable by itself, but under the wrong circumstances, it could turn into hydrogen gas, the same type of gas that had taken down the *Hindenburg*.

Andrea grabbed onto the handle. The hot metal seared into

her hand. The bucket was almost full, which meant it weighed about seventy pounds. They both tried to lift it together. Andrea groaned from the strain. The metal ring was like a razor cutting into her palms. Her teeth rattled from the effort. Her lungs couldn't expand any longer. Her vision started to go.

"Lift!" Judith screamed.

Andrea lifted. Her legs were shaking as she dragged the acid across the lawn. She heard a loud crack behind her. The earth shuddered beneath her feet. The supports for the balcony had started to fall. The upper floor was about to slide directly into the studio.

"Go!" Andrea yelled, straining against the weight.

And then the weight was suddenly gone.

Andrea felt a moment of lightness as she was launched into the air, then the cold slap of the water as her head went under. She fell sideways, her shoulder jarring against the bottom of the pool. Blood came into her mouth. She had bitten her lip. Judith floated limply beside her, hands drifting above her shoulders. The bucket gently settled to the bottom. Andrea turned, looking up at the surface. She saw flames shooting across the water. Then pieces of twisted metal rained down. Then sparkling shards of glass.

Then everything went black.

OCTOBER 21, 1981

Emily trekked toward home. She felt hot and sticky. Her bladder was going to pop. Today had been the longest day she had ever experienced. From the moment she'd left her hiding place in the back of the library, every minute had felt like an hour. Every hour had felt like a day. At lunch, she had tried to eat, but the food had taken on a metallic taste. By fourth period, she was so exhausted that she could barely put one foot in front of the other. Then fifth period rolled around and Emily had found herself startled awake by the teacher clapping together his hands for her attention.

Emily had said that she wasn't feeling well. There was no argument from the teacher. He'd let her leave twenty minutes before the final bell. In retrospect, slipping out into an empty hallway was the best thing for all concerned. As the day had dragged on, the giggles and stares had ebbed away and an open hostility had washed over the school. Even her math teacher had looked down his nose at her.

Why?

Until a few days ago, Emily had spent her entire nearly eighteen years of existence being the good girl, the teacher's pet, the great student, the friendly girl-next-door type who would always lend you her class notes or gladly offer to sit with you in the parking lot while you cried over a boy.

Now, she was a pariah.

Except for Melody Brickel, but Emily wasn't sure what to make of that.

The two of them had been periphery friends for years, always smiling to each other in the halls, talking about music and laughing along to silly jokes in band practice. They'd even bunked together a few times at band camp, though Emily had felt the pull back to the clique the second the bus had dropped them off back home.

And now, Melody had written her a letter. Emily didn't need to pull it out of her book bag to know what it said. She had read it over and over throughout the day, even hiding in the bathroom stall so she could analyze every word.

Hello!

I am sorry about what is happening to you. It is VERY unfair. You should know that I am STILL your friend even if I can't talk to you anymore. Or at least for the time being. Everything is so complicated. My mother is worried about me being around you. NOT that she thinks that you did ANYTHING wrong. She wanted me to make it CLEAR to you that what happened is NOT YOUR FAULT. Someone took advantage of you! The thing Mom is worried about is ME being hurt by association. Because people are SO MEAN, and I am already the subject of a lot of abuse because everyone thinks that I am weird. I always thought weirdness was one thing you and I had in common. But YOU are NOT weird because you don't belong (like ME). Your weirdness comes from your LOVE and ACCEPTANCE of all kinds of people. No one else at school is NICE to everybody no matter who they are or where they live or if they are smart or whatever. You are so genuinely KIND. You DO NOT deserve what people are saying. Maybe when this is over we can be friends again. I am still going to be a world-famous musician one day and you will be a lawyer who helps people and everything will be awesome again. Until that happens I LOVE YOU and I am SO SORRY!!! Keep working it out! YOU WILL FIND THE TRUTH!!!
—Your Friend

PS: Sorry this is messy I was LITERALLY CRYING!!! the whole time I wrote this.

The notebook paper was crinkled where Melody's tears had dried. She had circled them like crime scene exhibits, as if she needed to prove beyond a reasonable doubt that she was heartbroken.

What was Emily supposed to do with the letter? What was she supposed to think? She couldn't very well go up to Melody and ask her.

. . . I am STILL your friend even if I can't talk to you anymore.

The note had been wrapped around a cassette tape, secured by a green rubber band. Melody had made Emily a copy of the Go-Go's album. She'd done a very good mock-up of the cover art using a fountain pen and magic markers. Her usual block print had been replaced by a cool, funky script.

Keep working it out! YOU WILL FIND THE TRUTH!!!

She meant Emily's Columbo Investigation. She had seen Emily furiously working the pages as if she could somehow manage to put together the puzzle. In a moment of weakness, Emily had confessed that she was trying to find out who had taken advantage of her at the party. She had even shown Melody some of the passages.

"'Took advantage of,'" Emily quoted from Melody's letter. What a phrase. As if Emily had been a two-for-one coupon or a half-priced steak dinner that someone had availed themselves of.

Not someone—

Clay, Nardo, Blake. Maybe Dean. Maybe Jack.

A car drove by at a slow pace.

Emily looked away because she didn't want to see the faces staring back. Her throat burned as she swallowed back tears. She really was a pariah now. She had lost the clique. She had one friend she could never speak to. The entire school had turned against her. And Cheese—

Jack.

The tears finally broke through. Nardo had said that Jack was at The Party. He'd said that Jack was *standing right there* when Emily had walked into the house.

Her eyes squeezed shut. She tried to take herself back to that moment. She walked through Nardo's front door. She stuck out her tongue for Clay to give her the tab of acid. She saw the Fontaines' sunken living room, the heavy drapes across the large windows, the sectional sofa that curved around a large projection screen.

She could not conjure any memories of Jack being at Nardo's. *Ever.*

Her eyes opened. She stared up at the beautiful, blue sky.

Jack sold pre-rolled joints. Emily knew that was a fact. He kept a sandwich bag full of them inside his coat pocket. It was common knowledge that Jack could hook you up. Everyone said he stole pot from the evidence room at the police station, but Emily knew that he got the weed from a cousin in Maryland and hand-rolled them himself. What she didn't know was whether or not Jack sold harder drugs.

She tried to take herself back to that night again.

Walking through the front door. Sticking out her tongue. Clay brandishing the tab of acid like a conductor summoning the orchestra's attention.

Jack had not been there. This was not a memory issue, or an LSD-induced black hole. This was common sense. Nardo hated Jack. All of the boys did, especially Clay. They went out of their way to be cruel to Jack, tripping him in the hall, slamming his lunch tray out of his hands, stealing his clothes out of his gym locker. And Jack went out of his way to avoid them at all costs. No matter how much money Nardo had offered, she could not see Jack willingly going to his house.

Emily thought about her Columbo conversation with Jack. One thing he'd said seemed to have particular relevance now—

Sometimes, they make up lies to throw the heat onto somebody else.

Nardo was definitely a liar. He lied to his parents about where he was going. He lied to Clay about not having any cigarettes left. He lied to Blake about not failing a history exam. He lied to Ricky all the time by not coming out and saying that he didn't have feelings for her and it was never going to happen. It was a game to him, telling people what he wanted them to know rather than simply giving the truth.

So why would Emily ever think that Nardo was telling the truth about Jack being at The Party?

And if Nardo was lying about The Party, was he lying for the sake of lying, or was he lying to cover his own ass?

The best person to talk about this with could possibly be the worst person to approach, but Emily was almost home and Jack was probably in the shed. Things had been particularly hard at home for him lately. She coached herself on how to question him as she walked up the long driveway. Jack had told her how to implement the Columbo strategy, so it likely wouldn't work on him. There would be no *one more thing*. Emily had to be honest with him and hope that, in return, he was honest with her.

She practiced aloud, trying to keep her tone even, her cadence light, almost whispering, "Did you do this to me?"

Emily closed her eyes and repeated the question. She listened carefully to her voice. She didn't want to be accusatory. She wasn't angry. In fact, she would probably be relieved to find out it was Cheese because it made a certain kind of sense that he would take advantage of a situation. He was so desperately lonely. He had very few friends. As far as Emily knew, he had never been on a date. Except for his weed business, he could probably go days without anyone his own age speaking to him.

Emily felt her head shaking. Even if she accepted that Jack had been at The Party, there was no way that the boys or even Ricky would've let Jack *take advantage of* Emily.

But Ricky had been passed out on the front lawn, according to Dean. And Blake and Nardo had both backed the story that they were in the upstairs bathroom. Everyone so far agreed that Clay and Emily had been out by the pool. They had been arguing. Were they arguing about Jack?

They had argued about him so many times before.

She heard a guttural sound come out of her throat. All of this endless speculation was exhausting. Her brain was on a carousel again. The house receded and plastic horses on poles started moving up and down. Tinny music drowned out the distant roar of the ocean. Tears rolled down her face. The carousel spun faster and faster. The world was blurring. Her eyes could barely stay open. Her brain finally, blissfully, turned itself off.

She had no idea how much time passed. One minute she was

trudging around the side of the house, the next she was sitting on the wooden bench inside her mother's English garden. When it was in season, flowers and plants spilled over into the walkway. Goldenrod. Black-eyed Susans. Milkweed. Great blue lobelia. The style of garden dated back to the eighteenth century, a rebellion against the symmetry and formality of the classic architectural garden.

That Esther allowed, let alone encouraged, something so wild and unstructured to grow in her yard had always struck Emily as odd. Given her mother's strict personality, it seemed like she would be more drawn toward tightly trimmed boxwoods and rectilinear patterns. The garden had always made Emily sad. It was a reminder that there was a part of her mother that she would never know.

"Emily?"

Clay sounded surprised to see her, though he was the one who was trespassing.

She asked, "What are you doing here?"

"I—" His eyes flickered toward the shed. "I needed something to take the edge off."

Emily smoothed together her lips. He'd come to score some pot and ended up seeing the last person on earth he wanted to see.

There were worse things that could happen to a person.

"Jack isn't here," she told him, though she had no idea whether or not Jack was in the shed. "I can tell him you came by."

"Forget about it. I'll catch up with him later." Instead of leaving, Clay shoved his hands in his pockets. He looked back at the shed with real longing. "It's been a rough couple of days."

She laughed. "Sorry it's been so hard on you."

He gave a heavy groan as he sat down beside her on the bench. "Aren't you going to ask me?"

Emily shook her head, because she finally just now realized that it was pointless to ask. No one was going to be honest with her.

"It wasn't me," Clay said, uselessly. "You know I don't—"

"Feel that way about me," Emily finished. "Yes, I know. Your minions have all repeated the line."

Clay sighed again. He kicked at the gravel. A streak of dirt was left in his wake. Emily would have to smooth over the mark after he left. Which was unsurprising. She and everyone else in the clique had been smoothing over Clay's mistakes for almost their entire lives.

He asked, "What are you going to do?"

Emily shrugged. No one had asked her what she was going to do. Her parents had decided, and now she was doing it.

He asked, "Can you feel it?"

Emily followed his gaze. He was looking at her stomach. Without thinking, she had rested her palm flat to her belly.

"No." She moved her hand away, slightly sickened by the thought of something moving around inside of her body. She didn't even know what a baby looked like at six weeks. Was it still considered a zygote? She had learned enough about gestation in health class to pass the exam, but the details had seemed esoteric back then. Emily imagined a cluster of cells pulsing around in a blob of liquid as they waited for a shot of hormones to tell them whether or not to turn into a kidney or a heart.

"I heard you got a marriage proposal."

Emily felt her brain reaching back for the calmness of the carousel. She forced herself to stay in the present, asking Clay, "Did they send you here?"

"Who?"

"The clique." She normally appreciated his coyness, but now she found it annoying. "Ricky, Blake, Nardo. Are they worried I'll ruin your life?"

Clay looked down at the ground. He kicked a deeper furrow into the gravel. "I'm sorry, Emily. I know this isn't what you wanted."

She would've laughed if she'd the energy.

"Are you . . ." Clay's voice trailed off. "Are you going to name someone?"

"Name someone?" she asked. It sounded like McCarthyism. "Who would I name?"

Clay shrugged, but he had to know the list. Nardo, Blake, Dean, Jack. Not to mention himself, because even though he kept saying he wasn't interested in Emily, he'd still been at The Party and they had clearly argued about something.

She felt a spark of Columbo. Maybe Emily wasn't so resigned

to her state after all. "Clay, I'm sorry about arguing with you the night of The Party. It wasn't—it wasn't your fault."

His mouth twisted to the side. "I thought you didn't remember anything."

"I remember yelling at you," she lied. And then she tried to build on the lie. "I shouldn't have said all of those things."

"Maybe." His shoulders shrugged. "I know I can be selfish, Em. Maybe it's because I'm an only child."

She had always found it cold-blooded that he so easily dismissed his other siblings, even though they hadn't grown up together.

He said, "I can say that I'll try to do better, but you're right about that, too. I probably won't. Maybe I should accept who I am. You seem to."

Emily felt an echo of a memory. They were standing by Nardo's swimming pool. She had screamed at Clay that he always promised to do better but then he never actually did. He simply made the same mistakes over and over again and expected other people to change.

He added, "At least I'm not as bad as Blake, right?"

Emily was at a loss as to how to answer. Was he talking about what Blake had done yesterday or Blake in general? Because either could work. Blake had been a sleazeball yesterday. But as with Clay, he was never going to change. His ego wouldn't let him ever admit that he was wrong.

"You should know," Clay said. "Blake is telling people you're into drugs and partying."

Emily took a deep breath and held it in her lungs. The news was unsurprising. Blake had a level of cruelty that none of them could fathom. Jack had called it this morning. Nardo was just mean. Clay was easily bored. But when Blake took against you, he *really* took against you. Not to mention Ricky, who was part Wicked Witch, part flying monkeys.

She said, "Nardo told me—he said that Jack—Cheese was at The Party."

Clay turned to look at her. The light blue of his eyes was bleached out by the sun. She could see the fuzz of hair beneath his chin. He was so handsome, but she didn't feel the same stir she had before.

He said, "You were stoned that night."

Emily had never claimed otherwise, but she had no idea why he sounded angry.

"You were really fucked up," he said. "You could barely remember how you got home. You didn't even know it until your grandmother told you."

"Okay?" she asked, wondering where this was going.

"I mean, so, technically, what Blake is saying isn't that far off base." Clay looked down, watching the toe of his sneaker dig into the earth. "You're into drugs. You're into partying. You played the game. You need to take the loss. Have some dignity."

Emily's only surprise was that she kept being shocked every time this happened. They had all turned on her in the exact same way—first Dean, then Ricky, then Blake, then Nardo and now Clay. They really were all following a script. Friendliness. Obsequiousness. Fury. Contempt.

Clay stood up. His hands were still in his pockets. "Don't talk to me again, Emily."

She stood up, too. "Why would I want to talk to you when all you do is lie?"

He grabbed her arms. He wrenched her forward. She braced herself, expecting a threat or a warning or something—anything—other than what he actually did.

Clay kissed her.

He tasted of nicotine and stale beer. She could feel the roughness of his skin against her own. His tongue probed her mouth. Their bodies were practically clamped together. It was Emily's first real kiss. At least the first real kiss that Emily could remember.

And it felt like nothing.

Clay pushed her away. He wiped his mouth with the back of his hand.

"Goodbye, Emily."

She watched him leave. His shoulders were hunched. His feet scuffed the ground.

Emily's fingers went to her mouth. She gently touched her lips. She had expected that a kiss made you feel—something. Nothing tingled. Her heart wasn't lurching. She had felt the same passive disinterest she'd felt when Blake had drunkenly tried to kiss her in the alley two years ago.

She watched Clay turn the corner of the house. His shoulders were still hunched. He looked guilty of something but there was no telling what.

Emily felt a laugh come from deep inside her soul. If only she could get back all the time from the last decade she had wasted obsessing over how Clayton Morrow was feeling.

Emily used her foot to cover up the gouge he'd made in the gravel. She looked up at the house. By chance, she caught a glimpse of her father walking back into the bedroom. He had been on the balcony that overlooked the shed and garden. She had no idea how long he'd been there or what he'd seen. She tracked his progress through the windows. He went to the sideboard table and poured himself a drink.

Emily looked down. Without realizing it, she had put her hand to her stomach again. She had thought of herself as alone in all of this, but there was someone else making the arduous journey alongside her. Or inside of her, to be accurate. She felt no attachment to the cluster of cells, but she did feel a sense of duty. It was exactly what Melody had written in her letter—

Your weirdness comes from your LOVE and ACCEPTANCE of all kinds of people.

Emily felt no love for the cells, at least not yet, but she had resigned herself to acceptance. Clay was not altogether wrong when he implied that Emily's pregnancy was her problem to deal with. She was the one who was going to live with it for the rest of her life. She sat back down on the bench. She stared out at the fallow garden.

She cleared her throat. She said, "I will—"

Her voice gave out.

Again, Emily felt strange to be alone and speaking out loud, but she needed to hear the words as much as she needed to say them. It was a wish list, to be honest, enumerating all of the precious things that she had lost in the short span of a few days. It was also a promise to give all of those lost things back to her eventual baby.

She cleared her throat again. The pledge came freely this time, and loudly, because it mattered.

"I will protect you. No one will ever hurt you. You will always be safe."

For the first time in days, Emily felt as if some of the stress had finally left her body.

Behind her, she heard the balcony door slam closed.

8

The salty water had a calming tint of French blue. Andrea floated upside down, weightless and free. She could stay down here, languid and warm, but something told her not to. Her hands reached up. Her feet pushed off. She broke through the surface. The sun kissed her shoulders. She wiped the water out of her eyes as waves lapped at her chin. She turned, looking back at the beach. Laura was underneath a large rainbow-colored umbrella. She was sitting up so that she could keep an eye on Andrea. Her top was off. The scars from her mastectomy showed. A man wearing a dark hoodie was sneaking up behind her.

"Mom!"

Andrea startled awake.

Her eyes darted around the room. She wasn't swimming in the ocean. She was in a hospital bed. An IV was in her arm. An oxygen mask covered her mouth and nose but she still felt like she couldn't draw in enough air. The panic built like a cresting wave.

"Hey." Mike's hand was steady on her shoulder. He straightened the mask on her face. "You're okay. Just breathe."

Her panic slowly dissolved at the sight of him. There was a look of concern in his eyes that reached straight into her heart.

He asked, "Did you do something different with your hair?"

Andrea couldn't laugh. The last hour flooded back in—the fire, the ride in the ambulance, the endless tests, the total lack of information. The doctor had said that Andrea needed fluids, not pain medication. Andrea disagreed. Her nose was throbbing. Her chest felt as if it was bound by rope. There was a pinching sensation in her forehead. Her lip was swollen. She reached up to touch it.

And then she coughed so hard that her eyes watered. The mask turned disgusting. She tried to push it away, but Mike lifted it off her head. Andrea rolled to her side, seized by a fit of coughs that felt like her lungs were trying to come out of her face. She tried to cover her mouth, but the IV tugged at her arm. Her feet got caught up in the sheets. The pulse oximeter clipped to her finger snapped off.

Mike was kneeling beside her, his hand rubbing her back. "You want some water?"

Andrea nodded. She watched him pick up a large pitcher by the sink. Her eyes were still burning from the smoke. She pulled a tissue from the box. She blew her nose so hard that her ears popped. The residue looked like the inside of a fireplace. She took another tissue and blew until her ears popped again.

She asked, "Is my mom okay?"

"As far as I know." He held the straw so she could sip from the cup. Her fingernails were rimmed in black. The smoke and soot from the fire had absorbed into her skin. The nurse had given Andrea a pair of scrubs to change into, but they were already filthy.

Mike asked, "Do you want me to call Laura?"

"God, no." Andrea gave up on the water. It hurt too much to swallow. "The fire. Did anyone—"

"Everybody got out. Bible's hand was burned a little. Judith's daughter ran back into the house to rescue the family parakeet. Bible ended up saving them both." Mike sat on the edge of the bed. "You're the one who's good at bird jokes. Maybe you can tease him about it later."

Andrea felt a flush of shame. He was talking about their exchange at Glynco. Mike had asked her why she had ghosted him and Andrea had hidden behind a pun.

"Syd," was all that she could think to say now. "The parakeet's name is Syd."

Mike let out a long sigh. He stood up from the bed. He went to the sink to wash the soot from his hands. "The fire chief already ruled out arson. The judge never upgraded the electrical service. The box was still running on fuses. There was some medical equipment upstairs for the husband. They used one extension cord too many."

"Yankee Cheap." Andrea rubbed her eyes, then thought better of it. "Can you help me sit up?"

Mike's hands were steady on her shoulders, but there was nothing he could do to keep the room from slipping sideways. Andrea nearly tumbled off the bed.

"Hey, steady now." The concern was back in his eyes. But then a shade came down and he held up his hands in surrender. "Sorry, I know you can take care of yourself."

She felt like a rock had settled on her chest. "Mike, I—"

"You managed to impress the boss." Mike's tone changed again. "Running into a burning building. Keeping an entire neighborhood from being leveled. You sure put all those *helpless little girl* rumors to rest."

He really remembered every stupid thing she had said.

Mike returned to the sink. He pulled a handful of paper towels from the dispenser and wet them under the faucet. "They took a chunk of glass out of your forehead. Four stitches."

Andrea touched the stiff threads holding together her skin. She had only a vague recollection of the doctor sewing her up. "Why does my nose feel like it's stuffed with bees?"

"It's not broken. Maybe you smacked it when you went into the pool?"

The memory of falling into the water felt like it had happened to someone else.

"Hold still." Mike used the wet towels to gently wipe her face. "You do not wanna be posting pictures of yourself on social media right now."

Andrea closed her eyes. The towel felt warm on her skin. He carefully blotted her forehead, then traced along the left side of her face. She felt the tension start to drain out of her body. She longed to press her forehead against his chest again.

"The judge's husband," Mike said. "It's not looking good for him."

Andrea's eyes opened.

"He wasn't in great shape to begin with." Mike stroked gently down the other side of her face. "Is this okay?"

It hurt a little, but she told him, "Yeah."

Mike gently dabbed around her mouth. Her bottom lip ached where it had been split open. Andrea figured that she deserved the pain.

He said, "There's a difference between needing to be saved and asking somebody who cares about you for help."

She couldn't find the words to answer him.

Mike folded the towel to a fresh square. "How's it going with Bible?"

"He—" Her throat rasped with a cough. "He's a legend."

Mike had moved down to her neck, almost grooming her like a cat. "Did he tell you he was my first partner when I joined WitSec?"

Andrea wasn't surprised that Bible hadn't shared the information, but she was surprised that he'd been in WitSec. "Does he know about . . . ?"

"I never told him your status," Mike said. "But I wouldn't be surprised if he figured it out. He's pretty damn smart."

Bible was more than that. "He's a damn wizard."

Mike's smile was strained. He didn't want to talk about Catfish Bible. "For the record, only one of my sisters always needs to be bailed out. And I wait on my mom hand and foot because she's worked hard all of her life and she's earned it."

Andrea forced herself not to look away from him. "I shouldn't have said that. Any of it."

"Do you think it's true?"

She felt her head shaking. "No. I love your mom. And your sisters are great."

Their gaze met for a second before Mike walked back to the sink. He wet a fresh paper towel. "I've never rescued you. Actually, if you think about what happened two years ago, you pretty much ran rings around me. I didn't know which end was up."

Andrea shook her head, because what she remembered most was feeling completely lost.

He said, "You went through a trauma, Andy. Anybody else would've given up. I'm in awe that you made it out alive."

She felt tears spring into her eyes. She desperately wanted that to be true.

Mike walked back to the bed. He started to clean her hands, though she had already washed them. "I understood why you bailed on me. Things were bad. You needed time to figure out who you were, what you were going to do with your life. I wanted to give you that time. I knew you were worth the wait. But you never came back."

Andrea tasted blood when she bit her lip.

"The rumors Bible was talking about—" Mike lightly held her hands. He was nervous. She had never seen him nervous before. "I was a mess when you disappeared. Everybody was teasing me about mooning over a girl, but the truth is, you kind of broke my heart."

Andrea bit her lip harder. She had made such a huge, hurtful mistake.

"I mean—I didn't pine for you or anything like that." Mike tried to hide his vulnerability with one of his grins, but it lacked his usual cockiness. "Sure, I wrote some poetry, but I wasn't wandering around aimlessly wailing your name."

Andrea laughed, but only to let out some of the regret swelling inside of her chest.

He shrugged. "All I could do was throw myself into a bunch of meaningless sex."

She laughed for real this time.

"Don't get me wrong. I was grateful for all the sex. I learned a lot." His playful tone had returned. "The stewardess who got me back into journaling. The ballerina who worked on my interpretive dance. The tender moments with an empty nester down the street from my nana. And the supermodels—so many supermodels."

Andrea laced her fingers through his. Her heart was pounding so hard she was certain he could hear it.

"Weird," she said. "That's exactly how I coped without you."

Mike's eyebrow arched. "Men supermodels or women supermodels?"

She shrugged. "When you're in an orgy, you go where you're needed."

"Sure. You don't want to be rude."

She kissed him.

Her arms went around his shoulders. She wrapped her legs around his waist. Everything about his body felt new and familiar at the same time. His beard was as luxurious as she'd imagined. His mouth was like honey.

"Mike—" Andrea was breathless when she managed to pull away. "I'm sorry. I'm so stupid, and I'm so sorry."

The curtain raked back.

"Time to go, folks. We need the bed." The nurse didn't seem to mind ruining the tender moment. She unceremoniously yanked the IV out of Andrea's arm. "If you experience hoarseness, prolonged coughing spells, mental confusion, or difficulty breathing, call 911 immediately. Is this your husband or partner?"

Mike said, "It's complicated."

"She has a mild concussion." The nurse held up a clipboard. "I need somebody who isn't her to sign this."

"That's me," Mike said.

"Breathing exercises. Do them once every waking hour." She checked a box on the paperwork. "No smoking or drinking for the next seventy-two hours. Use throat lozenges or spray for the pain. Tylenol as needed. No strenuous exercise."

"Can she work?" The question had come from Deputy Chief Cecelia Compton. She was still dressed in her blue power suit. Her arms were crossed over her chest. "Or should she take time off?"

"Desk duty is fine if she's up to it." The nurse reached into her pocket and handed Andrea some cough drops. "You're due for Tylenol in six hours. Don't exceed more than four thousand milligrams in a twenty-four-hour period."

Andrea would take heroin if her throat stopped hurting. She unwrapped one of the cough drops. "Thank you."

"Oliver?" Compton said. "Can you follow me?"

Mike helped Andrea down from the bed. She held onto his hand until she had to let him go. Then she had to jog to catch up with Compton.

"I'm glad Mike was in town." Compton's arms swung as she walked at a brisk clip. "Leonard worked with him a few years ago. Mike's a stand-up guy. I never believed those rumors. No woman in her right mind would break his heart."

Andrea rolled the cough drop in her mouth.

"Here's the deal." Compton was back in boss mode. "Bible's idiotic parakeet rescue put him on the injured list. And I don't care what your nurse said. You're both on medical leave for the remainder of the week. Get some sleep. Walk on the beach. I've got another team taking over security for the judge and her family."

Andrea should've been used to disappointment by now, but the thought of sitting in a motel room while Dean Wexler happily went about his sick business felt like a blow from a hammer.

Compton sensed her mood. "Bible brought me up to speed on your conversations with Ricky Fontaine and Melody Brickel. Sorry they didn't pan out. Something will break eventually. It always does."

Nothing had broken in twenty years. Forty, if you counted Emily Vaughn. Andrea wasn't ready to give up. She hadn't become a Marshal so that bad people could keep doing bad things. "Ma'am, I—"

"Hold on." Compton knocked loudly on the door to the men's bathroom. She asked Andrea, "You up for sticking around a tad longer?"

Before she could answer, the bathroom door swung open. Unlike Andrea, Leonard Bible looked no worse for the wear. The only indication that he'd been inside a burning house was a bright white bandage that covered his right hand.

He held it up for Andrea to see. "Bird brain."

"Silence," Compton ordered.

Bible winked at Andrea. "I wish my wife was here to tell my boss to stop breaking my balls."

"Well your wife sure as fuck ain't gonna kiss 'em and make 'em better." Compton took a deep breath, transitioning back into her boss role, telling Andrea, "The judge asked to speak with you. I believe she wants to offer her thanks, but keep it brief. Dr. Vaughn is circling the drain. He won't last through the night."

"Yes, ma'am."

Compton gestured up the hallway, but it was easy to spot Franklin Vaughn's hospital room. Two Marshals flanked the door, their chests so muscled that they looked like hot air balloons. Somehow, they recognized Andrea. One gave her a nod. The other opened the door.

She had expected to hear the whirs and beeps of machinery, but the room was silent. The only light came from the fixture over the bathroom mirror. Someone had left the door ajar to keep out the darkness.

Judge Esther Vaughn was seated in a wooden chair facing her husband's bed. The large briefcase she had saved from the fire was at her feet. Her attention was squarely on her husband. Franklin Vaughn had no tubes or IVs hooked into his body, not even a cannula for supplemental oxygen. He was clearly receiving palliative care.

Andrea moved the cough drop to her cheek. "Ma'am?"

The judge's shoulders flinched as if Andrea had shouted the word. But she didn't turn around. She said, "Sit down, Marshal."

Andrea hesitated. There was a large, upholstered chair on the other side of the bed that you'd find in almost every hospital room across the country. Andrea had sat in a similar one for untold hours while her mother was recovering from multiple breast cancer surgeries.

She walked around the bed. She didn't sit down. Nor did she look at Franklin Vaughn. "Chief Compton said you wanted to speak to me, ma'am?"

Esther slowly tilted up her chin. She studied Andrea, taking in her soot-covered skin and dirty scrubs. "Thank you."

"You're welcome, ma'am." Andrea felt her throat tighten with the need to cough. "I'm sorry Dr. Vaughn isn't well. Can I get you anything before I leave?"

The judge fell silent. Andrea listened to Franklin Vaughn's shallow breathing. Without thinking, she started to count his breaths. She was taken back to her mother's hospital room. For days, Andrea had monitored Laura's every inhalation, written down every medication and test, jumped up to help every time Laura moved, for fear if she let her guard down her mother would die.

Andrea blinked. She couldn't tell if the tears in her eyes came from her memories or the fire. "Ma'am, if you don't need anything else, I'll—"

"I was thinking about when Judith was delivered," Esther began. "The birth of a child should be a celebration. Don't you agree?"

Andrea pressed together her lips. The judge was looking at her husband again. Esther's hand reached out, but only to hold onto the bed rail.

"The doctors came to us for our decision. Franklin and I had argued so many times over whether or not we would let Emily go once the child was safe," Esther said. "I wanted to turn off the machines. Franklin said that we could not. The world was watching. *Our world* was watching. But Emily made the decision for us. She developed a postpartum bacterial infection in her uterus. Puerperal fever, they called it. The infection turned septic. Everything happened very fast."

Andrea watched Esther's fingers tighten around the bed rail.

"When Franklin suffered his stroke last year, the doctors came to me for a decision." Esther's voice had grown harder. "I had such a vivid memory come back to me. He and I were in the study. He was so angry, so insistent, that we should keep her alive. I asked him what he would want for himself were he in Emily's place. His face turned completely pale, and he said— 'Promise me, Esther. You must *never* let me linger.'"

Andrea watched Esther's hand slowly fall away. The woman's head bent down as she stared at the floor.

"I broke my promise. I made the doctors take extraordinary measures. I let him linger," Esther said. "At the time, I told myself—Franklin was still alive, wasn't he? His heart was still beating. He was still able to draw breath. Only God can take a life."

Andrea saw the judge's hands clench in her lap.

"In truth, I wanted him to suffer." Esther paused, as if the admission had taken too much out of her. "I should have defended Emily when she was alive. From his anger. From his fists. At the time, I told myself that he wasn't as bad with her. If I could stand it, so could she. Only when she was gone did I realize that I had failed her so profoundly. She was my daughter. I did nothing to protect her."

Andrea thought about the first letter that had been mailed to the judge—

HOW WOULD YOU LIKE THE WORLD TO KNOW THAT YOUR HUSBAND PHYSICALLY ABUSED YOU AND YOUR DAUGHTER BUT YOU DID NOTHING TO PROTECT HER?

"I told myself that my career emasculated him," Esther said. "What did a bruise matter? A slap? My ambition was an affront. Franklin was never successful in his own right. At home, he needed to assert himself. My pain was a small price to pay. I had no right to drag Emily into our devil's bargain. Nor to use her tragedy as a cudgel against my detractors."

Andrea heard echoes from the second letter—

YOU SACRIFICED YOUR CHILD FOR YOUR CAREER! YOU DESERVE YOUR CANCEROUS DEATH SENTENCE!

"I put my foot down with Judith. I told Franklin that I would leave if he ever harmed her. He acquiesced so easily." Her forehead wrinkled, as if she still did not understand his capitulation. "Why couldn't I do that for Emily? Why couldn't I do that for myself?"

Andrea chewed the inside of her cheek.

"After Emily was attacked, Reagan suggested I withdraw my name. I was furious. I couldn't give up everything I had worked for. I felt that, should I back out, Reagan would think twice before nominating another woman. Any president would. I wanted to create a judicial legacy." Esther's gaze settled on her husband. "All of the anger and drive, all to find ourselves both nothing but fragile, mortal beings."

YOU'RE DYING OF CANCER AND YOUR HUSBAND IS A VEGETABLE, BUT ALL YOU CARE ABOUT IS YOUR SO-CALLED LEGACY!

"I have told myself for far too long that my life has been built on pillars of strength, honesty and integrity, but that's never been the case." Esther's tone was never so sharp as when she turned it on herself. "In those last few months before the attack, Emily had been entirely stripped of artifice. She understood the world better than I did. She saw me more accurately than anyone else ever has. The closer I get to my own death, the better I understand her clarity. I was blinded by my own arrogance. I was a hypocrite. A fraud."

YOU ARE GOING TO DIE, YOU ARROGANT, NEEDY, AND WORTHLESS BITCH! EVERYONE WILL KNOW WHAT A FRAUD YOU ARE. I WILL MAKE SURE YOU SUFFER!

"I have never spoken those words aloud before. Not even to Judith," Esther said. "I'm not sure why I'm telling you now."

Andrea could barely hear the woman's voice. She had shrunk into herself, hands clasped in her lap, back bent as she stared down at the floor. A sense of longing had filled the room. The judge's husband was going to die in a few hours. Esther only had a few months left of her own life. She had confessed more to a stranger than she had ever confessed to herself.

Andrea should have felt pity for the old woman, but she found herself thinking back to Ricky Blakely's 1982 witness statement. The cartoonish cursive. The large circles dotting her 'i's. Ricky was a teenager when she wrote the long, meandering sentences, but if Andrea had learned anything in her life, it was that people did not change that much after they left high school.

There were so many things that had bothered Andrea about the death threats. The lack of swear words. The absence of sexual threats. The exacting punctuation. The use of an Oxford, or serial, comma before the *and* at the end of a list. Understandably, someone writing a death threat would try to conceal their identity, but it was hard to hide the fact that you were *imposing, imperious, intelligent*, and, most importantly, *indomitable*.

"Ma'am?" Andrea asked. "Why did you send those death threats to yourself?"

Esther's lips parted, though not in surprise. Andrea recognized the coping mechanism. Take a breath, calm your fluttering heart, focus on anything but the trauma at hand.

When Esther finally looked up at Andrea, it was not to answer the question, but to ask one of her own. "Why aren't you afraid of me?"

"I don't know," Andrea admitted. "When I think about you, I'm afraid, but then I see you in person, I realize that you're just a lost old woman whose daughter was murdered and whose husband used to beat her."

Esther's chin dropped, but only slightly. "Does Leonard know?"

"He still thinks Ricky wrote the letters."

Esther looked down. Her gaze had found the briefcase at her feet. The judge's house had been consumed by fire, yet the only thing she had rescued was the briefcase.

Esther said, "I should not have manipulated the system. I can see now how selfishly I behaved. I apologize."

Andrea wasn't looking for an apology. She wanted an explanation. The judge had been around almost as long as the Marshals. She knew how Judicial Security worked. The first priority when a credible death threat was received was to ensure the judge's safety. Esther had obviously felt threatened enough to want protection, but she had also been afraid to explain why. Andrea felt like a piece of the puzzle was finally about to click into place.

She asked the woman, "Who did you need protection from?"

Esther's frail shoulders rose as she took a deep breath. Then she exhaled a name like it was a disease. "Dean Wexler."

Andrea had to steady herself on the back of the upholstered chair. Every awful thing that happened to a woman in this town seemed to always lead back to Wexler.

"'Your adversary the devil prowls around like a roaring lion seeking someone to devour.'" Esther's voice had started to tremble on the last few words. "1 Peter 5:8."

Andrea kept her grip on the chair. She could think of only one reason that Dean Wexler would be able to incite fear in Esther Vaughn, but she could not bring herself to say it.

Instead, she asked, "Tell me."

Again, Esther had to fortify herself with another deep breath. "In the first year of Judith's life, I would have her playpen set up in the garden so we could spend time together. I was in the potting shed when I realized she had gone silent. I ran outside to find Wexler holding her."

Andrea watched tears flood into the woman's eyes. She was still clearly haunted by the memory.

"Judith had no idea that she was in a stranger's arms. She was always such a trusting, happy child. But I could see the look on Wexler's face—as if he wanted to harm her. He'd gone out of his way to grip her arm as if he wanted to wrench it away. The malevolence in his eyes, the sheer evil—"

Esther stopped as her emotions threatened to take over.

"I had never screamed like that before. Not when we learned about Emily's attack. Not even when Franklin . . ." She let the words trail off, but Andrea knew that she was talking about the beatings. "For the entirety of my life, I saw myself as strong, impenetrable. You get harder in the broken places, and you carry on. But seeing that vile demon holding my Judith broke me completely in two. I was on my knees in front of him, begging him to give me Judith, when Franklin came outside."

Andrea watched the judge try to collect herself. Her hands had started to shake. Tears wept from her eyes.

"I—I rushed into the house with Judith. My heart felt as if it was on fire. By the time Franklin returned, I was hiding with Judith in the upstairs closet." Esther paused as she struggled with the memory. "That is when Franklin told me that Dean Wexler is Judith's father."

Andrea felt the world slip sideways again, though she had known that this was coming. Her thoughts threatened to spin out of control—*if Dean was Judith's father, that meant he'd lied about his sterility, and if he had lied about that, what else was he hiding?*

"Franklin told me that we had to pay Wexler to go away. They had made a bargain, and Franklin would handle it." Esther clasped together her hands to keep them from shaking. "I should have immediately called the police. I can see that so clearly now, but, at the time, I did nothing."

Andrea could only ask, "Why?"

"I was terrified that Wexler would find a way to get Judith. You can't imagine the vicious look on his face that day in the garden. To this day, I truly believe he is a manifestation of evil." Her fingers returned to the cross around her neck, working it like a talisman. "Wexler could have sued for parental rights, you see. He could have taken Judith away from us. Or been granted visitation. Or somehow had a say in how she was raised. The most expedient way to rid ourselves of the threat was to pay him to stay away."

"But," Andrea said. "If Wexler had tried to claim parental rights, he was basically admitting to statutory rape."

"You must put that admission in the context of the times. The constitutionality of statutory rape laws was not upheld by the Supreme Court until March of 1981. Delaware state law held age of consent at seven years of age until the 1970s. Rape shield laws were only a few years older. When I first sat on the bench, the woman's claim of assault had to be corroborated by an eyewitness in order to be considered credible."

Andrea had to say, "Excuse me, judge, but not that much has changed. A tragically raped and murdered white woman is still a tragically raped and murdered white woman."

"You're speaking to the tabloids, not the court of law." Esther paused, her fingers gripping the tiny cross. "How do you get from A to B? Dean was admitting to sex, not murder, and he could always recant the confession. My stature and the salacious details alone would make any prosecutor wary of trying an iffy case with no corroborating evidence. Franklin and I had already hired a private detective who'd had no success finding Emily's killer. We were faced with the same problem as always—the glaring lack of evidence."

Andrea spoke carefully. "The police get informers to flip on suspects all the time."

"You mean pay or induce someone to corroborate Dean's guilt?" Esther did not sound offended by the prospect, which meant she had considered it. "What if that person recanted? What if they ended up blackmailing us? Better the devil you know, and Wexler was the devil incarnate."

Andrea knew that Esther had likely made the best of all the bad decisions available. She also knew something else that had happened around that same time. "Wexler told us he inherited money from a dead relative. That's how he was able to purchase the farm."

Esther slowly began to nod. "The property had belonged to Franklin's mother. Upon her death, it was meant to go to Emily, then pass to Judith."

Andrea watched Esther pull a tissue from the sleeve of her dress. She carefully wiped away her tears before continuing.

"Franklin deeded the land into a partnership. The partnership sold the land to a shell corporation for a nominal price. Then the shell corp made non-public transfers into a trust that was controlled by Dean Wexler." Esther looked at Andrea, explaining in simple terms, "Tax fraud, tax evasion, embezzlement, forgery, perhaps money laundering, but I would need to look up the 1983 statute."

Andrea knew that Wexler hadn't stopped there. "Did you have anything to do with the labor board case?"

Esther nodded again. "Franklin told me that I would have to call in some favors. That was always how he phrased it—you need to call in a favor. I never questioned him. I did as I was told because I wanted to protect Judith."

Andrea pointed out a flaw in the judge's story. "According to Bob Stilton's case file, Wexler maintained that he couldn't be the father. He had some kind of childhood illness that caused him to be sterile."

"Again, there was no proof." Esther had clearly read the case file, too. "Franklin told me we had to take Wexler at his word. The risk was too big. I was so desperate to protect Judith that I didn't ask questions. By the time I started to wonder, it was too late."

"You never asked Wexler for DNA?"

"To what end? After one submits to blackmail, one must always submit to blackmail. Both Franklin and I had incriminated ourselves with the original land deal. Dean had proof that we broke the law. We had no proof that he had murdered our daughter." Esther's sigh was filled with exhaustion. She had spent decades hitting the same brick walls that Andrea had banged up against for only a couple of days. "I told myself that the threat was too personal to risk breaking our pact. Wexler could always find a way to get to Judith. And then when Guinevere was born, the stakes were even higher."

Andrea looked down at her swollen left wrist. "Do you know what Dean is doing to the women at the farm?"

"For years, I chose not to know. Emily called it my *gift of willful blindness.*"

Andrea wanted to be tactful, but then she thought about Star
Bonaire and Alice Poulsen. "Ma'am, you seem to have a lot of
details for someone who claims they were left out of the details."

Esther's gaze settled on her husband. His breath had turned
raspy. The seconds in between had grown farther apart. "After
Franklin suffered his stroke, there was no longer a buffer. Wexler
came to me directly. I told him I was finished. I knew that my
cancer was inoperable. I wanted to spend the remainder of what
little time I had left with Judith and Guinevere."

Andrea had seen how Dean Wexler treated women who stood
up to him. "What did he do?"

"A piece of mail was sent to the house addressed to Guinevere."
Esther's hand went to her throat again. She held onto the gold
cross. "I recognized the return address. Wexler had sent an application to apply for a volunteer position at the farm. Guinevere's
name and address were pre-entered into the form."

"That's all?" Andrea asked. She didn't see Dean Wexler being
that subtle.

"The envelope included photographs of Guinevere. Someone
had followed her from school to home. One photograph was
taken through the open curtains of her bedroom window."

Andrea could feel the desperation in her voice. "What did you
do?"

"I panicked again," Esther said. "I had learned nothing from
the first time. Instead of finally coming forward with the truth, I
manipulated the system. It's as you said. I wrote the death threats.
I knew Judicial Security would intervene."

Andrea gently corrected her story, because she hadn't taken the
first few offers of protection. "You wanted Bible."

"Leonard is a good man," Esther said. "So much of my life
has been spent in fear of bad men. Of my husband. Of Wexler.
Of my own people. I've lived with the terror of losing—always
losing. Emily saw my fear and called it cowardice. She was right,
of course. I have no delusions that I will not suffer in the afterlife
for my sins. I wanted to spend what little time I have left
surrounded by people who love me."

"And after you're gone?" Andrea asked, because the judge
clearly had a plan.

Esther shook her head, but said, "I should apologize for underestimating you. Leonard told me that you had the spark of brilliance."

Andrea didn't take the compliment. There were too many other women who were suffering at Wexler's hands. "Judge, what's in your briefcase?"

NOVEMBER 26, 1981

Emily sat beside Gram at the kitchen table. They were both shelling pumpkin seeds for the annual Vaughn Thanksgiving get-together, though this year, instead of fifty people drinking cocktails in the formal living room and another twenty jammed into the tiny den where the TV was kept to watch football, only four people would be in attendance. And one of them didn't quite know who the others were.

Gram told Emily, "My father taught me how to do this. He loved pumpkin seeds."

"What was he like?" Emily asked, though she could recite the story herself.

"Well, he wasn't very tall." Gram started by describing her father's hair, which was soft and thin, much to his disappointment because he had styled himself as a Clark Gable. When she moved on to his love of haberdashery, Emily let herself zone out. She watched her hands move as she shelled the pumpkin seeds. Esther had already roasted them in the oven. Most people shelled them one at a time as with peanuts, but Gram insisted it was better to put in the work now so that you could fully enjoy them later. They had nearly filled the bowl.

"Papa said to do it like this." Gram showed her how to gently squeeze the shell until it cracked open. The meat was green inside. "But you mustn't eat it yet. You must put them all in the bowl."

"That's a good idea," Emily agreed. She reached for another handful of seeds, but a sharp spasm in her back brought out a loud yelp. She resisted the impulse to double over, leaning back instead to stretch the muscle.

"Oh," Gram said. "Are you okay, dear?"

Emily was not okay. She hissed out air between her teeth. She wasn't sure if the pulled muscle was a result of her pregnancy or from carrying her heavy book bag or from not being able to sleep at night because she was so anxious about the way things were going at school.

"You're a little early for muscle cramps." Esther had appeared from the pantry. She put the can of sauerkraut on the table and kneaded her fist into Emily's back. "Push through it."

Emily didn't want to push through anything. She wanted this to be over.

"Better?" Esther asked.

Emily nodded, because the spasm had eased. She leaned into her mother's hip, eyes closed. Esther held onto her, stroking back her hair. This was something new for both of them. Gram had always been the one to dry Emily's tears or kiss a scrape on her knee. Esther was the one who drilled her on vocabulary and coached her on debate team prep. It was as if Emily's pregnancy had brought out a maternal side of Esther that none of them knew existed. Or maybe Gram's dementia had left an opening that Esther had never felt required to fill.

"Dear," Gram said to Emily. "You're a bit young to be with child."

Emily laughed. "That's the truth."

Gram looked confused, but she laughed, too.

Esther's lips pressed against the top of Emily's head. "All right. I should make dinner. Your father will be back from the club soon."

Emily watched her mother move around the kitchen. Technically, Esther wasn't *making* dinner. She was heating up what had already been prepared by the cook, who favored Maryland dishes. Crab cakes. Corn on the cob. Clam and oyster stuffing. Cranberry relish. Green beans with tomatoes. Baked ham.

The ham was the clearest indication of their change in circumstances. Normally, Emily was put off by the sight of the plump, pink meat simmering in its own juices. The shape was too reminiscent of the actual pig. The ham that Esther had taken out of the refrigerator was small, more like a loaf of bread. And still, it was ample enough to feed more than four people.

No one would say the words, but the lack of celebration was Emily's fault.

Her original sin had far-reaching implications well beyond the reduced number of guests at the party. Esther's judicial appointment had turned iffy. She was constantly on the phone, taking meetings in DC, scrambling to show that she was still deserving of a lifetime appointment. The pressure was immense, though her mother never spoke about it openly. There were harried conversations with Franklin that quickly sputtered out when Emily entered the room. At night, she could hear their muffled voices through the bedroom wall as Franklin paced across the creaky floor and Esther strategized at her desk.

This past week had been particularly bad. Emily had read an op-ed in the *Wilmington News Journal* asking whether Esther Vaughn's judicial ambitions had overshadowed her duties as a mother. Franklin had left the paper folded open on the breakfast table so that Emily would find it.

Emily stood from the table. She felt a sudden weepiness. There was no tissue in the kitchen, so she used a paper towel to blow her nose. Esther's smile acknowledged that she knew that Emily was crying and there was nothing that could be done about it.

She asked her mother, "What can I do to help?"

"The hasty pudding is in the fridge outside. Do you mind—"

"Goodness." Gram was looking at them both. "I think I'll retire to my room for a nap."

Emily could tell she had no idea who was standing across from her in the kitchen. Thankfully, Gram had lived in the house long enough that she found her surroundings familiar. She ambled up the back hallway absently humming "Yankee Doodle." By the time she hit the stairs, she was marching to the beat.

Esther exchanged an amused look with Emily. Her mother had been in an incredibly good mood since this morning. Emily wondered if her pregnancy had actually managed to bring them closer together. It was very difficult to tell. At times, their mother–child relationship felt like it was entering a new phase. And then, at other times, Esther was lecturing Emily about turning the thermostat too high or leaving a wet towel on the floor.

"Pudding?" Esther prompted.

"Right." Emily knew she couldn't blame her memory loss on her pregnancy. She was easily distracted because focusing on the here and now was generally too depressing.

The garage felt cold as a polar bear's rump, to borrow a quote from Gram. Emily didn't bother to go back inside for her coat. Her body temperature was running hot at the moment. Of course that changed as soon as she'd reached the far side of the garage.

Emily shuddered as she opened the refrigerator. Thanks to Gram, she started humming "Yankee Doodle," an annoying thing to have in your head on any day of the year. She remembered reading Louisa May Alcott's *Little Men* for extra credit in the sixth grade. Emil and Franz had gone to the corn mill and brought home enough for the family to eat hasty pudding and Johnny cake for months. Emily had gotten a star from the teacher for making a connection to the song.

She wasn't getting any stars from teachers now.

Emily had become completely ostracized at school. Even the janitors looked away when she walked past. It was as if her pregnancy was putting out a force field. The more the nasty rumors spread, the more people kept their distance. Teachers shook their heads in dismay. Someone had cut a giant hole in the T-shirt she wore for PE. The word WHORE had been carved into her desk in homeroom. Before Thanksgiving break, some idiot had peeled off the liner to a maxi-pad and taped it to her locker. They'd used a red magic marker to indicate blood. A black marker had been used to box it in, making it look like a postcard with the words scrawled below—

WISH YOU WERE HERE?

Emily suspected that Ricky was behind the maxi-pad if not the rest of the destruction. The most savage abuse seemed to be coming from the clique. Blake's rumors about Emily's drug and alcohol consumption had taken on their own life. She was not just a user but a dealer. Not just a stoner but a junkie. Ricky had layered in her own lies, telling anyone who would listen that she had seen Emily giving blowjobs to several boys behind the gym. Then of course several boys had volunteered that they were the ones on the receiving end. Nardo was predictably cruel, making snide comments every single time he passed within hearing distance—

Plebe one day.

Fucking cunt the next.

And, on the days when Emily looked particularly down, *Fat bitch*.

Clay was completely ignoring her, which was far more hurtful than Nardo's nasty asides. As far as Clay seemed concerned, Emily was a nonentity. Her presence in the cafeteria or on the street had as much impact on him as the payphone on the wall or the mailbox on the corner.

Then there were the others. Melody Brickel offered a smile every time she saw Emily, but the smiles were only a reminder of what had been lost.

Dean Wexler had demanded that Emily be transferred out of his class. Because the school year was so late in the term, she now spent that period in a makeshift study hall, alone in the library.

Then there was Cheese—or Jack, as Emily had to think of him now.

Jack went out of his way to avoid her at school. He barely talked to her outside of class, and during non-school hours, he was always tied up. He had told Emily it was because his father was making him work at the station. The excuse felt weak. Jack had said many times that he was not going to the state police academy this summer. He was going to leave town as soon as he graduated.

Emily thought that her unexplained pregnancy was the reason that there was a noticeable strain between them. She had never asked Jack if he was at The Party. She'd told herself this was because she wasn't going to fall into Nardo's trap, but part of her was secretly afraid of what Jack's answer might be.

Had Jack been at Nardo's?

Had he done something to Emily?

Emily caught herself staring blankly into the refrigerator. She had forgotten what she was here for.

Beer, Cool Whip, sodas, milk.

She should go talk to Jack. They had never kept secrets between them. Not about the important stuff. She had seen him slip into the shed last night. Emily had left him a pillow and fresh blanket because she knew the holidays were always bad at his house. His mother would open the alcohol shortly after breakfast. The Chief would join in by noon. By the time dinner time rolled around, they were either screaming at each other, involved in a physical altercation, or both passed out on the floor.

"Pudding," Emily said, finally remembering why she was freezing her ass off in the garage.

She placed the bucket of Cool Whip on top of the pan and used her hip to shut the fridge door. She cut across the empty space where her father's car was normally parked. She wondered if he was really at the club. They did shotgun starts on Thanksgiving morning so that the staff could have some semblance of a holiday. She knew he'd signed up for nine holes, but she also knew it didn't take four hours to play the back nine.

"Did you get lost?" Esther was waiting for her at the door.

She hefted up the pudding. "I couldn't get that stupid song out of my head."

Esther took a breath, then belted out, "'Fath'r and I went down to camp along with Captain Goodin'"

Emily joined in. "'And there we saw the men and boys as thick as hasty puddin'.'"

Esther stomped her feet along with Emily as they marched back into the house, both singing at the top of their lungs—

"'And there was Captain Washington and gentle folks about him . . . they say he's grown so tarnal proud he will not ride without them!'"

Emily felt giddy as her mother pulled her into a side hug. Esther really was in a brilliant mood. They hadn't sung together in ages.

"Oh, dear." Esther wiped tears of laughter from her eyes. "That was fun, wasn't it?"

Emily felt like she was preening. "You're very happy today."

"Why wouldn't I be happy? I get to spend the entire day with my family." She held onto Emily's arm for a few seconds, then returned to the dinner preparation. "Sit down. I think I can manage the rest."

Emily was grateful for the reprieve. She propped her feet on Gram's empty chair. Her back was no longer in spasm, but now she felt her toes were swelling into hurtful sausages.

She told her mother, "I should work on my English assignment. The paper is half my grade."

"Don't worry about that today." Esther had her back to Emily, but her spine had stiffened. She turned around, crossed her arms over her chest. "Actually, perhaps you shouldn't worry about any of it. You should leave school now on your own terms rather than waiting until it becomes impossible."

Emily felt breathless from the very idea. "Mom, I can't leave school. If I make it into next year, I'll have enough credits to graduate."

"You'll have a baby by graduation, Emily. Surely you don't expect to walk across the stage with the rest of the class."

Emily felt the lightness of the last few moments being snuffed out. The two of them were not contemporaries, nor were they friends. Esther was her mother, and her mother was passing down an edict.

"That's not fair," Emily said. If Esther was going to sound like an adult, she was going to sound like a child. "You're making it out like I have no choice."

"You do have a choice," Esther said. "You can choose to focus on what is important."

"My education isn't important?"

"Of course it is. Or, rather, it will be."

"Mom, I—" Emily hadn't said the words out loud before, but she had been thinking them for the last month. "I can still go to college. We could hire a nanny and—"

"With what money?" Esther's hands were raised in the air, unwittingly gesturing toward the mansion that had been in Franklin's family for over half a century. "Who is going to pay for this nanny, Emily? Will you have a job in addition to attending classes? Will she be there when you have to prepare for your courses and write your papers?"

"I—" Emily saw now that she should have planned out this conversation ahead of time. She needed actual numbers to show her parents, an explanation of how a small investment now could pay dividends in the future. "I can't *not* go to college."

"Yes, you *will* go to college," Esther said. "Eventually. When the baby is old enough to go to school. After he's been successfully enrolled for a few years, you can—"

"That's eight years!" Emily was flabbergasted. "You want me to go to college when I'm nearly thirty?"

"It's not entirely unheard of," Esther said, but she glaringly left out any examples. "You can't take care of an infant while you're in college, dear. That's not possible."

Emily could not believe the hypocrisy. "That's exactly what you did!"

"Lower your voice," Esther cautioned. "It was different for me. Your grandmother was home with you while I was at Harvard. And I had a husband. Your father gave me legitimacy. He allowed me to seek a career outside of the home."

"Allowed?" Emily couldn't help but laugh. "You're always telling me that women can do anything."

"They can," Esther said. "But within reason."

Her hands flew into the air in exasperation. "Mom!"

"Emily," Esther said, her voice tightly controlled. "I know that we said we were not going to discuss the circumstances surrounding the genesis of your condition."

"Christ, you sound like a lawyer."

They both looked stunned. Emily's hand slapped to her mouth. She thought things like that all of the time, but she never, ever said them out loud.

Instead of admonishing her, Esther sat down at the table. She dried her hands on her apron. "You have to earn your way back, Emily. You broke a rule—a cardinal rule—that women are not allowed to break. Those doors that were once open to you are now closed. These are the consequences you must suffer for your actions."

"What actions? I didn't—"

"You're not returning to school," Esther said. "Principal Lampert called your father last week. The decision has been made. There is nothing you can do about it. You have been dis-enrolled."

Emily felt tears moisten her eyes. From birth, Esther had pounded into her the value of an education. Emily had spent hours studying and memorizing and drilling for every test, every paper, so that her mother would be proud.

And now, Esther was telling her that it was all for nothing.

"Emily, this isn't the end of world," Esther said, though clearly it was the end of something. "Your father and I have discussed this, and we are in agreement."

"Oh, if Father says it, okay."

Esther ignored her sarcasm. "What you will do is bide your time. You will stay in the house, keep yourself out of the public eye, and then, when enough time has passed, we will come up with a way to reintroduce you into the world."

"You want me to stay locked in the house for eight years?"

"Stop being dramatic," Esther said. "You'll have a confinement until the baby arrives. You may walk in the back garden or, when school is in session, up and down the street. You should maintain a healthy exercise regime."

Emily heard the practiced tone in her voice. She could see her parents hashing this out late at night, Franklin pacing the room with a glass of Scotch in his hand, Esther making a list of what Emily could and could not do, neither of them bothering to question what their pregnant daughter wanted.

The same way they had decided on her behalf that she would carry this baby.

The same way that they were making her leave school, give up graduating, defer college, postpone her life.

"And then?" Emily asked, because she wanted to know what else they had decided.

Esther seemed relieved by the question, which she clearly inferred as consent. "When the time feels right, your father and I will start taking you to functions. Something easy at first, only with our people. We'll choose those who are most amenable to your reintroduction. Perhaps once the child is old enough, you could get an internship. Or a secretarial position."

"You're such a hypocrite."

Esther looked more amused than insulted. "I beg your pardon?"

Emily was tired of keeping all of the thoughts in her head from coming out of her mouth. It was exhausting to be considerate, especially when no one—ever—thought to be considerate to her in return.

She told her mother, "You preach from on high about how important it is for women to be strong. You project this sense of invincibility. You let everyone think that you're fearless, but everything you do, every choice you make, is because you're afraid."

"I'm afraid?" Esther huffed a laugh. "Young lady, I've never been afraid of anything in my life."

"How many times has Dad hit you?"

Esther locked her in with a steely gaze. "Be careful."

"Or what?" Emily asked. "Dad will give me another bruise? He'll twist Gram's wrist until she shouts? He'll drag you up the stairs by your arm and beat you with your hairbrush?"

Esther did not look away, but nor did she see Emily.

"You are so terrified of what people will think of you," Emily said. "That's why you stay with Dad. That's why you want to lock me inside the house. You have wasted your entire life trying to act the way they want you to."

"My entire life," Esther mocked. "Pray tell, who is *they*?"

"*They* is *everybody*," Emily said. "You wouldn't let me get an abortion because *they* might find out. You wouldn't let me pursue adoption because *they* would use it against you. I'm being forced out of school because *they* told you it was time. You act as if you are in complete control of your life, your legacy, but you are terrified that *they* can take everything away from you at any time."

Esther pursed her lips. "Go on. Get it all out."

She was acting like Emily just needed a punching bag when Emily was deadly serious. "I'm not suffering the consequences of my actions, Mother. I am suffering the consequences of your cowardice."

Esther raised an eyebrow, the same way she did when she was humoring someone.

"You're a hypocrite." Emily was repeating herself, but now, the words felt like a revelation. She had never before spoken to anyone so plainly. Why had she been so silent for so many years? Why had she worried so much about saying the wrong thing, doing the wrong thing, making the wrong people upset?

What were *they* going to do?

Emily stood up, fists on the table. "You have this amazing gift of willful blindness. You think you're so smart, so clever, but you never see the things that you don't want to see."

"What don't I want to see?"

"That you're terrified," Emily said. "You walk around holding fear in your mouth all the time."

"Really?"

"Really," Emily said. "You've got lines around your mouth from holding it in, pursing your lips the same way you're doing right now."

Esther's lips unpursed. She tried to laugh it off, but there was nothing to laugh at.

Emily said, "I see you choking on your fear all of the time. With Father. With your friends. Even with me and Gram. You try so hard to swallow it down, but it won't go. All it does is turn your words into a weapon every time you speak. And what you say is bullshit, Mother. It's all bullshit because you are terrified that people will see the truth about you."

"And what is this truth?"

"That you're a coward."

Esther sat back in the chair. Her legs were crossed. "I'm a coward, am I?"

"Why else is this happening?" Emily demanded. "Why aren't you standing up for me? Why aren't you telling Principal Lampert to fuck off? Why aren't you down at Georgetown demanding they honor their acceptance letter? Telling the senator that I'll be reporting for my internship? Telling Dad that he has to—"

"You have no idea what I've done for you."

"Then tell me!" Emily yelled. "You talk all the time about being a model for other women. What are you modeling for me, Mom?"

Emily had pounded the table so hard that the pumpkin seeds had spilled from the bowl. She watched her mother gather them together, scraping them to the edge so that they would drop into her hand. She didn't speak until everything was back in its place.

"My dear, to be perfectly honest, you are not the type of woman I am modeling for," Esther said. "No matter how your pregnancy happened, it happened. You *let* it happen by putting yourself in a precarious situation. Now, if you were some poor girl living in a trailer in Alabama, your choices would be different."

Her words were so close to what Ricky had screamed at Emily a few weeks ago that Emily felt a physical weight on her shoulders.

"I acknowledge that the next few years will be a difficult period of your life," Esther said. "But one day you will realize the gift that your father and I are giving you. If you make these sacrifices now, if you use your time wisely, you will eventually be welcomed back into the fold."

Emily wiped her mouth. She had been so mad that spit had flown out of her mouth. "And if I don't?"

Esther shrugged as if to say it was obvious. "*They* will cast you out."

Emily's throat worked. She could not imagine how it was possible for her to be more cast out than she was right now.

"What if—" Emily flailed around, trying to form a cogent alternative. "What if we just played by their rules until you're confirmed? Dad is always saying it's for your lifetime. Once you're on the bench, what does it matter?"

Esther looked at her as if she could not believe Emily had come from her own body. "Do you really think that my most ardent ambition is to spend my lifetime merely as a federal judge?"

Emily knew that it was not.

"You watched Sandy O'Connor's confirmation on television. Jesse Helms nearly took her down over her views on abortion." Esther jabbed her finger into the table. "You think that your life is hard? Sandy couldn't find a job when she graduated Columbia Law. She had to forgo a salary and sit with the secretaries just to get her foot in the door. And now she's a sitting Supreme Court justice."

"But—" Emily tried to parry. "You can change that, Mother. Can't you see that—"

"I can't do anything from the outside."

"There won't be another opening for years, and even then, it could be a decade or more before another woman is nominated, let alone confirmed. This is about what you have an opportunity to do right now, Mother." Emily tried to take the begging tone out of her voice. "We could pretend that we're doing what you said. I'll go ahead and drop out of school. Once the senate hearings are over and you're sworn in, I can take summer school classes and then I could—"

"The federal judgeship is already locked down," Esther said. "I had prepared to make the announcement in a toast before dinner. Reagan himself called me this morning. Not even your father knows."

Emily was knocked back by the news, which neatly explained her mother's ebullient mood. She hadn't been pleased to have her family around her for the holiday. She had been elated because she had gotten what she wanted.

For now.

"Reagan says the process will take longer than I'd like, but that can't be helped. The announcement will come in March, before the Easter break. There will be a period of vetting, I'll take meetings at the Capitol, then the confirmation hearing will begin in late April." Esther sounded positively effusive. "Ronnie wants to set a standard, to show the country he's not merely elevating women for the sake of elevating women. He's elevating the *right* women."

"Jesus," Emily muttered. She felt utterly defeated.

"Language," Esther cautioned. "Emily, when he called this morning, Ronnie referred to the Pericope Adulterae. John 8:1–20. Do you know what that means?"

Emily had nothing to say. Her mother was almost giddy as she relayed the conversation. Nothing Emily had said in the last ten minutes had cracked Esther's hard shell. Emily had challenged her, she had called her mother out for her hypocrisy, and now Esther was quoting John the Apostle as if none of it had happened.

"You know the passage," Esther said. "The Pharisees brought to Jesus an adulterous woman. They told Him, 'The Law of Moses commanded us to stone such a woman. What do you say?'"

Emily felt her mind going back through the conversation as she tried to find the moment Esther had climbed back onto her high horse. She was clearly expecting Emily to play the game, to do the same thing they did with Franklin. Ignore the bruises. Forget about the yelling. Pretend like the sobbing and begging Emily heard through their bedroom wall had come from the television and not her mother.

Esther said, "The Pharisees were trying to test Jesus. To see how strongly His morals would hold. Do you know what Jesus said? Do you?"

Emily was disgusted with herself for knowing the answer. She had learned it in Sunday School, but had not until this moment wondered why the Pharisees were ready to stone the woman but never deigned to consider punishing the man with whom she'd been caught red-handed.

"Do you know the verse?" Esther asked.

Emily recited by rote. "'He lifted up Himself and said unto them, he that is without sin among you, let him first cast a stone at her.'"

"Precisely." Esther nodded approvingly. "Reagan understands that good people can sometimes make mistakes. You know that he was divorced before he married Nancy."

Emily nodded along with her mother as if she gave a shit about Ronald Reagan's personal life. Emily was not an adulterous woman. She had not knowingly made a mistake.

"Ronnie told me that your father and I have set an admirable example by supporting you through this difficult time. He said it showed great strength of character."

"Oh," Emily said, as if everything was clear now. "If Reagan says you're not a hypocritical coward, then what the fuck does your own daughter know?"

"I told you to watch your language." Esther stood up from the table. The conversation ended that abruptly. "Place the pumpkin seeds by the bar in the parlor. Your father will be home soon. I want to make sure dinner is on the table by the time he is out of the shower. Your grandmother will probably . . ."

Esther's entreaties faded away as Emily carried the bowl of pumpkin seeds toward the parlor. She should've known better than to attempt to argue with a woman whose career had been built on winning arguments.

But it was more than that.

Emily would never get through to her mother, mostly because the judge would always stand in the way. Esther was the house-wife, the gardener, the food heater-upper, the mom, the daughter-in-law, the occasional field trip chaperone. The judge was the one whose principal design was to project strength. Everyone described her as intimidating. She held forth at parties like a scholar. Her opinions were circulated as if she was a deity. She wielded her intelligence like a sword. She ruled over her courtroom like a queen.

And then she came home and her husband pounded the shit out of her.

Emily ate a handful of pumpkin seeds. They crunched between her teeth. Instead of going into the parlor, she pushed open the patio door. Cold air whipped her hair around her face. She hugged the pumpkin seeds close to her chest.

Despite Sisyphus repeatedly rolling his rock across her body in the family kitchen, Emily smiled at the thought of seeing Jack. She would take him a plate of food once dinner was over. He generally subsisted on candy bars and beef jerky when he spent nights in the shed. At least going by the wrappers Emily cleaned out the next day. The pumpkin seeds would tide him over for a while.

The warped shed door hadn't shut all the way. Emily would bring Jack one of the spare duvets from the closet. He never complained about the cold, but it was particularly brutal this time of year. There was no insulation in the shed. Even a slight breeze could rattle the single-paned glass like a train chugging down the tracks.

Emily paused outside the door, listening. Her heart felt shattered when she heard a low moan. Every time she told herself she was completely alone in the world, she should remind herself of what Jack was going through. Esther was a sanctimonious hypocrite and Franklin was a tyrant, but at least Emily wasn't spending Thanksgiving in a cold shed.

She leaned down, thinking she could leave the bowl of seeds for him, but then she heard the moan again. Her heart ached for him. Emily had seen Jack cry before. More than a few times, to be honest. The distance he was keeping from her at school had been hurtful, but he was still her friend.

Emily pushed open the door.

At first, she wasn't sure what she was seeing. Her mind could not make sense of it.

Clay's back was to the door. Jack's hands were braced against the workbench. She thought they were fighting. Wrestling. Playing. But then she saw that Clay's pants were down around his ankles. Jack moaned again. The bench shook as Clay thrust into him.

They were having sex.

9

Andrea repeated her question. "What's in the briefcase?"

Instead of responding, the judge's gaze rested on Franklin Vaughn. There was no emotion on her face, no gesture of love between them. The man who had been her husband for almost half a century was going to be dead in a matter of hours. Esther herself was not going to be long behind him.

She told Andrea, "When I was given the news about my cancer, I attempted to put my affairs in order. Franklin had always managed that aspect of our lives. I assumed that the wills were in the safe along with all the financial documents. I was correct, but I had not anticipated that I would find this as well."

Esther reached down, struggling to lift the briefcase from the floor. Andrea went around the bed to help her. The case was lighter than she expected. She lifted it with one hand onto the judge's lap.

"Thank you." Esther's fingers rolled the combination. The locks clicked open.

Andrea was standing over her, so she could see inside. Sheafs of papers, a few manila envelopes, and an older-looking laptop with the power cord still attached.

"Franklin was always far more technically inclined than I." Esther looked up at Andrea. "He recorded all of his conversations with Wexler. The Fontaine boy makes several appearances, too. There are audio recordings of the earlier meetings. Later, it appears that Franklin secreted a video camera in the bookcase so he could capture the negotiations. One in particular is very damning. They structured a land charity using Fontaine to hide a conservation easement that netted Wexler over three million dollars. The federal statute of limitations for conspiracy and continuing offenses begins not with the original act, but upon abandonment, withdrawal, or the accomplishment of the conspiracy's objectives. The black-mail alone has lasted nearly four decades. The trick with fraud is to prove intent. The video recordings provide ample proof. You have them dead to rights."

Andrea should have felt elated, but all she could summon was anger. This information had been available for decades. "Why didn't Franklin—he could have—"

"Yes, Franklin could have exposed them years ago. He shares the legal blame, but the moral failure is entirely mine." Esther's lips pursed as she tried to collect herself. "I told myself that the difference of a few months would be inconsequential. Thanks to the death threats, Judith and Guinevere would be under twenty-four-hour protection. Bible would go to the literal ends of the earth to ensure their safety. I would reach the end of my life on my own terms. Wexler and Fontaine would be exposed after I was gone. No one else would be hurt. At least I told myself that, but I was wrong, wasn't I?"

Andrea felt the lump come back into her throat. "Alice Poulsen."

"Yes, Alice Poulsen." Esther reached into the briefcase, but only to rest her hand on a thick manila envelope. She looked Andrea in the eye. "My cowardice cost another parent their child. I did not earn a peaceful death. I do not deserve it."

Andrea watched her pull the envelope from the briefcase. The label was handwritten—

To be delivered to Leonard Bible upon my death.

Esther said, "This contains copies of all of the supporting docu-ments for the original land transfer, the conservation easement and the charitable land trust. The laptop has all of the recordings, video and audio, as well as pertinent emails, wire transactions, bank account routing numbers and tax documents. You'll find dates, times, locations, steps taken when they forced me to intervene in legal matters. I've included a summation on top outlining the case. Dean Wexler and Bernard Fontaine can be charged for tax evasion, tax fraud, wire fraud—countless other crimes. It's all in here."

Andrea was too stunned to take the envelope. Esther was literally offering everything they needed to stop Wexler and Nardo.

"As long as I am capable, the government will have my full cooperation." Now that she had made up her mind, Esther seemed eager to get it over with. She returned the envelope to the briefcase and waited for Andrea to take it all away.

There was nothing more to be said.

Andrea's hands had started to shake. She felt sweaty and cold at the same time. She clutched the briefcase to her chest. The weight was heavier this time. Alice Poulsen's restless soul was inside. Star Bonaire's shaky future. Esther Vaughn's undeserved peaceful death.

The Marshals nodded to Andrea as she left Franklin Vaughn's room. Only when she had reached the end of the corridor did Andrea let herself acknowledge what she was holding.

Evidence of Wexler and Nardo's crimes.

Enough to put them in prison. Enough to shut down the farm.

The elation finally came. Her brain was dizzy with it. Adrenaline sharpened everything to a point. She was jogging as she turned the corner, her head swiveling in search of Bible. She saw him near the elevators talking to Mike. They were both leaning against the high counter of the nurses' station. Bible cradled his bandaged hand. Compton was a few feet away typing on her phone.

"Andy?" Mike saw her first. "What's wrong?"

Andrea could barely speak. Her hands almost slipped on the briefcase. She stumbled the last few feet to reach them.

"Andy?" Mike took the briefcase. "Are you okay?"

"I'm—" She had to stop to take a breath. "The judge wrote the death threats to herself."

Compton looked up from her phone. Bible's jaw was clenched, but he said nothing.

"She—" Andrea had to stop again. She took another breath. She placed her hand to her chest, coaxing her heart to slow. "The judge was being blackmailed by Wexler. For decades. Since Judith was a baby. Wexler told her that he was the father, but I don't know. He could be lying. But it doesn't matter because we've— we've got them. Both of them. Nardo was in on it, too."

"Oliver, take me through this." Compton had knelt on the

floor with the briefcase so she could go through the contents. "What am I looking at here?"

"The laptop. Franklin Vaughn recorded everything. There's enough in there to send Wexler and Fontaine to prison for fraud, at least." Andrea was on her knees, too. She found the envelope that had been meant for Bible. "Esther outlined—everything is outlined in here. She said she built a case for us. That both Wexler and Fontaine were implicated."

Compton was silent as her eyes scanned the bullet-pointed pages. Her head started shaking when she got to the last item. "Son of a fucking bitch. She practically wrote the warrant applications for us. Leonard—"

They all looked up at Bible. His jaw was still set.

Compton stood up. She pressed her hand to the side of his face. "Put it in the trash, baby. Take it out tomorrow. All right?"

Bible gave a curt nod, but the look of betrayal did not go away. "She give us enough?"

"She did." Compton searched for Mike, who was plugging the laptop into an outlet behind the nurses' station. "Mike, you're seconded to me for the duration. Chain of custody starts now. We need to do this by the book. Upload those videos to DOJ. I want search warrants for the farm. Arrest warrants for Wexler and Fontaine. We need to do this tonight. I've got some Marshals in the area I can pull in for surveillance on the farm. We've gotta make sure Wexler and Fontaine don't bolt before we can scoop them up. Men like that always have an escape plan. Can Stilton be trusted?"

The question had been directed at Bible. He shook his head, but said, "Unknown."

"All right, we'll leave Stilton on the bench until the arrests are made. Fontaine was carrying concealed. We have to assume they're armed. I'll call down the strike team from Baltimore. We don't want this turning into a hostage situation. Priority one is securing those girls, right?"

Compton was waiting for Bible.

He said, "Right."

"Good," she said. "I'll have ambulances at the ready in case anyone chooses to leave. They'll be taken to Johns Hopkins.

Hopefully, there's a way to break Wexler's hold on them. Same with Fontaine. If Esther's right, he's staring down Big Boy Prison. He'll want a deal to turn against Wexler. We'll transfer him to Baltimore, give him time to sweat it out. Bible, I'll need you to take the lead on Fontaine. Give him twenty-four hours in a holding cell and he'll be ready to talk."

"No, ma'am," Bible said. "I want Wexler, and I want him tonight."

Compton asked, "Why?"

"We're never gonna have him this scared again," Bible said. "We yank him out of bed, pop him into Stilton's holding cell, go at him hard, get him to confess. That's the quickest way to get this over and done with."

"Or we throw him into holding, he shits himself, asks for a lawyer, and we see him at trial in three years," Compton said. "We only get one bite at this apple. If we give Wexler some time on the ride to Baltimore, he might start thinking he can talk his way out of this big misunderstanding. That's what we want, right? We want him talking to us, explaining things."

"He's a psychopath," Bible said. "You give him time to regroup, he's gonna come up with a plan."

"I hear you." Compton turned to Mike. "You're on the team. What do you think—push Wexler tonight or give him some time?"

"My gut says tonight. And not that you asked, but I don't want Fontaine to get a deal." Mike shrugged. "Why go after Renfield when you can drive a stake through Dracula's heart?"

Andrea felt herself nodding. She didn't want Nardo to get away with anything, either. Renfield was almost too accurate a description. Nardo wasn't only Dean's acolyte. He literally procured victims for his malevolent master.

"Oliver." Compton had turned to Andrea. "Chime in."

Andrea could only share what she knew to be true. "Nardo will lawyer up. That's what he always does. If the plan is to get him to turn on Wexler, I don't think that will happen until his back is against the wall. And maybe not even then. He's a nihilist."

"Okay, take Fontaine off the board," Compton said. "What's the best way to go at Wexler?"

"He only makes mistakes when he's angry." Andrea had seen Wexler out of control. She had also seen him less than ten minutes later when he was bragging about single-handedly ushering in the organic farming movement. "If you give him time to calm down, he'll use it to find a way out."

"All right, decision made," Compton said. "Bible, you and Oliver will take Wexler tonight. We'll snatch him up at the farm and take him directly to Stilton's shop. Fontaine will go to Baltimore. Oliver, go back to the motel and get a shower. Once we have Wexler in custody, we'll swing by on our way to the police station. Plan for three hours. Be ready in two."

Andrea was not going to sit around for two more hours. "Ma'am, I—"

"You'll follow orders," Compton said. "I don't need another muscle. I need a brain. You've dealt with Wexler before. He knows you're not afraid of him. You can't look like you've just run out of a fire and jumped into a swimming pool when he sees you. Bible, help her figure this out, then come find me. Mike, let's get some privacy so we can watch those videos."

Mike closed the laptop. He caught Andrea's eye again before he left with Compton.

Andrea's weight had shifted to the balls of her feet. She felt like her body was coiled. She was desperate to go after them, to be doing something instead of this interminable waiting.

She asked Bible, "What's the strategy? How are we going to get Wexler to confess?"

"You can't strategize with a psychopath. They're always gonna come at you from a different angle."

Andrea had not really thought about Wexler as a psychopath until now. He fit the criteria: lack of shame or remorse, grandiose sense of self-importance, manipulative, poor impulse control. She was intimately familiar with the list because she had noted the same attributes in her father.

"All right," she said. "But we have to have some kind of plan or framework or—"

"No lesson plan for this, partner." Bible shrugged, as if it was inconsequential. "You're just playing hopscotch, all right? Throw a rock onto the square, wait for Wexler to jump to it."

Andrea didn't want another homily. She wanted details. "So—what? We let him lecture us on fava beans and hope he says by-the-way yeah I committed a bunch of fraud where do I sign my confession?"

"That'd be great, but I don't think that's gonna happen," Bible said. "We steer the conversation. We keep nudging him along the way. Eventually, he'll get to the right square."

"I can't do metaphors right now, Bible. This is too important. Every time you've thrown me into the deep end, I've figured out how to swim. This time is different. I need broad strokes."

"Okay, I hear ya," he said. "Let's plan this out. I'll take the lead in the interview. That good by you?"

Andrea had expected as much. "Yes."

"Then ol' Dean comes in and he says, 'I'll only talk to her.'" Bible pointed his finger at Andrea's chest. "So, I get up and leave you two alone. Then what?"

Andrea chewed her lip.

"Or we decide you're gonna take the lead, right?" Bible didn't expect an answer. "And ol' Dean says, 'Nope, not talking to that girl. I only talk to men.' And you have to get up and leave."

"Then we both—"

"We both spend the next two hours getting our heads on straight," Bible said. "That's how we prepare. That's the strategy. We can't anticipate what he's gonna say. We think he'll wanna talk about the farm? Maybe he wants to talk about Emily. We think he wants to talk about Emily? Maybe he wants to talk about how his mama never loved him or his daddy shot a mock-ingbird."

"So we just let him talk about whatever he wants to talk about?"

"Correct," Bible said. "You heard the Boss. Talking is exactly what we want him to do. We get him wound up, we give him an audience, he makes a mistake. We can only keep in mind where we need to end up. And where is that?"

"Jesus." Andrea wasn't up for the Socratic method, either. "The blackmail. The bogus land deal. The labor board case. The conservation easement. The tax evasion. The bogus charity. Emily fucking Vaughn."

"We just need one of those." Bible held up his finger. "We get him to admit to one bad thing. Then we walk him through it, and we get him to another bad thing. Then another bad thing. Throw the rock, jump to the square. That's how we win. It takes time."

She told Bible, "I'm so fucking tired of all this hurry up and wait."

"It's the nature of the beast."

"It's fucking annoying." Andrea's frustration gave way to anger. "Wexler either raped and killed Emily Vaughn or he knows who did. He's terrorized Esther's family for forty years. He's got his foot on Star Bonaire's neck. He's pushed Melody Brickel to the brink of bankruptcy. Alice Poulsen killed herself to get away from him. He's got at least a dozen more girls who are living corpses on the farm. Every fucking thing that guy touches either withers away or dies and he always manages to get away with it."

Bible studied her carefully. "Sounds to me like you're making this personal."

"You're damn right I am."

Andrea had been too impatient to wait around for a ride back to the motel. She'd walked the short distance from the hospital, the bag marked PATIENT BELONGINGS swinging from her hand. She shouldn't have bothered. Her clothes could not be saved. Her waterlogged service weapon was being sent back to Baltimore and she wouldn't get a replacement until tomorrow morning. Her Android was still in her backpack in Bible's SUV. Her iPhone was so damaged that parts of the guts were showing through the broken glass. Even her shoes were trashed. Pool water squicked out with every step.

The longest, hottest shower in the world had finally made her feel clean, but nothing could clear Andrea's mind of Dean Wexler. She kept silently going back over what Esther Vaughn had told her. Not about the blackmail and fraud, but about losing her shit when she'd found Wexler holding Judith in the garden. At a molecular level, Andrea understood that kind of terror. She also understood what it felt like to think of yourself as one kind of person, then have trauma split you into another.

As with Laura, as with Esther and Star and Alice, Andrea had led two different lives: the one before she had met a psychopath and the one after.

She walked over to the window and peered through the curtains. The road was empty, the forest behind was cast in total darkness. The surveillance teams would be set up by now. Six Marshals would be guarding all the roads leading into and out of the farm, watching the activities, trying to ascertain the locations of Wexler and Nardo. The strike team would be en route from Baltimore. The warrants would be in process, maybe already signed. There was nothing for Andrea to do but try not to pull out her hair while she waited, waited, waited.

She looked at the clock: 11:10 p.m. She had at least ninety more minutes before she was face-to-face with Dean Wexler again.

Andrea pressed her forehead to the cold glass. Bible had told her not to plan, but she had to plan. She didn't have his natural self-confidence, let alone his decades of experience. She conjured up the cramped interrogation room at the back of Stilton's police station. She tried to imagine herself sitting across from Wexler. Instead, she found herself back in the farmhouse kitchen. Star assembling the ingredients for bread. Wexler droning on like a televangelist. The self-satisfied look on his face. The long pause he had taken before allowing Star to place his glass of water on the table.

He liked being in control. He liked other people witnessing it.

Which meant he would want both Andrea and Bible in the room.

Bible would do most of the talking. What would Andrea do?

She walked to the desk. The notebook was no longer blank. She had written down some observations about her short time alone with Dean Wexler. Bible had his hopscotch, but Andrea had her triggers. The goal tonight was to make Wexler feel out of control. That was when he would make his first mistake. Andrea had three previous examples of Wexler's façade dropping, and they had all happened inside of his old Ford truck.

The first time was when Andrea had said Emily Vaughn's name. Without warning, Wexler had slammed on the brakes, almost sending Andrea's head into the dash.

He had hit the brakes a second time when Andrea had pointed out that, though Wexler had left teaching, he had still found a way to surround himself with vulnerable young women.

The third incident was both more straightforward and more complicated. Wexler had told Andrea that he took shits bigger than her. Andrea had basically told him to get his head out of his ass.

That was when Wexler had escalated. He'd grabbed Andrea's wrist to silence her.

She tapped her pen on the notepad. Wexler's triggers were easy to spot. He didn't want to hear Emily's name. He didn't like being called a predator. And he sure as hell didn't like being called out on his bullshit.

Andrea didn't know where this information got her to. Were they hopscotch boxes or were they the rocks? She put down the pen. She walked back to the window and peered out at the desolate road again. She crossed her arms. She put her back to the window. She let her eyes close.

There was a fine line between prodding Wexler's ego and bringing out his rage. Andrea wasn't worried about his violence. She could handle herself, though she doubted Bible would let it get that far. The problem was, if she pushed Wexler too hard or in the wrong direction, she'd end up ruining everything. On the other hand, if she didn't push hard enough, Wexler might think that Andrea was afraid. If his behavior had proven anything it was that Dean Wexler liked it when women were afraid.

Andrea opened her eyes. The clock told her that only two more minutes had passed. Eighty-eight more minutes of pacing and looking out the window would not get her any closer to a strategy. She knew how to piss off Wexler, but she did not know how to get information out of him. Melody Brickel had said that Wexler was a cheap copy of Clayton Morrow. Andrea knew of only one person on earth who had faced down Clayton Morrow and lived to talk about it.

She picked up the desk telephone and dialed the number before she could change her mind.

Her mother answered on the fourth ring. "Darling? Are you okay? What time is it?"

"I'm fine, Mom. I'm sorry I—" Something occurred to her. "Did the Caller ID come up?"

Laura took a long pause before answering. "I know you're in Longbill Beach."

Andrea muttered a curse. She was supposed to help trick Dean Wexler into confessing, but she hadn't been clever enough to turn off the location services on her iPhone. "So you've been lying this whole time?"

"You mean the same way you've been lying to me?"

Fair.

"Darling, are you okay?"

Andrea rested her head in her hand. She could feel the thick threads stitching together the cut in her forehead. Her nose was throbbing. Her throat ached. "I'm sorry I lied to you."

"Well, I'm not sorry I lied to you. It was fun listening to your voice squeak."

Also fair.

Laura asked, "Why are you calling from your motel room? What's wrong?"

"Nothing." Andrea suppressed a cough. "Don't worry, I haven't flung myself over any cliffs lately."

"I believe it's *flinged*."

Andrea opened her mouth, then closed it. This was not the first time they had argued over past participles. The last two years had been riddled with petty disagreements. Andrea decided to finally take the razor out of her mouth.

"Mom, I need your help."

"Of course," Laura said. "What's wrong?"

"Nothing is wrong," she insisted. "Can you—would you mind—telling me some things about him?"

Laura didn't ask for a proper noun. Clayton Morrow was the Voldemort of their lives. "What do you want to know?"

"I—" Andrea wasn't sure where to start. In the past, she had always shut down whenever Laura brought up her father. The only way she could get through this was to remind herself that, over forty years ago, Dean Wexler had studied from the book of Clay Morrow. "What do you remember about him? I mean, when you first met him."

"The sex wasn't great."

"Mom."

"All right," Laura said. "I suppose there's a better way to say it. The sex really didn't matter. Being able to hold his attention was the aphrodisiac. Obviously, I wasn't the only one he kept in thrall. I saw him do it with men, other women, even children. He watches people, and he figures out what they need, and he finds a way to become the only person in the world who can give it to them. After that, they'll do anything he asks."

Andrea knew instinctively that Wexler followed the same pattern. He had denied having contact with the volunteers, but Star was clearly under his thumb. She was literally torturing herself into an early grave.

"Considering your current location," Laura continued, "I never believed your father killed that poor teenager. Not when I was told about it, and not now."

Andrea did not want to get sidetracked, but she couldn't help asking, "Why not?"

"I don't agree with your current career, but I'm still your mother. I looked at the syllabi you emailed me. Six of your courses at Glynco dealt with analyzing criminal psychology."

Andrea should not have been surprised. "And?"

"Look at the charges that were made against your father. At least the crimes that the government knew about. Everything was conspiracy this, conspiracy that. He never got his hands dirty. Committing acts of violence was beneath him."

Andrea knew that wasn't true. "I've seen a scar that tells me otherwise."

"Darling, it was the eighties. Everyone got a little rough."

Andrea was silent. Laura always spoke too lightly about the violence she had suffered at Clay's hands.

Laura said, "Your father's kink wasn't committing actual crimes. He got off on making other people commit crimes for him."

Andrea bit her lip. Another personality trait Wexler had mimicked. Nardo Fontaine screened all the prospective volunteers. His name was listed on the fake charity that had netted Wexler $3,000,000. Andrea could easily see Nardo coming up with the original plan to blackmail the judge. And she could see him following Guinevere around town with a camera, reveling in the chaos the photographs would bring.

"Andy?"

"You tricked him into incriminating himself," Andrea said. "How did you do that? How do you trick a psychopath into telling the truth?"

Laura kept silent for so long that Andrea wasn't sure she was still on the line. Eventually, her mother said, "You do the same thing that they do to you—you make them think that you believe in them."

Andrea knew that Laura had believed quite a lot of Clay Morrow's destructive philosophy.

"Your father was—" Laura seemed to be searching for a word. "He was so believable. He would tell you things that *sounded* true, but weren't necessarily accurate."

"Were you allowed to disagree with him?"

"Of course," Laura said. "He loved a healthy debate. But you can't have a logical discussion with someone who makes up their own facts. There was always a statistic or a data set that only he knew about. He was smarter than everyone else, you see. He had it all figured out. In the end, you felt embarrassed for not coming round to his point of view sooner. It takes a tremendous amount of arrogance to honestly believe that everyone else in the world is clueless and you're the only one who knows the truth."

Andrea felt herself nodding. That was Wexler, too. "So how do you make them think you believe what they're saying?"

"Start with skepticism, but make it clear that you're open to persuasion. After a while, concede some of their points. Expound upon some of their reasoning. Make them believe you've been swayed by their genius. The easiest way to make someone trust you is to parrot back everything they say." Laura stopped, as if she was afraid that she was giving away too much. "People think psychopaths are so clever, but they generally only go after the low-hanging fruit. I wanted to be persuaded. I needed something to believe in."

"How did you get away from him?"

"What do you mean?" Laura asked. "I told you how I—"

"Not physically." Andrea was thinking about Star Bonaire. "Mentally, how did you get away from him?"

"You," Laura said. "I thought I loved him, but I didn't know love until the first time I held you in my arms. After that, you were all that mattered. And I knew that I had to do everything within my power to keep you safe."

Andrea had heard her mother make similar declarations many times before, but instead of rolling her eyes or brushing it aside, she said, "I know what you gave up to keep me safe."

"Sweetheart, I gave up nothing and I gained everything," Laura said. "Are you sure you don't need me?"

"I needed to hear your voice." Andrea didn't know if it was stress or exhaustion that brought tears to her eyes. "So I've heard your voice, and I'm going to go. But I'll call you this weekend. And—and I really love you, Mom. I love you very much. Okay? I really do love you."

Laura was silent for a moment. It had been a long while since Andrea had said those words and actually meant them. "All right, my beautiful girl. You'll call me this weekend. Promise?"

"I promise."

Andrea rested the phone back in the cradle. She wiped her eyes with the back of her hand. Why she had started crying on the phone with her mother was something to think about another day.

For now, she needed to consider what her mother had told her. Maybe Wexler wasn't a cheap copy of Clay Morrow after all. He sounded more like an exact duplicate. She picked up her notebook and read through Wexler's triggers again. Should she avoid them or use them? Should Andrea try to piss him off or should she try to make him think that she was open to his philosophy?

Or maybe she should let herself accept that Bible was a lot better at this than Andrea was. There was no way to predict a psychopath's behavior. They had to let Wexler take the lead. The strategy would come when they had him talking. All that Andrea could do was mentally prepare herself for the unexpected.

She looked at the clock and let out a sharp, angry curse. Eighty more minutes. She was going to start climbing the walls if she stayed in this room a moment longer. The police station was a ten-minute walk away. Andrea could be waiting on the stairs when the Marshals arrived with Wexler.

She scribbled a note to hang on the door. Andrea was already wearing her only clean clothes, a pair of Cat & Jack pants for active boys and a black T-shirt she had found in the bottom of her duffel bag. Her still-wet sneakers bunched up her socks when she shoved them on. Out of habit, she put her broken iPhone in her back pocket. She closed the door on the edge of the note, hoping it was vague enough but also self-explanatory—

ALREADY AT LOCATION

The motel's welcome sign flickered off as Andrea crossed the road. There was no sidewalk, but she wanted to be under the streetlights. The scent of the ocean was a bitter salt in her busted nose. Her eyes started to sting. She turned away her head and took a deep breath of cold night air. Her wet hair plastered to the back of her neck. She stuck her hands into her pants pockets as she trudged along the straight yellow line.

The sound of a car made Andrea turn. She stepped onto the graveled shoulder. The forest was to her back. She thought about the surveillance teams again. The strike team from Baltimore. The arrest warrants, search warrants. All the girls at the farm.

Andrea continued her walk toward the police station. She mentally ran through the conversation she'd had with her mother. The main thing Andrea had learned two years ago was that psychopaths were like fire. They needed oxygen to burn. Maybe that was the key with Wexler. Andrea knew how to use silence as a weapon. If she could deprive Wexler of oxygen, he might end up burning himself out.

Another car passed. Andrea stepped aside again. She watched a BMW coast toward downtown. The brake lights didn't flash. The car drove to the end of Beach Road, then took a left away from the sea. She started to step back into the street, but a flash of motion stopped her.

Andrea's hand went up to shield her eyes from the streetlights as she looked back in the direction of the motel. She had no memory of walking past an old logging road. She only saw it now because a vehicle was slowly making its way along a narrow dirt path. She heard the low rumble of a muffler. The pops and cracks of tires rolling over tree roots and fallen limbs.

The front end of a blue pick-up truck appeared from the darkness.

Andrea felt her heart freeze at the sight of the old Ford.

The wheels crunched on the gravel shoulder. The headlights were off. Instinctively, Andrea darted across the street so that she could conceal herself in darkness.

The truck idled. Andrea couldn't make out the driver's face, only that his head turned left, then right, before the tires slowly bumped onto the asphalt. She had only a split second to see inside the truck as it turned toward downtown. The streetlight hit their faces. The driver. The passenger.

Bernard Fontaine.

Star Bonaire.

NOVEMBER 26, 1981

The bowl slipped from Emily's hands. Pumpkin seeds scattered across the shed floor.

Clay ripped himself away from Jack. His penis flopped against his jeans as he dragged them up around his hips. He stumbled backward, banging into one of the windows. The glass cracked. Emily could hear the fracture work its way into the next pane, then the next.

"Oh God!" Jack was kneeling on the floor. His hands covered his face in shame. He rocked back and forth. "Oh-God-oh-God-oh-God . . ."

Clay didn't say anything. He looked equal parts terrified and enraged.

"I'm—" Emily had no more words. Her brain was dizzy with what she had seen. She shouldn't be here. This was private. "I'm sorry."

She turned to leave, but Clay moved so quickly that he slammed the door closed before she reached it.

"Look at me!" He grabbed her arms and banged her back against the door. "If you tell anybody about this, I'll fucking kill you!"

Emily was too shaken to respond. She had not let herself understand it in the moment, but now she felt the knowledge settle deep into her mind. The two boys had been having sex. Clay and Jack. How long had they been doing it? Were they in love? Surely you had to love someone if you let them do that to you. Why did Clay treat Jack so badly if they were in love?

"Clay." Jack put his hand on Clay's shoulder.

"Get the fuck off of me!" Clay violently jerked away. "Jesus Christ, you queer piece of shit. Don't ever touch me again!"

Jack stood paralyzed, his hand still reaching into the air. He looked so hurt that Clay could have stabbed him and caused less pain.

"Clay," Emily said. She couldn't stand his cruelty. "You can't—"

"Shut the fuck up, Emily." Clay's finger was in her face. "I meant what I said! Don't you fucking tell anybody!"

"She won't—" Jack's voice was raspy. He had started to cry. "She won't tell."

"She better fucking not!" Clay wrenched away from Emily. He started pacing across the shed floor, hammering his fist into his open palm. His feet were heavy on the stone. "I'll tell everybody she came onto me. I'll say that she tried to blackmail me into marrying her. That she was going to lie to everybody about me being the father."

Emily watched him pacing back and forth the same way her father paced when he was deciding her future.

"Clay," she tried.

"I told you to shut your fucking mouth." Clay glared at her, jamming his finger in her direction again. "I'll destroy you, Emily. Don't think I won't."

"Go ahead." Emily's words were strong, but her voice was weak. She had done nothing to this person but care for him and love him for almost her entire life. "Tell them I tried to blackmail you. Tell them I'm a whore. Tell them I gave you a blowjob behind the gym. What possible damage could you do to my reputation? I'm already utterly destroyed."

"Emily," Jack whispered.

"What, Jack? They're already saying all of those things," Emily said. "Thanks to Blake and Ricky. Thanks to Nardo. Thanks to you, Clay."

Clay had the audacity to look offended. "I never repeated those rumors."

"You never stopped them." Emily was so tired of these cowards hiding behind their own twisted sense of morality. "You could've stopped everything, Clay. You could've made this okay."

"This?" He threw out his arms in an open shrug. "What the hell are you going on about?"

"This!" She held her stomach. "This baby. You could've set the tone with the clique. You could've made it clear to the school that I shouldn't be cast out."

"Cast out?" he repeated. "That's ridiculous."

"Is it?" She hated herself for using her mother's words, but they were so damn fitting. "Clay, you're the one who gets to decide who the *right* people are. Everyone looks up to you! One gesture, one word, can mean that someone is in or out. You could've protected me."

He looked away instead of trying to contradict her.

"You could do it now." For the first time in weeks, Emily saw a real way out of this. She had begged her mother for legitimacy, but Clay was far more powerful in Emily's small world than Esther. "The only reason people at school think it's wrong is because people think it's wrong. You could change everything for me. You could make it okay."

"How are you so stupid?" he demanded. "The only thing it would change is that people would think I'm the father. Why else would I be taking up for you?"

Desperation constricted her chest. "Because you're my friend!"

The word *friend* lingered, a distant echo in the small shed. They had been friends for more years than they could both remember. All of them, in some way, had always been in each other's lives.

Clay shook his head in disbelief. "I can't be your friend anymore, Emily. Surely you see that. Everything has changed."

She wanted to scream until her throat bled. Nothing had changed for him. He was still popular. He still had the clique. He was still going out West to college. He still had a future.

"Emily, you have to understand," Clay said. "My parents thought it was me. I had to swear on a Bible. They were going to force me to marry you."

"Force?" Emily said, as if she had no say in the matter. "I don't want to marry you. I don't want to marry anyone."

"Bullshit," Clay said. "If you get married, all of this will go away."

She pressed together her lips so that she didn't laugh in his face. Nothing was going to go away for Emily. The baby would still be growing inside of her. Instead of interning for a senator and learning about macroeconomics and tort reform, she would be cleaning vomit out of her hair and changing diapers.

Clay said, "I can't risk my parents thinking that I lied. They'll disown me. You know how religious they are. They'll put up with a lot of my shit, but not that. They made it damn clear to me. I'll have nothing."

She finally laughed. "Well God forbid you lose your beloved parents."

"Go fuck yourself, you stupid, conniving bitch." Clay's anger sparked like a warning flare. "I will not get stuck in this pissant town. I will not live the rest of my life surrounded by fucking bourgeois cocksuckers who don't read books or talk about art or understand the fucking world that we live in. And I sure as shit will never see either of your fucking faces ever again."

Emily heard a sob from Jack. He was staring at Clay, a mournful expression on his face. His devastation spread like a miasma straight into Emily's heart. Every day, over and over, they both lost the same things again and again.

"Clay," Jack said. "You said I could go with you. You said—"

Emily would have missed Clay's transformation had she not been watching him so closely. His handsome features contorted into a monstrous hideousness. Rage darkened his eyes. His elbow was cocked back as he ran across the room. And then he smashed his fist squarely into Jack's face.

"Fucking freak!" Clay punched Jack so hard that his head splintered the wall. Then he hit him again. And again. "You're not my fucking girlfriend!"

Jack held up his arms in vain, trying to block the punches, not hitting back though he was so much bigger and stronger than Clay. Even when a tooth chipped, a finger snapped back on his hand, he kept taking it.

"No—" Emily's hands went to her mouth. She was horrified by the violence, incapable of stopping it. Clay kept pummeling Jack until they were both on the ground. His fist was like a pile driver. Even when it became clear that Jack would do nothing to stop him, Clay kept hitting him. It was only when Clay's energy was spent that he reluctantly stopped.

His face was slashed with blood. He was sweating profusely. He pushed himself to standing. Instead of leaving, he swung back his foot to kick Jack in the head.

"No!" Emily screamed. "Stop!"

Her voice was so loud that the air seemed to shake with it.

Clay's head whipped around. His eyes were wild.

"Stop!" Emily said, her voice urgent with fear.

Clay had frozen, but only because he seemed to realize where he was—inside a shed that was on the Vaughn property with their pregnant daughter watching. His hand went to his face. Instead of wiping the blood away, he smeared it like horror make-up across his cold, hard features. He had finally, deliberately, showed himself.

His *real* self.

The boy she had met in elementary school, the cool kid who had talked about art and books and the world, was a disguise for the blood-covered fiend who had nearly beaten his lover to death.

Clay didn't bother to return the mask to his face. Emily had seen him now. She knew exactly who he was. He pointed his finger at her chest one last time. "If you tell anybody about this, I'll do the same fucking thing to you."

He shoved her away from the door. Emily stumbled, catching herself against the wall. The door slammed so hard the fractured glass panes finally toppled over, splintering onto the floor. Clay would go home to the Morrows now. He would clean himself up before he saw them. He would sit at the dinner table and eat his mother's Thanksgiving dinner and watch football with his father and neither of them would know that they were harboring a cunning, sadistic animal.

Jack rolled over onto his back. He let out a pained cry.

Emily rushed over to him. She dropped to her knees. She used the hem of her blouse to wipe the blood out of his eyes. "Oh, Jack . . . are you okay? Look at me."

His eyes rolled. He was panting. Blood poured from his nose, his mouth. An angry gash split his eyebrow in two. His front

tooth was chipped. The pinky finger on his left hand bent
awkwardly to the side.

Emily strained to help him sit up. He was too heavy. She ended
up sitting on the floor. His head was in her lap. He was sobbing
so hard that she started crying, too.

"I'm sorry," he whispered.

"It's all right." She stroked his hair behind his ear the way
Gram used to do when Emily was feeling bad. "Everything's going
to be okay."

"We-we weren't—"

"I don't care, Jack. I'm only sorry he hurt you."

"It's not—" He groaned again, forcing himself upright. Blood
streamed down his face along with his tears. "I'm so sorry, Emily.
I never wanted you to know what—what I am."

Gently, Emily took his uninjured hand. She knew how lonely
it could be when no one touched you in kindness. "You're my
friend, Jack. That's who you are."

"I'm not—" Jack took a halting breath. "I'm not who you
think I am."

"You're my friend," she repeated. "And I love you. There's
nothing wrong with you."

Emily knew she had to be strong for him. She wiped away her
tears. She heard the *thunk* of her father's car door slamming shut
in the garage. He would shower and have a few drinks before
she was expected at the dinner table.

"I won't tell anyone," Emily promised Jack. "I would never
tell."

"It's too late," he whispered. "Clay hates me. You heard what
he said. I thought I could go to college with him, maybe find
work, but . . ."

Emily felt her mind flood with reassurances, but they were all
false. Clay was as finished with Jack as he was with Emily. She
should count herself lucky that all he had done was turn his back
on her. She had seen her father lose control so many times, but
she had never seen a human being turn into a monster right before
her eyes.

"I won't tell," Emily said. "Not that I think you should be
ashamed, but if you—"

"Nardo knows." Jack leaned his back against the door. He looked up at the ceiling. His tears ran unabated. "He saw me and Clay together. He knows."

Emily's mouth opened, though the real surprise was that Nardo hadn't told the entire school. "What?"

"I—" Jack had to stop to swallow. "I asked Nardo if he's the father."

Emily leaned her head back against the wall and stared up at the ceiling. She had spent hours poring over her Columbo Investigation. Had Jack figured it out? Why hadn't he told her?

"I'm sorry," Jack said. "Nardo didn't—he didn't confess. He told me to fuck off, and then he said that he'd seen me and Clay together, and if I kept asking questions, he would . . ."

Emily felt her heart thumping inside of her chest. She knew the malice that Nardo was capable of. It made no sense that he would keep such a salacious secret.

Jack sniffed. "But I had already asked everybody. Even Clay."

"But—" Emily didn't know how to say it other than to be blunt. "Clay is clearly not into girls."

Jack shook his head. "He likes girls, too. He's not like me. He can pass for normal."

Emily could hear the self-condemnation in Jack's voice.

He said, "Everybody denied it, for what it's worth. They all had their stories pretty much down pat."

"Who is everybody?" Emily was having trouble understanding what he had done. She had shown him her Columbo Investigation last month and he'd said nothing. "Who did you talk to?"

"Nardo, Blake, Clay, Ricky, Wexler. The same people you talked to." His breath wheezed through his nose. "I'm sorry, Emily. I know you were working on your own investigation, but you were so obsessed with it—obviously, for a reason—but I thought I could figure it out because I could look at it more clearly. Like, without the emotions you have. Nobody thinks much of me. I'm invisible at school, and I hear things sometimes, and I thought I could put it together, but I failed. I failed you."

"You didn't fail me, Jack." Emily took a deep breath. "Nardo implied that it was you."

Jack gave a humorless laugh. "Yeah, well, consider the source."

"He said you sold him the acid we all took at The Party."

"I did," Jack said. "I got it from my cousin."

Emily turned her head to look at him again. He hadn't been avoiding her because things were tense. He had been hiding something. "Were you there, Jack? Did you see something?"

"No, I promise. I would've told you." Jack turned to look at her, too. "Nardo made me leave before anybody got there. But after it happened, Clay was really upset. He told me that you got really mad at him at The Party. He saw you through those big windows that overlook the pool. You were outside, and you had taken your dress off. He made you put it back on. It was really cold. And you started screaming at him."

"About what?"

"He couldn't tell why you were so mad. He said you were hysterical. All he could do was go find Nardo."

Emily conjured the scene in her head, not from memory but as a sort of projection of what could be the truth. Her standing naked by the pool, Clay rushing out to dress her. No—that was too chivalrous. He'd wanted to know what happened. He would've made some joke about her nudity. And then he would've gotten annoyed because she was overwrought, but she had been over-wrought because someone had raped her.

She asked, "What did Clay tell you happened next?"

"They were all too fucked up to drive you home." Jack used his arm to wipe blood from his face. "Nardo called Mr. Wexler because he knew Wexler would shut up about it. They didn't know what else to do. You were out of your mind. Blake had to give you a couple of bennies to calm you down. You were still yelling at Clay when Wexler and Nardo dragged you into the car."

Emily looked away from him. She hadn't only been on acid. Her friends had given her a psychoactive drug that was prescribed to prevent anxiety and seizures. And then they had handed her over to ghastly Dean Wexler so he could be alone with her in his car.

She asked, "Do you think Clay was telling the truth?"

"I don't know. He's a liar, but they're all liars." Jack had started to weep again. "I'm sorry, Emily. I should've told you all of this before. I was ashamed, and I didn't know how to explain why Clay had confided in me without telling you about—about what I am."

"I know what it's like to be judged by people," Emily told him. "I'm not going to judge you, Jack. It's none of my business."

Jack took a sharp breath. "I'm so sorry."

"You have nothing to be sorry about." Emily could not let him spiral into self-hatred. She knew there was literally no bottom to the darkness. "How did Nardo find out about you and Clay?"

Jack shrugged, but said, "The only time I can think of was when Clay and I were in my dad's hunting truck. We took it to the logging road off the farm property. The one that comes out close to downtown."

Emily knew the road. The old farm property belonged to Gram. She had created a trust so that one day it would pass to Emily.

She asked, "Does Clay know that Nardo saw you?"

Jack nodded, but asked, "What are you thinking?"

Emily wished that she had her Columbo Investigation, but she always kept it in her purse because that was the only place her parents would not look.

She told Jack, "It's odd that Nardo has kept a secret from everybody else."

Jack's lips parted in surprise. "You think Clay knows something about Nardo?"

"Maybe." Emily thought it made sense, but then a lot of theories had made sense at various times. "Nardo would never turn on Clay. He's terrified of being alone. He needs someone to prop him up, tell him what to do, who to be. And Clay could turn the whole school against Nardo. No one would believe that he's—"

"Queer," Jack finished. The word sounded dirty in his mouth. "You're right. They'd end up turning on Nardo. And lots of kids are going to Penn. That kind of stink would follow Nardo all the way to college. He'd keep his mouth shut no matter what."

Emily sighed, because she had reached the same conclusion. "I feel like there's a wheel in my head, and it spins round and round trying to point to the right person. Sometimes it's Clay, then Nardo, then Blake, then—"

"Me?"

"I never believed that," Emily said. "Unless I was telling myself that you're the best possible person it could be."

"I do love you, Emily," Jack said. "I could marry you. So long as you know what I am. I can't change it. I've tried so hard."

"I love you, too, Jack, but you deserve someone who loves you the way you want to be loved." Emily added, "We both do."

He covered his face with his hands. His life had been so difficult. She had always known he was lonely, but she had not realized until now that he'd been utterly alone.

"Jack, it's not your fault." She gently took away his hands and held onto them. "All I want is to know who hurt me. I've given up on the person being punished for it. And I don't want to marry any of them, or even know them anymore, to be honest. The thought of any of those jerks being in my life, making decisions for me or my baby, is not only terrifying. It's disgusting."

"I want to find out, too." Jack used his arm to wipe his tears. "What about your Columbo Investigation? Is there anything new?"

"I thought it was Blake for a while," she admitted. "He's so transactional, isn't he? He manipulates people like game pieces around the board. He was so quick to offer a solution that would get him all of the glory and none of the blame."

Jack nodded. "What made you rule him out?"

"He's the least popular of the three boys. I honestly don't think that Clay and Nardo would protect him. Like I said before, they feed off each other. Clay needs Nardo's adulation and Nardo needs Clay's coolness, if that's what you want to call it. Blake is the obvious sacrificial lamb."

"It'd be the easiest way out," Jack agreed. "I mean, if they blamed Blake, it would take the heat off them."

Emily shrugged, but she had come to the same conclusion. Until she talked herself out of it and the circle started to spin again. "Sometimes I think it could have been Nardo. He's so merciless and selfish. He always takes what he wants. But I figured if it was him, Clay would turn on him, right? Clay always protects himself."

"Nardo saw me and Clay together," Jack reminded her. "They're both holding loaded guns on each other."

"There's no guarantee with Nardo. He is very bad at keeping secrets," Emily said. "It's almost pathological. If he sees an opportunity to hurt someone, the poison spills out before he can stop it. The thing inside his brain that warns him about consequences is broken."

"That's a good point," Jack said. "It's why Clay is graduating early, heading out west as soon as he can. He said he can't trust Nardo to keep his mouth shut."

"What about Clay? You said he's into girls, too." Emily felt her face flush, but she had come this far. "I thought that maybe I—I could've done something to provoke him? Maybe I threw myself at him? And he gave in, but he was angry after the fact."

Jack gave her a look. "Emily, you weigh about a hundred pounds, even pregnant. I think Clay could fend you off. And he's had plenty of opportunities before."

Emily felt heat coming off her skin. Clay must have laughed about the crush with Jack.

"What about Wexler?" Jack asked. "He's a creep. The way he looks at the girls at school is gross. And he's always trying to find ways to talk about sex stuff with them, even in class."

Emily didn't want to think about being in Dean Wexler's car the night of The Party. She had been nearly comatose. He could've done anything. And Nardo probably had known that when he'd loaded Emily into the car.

She told Jack, "Remember, Dean told me that he can't father children."

"No offense, but that sounds like something a guy would say so he doesn't have to wear a condom."

Emily laughed. "I think you know as much about condoms as I do."

Jack looked at the ground. The joke had hit too close. "I told you I'm invisible. I hear them talking in the locker room about sex and girls all the time. It's not nice what they say. Nardo especially, but Clay always laughs at his jokes, and Blake's usually there to twist the knife."

Emily had seen this happen in real time. The more Clay could push Nardo toward acts of maliciousness, the happier Clay was. And Blake was always a willing participant in the destruction, alternately egging Nardo on and despising him for his cruelty. She supposed she should add Ricky to the depraved cabal. In many ways, she was the most vicious of them all.

She asked Jack, "Why did I never see that they're all such reprehensible human beings? I loved them so much. They were my best friends. I trusted them completely."

Jack suddenly turned bashful.

"Say it," she told him. "We literally have no secrets between us."

He nodded because it was true. "I'm sorry, Emily. Nobody ever understood why someone as nice as you was hanging out with them."

Emily didn't understand why herself. Or maybe she didn't want to admit the reason. Clay had made them all feel so special, so cool. "Why didn't you ever tell me?"

"I mean—" Jack shrugged. "It was pretty obvious that they were terrible."

Emily could only see that in hindsight, which was doubly depressing because, just weeks ago, Ricky had accused her of being a Pollyanna.

Still Emily felt the need to defend them, at least partially. They hadn't all started out bad. Only Nardo had shown signs of his later brutishness, always yanking Emily's hair or snapping Ricky's bra strap. Clay had once been kind. Long ago, Blake had been sensitive. Even Ricky had been sweet, taking up for Emily in third grade when someone had ruined her art project. Though, looking back, Ricky was probably the person who'd ruined it in the first place. She was such a spiteful bitch.

"Emily, you're not going to be alone in all this, okay? I'm going to be here if you need me. When you need me," Jack said. "I've already been accepted into the police academy for summer term. I only applied to get my dad off my back, but Clay doesn't want me to go with him and I don't have any other options. I'm going to stay in Longbill and work for my dad when I get out of the academy."

Emily's heart sank. If anybody ever needed to get out of this place, it was Jack Stilton. He needed to go to Baltimore or some other big city where he could find people like himself who were living happier lives.

"No," she said. "Jack, don't do the easy thing. Fight for your happiness. You've wanted to get out of here since we were in elementary school."

"What else am I going to do?" he asked. "You heard Clay. He's not going to change his mind. And my grades are shit. I'm barely graduating fucking high school. I can't join the army because they outright ask you who you are, and I can't tell them. I mean, I could, but hell, I could end up in prison. Or dead, if my dad finds out. At least in Longbill, I know the people I'm dealing with. And they think they know me."

"Jack—" Emily couldn't argue with him. He was just as trapped as she was. "If you really do become a cop, if you can stomach it, will you make me a promise?"

"Of course. You know I'd do anything for you."

"I want you to find out who did this to me," Emily said. "Not for my sake, because I don't want any of those callous, hateful bastards in my life. I want you to catch him for the sake of the girls who come next."

Jack seemed surprised by the observation, but not because he disagreed. "You're right. Criminals have a modus operandi. They repeat their patterns. That's how you catch them."

"Promise me." Emily's voice cracked. She could not imagine another girl having to go through what she was going through. "Please, Jack. Promise me."

"Emily, you know I'll—"

"No, don't make a promise because I'm crying. Make it because it matters. What he did to me matters. *I* matter." Emily got on her knees, hands clasped in front of her. She was suddenly overwhelmed by sorrow for everything she had lost. "He didn't just rape me, Jack. He knew that I wasn't really there, that I was more like a—a receptacle."

"Emily—"

"No, don't tell me that's not what happened." Emily fought back the wave of devastation. "It wasn't only that one night that he hurt me. The stain is on my soul. He turned me into nothing. I am ruined because of him. My life that I worked for, that I planned for, is gone. All because he decided that my wants, my desires, were nothing compared to his. You can't let that happen to another girl. You can't."

"I won't, Emily. I'll find out who did this if it kills me." Jack was on his knees, too. He carefully wrapped his broken hands around hers. "I promise."

10

Andrea kept to the shadows as she followed the beat-up old Ford truck.

Nardo was behind the wheel. Star had pushed her body against the passenger's side door, putting as much space as she could between her and Nardo. He didn't seem to care. He drove slowly down the road, his arm hanging lazily out the window as he smoked a cigarette.

Andrea searched the dark expanse of road behind her, hoping to spot a government-issued black SUV that told her one of the six surveillance teams had followed the truck from the farm. But the teams were set up on the entrances and exits. They weren't monitoring an old logging road that had probably been wiped off the map during the last century.

She turned back around. The truck was still moving. There were no payphones on the street. The motel was ten minutes away. This was what Compton had been afraid of, that men like Wexler and Nardo always had an escape plan. Andrea was not surprised to find Nardo making a run for it. He had moved on from Clay Morrow. He could move on from Dean Wexler.

Andrea bolted out in the open, taking a chance as she sprinted up the stairs to the police station. She yanked on the locked door. She looked inside the lobby. There were no lights on inside. She knocked on the glass.

Nothing.

"Shit," she muttered, running down the stairs. The arrest warrant had to be in front of a judge by now. Any moment, Bernard Fontaine would go from being a person of interest to a fugitive. If Andrea lost sight of him, they might never find him again. He would never face justice. Melody Brickel might not ever see her daughter again.

There was a phone in the restaurant.

The diner was one hundred yards away. Andrea let all the catastrophes rain down in her head as she jogged toward the pink glow of the neon lights.

She had no back-up. Her waterlogged gun was on its way to Baltimore. Nardo had a history of carrying a concealed weapon. She knew by the shape that it was a micro gun, which narrowed it down to one of the most popular 9mms, the SIG Sauer P365. That meant ten in the magazine, one in the chamber. He also had Star in the vehicle with him. In seconds, she could turn from passenger to hostage.

Andrea darted into a doorway as the brake lights glowed. She watched Nardo pull into a space a few yards from the diner. The rumble of the Ford's engine cut. The emergency brake raked up. Nardo flicked his cigarette onto the sidewalk. He got out of the truck and slammed the door. He stretched up his arms to the sky, bending his back in a stretch that pulled the white T-shirt out from his cargo pants.

Andrea held her breath, waiting.

Star sat in the truck. She didn't move until Nardo gave her permission by way of a flick of his wrist. She pushed open the door. She turned her body. She slid off the seat. Her feet touched the ground. She trailed several feet behind Nardo as they both disappeared inside the diner.

Andrea did another quick inventory, not to catastrophize but to make herself aware of her physical state. Her fight or flight was going berserk. She was sweating. Her heartbeat was as tight as a cymbal. Adrenaline was making her dizzy. She was on the balls of her feet. Her muscles were tight. Her fists were clenched. She was holding her breath.

She opened her mouth. She sucked in air.

She exhaled, then inhaled, then out, then in again, until the dizziness passed.

Andrea silently listed the things she had *not* observed. The truck had not been speeding. Nardo had not been constantly turning, looking for tails. He had not continued down the road on his way out of town. Star was not driving while Nardo hid in the back of the truck. There was nothing frantic about either of their actions.

She felt jarred by a sudden realization. Nardo wasn't making his escape. He was fucking with Ricky. Melody Brickel had told Andrea he was in the diner at least once a week. He always dragged Star along to serve as his audience.

Andrea pushed herself away from the building. She took one last look over her shoulder. The road was clear. There was no one coming. She kept her arms loose at her side as she walked down the sidewalk. Ten more paces and she was in front of the diner. She looked past the neon signs. There were only three people inside. They were arrayed in a lopsided triangle across the restaurant.

Nardo was at the sharpest point, taking up space in the semi-circular booth. Ricky was standing behind the counter near the cash register. Star was sitting on a stool at the far end. She was staring straight ahead at the tiled wall. Her hands were clasped in front of her, which made her angular shoulder blades stick out from her back like two shark fins.

Andrea had reached the entrance. She looked through the glass door. Her eyes found the security camera in the corner. The full bar behind the cash register. The long hallway that led past the bathroom, the kitchen, and exited onto the boardwalk and the Atlantic. Andrea reached for the door handle. Her fight or flight tried to overrule her. Her skin felt clammy. Sweat had pooled into the band of her pants. Her vision was so crisp that her eyes ached.

She reminded herself that they wouldn't know any of these things. All that mattered was how Andrea looked when she walked into the diner.

She opened the door.

"Oh, shit," Ricky said.

Andrea looked awful. She had survived a fire. She'd nearly broken her nose. She'd cut open her forehead. She'd split her lip. If she looked sweaty and shaky, there was a damn good reason for it.

Nardo bellowed, "Wut woah Ricky Jo, Porky Pig just showed up. Better not *viowate* your *westraining* order."

Star said nothing. She didn't even turn around.

"Ignore the asshole." Ricky used the knife in her hand like a pointer, indicating a red line of tape on the floor. "Twenty-five feet."

The restraining order. Nardo kept coming to the diner because he wanted Ricky to violate it. Ricky had marked the line so that she wouldn't. The camera in the corner kept them both honest. Star was there because the game would mean nothing if no one could watch it.

None of which mattered because all that Andrea needed was a telephone.

She walked toward the counter. She let herself look at Nardo. His arms were splayed across the back of the booth. A large plate of spaghetti was on the table. While Andrea watched, he lifted a stein of beer as if to toast her.

Ricky had kept his plate warm. She had known he was coming.

"You okay, hon?" Ricky's jaw worked her chewing gum. She was slicing fruit for the breakfast rush. The bangles on her wrists tapped against the counter. She was like her own percussion section. The knife hit the cutting board, then her gum popped, then the bangles clicked, then the knife hit the cutting board.

"I'm good." Andrea positioned herself at the counter so she could keep an eye on Nardo. The mirror behind the bar gave her a full view of the restaurant. The cash register was on her left. Ricky was at a diagonal across the counter on Andrea's right. Star was in her periphery. The woman had taken no notice of Andrea's entrance. The counter was empty in front of her. She had not moved since Andrea had walked through the door.

"Heard about the fire, hon." Ricky was keeping one eye on Andrea as she sliced a cantaloupe. Their discussion at Ricky's house had not ended well. She was clearly still on guard. "I can fix you a sandwich. We're out of pasta."

Andrea noticed the sign taped to the cash register—

PHONE IS NOT FOR CUSTOMER USE.

"Hon?" Ricky asked.

Andrea had to swallow before she could speak. "No thanks. Can I have some tequila?"

"Looks like you need it." Ricky let the knife clatter onto the cutting board. Without asking for a brand, she grabbed the Milagro

Silver off the bottom shelf. "I could smell the smoke from my place. Damn, that house has been around for yonks. Hard to believe it's gone. Everybody's okay, right?"

"Yes." Andrea could see the sweat from her hands had dripped onto the counter. She had to get Ricky back on her side. "I'm not supposed to tell anybody—"

Ricky perked up as she filled a shot glass to the rim.

"The judge's husband—"

"Franklin."

"Right." Andrea leaned forward, kept her voice low. "He wasn't doing well to begin with, but after the fire . . ."

Ricky gave a slow nod to say that she understood. "It's sad the amount of tragedy that family has had to put up with over the years. Is Judith okay?"

"She's sad. It might help if she heard from you."

Ricky nodded again. "I'll make some food. People always need food."

"I'm sure the judge will be grateful." Andrea reached into her back pocket and pulled out her phone. She tried to look as if she'd just remembered it was broken. "Crap."

"Crap is right." Ricky placed the tequila in front of Andrea. "You stick that thing in a microwave?"

"It got damaged during the fire." Andrea felt her voice growing thin. She cleared her throat. "I know you've got a sign, but can I use your phone?"

"The sign's for tourists." Ricky reached under the cash register. She lifted up the phone and plopped it down on the counter.

Andrea stared at the ancient-looking machine. A cord ran out the back. The receiver was connected by a springy cord. The number keys were on the base. Andrea's plan had been to take the cordless phone into the back hall for privacy. The corded landline wasn't going anywhere.

"You okay, hon?" Ricky was back to the cutting board. She gave Nardo a telling glance.

"Yeah, rough day." Andrea looked at the mirror. Nardo was watching. Ricky was watching. Only Star seemed to not care.

Andrea picked up the phone. She told Ricky, "I forgot to say the call is long distance, but I can give you cash."

"That's cool." Ricky grabbed a handful of strawberries. "Just make it quick."

Andrea dialed the only number she had ever memorized. The phone rang once before it was answered.

"Darling?" Laura sounded like she hadn't gone back to sleep. "What is it?"

"Hey, Mom. I'm sorry I didn't call you back after I left the hospital."

"What?" Her voice trilled up in alarm. "When were you at the hospital?"

"No, I couldn't fall asleep." Andrea could see that Ricky was openly listening to the call. "I forgot to ask. Do you mind calling Mike for me? His number is stored in my stupid phone."

Ricky made a face at the broken iPhone, as if she was part of the conversation.

"Mike?" Laura demanded. "My Mike? What does Mike have to do with the hospital?"

"Tell him I walked down to the diner to get a drink." Andrea's hands were steady as she rolled the shot glass between her fingers. "I got a message at work from our neighbor. He needs Mike's help. Renfield got out."

"Okay." Laura's voice had turned deadly calm. During her criminal days, she had communicated exclusively through codes and cyphers. "I'm writing this down. I'm supposed to call Mike and tell him you're at the diner. Correct?"

"Sure."

"And I don't know what the other part means, but I'll tell him verbatim, 'I got a call from our neighbor. He needs Mike's help. Renfield got out.'"

"That's right," Andrea said. "Thanks, Mom. I love you."

The receiver went back into the cradle. Andrea took a sip of tequila. Her fingers were slick on the glass.

Ricky left the phone on the counter. She kept the knife moving back and forth, but her eyes had never left Andrea. "That was your mom?"

Andrea nodded. "My cat got out. He only comes when my boyfriend calls him."

"I wish I had time for a pet." Ricky was smiling, but there was an edge to her tone. "Bit late for a phone call, isn't it?"

Ricky glanced at Nardo again. Her curiosity had crossed into suspicion.

Andrea knew that Ricky had seen her dial the number. "Mom used to live in Georgia, but she moved to Portland last year."

"Maine?"

"Oregon." Andrea resisted the temptation to check on Nardo. She felt like he was staring a hole into her back. "They're three hours behind. She was watching TV."

"I love Oregon." Ricky wasn't going to let up. "What part?"

"Laurelhurst," Andrea said. "It's on the eastern side of Portland. She lives near the park with the Joan of Arc statue. There's some great live music at the coffee house."

Ricky relaxed, but only slightly. "Sounds nice."

"It is." Andrea finished her tequila. She let herself find Nardo in the mirror.

He had pushed away his plate. He dropped his empty stein onto the table. "Waitress?"

Ricky ignored him, but the blade struck the cutting board with tellingly loud *thunks*.

"Hey, waitress," Nardo called. "You got any more of that tequila?"

Ricky forced the knife down on the counter as if she was keeping herself from using it on Nardo. She grabbed the bottle. She slammed a shot glass down on the counter.

Andrea looked at Nardo. He was smirking. Andrea was calculating. Laura would've called Mike immediately. Andrea had no doubt that he would pick up the phone. Protectees only called during life and death situations—

Andrea is at the diner. Renfield got out. She needs your help.

At the hospital, Mike had used the name *Renfield* to describe Nardo. And he sure as hell would know something was wrong if Andrea was asking for help.

Her gaze traveled to the clock on the wall. She watched the second hand tick between the numbers. Two minutes for Laura to relay the message to Mike. Two more minutes for Mike to relay it to Compton. Four minutes for Compton to mobilize teams. The closest Marshals were at the farm, but that fifteen-minute drive would be cut down to ten with lights and sirens.

Eighteen minutes in all, if everything went exactly as Andrea had guessed. The call to Laura had ended at 11:59. The soonest someone could get here would be 12:17.

"Heads up," Ricky slid the tequila shot down the length of the counter.

The glass stopped shy of Star's pointy elbow.

This was clearly part of the game that Ricky played with Nardo. She couldn't cross the red line. Star wasn't only there as an audience. She was there to serve him.

"Let's go, girl." Nardo rapped his knuckles on the table. "You need to lift those spirits."

Improbably, Ricky laughed. She was watching Star with a look of sick satisfaction on her face. The sound of her knife hitting the cutting board turned into a staccato as Star went through the slow mechanics of delivering the drink to Nardo. Her yellow dress swayed back and forth on her angular frame. Her bare feet sounded like a whisper as they brushed across the floor.

Andrea's eyes found the mirror again, but this time she wanted to see outside. The blue truck was the only vehicle in the street. She looked at the clock again. Only a minute had passed.

"Waitress," Nardo called to Ricky again. "Where's my dessert, old girl? Maybe I should speak to the manager. The service here is atrocious."

Ricky rolled her eyes for Andrea's benefit, but she followed his order. She used a chef's knife to cut off a large chunk of chocolate cake. Then she dropped the plate on the counter for Star to retrieve.

Andrea clenched her teeth as Star haltingly traversed the room. Silently, she ran through the timeline again. Laura to Mike. Mike to Compton. Compton to the surveillance team. They wouldn't rush into the building. They would see three potential hostages. They would assume that Nardo was armed. Like Andrea, they would assume it was a SIG Sauer P365 with ten opportunities to take out three different hostages.

Andrea couldn't do anything about Ricky or herself, but Star was inches away. She was reaching for the plate with Nardo's slice of cake. Her chapped lips were parted. Andrea could smell the sickly, medicine odor of her breath.

Andrea said, "I talked to your mother."

Star said nothing.

"She misses you. She wants to see you."

"Hon," Ricky told Andrea. "I know you're trying to help, but—"

The plate dropped from Star's hand. The thin china broke in two. The cake rolled off the edge, smearing across the counter.

"Fucksakes." Ricky reached for a bar rag to clean up the mess.

Nardo asked, "What happened over there?"

"Your fucking Skeletor broke a plate is what happened." Ricky turned around to wet the rag at the bar sink. "Jesus, Nardo. Why can't you just leave?"

Star's head was bowed. Her eyes glistened with tears that would not fall.

Andrea told the girl, "Go down the hall. Walk out the back door."

"Walk out what, you say?" Nardo was pushing himself up from the table. "Star, heel. Back to your spot. Be a good little doggie."

Andrea could not stop Star from returning to her place at the end of the counter. She watched the woman slowly spin around on the stool to face the blank tile wall again.

"Come now, southern gal." Nardo slowly walked across the room. "I've only taken dear Star out on loan. She's expected back in one piece."

Andrea stood up. She wasn't going to be sitting when Nardo reached her.

"Keep it cool, Robocop." Nardo showed her his hands, but he kept walking. "Star's the best girl on the farm. Didn't you hear? She won *a-trophy*."

Andrea had no time to form a response.

Two things happened in quick succession.

Ricky started laughing.

Jack Stilton walked through the door.

He was wearing jeans and a faded Bon Jovi T-shirt that stretched over his beer belly and dipped into his waistband. His gun was on his belt. Not his service weapon, but a revolver. The single-action Ruger Blackhawk chambered a .454 Casull. One shot could literally crack open a bowling ball.

Andrea felt her heart sink as Stilton nervously glanced around.

He wasn't here to save the day. He was annoyed to find that he wasn't the only customer in the diner. He was also drunk. She could smell the alcohol from fifteen feet away.

"Look at that doe-eyed fuck." Nardo scooped the piece of cake off the counter with his hand. "Waitress, I'll expect a discount."

Ricky ignored him, asking Stilton, "What do you want, Cheese?"

"A drink." He said it like a question, the words slightly slurred. Andrea could see his cruiser parked in the street. He was off-duty. He was intoxicated. Compton had said she would call Stilton when Wexler and Nardo were in custody. He clearly had no idea what was going on.

"Fucksakes," Ricky said. "Can any of you assholes read the giant neon sign in the window? We close at midnight. Sorry, hon. I don't mean you."

Andrea didn't acknowledge the apology. She watched Nardo walk toward Star. The outline of the SIG Sauer was visible under the back of his shirt. He made a loud groan as he sat beside her at the counter. He bit into the cake, eating it with both hands.

Ricky made a disgusted noise before telling Stilton, "Make it fast, Cheese. You want Blue Earl or tap?"

"Whatever's easy." Stilton sat at a table with his back to the door. He gave Andrea a wary appraisal. "What are you doing here?"

Nardo said, "Cheese smells a mouse."

"Shut up, asshole." Stilton was still turned toward Andrea. "I thought you were supposed to be watching the judge."

Andrea made her fists unclench. Her heart was beating so hard she could feel it against her shirt. "There's another team guarding her family at the hospital."

"Come now, deputy pig. That's not the whole story." Nardo had finished the cake. He wiped his hands on his shirt, leaving chocolate stripes across his chest. "Cheese, your friendly Marshal was trying to save poor Star. Isn't that right, Ricky? Star's mommy wants her back."

Ricky rolled her eyes as she placed a can of beer on the counter. She asked Andrea, "You mind doing the honors, hon?"

Andrea was grateful for the excuse to go to Stilton. She handed him the beer, but instead of returning to her place, she sat beside him at the table.

"Look at that, Ricky, Cheese has a girlfriend," Nardo said. "Sorry to burst your bubble, deputy pig, but Cheese curdles at the sight of pussy."

Ricky laughed as she packed the fruit into containers.

Andrea didn't care about the woman's bizarre sense of humor. She glanced down at Stilton's giant cowboy revolver. The strap across the handle was unsnapped. She tried to get his attention, but he was busy gulping down his beer.

She looked at the clock. 12:05 a.m. Eight more minutes. At least.

Could she take Stilton's gun off him? Would he struggle? Could Andrea get the revolver in her hands, stand up, line the sights, before Nardo reached behind his back and pulled his own weapon?

Star was the problem. She was sitting directly beside Nardo. Andrea was a good shot at the range, but this was real life. Every nerve in her body was tingling. Her breaths were shallow. Sweat dripped down her back. She wasn't sure she could hit one without endangering the other.

She looked at the clock: 12:05 a.m. The second hand had barely moved.

"Dammit." Ricky was looking at the clock, too. "Last orders, people. I have to wake up in six hours to do this shit all over again."

"Don't be a party pooper, old girl." Nardo had spun around on the stool to face Andrea and Stilton. He had an animal instinct that something was off. A sane person would heed the warning and leave. Nardo leaned his back against the counter, elbows resting on the edge. "Waitress, how about one of those beers?"

Andrea tuned out Ricky's sarcastic response. She waited for Stilton to look at her. Then she glanced down at his gun. He could take Nardo into custody. He could end this right now.

Stilton's eyes narrowed. The cop part of him was drowning in alcohol, but he had to be picking up on the stress. Andrea couldn't stop herself from looking at the clock again, begging the hands to move. She stared until the second hand clicked to the next marker.

12:06 a.m.

A phone trilled.

The air turned so thick with tension that Andrea could hardly breathe.

The phone rang again. Stilton dug into his pocket. Andrea saw the caller ID.

USMS COMPTON.

He looked at her for clarification. She gave the smallest shake of her head, begging his mind to clear so that he didn't make a mistake that got them both killed.

Stilton cleared his throat. "Hello?"

The phone was loose against his ear, propped up on his crooked pinky finger. Andrea could hear the murmur of Compton's voice, but could not make out the words.

"Huh," Stilton said.

There was a long pause as he listened to Compton. Andrea could guess what the boss was saying. Wexler in custody. Nardo at the diner. Arrest warrant in place. Could be armed and dangerous.

Stilton did the exact wrong thing. He looked at Nardo as he responded.

"I'm at the diner now," he said. "Sure. Sure. I get what you're saying. No problem."

Andrea watched Stilton end the call. He placed the phone face down on the table. He moved slowly, resting his arm on the back of his chair. His fingers were inches from the handle of the revolver.

But he left the gun in its holster.

"Nardo," Stilton said. "Why don't you tell me about Emily?"

Andrea bit her lip so hard that blood swirled into her mouth.

"Fuck me," Ricky said. "Let it go, Jack."

Nardo snorted. His elbows were still cocked back on the counter. Either he or Stilton could reach for their weapon at any time. "Bit of a slut, wasn't she?"

Andrea felt her jaw ache from clenching together her teeth. Why was Stilton asking about Emily? Compton had clearly given him the go-ahead. Why wasn't he making the arrest?

Stilton said, "I know you raped her."

"Do you?" Nardo turned his head to the side, making it clear that he knew Stilton was armed. "I'm not up on the law, old boy, but I believe the statute of limitations ran out—oh, maybe thirty-five years ago."

"So admit it," Stilton said. "You raped her."

"All right, that's it." Ricky rapped her knuckles on the counter for attention. "Cheese, you're drunk. Nardo, I'm tired of your shit. I want everybody out of here. You, too, hon."

No one moved. The room turned so quiet that Andrea could hear the blood rushing through her body.

Nardo said, "Hell yes, I fucked her."

Ricky gasped. Andrea's heart stopped. Stilton didn't move.

"What?" Nardo looked delighted by their responses. "Don't tell me no one's ever thought it before. Of course I fucked her. Did you see her tits?"

Andrea tried to quell a sudden, staggering panic. She had chased a confession for days, and now that it was here, all she could think was that none of them were going to get out of this alive.

"Stilton," she said. "Nardo has a gun."

"So do I." Stilton wrapped his fingers around the handle of the revolver, but he inexplicably left it holstered. He told Nardo, "You didn't fuck her. You raped her."

"What I did was fill every single hole that young lady had with my cock." Nardo drank in Stilton's look of horror. "She was gagging for it. She couldn't get enough."

"Nardo," Ricky warned.

"Here." Nardo cleared his throat and hurled a wad of phlegm on the floor. "Test my DNA against Judith's. All that it will prove is that I came inside of her mother. Though if you must know, I came inside of Emily several times."

The nerve at Stilton's temple started to twitch. His fingers were so tightly wrapped around the grip of the revolver that his knuckles were white. He was going to shoot Nardo. There was no way around it. And he was so drunk he would probably end up killing Star in the process.

"Jack," Andrea tried. "You need to—"

"What about Dean?" Stilton's voice had caught on the man's name. He looked stricken, as if he couldn't believe what he was hearing. "Dean drove her home."

Nardo's smirk turned into a sadistic grin. "Well, who knows what the old boy did in the car? Our Mr. Wexler certainly does like a girl who can't say no."

"Fucking hell," Ricky said. "Nardo, shut your mouth."

"As a point of interest, I think all the ladies at the farm are proof of the concept that the old boy can't father a child." Nardo couldn't stop himself. He was reveling in Stilton's anguish. "Tell me, Cheese. Is Emily why you turned to the bottle? Are you still mourning the loss of a brain-dead baby breeder?"

"Nardo!" Ricky yelled. "There's a goddamn United States Marshal listening to every word you're saying."

"I am so fucking bored with this stupid fucking town. It's been forty years and all anyone ever whines about is *who's-the-father-who's-the-father?*" Nardo's voice had taken on a whiny mimic. "So now the deep, dark secret is out. Big fucking deal. Worst-case scenario, I get visitation rights with my gorgeous granddaughter."

Stilton stood up so quickly he knocked over his chair. His gun was finally out. He pointed the revolver at Nardo's chest. Cocked the hammer with his thumb. "It's over, cocksucker. They know about the blackmail."

"Star!" Andrea tried in vain to get her attention. She was downrange. Her back was a target. "Star, move!"

"Blackmail?" Nardo seemed unconcerned. "It's been twenty years since you fixed that DUI for me. You're the one who'll get in trouble."

Stilton laughed. "Not me, you dumb fuck. The judge. She gave them everything."

For once, Nardo didn't have a quick response.

Ricky was the one who answered. "What are you talking about?"

The knife was back in Ricky's hand. Star was still in the line of fire. Andrea felt like her heart was shaking inside of her chest.

Star would not move. Ricky was unpredictable. Stilton could barely hold his gun. Nardo was seconds away from having his hands on a weapon that could kill all of them.

"Cheese," Nardo said. "You need to think about what you're doing. Think about what I know."

"Tell it to the Marshals. I don't give a fuck anymore." Stilton's voice cracked again. He had started to cry. "That call I just got? That was the deputy chief Marshal. They already dragged Wexler out in handcuffs. They're coming for your sorry ass right now. The next time you see daylight, it's gonna be through prison bars."

Star finally moved, but only to turn around. She asked Stilton, "Is Dean okay?"

"Nobody is okay." Stilton walked toward Nardo. Tears streamed down his face. He had to use both hands to steady the revolver. "I promised Emily forty years ago that I would find the asshole who raped her. Forty years I've been hounded by that promise, you piece of shit. Forty goddamn years, and I got you. I finally got you."

Nardo's smirk was back. "Fuck you."

Again, two things happened quickly, one right after the other.

Nardo reached his hand behind his back.

Stilton pulled the trigger.

The explosion was like a cannon going off. Andrea ducked down, hands covering her ears. She saw the right side of Nardo's body jerk back. The bullet had ripped open his neck. Blood spattered Star's face and chest.

Ricky started screaming.

"Fuh—" Nardo slapped his hand to the side of his neck. The SIG Sauer P365 clattered to the floor. His eyes had gone wide. His lips were trembling.

"Don't move!" Stilton cocked back the hammer again, lining up for a second shot.

"No!" Andrea pushed down the muzzle. Nardo was unarmed. He was not going to pick up the SIG Sauer. He was not going to do anything for much longer.

There were two common carotid arteries, one on each side of the neck. The structures varied, but the point of each was to deliver oxygenated blood at a high volume from the heart to the brain. An aneurism, clot or obstruction to blood flow could cause a massive stroke. If the supply was diverted outside the body, then death by exsanguination could occur in five to fifteen seconds.

Nardo's hand was the only thing keeping the blood inside of his artery.

"I'll c-call an ambulance." Ricky scrambled for the phone. She punched in the number.

"You murdered Emily," Stilton told Nardo. "Tell me the words. Let me hear you say it."

Nardo's mouth opened. A gurgling sound came up from his throat. His teeth had started to chatter. His skin had turned waxy. Blood was seeping between his fingers like water through a sponge.

"Please," Stilton begged. "You're not going to make it. Just tell me the truth. I know you murdered her."

"Help!" Ricky screamed into the phone. "My husband—he's—oh, God! Help!"

"Say it," Stilton said. "Look at me and say it."

Nardo's eyes focused, but only for a moment. He looked directly at Jack Stilton. The corner of his mouth quivered in a smile.

Stilton said, "Please—"

Nardo took away his hand, the gesture like a showman introducing the final act. A torrent of blood sprayed from the severed artery.

He was dead before he hit the ground.

Bible drove while Andrea sat in the back seat of the SUV with Ricky. The woman could not stop sobbing. She was shuddering under the thin cotton blanket from the ambulance. She had refused to go to the hospital. She had refused to make a statement. She had told them that all she wanted was to go home.

There was no legal reason to deny her wishes. Honestly, Andrea wanted nothing more than to get away from the diner. She knew she should be glad that Nardo was dead, but she could not get past the feeling of injustice. He would never pay for raping Emily. He would not stand trial for her murder. Even though his death had been violent, he had still somehow managed to go out on his own terms. He did not deserve a peaceful ending. As Esther Vaughn would say, he hadn't earned it.

"Wha—" Ricky bit back another sob. "What will they do with—with the body?"

Andrea exchanged a look with Bible. There was a reason they had volunteered to drive Ricky Fontaine home. Nardo had admitted to the rape, but not the murder. On the surface, the difference didn't have a distinction, but to make a case beyond a reasonable doubt, they needed independent verification. Eric Blakely had drowned forty years ago. Clay Morrow was in prison. Bernard Fontaine certainly wasn't talking. Jack Stilton had all but proven that he'd had no hand in Emily's murder. Dean Wexler had invoked his right to remain silent while four Marshals were escorting him down the stairs from the farmhouse.

Ricky might be the only person on earth who could confirm that Bernard Fontaine had murdered Emily Vaughn.

Andrea told her, "Nardo's body will be taken to the state morgue. They'll do a full investigation."

Ricky cried out again. The shaking worsened. She clutched the thin blanket around her shoulders. For once, the silver bangles around her wrists were silent. Ricky had tried in vain to resuscitate Nardo. His blood had formed a glue around the bracelets.

"Here we are." Bible pulled up the steep driveway to Ricky's house. He turned to the back seat, telling them both, "Sorry, I need to make a phone call. You ladies let me know if you need anything. Ma'am—"

Ricky looked down when Bible rested his hand on her arm.

He said, "I'm very sorry for your loss."

Andrea got out of the SUV. She walked around to the other side to help Ricky. The harsh floodlights did the woman no favors. She had aged in the last hour. The lines in her face were deeper. Dark circles ringed her eyes. She leaned heavily on Andrea as they climbed the stairs. The door wasn't locked. Ricky pulled it open.

Andrea didn't wait for an invitation. She went around the living room turning on lamps. Then she climbed the short flight of stairs into the kitchen. The chandelier over the table glowed as she walked to the stove. The kettle was already full. Andrea turned on the gas and waited for it to catch.

She called down to Ricky, "Tea will be ready in a minute."

She listened, but Ricky had no response. Andrea walked to the edge of the stairs. She could see the top of Ricky's head in the living room. The woman was sitting on the couch. She was rocking herself back and forth, the blanket still clutched tight around her shoulders. The paramedics had said that she was probably in shock.

Andrea was in shock, too, but she had put too much of herself into this effort to let herself give in.

She found a dirty mug in the sink, a sponge on the windowsill. She strained her ears to listen for Ricky. The sound of her soft cries traveled up from the living room. Andrea carefully washed and dried the mug. She walked to the fridge. She looked at the photos, the postcards, the reminders and receipts. Some of them were so old that the ink had faded. None of them felt particularly personal. Most of the postcards seemed to be from tourists who talked fondly about their time at the diner. They reminded Andrea of the anodyne notes in Ricky's yearbook—

Chorus was a blast! Remember Chemistry II! Don't ever change!

Andrea picked up one of the red pill bottles on the counter. Instinctively, she reached for her iPhone. She had no way of looking up the generic names on the labels. The only ones she recognized were diazepam, which was Valium, acetaminophen/codeine, which was Tylenol 3, and oxycodone, which was Percocet. Laura had tried all three at various stages of her cancer treatments, but only oral morphine had managed to lessen the pain.

The kettle started to shriek. Andrea turned off the gas. She reached up to search the cabinet, but then she thought better of it.

She walked to the top of the stairs again. She called down to Ricky, "Where do you keep the tea?"

Ricky had hooded the blanket over her head as if she wanted to disappear.

"The tea?" Andrea repeated.

"Cabinet—" Ricky's voice was scratchy. "Cabinet by the sink."

Girl, Forgotten

373

There was nothing but spices and a large box of chamomile tea in the cabinet. Andrea sloshed boiling water into the mug, dropped in the tea bag. She found a coaster on the counter. By the time she made it down the stairs, Ricky was no longer sitting on the couch. She was standing at the console table, blanket still clutched around her shoulders. Her face was bloated from crying. The paramedics had tried to clean her up, but Nardo's blood stained her shirt and clumped in her dyed hair.

Andrea placed the coaster and mug on the console table. She saw that both drawers were open. Ricky had laid out some of the snapshots—the birthday party, the wedding photos, Nardo and Clay sitting at the counter in the same diner where one of them had just died.

Ricky picked up the framed photo of the group. "Only two of us left now."

Andrea could hear the desolation in her voice. They had been her world, especially Nardo.

Ricky said, "I guess that's it, right? You'll tell the judge that Nardo did it."

Andrea nodded, but said, "I wish it was that simple, but Nardo didn't confess to everything."

Ricky took a shallow breath, but she didn't look up at Andrea.

"Nardo admitted that he had intercourse with her, and the DNA will prove that one way or another, but he didn't say anything about Emily's murder." Andrea waited, but Ricky only stared at the photo in her hands. "Ricky, did Nardo ever talk to you about her? Or about what happened the night of the prom? Did Emily say something or—"

"Clay was the one who brought her into the clique." Ricky's voice sounded flat. Her eyes had gone glassy. "Nardo never liked her. She was so boring. She didn't belong. Emily never belonged."

Andrea watched as Ricky gently placed the frame back on the table.

"Nardo was eighteen when it happened. I mean, you'll fuck anything at eighteen, right? Even a mousy little bitch."

Andrea could hear anger creeping into Ricky's tone. The woman still didn't want to believe Nardo had raped Emily.

"What Cheese said—he didn't know anything. Emily only told

her parents that she was raped because they were furious when she got pregnant. She was such a liar." Ricky looked down at the snapshot of Nardo and Clay in the diner. She traced her finger along Nardo's boyishly round face. "The night of the party, she was flirting with everybody. She started on Clay, then she tried it with my brother. He ended up locking himself in the bathroom to get away from her."

Andrea watched Ricky press her palm flat, covering Nardo as if she could somehow protect him.

"Emily was supposed to be my best friend. I hated her for fucking him. Nardo was *mine*. He belonged to *me*. And now—" her voice caught. "He's gone. I can't believe he's gone."

Andrea watched Ricky break down again. She covered her face with the blanket. Her cries were almost like a keening. Her shoulders bowed as if the burden of what she had carried all these years had finally broken her.

"Ricky," Andrea tried. "Did Nardo ever talk about it? About what happened?"

"Fuck." Ricky looked around the room. "I need a tissue."

Andrea gently placed her hand on Ricky's shoulder. "If you could—"

"Give me a minute." Ricky shrugged off the blanket before walking up the stairs. Her hand gripped the railing as she pulled herself up. She was still shaking her head when she disappeared into the kitchen

Andrea reached down to retrieve the blanket. Her head nearly banged into the corner of one of the console table drawers.

She looked inside.

Ricky had left the drawers open. She had shown Andrea some of the contents. She had no reasonable expectation that Andrea would not see the rest.

Andrea stood up, then she backed up a few steps, standing on the tips of her toes so that she could see into the kitchen. Ricky's back was to the stairs. She had braced her hands on either side of the kitchen sink. Her shoulders were shaking as she cried.

The blanket dropped from Andrea's hands as she walked back to the table. She picked up Eric Blakely's New Mexico death certificate. The document was old, but she could still feel the imprint where the typewriter had punched out the letters. She set it aside and rummaged around the left-hand drawer, finding receipts for a coffin, cremation, a black tux from Maggie's Formal Wear. Andrea remembered the metal case. Ricky had kept it in her shrine for a reason. She reached her hand to the back.

The pocket index looked exactly the same. The silver pointer was still lined up to A-B.

Andrea used her thumbnail to press the button on the bottom. The top of the case sprang open. She saw one name—Brickel, Melody. The street address was the one that Andrea had visited the day before with Bible. She imagined the seven-digit phone number had not changed.

The handwriting was beautiful, almost like a kindergarten teacher's. Andrea did not recognize the script from any of the witness statements—Jack Stilton's almost illegible cursive, Ricky's circles over the 'i's, Clay's randomly capitalized letters, Nardo's tight scribble, Eric Blakely's heavy-handed block that almost sliced through the paper. Nor did she recognize it from Melody's mixtape or what she had assumed were Emily Vaughn's affirmations.

Andrea tried to figure out how the device worked. The pages were hinged at the top. Alphabetized tabs ran top to bottom. Extra pages were in each section. The pointer had a clip that held up the previous pages out of the way. She closed the lid. She moved the pointer down to C-D. The case sprang open again. Her focus was drawn to two underlined words at the top of the page—

Columbo Investigation.

Andrea's heart went into her throat. The beautiful handwriting belonged to Emily Vaughn.

She backed up again. She checked on Ricky. The woman was still standing at the sink. She was still crying.

Andrea read the first word under the *Columbo* header—

Clay?

She had to swallow before she could continue to the next line—

Dean Wexler – October 20, 1981: Dean says that he's "not the fucking father." Admitted he picked me up at The Party. Said Nardo called him to take me home. Said I was fighting with Clay by the pool when he got there. He promised he would hurt me if I ever publicly accused him. He grabbed my wrist. It really hurt.

Update: I looked up the condition in the library and he could be telling the truth about not being the father but that doesn't mean he didn't do something, right?

Andrea read the next entry.

Ricky Blakely – October 20, 1981: She said I am a liar and that I have had sex with lots of people they don't know during band camp, debate club, etc, not only at The Party. She accused me of being a Pollyanna and said my parents would plot to make Nardo marry me because that's what rich people do. She also said I ruined everything for the clique. Oh, and that I want to force Clay to marry me, which doesn't make sense because my parents already struck a deal with Nardo's parents (apparently???). She never wants to talk to me again. She called me a stupid slut and told me to leave her house. I have always known that she can be spiteful but she was awful to me. Why did I ever think she was my friend?

Andrea flipped up the page. There was writing on the back. The cursive was smaller, the lines bunched together—

Blake (same day) – He said he was "zonked out" at The Party and that he pissed himself. He was locked in the bathroom the whole time. He says he isn't the one who did it. He asked me to marry him, but only to help himself politically. I told him no and he said that I should "flush" the baby. He made a pass at me and actually put my hand on his thing and it was gross. Blake is as bad as Nardo. Why did I never let myself accept what a horrid human being he is before now?

Andrea saw her hands were shaking as she turned the page.

Nardo Fontaine – October 21, 1981: I hate him so much. He's such a jerk. First his parents sent a stupid letter saying to stay away from him, then the same day he found me in the library and wouldn't shut up. Nardo admitted that he called Mr. Wexler the night of The Party, but said he had to bribe him with acid to get him to take me "off his hands." I was arguing with Clay, according to Nardo, but they've all clearly gotten their stories straight, and the story is that I am the bad person. Nardo told me that Jack was at The Party and sold us acid, the implication being that Jack is the one who hurt me. I don't believe him. Jack could have sold the acid, but he would never do that to me. Nardo is such a liar. Sometimes he says cruel things only to hurt people. It worked!

Andrea found Clay next, by far the shortest of the entries—

Clay—October 21, 1981: His EXACT words: You played the game. You need to take the loss. Have some dignity.

The notes had taken on the form of a diary after the Clay entry. The ink color changed. The dates skipped forward. The writing was more cramped, filling the margins on each side. Andrea skimmed rapidly through the pages, her eyes randomly picking up Emily Vaughn's thoughts from forty years ago—

Jack didn't do it. He promised he would help me and I know he will . . . On my last day at school, Clay told me he is sorry that this is happening, but I think he was only being nice to keep me quiet. He doesn't understand what this means for my future . . . Nardo grabbed my breast in front of the entire school and it really hurt but he laughed when I cried . . . I think Ricky is the person who taped maxi-pads to my locker and colored them red . . . I think Ricky cut a hole in my T-shirt . . . I know that Ricky tore up all of my notes from English class . . . Ricky is the only person who could've smeared shit on my flute case . . . Ricky said I deserve to die . . . Ricky was downtown when I went to pick up my stuff at Maggie's for tonight. She chased me down the street. I have never seen her so furious. She said if she saw me anywhere near Nardo tonight, she was going to beat me to death with her bare hands. I don't care. I'm going to the prom anyway. None of them will be there. They would never sully themselves with the plebs.

Andrea flipped up the page. She had reached the section for W-X. There were only blank lines after that. The date of the last entry was April 17, 1982, the day of the prom.

She picked up the receipt for the tux. $20 was not enough to buy a tuxedo, but it made sense for a rental. The logo at the top was for Maggie's Formal Wear. The date was April 17, 1982. The description read *b-tux*, which Andrea had assumed meant black tuxedo.

She was wrong.

Back in 1982, Eric Blakely was a fully grown man who would wear a man's tux. It was probably impossible to find rental tuxes for women. Much as today it was almost impossible to find work pants for female law enforcement. You had to make do with what was available in the kids' section. Andrea of all people should have realized that the b stood for *boys*. By Emily Vaughn's own hand, Ricky had been at Maggie's Formal Wear that day. She had been picking up a boys' tuxedo to wear to the prom so they would all match.

Andrea looked at the group photo again. She had never noticed before but they were all wearing shades of the same colors.

The clique.

Emily had been cropped out of the picture. Forty years had passed since Ricky had beaten the life out of Emily Vaughn and she still could not stand to look at the girl's face.

Andrea put down the photo. She walked up the stairs.

Ricky was still at the sink. Her back was to Andrea, but she asked, "Everything okay, hon?"

"Yeah." Andrea had heard a false ease in the woman's tone. "I was just thinking about something."

"What's that?" Ricky's voice still sounded off.

"They tell you at the academy to never make assumptions. I think someone made a really bad assumption about Emily's case."

Ricky kept her back to Andrea. "Yeah?"

"I don't think the person who raped her at the party is the same person who killed her."

Ricky looked into the window over the sink. She found Andrea's reflection in the glass, using it like a mirror.

"Emily had something she called her Columbo Investigation. She kept notes on everybody who might know what had happened to her at the party. I assumed it was a notebook, but it wasn't, was it? It was her address book." Andrea waited for a reaction, but there was none. "She had it with her when she was attacked, only the police never found it. She was naked. Her purse was missing. Do you know what happened to it?"

Ricky said nothing, but she had to know what was in the console drawer.

"There were black threads on the shipping pallet in the alley."
Andrea paused. "Did you wear a black tux that night, Ricky?
You already told me that you were at the prom."

Ricky's head dropped. She stared down at the sink. She was
still gripping the counter. The rubber bracelets and silver bangles
had settled around her hands. The light picked out the faded scars
where she had tried to slit her wrists.

Bible's words came back to Andrea—if they're homicidal,
they're suicidal.

"You should—" Ricky coughed. "You should go, okay? I need
to get some rest."

"It's been forty years," Andrea said. "Aren't you tired of living
with the guilt?"

"I—I don't—" Ricky coughed again. "I want you to leave.
Please leave."

"I'm not leaving, Ricky. You need to tell me what happened.
This isn't for the judge or Judith. You need to tell me for yourself."

"I—I don't know what you're—I can't, okay? I can't."

"You can," Andrea insisted. "You've suffered enough. How
many times have you tried to kill yourself because you can't live
with what you did?"

Ricky was bowed over by the weight of her guilt. She pressed
her forehead to the edge of the sink. "Please, don't make me."

"It's tearing you up inside," Andrea said. "Say the words,
Ricky. Just say the words."

The kitchen went silent. A clock ticked somewhere. Ricky finally
took a deep breath.

"Yes." She spoke in a raspy whisper. "I killed her, okay? I
killed Emily."

Andrea opened her mouth, but only for air.

"I told her to stay away from Nardo." Ricky leaned her elbows
on the sink. She put her face in her hands. "I saw her talking to
him outside the gym. Flirting with him. Pushing his buttons. She
couldn't—she couldn't stay away from him. Why didn't she just
stay away from him?"

Andrea said nothing.

"I didn't mean to—" Ricky coughed into her hands. "I only

wanted to warn her, but I—I lost control. She wasn't supposed to be there. I told her not to come and I—I couldn't stop myself. Everything happened so fast. I don't even remember going into the alley. Picking up the board. I was so angry. So fucking angry."

Andrea knew that Ricky was capable of that kind of rage. What she did not know was what had happened next. Emily Vaughn had weighed 152 pounds at the time of her attack. There was no way that Ricky had moved Emily on her own.

She asked, "Did your brother help you move her body from the alley?"

Ricky shook her head, but said, "That's why he left. He was terrified that someone had seen him or . . . that he would be arrested, and he knew he couldn't . . . that he would have to tell the truth about . . ."

Andrea listened to her voice trail off into more sobs. "Why did you take off her dress?"

"Blake said there could be evidence or . . . I don't know. I did what he said. We burned it all behind the house." Ricky sniffed. "He was good at that kind of thing, figuring out the angles, finding details that other people had overlooked."

Andrea couldn't disagree. He had managed to cover Ricky's tracks for forty years.

"I'm sorry," Ricky whispered. "I'm so fucking sorry."

Ricky's shoulders started to shake again as she cried. The woman never cried so hard as when she was crying for herself. She was docile for the moment, but there was no telling how long that would last. Andrea put a firm hand on Ricky's shoulder. She was about to escort her outside, but then she noticed a splatter of dark liquid across the dirty dishes in the sink.

Andrea's first thought was that it was dishwashing liquid, but then she noticed the partially dissolved pills streaking through the black like constellations.

Ricky coughed again. Bile dribbled from her lips, ran down her shirt. Her eyelids were fluttering. She was swaying on her feet.

Andrea's head swiveled toward the red pill bottles on the counter.

The Valium. The pain meds.

All three bottles were empty.

The gurgle from Ricky's throat was eerily similar to the one Nardo had made at the diner. She started to collapse. Andrea grabbed her around the waist. Instead of guiding her to the floor, Andrea gripped her left fist in her right hand and drove both hard into Ricky's abdomen.

"No—" Ricky heaved into the sink. Melted pills and chunks of undigested food splattered onto the dishes. "Please—"

Andrea gave her another quick upward thrust. Then again. Then again, until Ricky spewed a stream of vomit onto the floor. The orange and yellow pills formed a nauseating rainbow across the linoleum. Andrea put all of her strength into another vicious thrust.

Ricky gagged so hard that her body convulsed. She kept gagging, convulsing over and over until nothing more would come out. All she could do was start crying again, wailing like a lost child.

"Why?" she begged. "Why didn't you let me go?"

"Because," Andrea said. "You didn't earn it."

11

ONE MONTH LATER

Andrea sat at the bottom of the stairs inside her Baltimore apartment building. Her phone was to her ear as she listened to Bible describe Judge Esther Vaughn's funeral service. The cancer had taken her faster than anyone expected. Or maybe the woman knew when to make an exit. She had given a full statement to the prosecuting attorneys. She had recorded her dying declaration. Then she had gone home to her house in Baltimore, had a light lunch with Judith and Guinevere, then lain down for a nap and never woke up again.

"Weren't a lot of people there, considering all the Judge's criming," Bible said. "But Judith's friends from art school showed up by the boatload. Damn, those people can drink."

Andrea smiled. Drinking was in fact the only reason to go to art school.

She asked, "Did she talk about what happened with Nardo and Ricky?"

"Well, Judith, she's a practical lady," Bible said. "Not much of a surprise that her father was a bad man. As for Ricky—you know, I got no idea. Judith is glad the ol' gal's copped a plea and is going to prison for the rest of her life. I think it gave Esther some peace to finally know. And if Esther was happy, then that usually means Judith was happy."

Andrea thought that sounded a lot like Judith. For all of Judge

Esther Vaughn's indomitable, intimidating, illegal activity, she had always loved Judith. At her core, she had been nothing more than a lost old woman whose daughter was murdered and whose husband used to beat her.

"Partner, you should'a seen the spread they laid out. You ever had hasty pudding? It was the judge's favorite."

Andrea only knew about it from the worst ear-worm song ever. "What makes it hasty?"

"Hell if I know. Probably named after some Yankee farmer who liked pudding," Bible said. "Tell you what, I hoovered up so much of that stuff I'm gonna have to give up bread for the rest of the month. You know what they say—"

"The skinny Marshals love their wives," Andrea finished. "What the hell does that mean, anyway?"

Bible chuckled. "You know they make you take that physical fitness test once a year. Used to be they could fire you if you got a little on the tubby side. They can't do that anymore on account of it being discrimination, so now if you pass the test, you get two weeks off to spend with your beautiful wife. Or husband, if that's the case."

The inducement sounded familiar. Gordon had created a PowerPoint presentation to highlight important details from the USMS employee handbook. Andrea's only response had been that Citibank would probably take her last student loan payment out of her burial insurance.

"Hey, partner," Bible said. "You good?"

"I'm good," Andrea said, though she wouldn't be completely good until Dean Wexler's deal was signed off and the psychopath was in prison.

They couldn't prove he'd done anything to Emily Vaughn. Fortunately, tax fraud, tax evasion, wire fraud and various other tax-adjacent crimes were crimes that the United States government took very seriously. The best deal Wexler could get was twenty-five years in a federal prison. He was sixty-five years old. Even with good behavior, by the time he got out, Wexler would be in his eighties.

Andrea had been glad to hear that part of the agreement ensured that he wouldn't end up in a cushy Club Fed the same as Clay

Morrow had. Wexler would serve his time at FCI Berlin in New Hampshire, a medium-security institute with dormitory housing and a nationwide federal staffing crisis that made everything more dangerous. Wexler would have to wear a prison uniform, mop the floor and clean his own toilet, subsist on processed foods, wake at 6 every morning and have his bed made by 7:30. All his mail would be screened. His phone calls would be recorded. His visitation would be limited. Nothing he had would be his own, not even his free time.

And still, it wasn't enough.

The only consolation Andrea could give herself was to remember Wexler's happy pronouncement while they were riding in his old Ford truck the day that Alice Poulsen's body had been found. Wexler was bragging about how charmed his life had become after leaving his teaching position. If life really did make you pay for your personality, Dean Wexler would never raise his eyes and see an endless expanse of sky ever again.

Andrea cleared her throat. She got to the hard part. "How are the girls doing?"

"The girls," Bible repeated. This part was hard for him, too. Every other day, they talked about whatever assignment they were doing and the weather forecast and Cussy and the boss, but eventually, always, they got back to the girls on the farm.

After Wexler's arrest, ambulances had been on standby to take the girls to Johns Hopkins in Baltimore. Only three of the twelve had accepted the offer. One of them had passed away after failing to thrive. One had walked out of the hospital. The other was so malnourished that an expert from the CDC had been called in to manage her care.

Star Bonaire had rallied the remaining volunteers. She had somehow become their de facto leader. They were at the court-house every time Wexler made an appearance. When he was taken back to jail, they would return to their own prison at the farm.

Bible said, "You know, Cussy, my wife, she was over there this morning with Melody Brickel talking to Star. They were letting the girls know they got options when the government finally seizes the place. A group home, maybe, or they all got family somewhere. The Boss says she and Melody are banging their heads against the wall trying to get through to them, but I think it makes 'em feel better."

"I'm sure it does." Andrea heard footsteps on the stairs.

Mike held up a bottle of wine.

"Sorry, Bible. I need to go. Take care of your hand, bird brain."

"Aw, don't make another parakeet joke, partner. That's a cheep shot."

Andrea laughed as she hung up. Mike sat behind her on the stairs. She leaned against his leg as she looked up at him. "Mom and Gordon are unpacking my books."

Mike looked wary. "How's that going?"

"Gordon offered to make a spreadsheet. There's already been a heated discussion about whether to alphabetize or group by section."

"They ask your opinion?"

"Nope."

"You gonna organize them by color once they're gone?"

"Yep." She kissed him on the mouth. Her fingers scratched into his beard. She playfully tugged at his cheek. "Don't fuck with my mom."

"Baby, you know I would never do that."

Andrea knew he would do exactly that, but there was no reason to delay the inevitable.

The motion detectors triggered the lights as they walked down the long hallway. Her new apartment was smaller than her previous one, but at least it wasn't above her mother's garage. It wasn't above anything. Andrea had only been able to afford a basement unit in SOBO, which was what the locals called South Baltimore. The landlord had cut the rent when she'd found out that Andrea was a Marshal. Even with that, Andrea was going to be eating ramen noodles until she collected social security. If social security still existed when she was finally able to retire.

Andrea shot Mike a final look of warning as she opened the door.

He saw her parents and said, "Oh, look, Mom and Dad are here."

Laura clutched a book in her hands.

Gordon cleared his throat.

Mike plastered on his stupid grin as he walked around the room. "Nice place you got here, Andy. This is clearly the first time I am seeing it and I have no idea where the bedroom is."

Laura's nostrils flared.

Gordon cleared his throat again.

Andrea grabbed the bottle of wine. She couldn't do this without alcohol.

Her tiny kitchen was just off the living room and backed up to her even tinier bedroom. The bathroom was so narrow that the door scraped the toilet. She had exactly three windows. The one over the kitchen sink was long and skinny and offered a prime view of the footwear worn by the people traversing the sidewalk on the other side.

Andrea was pretty sure she loved the place.

She looked for the wine glasses but quickly gave up. She hadn't managed to unpack anything before her parents came to help, mostly because she knew that her parents were going to help. She found two water glasses, a jelly jar and a coffee mug in a box marked *stuff*.

Andrea turned on the kitchen faucet, squirted dishwashing liquid, grabbed the sponge. The dinner plates from last night were caked in sauce. Unbidden, her mind flashed up Nardo Fontaine taking his hand away from his neck. The blood had splattered all over Star. The woman hadn't screamed. She hadn't even wiped the blood from her face. She had sat down at the stool, clasped her hands on the counter, and stared ahead at the white tile wall as she waited for someone to tell her what to do.

Andrea closed her eyes. She took a deep breath.

This was how it happened sometimes. The trauma came back. Flashes of violence, flashes of pain. Instead of fighting it, instead of trying to change her whole life into something different because of it, Andrea had learned to accept it. The memories were part of who she was now, just like the memory of the triumph she'd felt when she'd taken Ricky Fontaine's full confession.

Andrea listened to the sounds in the other room. Her absence had brought down the temperature. She could hear Laura lecturing Mike, Gordon laughing at them both. She slipped her iPhone out of her back pocket. Andrea's iCloud account had backed up the photos she had surreptitiously captured of teenage Judith's collage. The original piece had been destroyed in the fire. Andrea had the only proof that it ever existed.

She scrolled past the liner notes from Melody Brickel's mixtape. The affirmations from what she'd later found out were from one of Melody's letters. The ultrasounds of infant Judith that fanned out from the center of the piece. The photos of Emily laughing and playing and doing everything but dying.

Andrea had been so desperate to persuade herself that Judith looked like Clay, but the fact was, she looked very much like her mother. Emily's light blue eyes were nothing like Clay's icy blue. As for Judith's sharp cheekbones and slight cleft to her chin, they could have come from some distant Vaughn or Fontaine the same way Andrea had drawn her own Piglet nose from her family's gene pool.

She swiped the screen, stopping at the group photo Judith had placed among the other candids in her collage. It was the same photo that Ricky had given a place of honor for forty years.

The clique.

Emily and Ricky were dressed alike, their liquid eyeliner and spiral perms placing them squarely in the eighties. The boys all had shaggy hair and wore their Members Only jackets with the sleeves pushed up. Ricky resembled Nardo more than her fraternal twin. Blake and Clay could be brothers. Together, the group looked like they were posing for a prequel to *The Breakfast Club*, though there wasn't a jock or a princess. Andrea only saw the nerd, the basket case, and of course all but one was an admitted criminal.

Gordon's loud laughter broke the spell. Andrea heard a teasing in Laura's voice when she responded. For once, Mike apparently had nothing to offer.

Andrea slid the phone back into her pocket. She stuck her hands into the sudsy water and started to wash the dishes. Her fingers curved along the smooth edge of a plate. Again, her mind started to wander back to the diner.

An investigation by the Delaware State Police had ruled that Jack Stilton's shooting of Bernard Fontaine was justifiable. Andrea couldn't disagree with the finding, though she wondered if Stilton

would've found a way to kill Nardo anyway. He had been ready
to take that second shot. The only thing that had stopped him
was Andrea. She understood his hatred of Nardo. Stilton had
been bullied by the asshole for years—including back in the late
nineties when, according to Stilton, Nardo had threatened to out
him as gay unless he made a DUI charge disappear. She couldn't
imagine how difficult his life had been. Tormented by the murder
of his high school best friend. Distraught over his lack of power
to bring her killer to justice. Knowing Nardo was the key to
solving the crime but too terrified to confront him. Andrea knew
that Stilton was an alcoholic and a misogynist, but he had also
been Emily Vaughn's only true friend.

"Hey." Mike's arms wrapped around her waist. He pressed his
lips to the back of her neck. "You all right?"

"Yeah." The lump in her throat reminded her not to lie to
him. "I keep thinking about Star."

Mike pressed his lips to her neck again. His three bossy sisters
had taught him that not every problem had a solution. He simply
said, "I'm sorry."

Laura cleared her throat. She held up three wine glasses. "I
found these in the box labeled *bathroom*."

Andrea shrugged. "Why take a bath if you're not going to
drink?"

Laura frowned when Mike took the glasses. "I read that judge's
obituary in the *Times*. No surprise that Reagan appointed her.
What a fucking hypocrite."

Mike said, "Criminals who live in glass houses . . ."

"Completely different," Laura scoffed. "You don't claw your
way up to those levels of power without corrupting your soul.
Look at my disgusting brother."

Andrea was enormously grateful when her phone started to
ring. The caller ID read BIBLE, LEONARD, which was strange,
because it usually came up as USMS BIBLE.

She told Mike and Laura, "I know you two can't play nice,
but play fair."

Andrea slipped out the door before her mother could argue.
She walked toward the stairs as she answered the phone. "Are
you calling me back about your chirpies?"

There was a long pause. She heard the rumble of shouts and profanities that served as the distinctive background chatter of a federal penitentiary.

Clayton Morrow said, "Hello, Andrea."

Andrea felt her hand go to her mouth.

He said, "I heard you visited the old hometown."

Andrea dropped away her hand. Her lips parted as she took in a deep breath. She did not cry out. She did not panic. She told herself the facts. Her father was in prison. Contraband cell phones were easy to obtain. Clay had spoofed Bible's number so that she would answer.

He wanted something.

"Andy?" Clay said. "I heard the news about Ricky and Nardo. Such a toxic relationship. They always did deserve each other."

Andrea took another deep breath. Dean Wexler might be a poor copy of Clay Morrow, but Clay's cruel tone reminded her of Bernard Fontaine.

"Did you find what you were looking for?"

Andrea stood up. She couldn't risk her mother coming into the hall. She climbed the steep stairs. She pushed open the door to the street. Traffic whizzed by. Horns blared. Pedestrians filled the sidewalk. Andrea leaned her back against the building. If Mike was still at the sink, he would be able to see her feet through the narrow window.

She asked Clay, "What do you want?"

"Ah, there's that beautiful voice," he said. "I'd like for you to come visit me, daughter. I've put you on my approved list."

She felt her head shaking. She would never visit him.

"Your uncle Jasper," he said. "I know you've been working with him."

"I wasn't working with Jasper," she told him. "I was trying to make sure you never get out of prison."

"Alas, I'm innocent," Clay said. "Though, correct me if I'm wrong, but it sounds as if you're wishing that I had actually killed her."

Andrea felt her fingers clench around the phone. His parole hearing was in another five months. She was certain that Jasper was scrambling to do the unseemly work to make sure it was denied. For Andrea's part, she had vowed not to let her world stop on a dime for her psychopathic father. She had failed at doing her part to keep him locked away, but she was not going to let Clayton Morrow make her feel like a failure.

"Nevertheless," he said. "I've got some very interesting stories about dear Jasper's gluttonous past that might interest you."

"Like what?" she demanded. "He's been at every parole hearing you've ever had. You didn't think to use this information to shut him up before?"

"Curious, isn't it? Why would I hold something back that could destroy him?" Clay chuckled in the silence. "Come see me, daughter. I promise you won't be disappointed."

Andrea's mouth opened to respond, but no words came out. She could feel the cold air inside of her mouth. She thought about the oxygen flowing around her. Circulating through her bloodstream. Bringing life into her body.

Clayton Morrow had not called because he wanted to spill dirt on Jasper. He was calling to pull Andrea back into his orbit. She could not let her world stop for him. He was a psychopath. His oxygen was attention. He needed Andrea to feed his fire.

"An-dree-ah," he sang. "I think you should—"

She ended the call.

She slipped the phone back into her pocket. She looked out into the street. A bike coasted by. People were rushing to do their shopping. Children were negotiating homework. Millennials drank lattes. A Great Dane on a long leash trotted in front of her like a show pony.

Andrea pushed away from the wall. She walked into the building. On the stairs, she could hear the low rumble of Mike's voice, the warmth of Laura's laughter, the constant clearing of Gordon's throat.

Last month, her mother had accused Andrea of approaching every challenge in life as if it was a cliff that she had to fling herself over. Completely out of control. Letting gravity take over.

Now, her life was more like a diving board.

Andrea had finally learned how to jump.

She'd already known how to fall.

ACKNOWLEDGMENTS

First thanks always goes to Kate Elton and Victoria Sanders for being there no matter what. And there has been a shit ton of *what* lately, so apologies and appreciations. Special thanks also to Diane Dickensheid for making sure the sails are correctly directed at all times; to Emily Krump for her amazing calmness; and to Bernadette Baker-Baughman, my confrere, for keeping me sane. Or at least punctual.

At HarperCollins: Liate Stehlik, Jen Hart, Heidi Richter-Ginger, Kaitlin Harri, Miranda Mettes, Kathryn Cheshire, Elizabeth Dawson, Sarah Shea, Izzy Coburn, Chantal Restivo-Alessi, Julianna Wojcik, and all my GPP peeps worldwide. At WME, Hilary Zaitz-Michael and Sylvie Rabineau. At Made Up Stories, the incredible Bruna Papandrea, Steve Hutensky, Janice Williams and Casey Haver. Also thanks to Charlotte Stoudt, Lesli Linka Glatter and Minkie Spiro for being such exceptional professionals and genuinely good people. Eric Rayman and Jeff Frankel were instrumental as usual. And of course I would be remiss not to mention the wonderful folks at Netflix.

At the United States Marshal Service, I owe a great deal of appreciation to Keith Booker, Marc Cameron, Brooke Davis, Van Grady, Chaz Johnson, Kevin R. Kamrowski, David Oney and J.B. Stevens for answering all my tedious questions. Any mistakes are completely and entirely my own—and not for lack of their trying.

Alafair Burke, Patricia Friedman, Charles Hodges and Greg Guthrie helped me with the legal stuff. Sara Blaedel confirmed the sophistication of the average Danish hedgehog. David Harper answered some tiny medical questions and is raring to go for the next Sara and Will, for those of you who are wondering what comes next. Kristian Bush and Melanie Hammet explained time signature changes, among other musical oddities, so I didn't embarrass myself in print. (I still might have, but what I am saying is that they tried.) Carly Place helped with Delaware facts, though the town of Longbill Beach is entirely fictional.

Last thanks always goes to my dad for hanging in there and D.A. for not hanging me—you are my heart. You are my home.

ABOUT THE AUTHOR

Karin Slaughter is one of the world's most popular storytellers. Published in 120 countries with more than 40 million copies sold across the globe, her novels have all been *New York Times* bestsellers. Slaughter lives in Atlanta, Georgia, and is the founder of the Save the Libraries project—a nonprofit organization established to support libraries and library programming. Her standalone novel *Pieces of Her* is now a Netflix series, and the Grant County and Will Trent series are in development for television.

For more information visit KarinSlaughter.com
AuthorKarinSlaughter
SlaughterKarin